T0044418

Also by Audrey Blake

The Girl in His Shadow

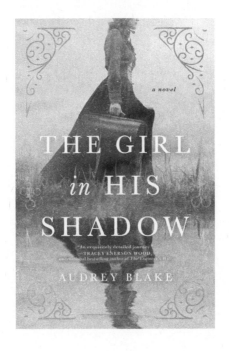

The
SURGEON'S
DAUGHTER

AUDREY
BLAKE

sourcebooks
landmark

Copyright © 2022 by Audrey Blake
Cover and internal design © 2022 by Sourcebooks
Cover design by James Iacobelli
Cover images by Crow's Eye Productions/Arcangel Images, Alex Korzun/
Shutterstock, Channarong Pherngjanda/Shutterstock, Ann Muse/Shutterstock
Internal design by Ashley Holstrom/Sourcebooks

Sourcebooks and the colophon are registered trademarks of Sourcebooks.

All rights reserved. No part of this book may be reproduced in any form or by
any electronic or mechanical means including information storage and retrieval
systems—except in the case of brief quotations embodied in critical articles or
reviews—without permission in writing from its publisher, Sourcebooks.

The characters and events portrayed in this book are fictitious or are used
fictitiously. Apart from well-known historical figures, any similarity to real
persons, living or dead, is purely coincidental and not intended by the author.

Published by Sourcebooks Landmark, an imprint of Sourcebooks
P.O. Box 4410, Naperville, Illinois 60567-4410
(630) 961-3900
sourcebooks.com

Library of Congress Cataloging-in-Publication Data

Names: Blake, Audrey, active 2020, author.
Title: The surgeon's daughter / Audrey Blake.
Description: Naperville, Illinois : Sourcebooks Landmark, [2022]
Identifiers: LCCN 2022000205 (print) | LCCN 2022000206 (ebook) |
   (trade paperback) | (epub)
Classification: LCC PS3602.L3415 S87 2022 (print) | LCC PS3602.L3415
   (ebook) | DDC 813/.6--dc23
LC record available at https://lccn.loc.gov/2022000205
LC ebook record available at https://lccn.loc.gov/2022000206

Printed and bound in the United States of America.
WOZ 10 9 8 7 6 5 4 3 2

To Jeff. You're such an enabler. XO

For Karina and Keisha, a mother and daughter who know a love stronger than death. You have inspired and changed me.

CHAPTER 1

PAIN WAS NOT UNUSUAL IN THOSE WHO CAME TO THE Grande Ospedale della Vita e della Morte in Bologna, Italy, but never more evident than in the horde waiting for treatment today. Nora was used to these beleaguered souls who hobbled, limped, or were carried to Via Riva di Reno from the alleys of the Quadrilatero. She'd walked those narrow, medieval streets herself this morning to the aptly named Grand Hospital of Life and Death, but with a brisk and resolute step, not like the fearful, sick, and bleeding sufferers who came from that slum in endless succession, day after day.

The trouble was, even with her best attention, a brilliantly deduced diagnosis, and skilled treatment, too much depended on chance. She surveyed the registration room with a practiced eye, silently praying she'd be accurate in her winnowing. *Life and death.* Screams, pleas, and whimpers, however striking, were less important than their causes, and causes needed to be determined quickly. A quiet fever, if ignored, would spread through the air if the patient wasn't quarantined. Broken arms, though agonizing, must be forced to wait.

"Dottoressa." A boy holding a younger child reached for Nora's arm. She wasn't a doctor, not yet, but the title brought a flush to her cheeks. *Soon.*

"*Un momento*," Nora said, her eyes flying past him to a woman leaning against the hospital door, silhouetted against the late afternoon sun. Her breath was as labored and ponderous as the music of a child forced to thump out exercises on the piano. Forgetting the seeping wound on the cheek of the young child in front of her, Nora hurried to the woman's side. "Signora, what's wrong?"

She was poor, obviously; in labor, obviously; but women delivered their babies at home. They did not shuffle down hot, dusty streets, shielding their bellies one-handed, to this hospital, especially when there were so many cases of erysipelas in the wards. The highly contagious fever kept many would-be patients from seeking help, because the people of this city seized and scattered bad news of the hospital before even the doctors caught wind of it.

"It's been a day and a night. I need help." The woman gasped, then gritted her teeth as a contraction sized her, only moments after the last.

"Piero! Quick!" Nora called, as she took the woman's weight on her arm. At this rate, they might not make it inside. Piero, the burliest orderly, swooped in with a wheeled chair, collected the woman, and swerved past the registration desk without breaking his stride. Impervious to protests from the crowd of waiting patients, he wheeled the woman down the corridor to the women's ward. Nora raced after him. Unable to find an empty bed, she hastily erected a screen.

"Not much time with this one, eh?" Piero whispered to Nora. "Maybe I should just leave her in the chair."

Nora frowned, recalling the woman's statement. *It's been a day and a night.* "It won't be much longer," Nora said to the woman. What had she been thinking, trekking here? "Put her on the table so I can take a look," she told Piero.

In spite of the woman's ungainly shape and agonized groans, Piero swung her easily onto the table as Nora set aside bundles of fresh linen and the carefully blended bottles of liniment and neatly pressed pills from Sister Madonna Agnes's pharmacy. As soon as she had room to work, Nora lifted away the ragged skirts, the hems stained the same perpetual rusty brown as everything else in the city. She paused in surprise, for she fully expected to see the head crowning, but it didn't even look like the fluids had ruptured, and when Nora felt for the head, she found almost no cervical dilation at all.

Something must have shown in her face, because the woman pushed up on her elbows and clicked her tongue to get Nora's attention. "Will I die?" she demanded.

"Of course not," Nora said, pretending she wasn't both puzzled and dismayed. "What's your name?"

"It feels like this one is killing me," the woman answered instead, ending on another groan. Her hands crumpled into fists until the contraction passed, then she collapsed onto the tabletop.

"You've birthed children before?" Nora asked.

"Four. Two still living," she gasped. "Never had any trouble, but—" Her face contorted, and she was once again in another realm, a place of consuming focus and pain.

Piero sent Nora an inquiring look—one she couldn't answer. For the past thirty years, all female medical students at the University of Bologna had ended up focusing on obstetrics, if they weren't simply diverted to midwifery in the first place. It was considered natural for them to exercise their skills on other women, so Nora had attended extra lectures, studied, and worked to hone her skills. But she didn't know what to do now, and this woman's life was worth more than her pride.

"I don't know," Nora hissed. "In the name of... Fetch somebody!" This was beyond her, but it required little skill to know there wasn't much time. Though she'd never seen it, Nora knew the dangers of everlasting labor: fits, apoplexy, puerperal fever.

Piero returned a blank look. "Who?"

"Anyone. Does it look like I can help her?" Professor Perra was good with difficult births. So was Sister Paula Benedicta. Hopefully one of them wasn't far off. Nora's cheeks burned with shame and frustration as Piero jogged off. She called for the ward sister, Maria Celeste, and asked for hot water and rags. Together, she and the wiry nun eased the patient onto her side and applied counterpressure to her back, with little effect, until another woman strode past the screen, unbuttoning her cuffs, her skirts swinging.

Nora didn't recognize her from anywhere, though she carried a doctor's bag.

"What have you here?" the woman demanded. She was tall, with loose black curls gathered rather carelessly for working in a hospital. Her soft jawline made a stark contrast to her severe eyebrows, bent in concentration.

Sister Maria Celeste sighed in relief, and Nora relaxed a little. Whoever the woman was, she had the sister's confidence.

"I'm not sure," Nora admitted. "Contractions are fast, less than thirty seconds apart—"

"I can see that," the woman interrupted. "And no dilation, I suppose, or you wouldn't have sent for me. Have you measured her pelvis?"

"I only checked the cervix," Nora said with a flush. She was being ordered about, but by whom? "She's had other live births, so the distance should be adequate."

"Just because she's delivered before doesn't mean her body can't change. Look at her," the woman snapped. "Short neck, stooped back. You have to recognize these signs." She shouldered Nora away from the bottom of the table. "Let me examine her."

Without a word to the patient, she reached beneath her skirts. Nora shot a pained look at Piero who silently mouthed *Dottoressa* over the woman's bent back.

"Just as I thought," the *dottoressa* said a moment later. "Her bones are collapsing. Poor nutrition. She's got less than five centimeters anteroposteriorly, and not much more than that from side to side." She reached over and began rummaging through Nora's open bag.

Nora didn't stop her. She'd read of a case where a woman's pelvis had narrowed after numerous births, but until this mysterious doctor's sharp reminder, she'd forgotten it. "I don't have a crotchet," she said quietly. She'd seen craniotomies in London, where doctors killed and removed an infant piecemeal in hopes of saving a mother, but she hadn't thought to use one here since they weren't permitted by the Catholic church.

The doctor looked at her in surprise. "God in heaven, I hope not." She drew out her scalpel and examined the blade. "Crotchet," she muttered under her breath with contempt. "You must be the English girl who does ether experiments. Get your needles ready while I talk to the patient. We're going to do a cesarean."

Nora kept her hands and her gaze steady, nodding because it was impossible to speak. She'd read of cesarean sections the same way she'd read of fairy tales and sea monsters. In England, she knew of one reported case where mother and child survived. The story was close to a hundred years old, more legend than fact, of a country midwife named Alice O'Neil who had used a razor for the operation while a man ran a mile to bring her silk thread and tailor's needles. Cesarean sections were not the stuff of myth here on the Continent, but they were still rare and deadly. In the year she'd spent in Bologna, Nora hadn't witnessed one and didn't expect to.

Some of her fear must have shown. The *dottoressa* cocked her head. "You've not seen one before?"

"No," Nora admitted, shrinking in her shoes. Now she'd be banished or sent to fetch someone competent.

"Can you follow directions?"

Nora nodded, like a child promising obedience to avoid the switch.

"Good. I haven't tried this with ether yet, and I hear you've a wealth of experience there."

Nora opened her mouth, but the woman's eyebrows lifted. "Yes, at once," Nora said instead, and ran to fetch her vaporizer.

———

"She's asleep," Nora said five minutes later and lifted the inhaler from the patient's face. "I used twenty drops. That should give us—" Her voice broke off. The woman doctor was already cutting.

"Explain your wonder drug later. We need to work," the doctor snapped.

"We haven't checked to see if she's insensible!" Nora hissed, aghast at the size of the incision. Nor did she know the patient's pulse or rate of respiration, essential markers for using ether safely.

"She's insensible," the woman said. "Hasn't even twitched. After such a protracted labor there's no time to waste. I'll need your help with the retractors."

Nora jumped to her bag.

"Mine are out on the table. There, beside her leg." The doctor jerked her head impatiently, and Nora reached across her to grab them, groping until she located them beneath the tangle of skirts. "You're blocking the light," the doctor scolded. "I know you must have been in surgeries before, so try not to act as if this is your first."

Nora clenched her lips to school the trembling that threatened them and sponged as quickly and skillfully as she knew how. She poised the retractors to wait for the doctor's order.

"You need to be faster. I tied off the vessels ages ago."

"I'm sorry, Dr…" Nora waited for the woman or for Sister Maria Celeste to provide the missing name. No one answered.

"Sponge."

Nora sponged again. The incision ran lengthwise between the pubis and ribs, an inch to the right of the navel. Had this doctor cut blindly? Or had she done something to try to avoid the placenta? There was an alarming amount of blood, but

Nora's reading told her if the placenta had been cut, they'd be up to their elbows by now.

"How did—"

"I need more room. Pull harder."

Nora tugged on the retractors, eyeing the blood and fluid spilling from the wound. Even if she dared, there was no time to express her misgivings. The doctor thrust past her, plunging her hands deep. Nora flinched. This woman acted without an ounce of humility or caution, like Liston and Vickery, London surgeons famous for their speed and recklessness.

"Baby is face forward," the *dottoressa* muttered. "Nothing but trouble today." Her forearms tensed as she pulled, and the baby came free, smeared in blood and vernix. The spindly limbs snapped straight, spreading as wide as the points of the compass.

"She's alive." Nora let out the breath she'd been holding, her chest loosening.

"That one is," the doctor said briskly, thrusting the infant—squalling now—at Sister Maria Celeste. Then she snatched up a needle and elbowed past Nora. "You're in my way again," she snapped.

Not wishing to be told a third time, Nora stepped back, though she hated to lose sight of the incision margins and the rapidly—almost haphazardly—flying needle. Was she suturing in layers? What type of stitch? Nora knew one of the chief obstacles to a cesarean was a stitch strong enough to withstand the powerful contractions of afterbirth without being so invasive as to cause infection. Weak stitches tore free and left the womb gaping—a long and painful death.

You'll get a look before applying the dressing, Nora told herself, but when the time came, she was dispatched to the patient's head to check her pulse and her breathing, while Sister Maria Celeste was entrusted with the bandaging.

"How long until she wakes?" the doctor demanded.

"I can't say for certain, but it shouldn't be much longer now," Nora said, wishing she could give a more precise answer. Vagueness seemed better than being wrong, however, so she held her tongue when the doctor's lips compressed with irritation.

Quietly, Nora busied herself wiping instruments and washing out sponges between checks. The patient's pupils were reacting normally, and she stirred now when Nora pricked her finger.

"A minute or two longer, no more," Nora hazarded.

The doctor nodded and continued firing instructions to Sister Maria Celeste. "She's to have fluids only. Broth, milk, barley water, but as much of them as she can stand. And keep a close eye on the dressing."

The patient groaned.

"Everything is fine. You are well, and so is your baby," Nora said, bending close. Her words were thick and clumsy, because she hadn't expected to say them, and the relief of it seized her while she spoke. "Be still. You must rest."

The eyes fluttered open, searching the room blindly. A clammy hand fumbled for Nora's wrist, then closed around it with startling, but rapidly fading strength. Panic.

"Hush," Nora murmured, cutting off a terrified babble in an incomprehensible dialect of Italian. Seeing the doctor frowning beside her, she added, "Sometimes they are confused when waking."

"So I've been told."

The doctor watched as Nora calmed and questioned, verifying the woman's name. Lucia. She gave only the one. "You've had a surgery," Nora informed Lucia when she saw her fingers fumble over her deflated middle, searching for her baby. "Your daughter is safe and whole, and as soon as your stitches heal, you can go home," she assured her, walking beside the stretcher as two orderlies carried her away.

"There's an empty bed just there," Sister Maria Celeste told Nora. "Where your girl with the scalded arms used to be."

Erysipelas had claimed another.

"The sheets are fresh," Sister Maria Celeste said, her way of giving Nora a nudge.

"Of course. Thank you. I'll see Lucia settled."

When Nora returned to the table, the screens had already been cleared away and the woman doctor was returning her instruments to her bag.

"You shouldn't have given Lucia so many false promises," she said with a frown. "This was the easy part. Unwarranted optimism isn't good for a doctor's reputation."

"But the surgery was successful," Nora said. "Recovery is always complicated, but what harm is there in giving her a few words of encouragement?"

"I wouldn't get hopeful. She's exhausted. She labored too long. Never bodes well." The doctor closed the catch of her bag with a snap. "Your ether was helpful, though. Without it, I think shock and pain would have killed her already."

Nora eyed her sideways. "You haven't used it before?"

"No. I've been in Egypt to treat my consumption. I just returned to Bologna last week," she said matter-of-factly.

"Oh." Nora had been uncomfortable before, and this revelation only made it worse. What was the correct response when another doctor told you they had a deadly condition? But at least her color was good. She was, in fact, the picture of health, attractively plump, and she hadn't coughed once. "The time abroad seems to have done you good. I'd never have known," Nora said, for lack of anything better to say.

"Thank you. This time I think I stayed away long enough. I went two years ago, you know, but missing my work makes me impatient. Not that it doesn't find its way to me. It's uncanny how many women manage to go into labor within my earshot."

Nora fumbled again for a response and settled for a smile instead, for her imagination had failed her. Then she remembered what had surprised her just a moment before.

"You've done cesarean sections *without* anesthesia?"

The woman gave her a funny look. "How else was I to do them?"

Nora ran her mind back over the last hour, assembling information from this woman's curtly worded instructions. "But I thought you did it on live mothers."

"I did."

"And they survived?"

"A fair number." She rolled her eyes. "Trust me, it happens with the right skills and bit of luck. You English are so set in your ways."

"I'm not," Nora said, though it should have been obvious. If she were, would she be here?

"Yes, I admit your proficiency with ether is surprising. I'd like to know more." Her look, as she spoke, was the kindest she'd given, so Nora plucked up her courage with both hands.

"Perhaps, when you write up the case—" She halted at the doctor's dismissive snort.

"Write up? Who has time for that? Besides, I told you I'm not pleased with her chances. If there's no other way for the baby to come out, it's much better to cut as soon as they begin labor—before even—so they aren't worn out."

"Still, your skill in surgery—"

"Is certainly worth the attention of whatever moth-bag surgeons you knew in England. But they'll never read it, so what is the point? I've written up enough successful cases that they could have learned the technique."

"You have?"

Something in Nora's question annoyed the doctor. She replied, in a voice exactly even, "Yes. If you cannot find my book on obstetrics, you'll easily find my mother's. Perhaps you've heard of it? *The New Art of*—"

Nora cut her off. "Your mother is Doctor Marenco? From Bagnacavallo?" Nora had an old, secondhand copy, because no newer copies were available, and though Marenco's confident assertions on the subject of cesarean sections were as frightening as they were fascinating, they were of limited practical use to Nora, who didn't understand when Dr. Marenco simply wrote: *Signora B's incision was closed in the usual way.* The mystery of the uterine stitch scratched at her like a rash. She'd been so close…

The answering smile was more of a grimace. "Yes. She was."

"I didn't know she was a woman."

"You don't know much," the doctor said flatly. "Not enough to help the women who will need your care. You and I will have to work together again, and next time I'll appreciate it if you're better prepared and less in the way."

Nora swallowed. "Yes, Doctor—"

"Marenco." She reached for a towel and began drying her hands. "They told me about you—student of Horace Croft." She tossed the towel aside. "You're good, but not as good as I expected. Stay until the patient is able to drink some broth."

CHAPTER 2

NORA COULDN'T REMEMBER WHICH SAINT THE BOLOGNESI were celebrating today, but for once she didn't mind the interruption to the hospital and university routine. This opportunity to spend the day with Mrs. Phipps, the English housekeeper who'd accompanied her on her journey to Bologna, was more than welcome.

Upon arrival in Italy, Mrs. Phipps, in her resourceful way, had collected every English-speaking woman within walking distance of their rented rooms and now spent most of her days with a small flock of displaced British citizens, as well as one American and a Frenchwoman who spoke four languages. Today, though, Mrs. Phipps had insisted Nora join their excursion—or more truthfully, given the unseasonable heat, their escape—to the green hills outside the city. To the older woman's surprise, Nora was the first one with her boots on. She needed respite from the critical eyes trained on her from every corner, every day.

"I'm glad you're joining me," Mrs. Phipps said as Nora climbed into the cart carrying several of Mrs. Phipps's *signore inglesi*. "You need a chance to relax."

"It's a perfect day for it," Nora said, scanning the sky and taking a seat next to Madame Bouchard—who often helped

Nora interpret passages in her medical books. They exchanged greetings, but even before the cart was outside the town, Nora's mind was back in the hospital, hashing over the past week. Did her imagination fool her, or were the other students growing even more spiteful? Last night Umberto Sagese had put all of the medicants for enemas away on the very back of the highest shelf, inches from Nora's farthest reach. She'd had to fetch a stool to retrieve the castor oil, and even then, she'd missed the bottle and nearly toppled—then turned round to find a knot of fellow students snickering.

Disguising her anger as dignity, she pointed to Bartolomeo Pozzi, the youngest, tallest, and least visibly amused of the pack. "A patient is in need of medicine. Get it down and put it where it can be reached."

Sagese, chilly and superior as ever, blocked Pozzi's attempt to obey. "It can be reached by those who should reach it."

Pozzi had mumbled something about being helpful to the nuns and done as Nora said, but the embarrassment still burned her chest.

"It's good you brought your sketching things," Mrs. Phipps said, jogging Nora's elbow. "You haven't done any scenery in ages."

Nora felt a surge of inner amusement. Lately, she'd been drawing wombs in the hospital morgue and pondering the best ways to slice them open, then stitch them back together, but she wouldn't be admitting that to this circle of ladies.

Madame Bouchard nodded approvingly. "You didn't come with us last time, Nora, and the views are very fine."

"I'm sure I'll enjoy them." Nora pushed back her bonnet

to let the sun onto her face. Mrs. Phipps would never have consented to riding in a cart in London, like so much cabbage being taken to market, but here under the hot sun with their legs stretched out, watching the road disappear behind them instead of stretching ahead, Mrs. Phipps looked almost child-like in her serenity. She wore her stays looser than she had in London and had taken up sketching, something she'd never have bothered with before. She'd never had time.

When they arrived at the picnic site, another party of women greeted them and together Nora and Mrs. Phipps added their blanket to the patchwork collection spread out on the spiky grass. Others were already setting out food and fanning away greedy flies.

Nora reached into the comically large picnic basket assembled by their landlady, Signora Carnicelli. A child could have stowed away in it. Besides the blanket, it was crammed with tomato salad, ham, bottles of lemonade, a loaf of bread with a wreath pattern slashed in the thick, gold crust, another salad of cucumbers and melon, an assortment of Viennese-style pastries, grapes, a bottle of wine, forks, napkins, plates, serving spoons, and two different sizes of glasses.

"She must have thought she was feeding an army," Nora said. Beneath the napkins was a pot of olive paste and another of strawberry preserve, something wrapped in an oilcloth that might be cheese…

"There will be plenty to share," Mrs. Phipps said.

Nora sat on the quilt, spreading her skirt over her curled legs and glancing doubtfully at the other ladies, who all seemed similarly equipped and were busily passing out plates. It was both strange and comforting to hear English words flying around her.

Mrs. Cross, the American, was laying out slices of cake with the help of a young lady Nora didn't recognize. Mrs. Phipps gave the plump, pleasant-faced girl an appraising but not unkind look. "We have another young member in our company today. Who's your companion, Susan?"

Mrs. Cross straightened, answering before the girl could speak. "My niece, Miss Clara Parrish, from Philadelphia. She's come to spend a few months with me." She smiled at the girl indulgently.

"How lovely for you both," Nora said.

Clara's dark eyes flashed over the group self-consciously. "I was keen to see the art and the architecture. I'm hopeless at the language, but I wish I weren't. I would simply inhale the libraries if I could."

"Let me help you with your Italian," Madame Bouchard offered. "The libraries need not be inaccessible, if you are willing to work."

Clara's eyes lit up, and Nora's smile went from polite to sincere. Another student. "Madame Bouchard is an excellent translator," Nora said. "What subjects are you interested in, Clara?"

Clara diverted her eyes to her china plate. "All of them. But my father is an attorney. I wish I could read Italian books on government and laws. The comparison would be fascinating. I've read so much about the English Parliament and Civil War."

Mrs. Patrick adjusted her considerable bulk and dabbed at her glistening neck. "How unusual. Two female scholars amongst us." Seeing the question in Clara's face, she pointed to

Nora. "Miss Beady is attending the local medical school, if you can believe that."

Clara's gaze intensified. "I can't. How did you... I had no idea..."

Mrs. Phipps's pride made an appearance. "She's a great talent. Only natural, considering she was raised by the finest surgeon in London."

"And the kindest woman," Nora added quietly.

"Do you mean to say actual surgery? Such as sawing off legs?" Clara pinked as she looked around the circle.

"I study all branches of medicine," Nora said, neatly side-stepping any gory details.

"Which reminds me..." Mrs. Russell spoke up, her accent clipped and imperious. "I've been meaning to ask you to look at my shoulder. I can't cross my arm in front of me anymore and I can barely lift it above my chin, but I don't remember injuring it."

"Can you show me?" Nora asked, extending her hand tentatively.

Mrs. Russell nodded, and Nora rested her fingertips atop the silk-encased shoulder. Mrs. Russell raised her arm a mere sixty degrees before screwing her face up in pain, and Nora detected grating in the joint. "Most likely arthritis of the shoulder," Nora told her, shaking her head sympathetically. "I'm afraid there is little we can do. The joints seize over time. There are menthol salves that give some relief. I don't have the facilities here to make my own, but Sister Madonna Agnes from the hospital could mix you one."

And, as always happened, the impromptu clinic doors burst

open. Mrs. Patrick had a painful wart on the pad of her big toe, Mrs. Chatham asked after her daughter who'd not had menses for four months, and Mrs. Riley complained of headaches that arose in the midday heat. Because it was not a formal setting, Nora gave herself permission to continue eating and answered between bites, happy to nod and let them describe simple conditions in great detail. It gave her time to chew.

"I'd never have thought it," Clara said, marveling as the other women exhausted their questions. "I've dreamed of presenting a case before a judge, but even in America, where I like to think there is some freedom of ideas, it is impossible."

"You would be an attorney if you were able?" Nora asked, turning away from Madame Bouchard, who was asking for a way to fade the sunspots on her arm.

The group grew silent and Clara's eyebrows lowered apologetically. "I don't know that I would wish to be an attorney, but I would love to advocate for those denied access to the law through ignorance. The English poor law commission to advance medical rights of patients caught my attention from the beginning. In Philadelphia, there are places where the poor are the most oppressed, suffering souls you've ever seen. If something could be done—"

"Surely the answer is philanthropy," Mrs. Patrick suggested.

"Philanthropy is like a bandage and very needed, but I would like to stop them from being wounded. If more laws protected children from mistreatment in factories and orphanages…"

"The law cannot change behavior," pronounced Mrs. Russell. "Nor will it alleviate poverty."

Clara frowned, her round face stubborn. "Then why do you

hang murderers, Mrs. Russell, and imprison thieves? Surely it is to change behaviors, if not of the condemned, then of those who would imitate their mistakes."

"Hangings are hardly a topic for ladies' discussion." Mrs. Russell bristled. "And though I value Miss Beady's advice, I would not wish to hear of her dissections."

"If you ask me, it is very silly to have separate topics for men and women," Madame Bouchard interrupted. "Something is worth discussing or it is not."

Mrs. Russell's nose wrinkled, and it was easy to see what she thought of the French way of things.

Miss Bunning, an unmarried woman in her late thirties, turned wistful eyes to the group. "I think you should read what you like, Miss Parrish. I wished to study music when I was young. I played cello alongside my brother. I was the more talented, but my father sent him to Austria to study music. What I would have given to play in an orchestra."

"There are some women who do," Nora offered softly.

"I missed my chance." Her smile was forlorn, fading. "My father had tears in his eyes when he refused me. He regretted it, he said, but the expense could never be justified for a daughter." Her eyes focused on Nora. "I wish he could have seen you. You may have changed his mind. But that was over twenty years ago. Times have changed."

"Have they?" Clara whispered. She turned to Nora. "I still don't understand how you obtained permission. American colleges won't let women in—"

"Nor will they in England. I was run out of London when the surgeons' guild found out my guardian, Dr. Croft, trained me."

"Were you prosecuted?" Clara was on her knees, leaning forward.

"No, thankfully, though they threatened to fine and prosecute Dr. Croft. Perhaps that's worse in a way—punished and ignored at the same time, like an animal or a young child. I was made an example, even though I had performed a successful surgery and saved a man's life." Nora willed herself not to pink, not to let her jaw tighten, but she failed at both. "I was no heroine to them. I was a laughingstock."

"Not everyone feels that way," Mrs. Phipps interrupted. "Which is why you are here."

Nora straightened her smile. "That's true. Professor Perra, who teaches at the University of Bologna but was in London at the time, offered me a place and insisted Dr. Croft pay for my schooling here, where women are allowed."

Though not welcomed, she added silently with a bitter taste in her mouth.

Mrs. Patrick refilled her glass of lemonade. "I never imagined how convenient it would be to have a woman in our tea circle trained in medicine. Perhaps a lady trained in other subjects would be useful as well?" She laughed at her own impracticality.

Mrs. Russell cast her eyes sideways and pinched her lips. Her doubtful expression made it clear that although consulting Nora about her shoulder pain was convenient, suggesting other women follow her lead was too radical a leap.

"Shall we bring out the drawing boards?" Mrs. Patrick surveyed the view. "It is why we came, after all, and I don't want to miss the chance to capture this."

Murmurs of assent and many rustlings of skirts filled the air as most of the women followed suit.

Watching Mrs. Phipps working between Mrs. Russell and Mrs. Patrick, Nora decided to draw the diminutive woman instead of the hazy city in the distance, framed by the ancient hills. She liked this view of Mrs. Phipps, quiet and content in a place she'd never have imagined herself. Later on, she could reproduce the sketch in miniature to send to Daniel. He and Horace would enjoy receiving a picture of Mrs. Phipps, who they sorely missed. And if she softened Mrs. Russell's features and omitted a few of her wrinkles, (an accurate portrait of her wasn't strictly necessary), it might charm her more than Nora's knowledge of ball and socket joints had done. She laid out her charcoals and scooted over to remain in her patch of shade, which was quickly shrinking as the sun marched to the apex of the sky.

Clara, who'd declared she was no artist, positioned herself at Nora's side. "What do your family think of your unusual pursuits?" she asked, her forehead creasing.

"I'm an orphan. And though my guardian, Dr. Croft, was not initially in favor of me leaving England, he agreed to it. He's never discouraged my interest in medicine. I don't think he'd know what to do with me if we didn't share that pursuit."

"How fortunate!" Clara's eyes grew wide. "I mean, not your parents, of course. Only that you had family to take you in and encourage you—"

"I knew what you meant," Nora assured her. "But Dr. Croft wasn't family. He was the physician who treated my family during the cholera epidemic in '32. My parents, grandmother, and younger brother all perished, leaving no one to care for me, so Dr. Croft brought me to his home. He and Mrs. Phipps saved me first from death, then life as a London orphan, which is most likely worse." When Horace Croft carelessly brought her home for lack of a better idea, Mrs. Phipps had kept him from jettisoning her once she'd recovered. Yet somehow she'd become dear to them, as they had to her.

Picturing Horace's unkempt beard, his white hair rebelling in boyish cowlicks, and his blue eyes burning with the excitement of discovery, Nora smiled. "It was hardly a conventional life for a child. Dr. Croft was not overly cautious about leaving around parts and pieces of his work. There was always a patient or a dissection. But if he had been conventional and shielded me from his work, I would have never learned." Her voice lowered. "I thank God for him."

Nora glanced at the other women. All were engaged in their drawings or other conversations. She and Clara could speak quietly without being overheard. "How old are you?"

"Twenty-two," Clara said.

"I'm twenty-five. You should study the law. Unless we try to find ways for ourselves, there won't be any." She looked past Clara and studied Mrs. Phipps's profile before making a sweeping curve that would become her hairline.

Clara shifted on her folded knees. "My mother assures me I will ruin my chances for marriage if I pursue anything so unnatural."

Nora cleared her throat. "I don't know anything about America, but I am attached to a successful surgeon—" With no warning, the thought of Daniel's face stole her words. She closed her eyes against the pang of missing him. How he would have lambasted those students yesterday evening for mocking her.

"You will be married and a surgeon?"

"I see no reason why I shouldn't," Nora said, rankled by Clara's skepticism. "I don't know if you will practice law as a man might. Even if I succeed and earn my medical degree— and I will, if sheer stubbornness has any part in it—my opportunities will never be as broad as my fellow students. But there are ways." She pictured Dr. Marenco ordering patients, nuns, orderlies, and fellow doctors about with fierce authority. "We must be inventive."

Clara pressed her thin lips out of existence as she watched Nora draw. "And the doctor you're attached to, he doesn't mind?"

"He did." Nora brushed a crumb from her wrist and inhaled the warm scent of vineyard air. Her memory of his first haughty glance, when he'd arrived as Horace's under surgeon, was so different from the way he'd looked at her when she boarded the ship to Italy that it seemed a caricature and not her own Daniel. "When he discovered my talents, he was appalled. But because he worked for Dr. Croft, he could hardly protest too loudly and keep his place at the practice. We came to an understanding eventually."

Understanding? What a tame word to describe the way he kissed her after their first surgery together, but Nora wasn't sharing more with Miss Clara Parrish, no matter how similar their struggles. That moment was private, as was the time he'd discovered her working late at night at a dissection. He'd demanded that she leave, they'd argued, and somehow ended up with her wielding the scalpel while he held back the lungs with a pair of spoons.

Submerging into memory, Nora's drawing hand fell still. Instead of the bright frocks spread out on the blankets around her, she saw—felt—Daniel, sitting beside her on the worn brocade sofa her last night in London. "Keep still," Nora had told him, raising his chin with her forefinger a mere half inch. "Yes, just there."

She exchanged a chestnut-brown pastel for a gold one and returned her attention to her drawing, blending highlights into his hair. Over the last half hour, he'd gradually shifted closer—he might not notice the diminishing space between them, but she felt each hairbreadth that vanished. She ought to put aside the pastels and hold him instead while he was within such easy reach. Tomorrow, she'd be gone.

But she couldn't take kisses with her and memories would fade. This drawing would comfort her, smiling at her from some Italian wall. "Almost finished," she murmured, to herself as much as him.

She wasn't leaving without a reproduction of his wide forehead and fine chestnut hair. His mouth—usually stern—had learned to settle comfortably into smiles, and it was this soft, private one she wanted to take away with her.

"You can't let anyone see this portrait," Daniel said, leaning closer to peer over her shoulder.

Her hand stilled. "Whyever not? You aren't—" She broke off, blushing, unable to speak the thought. She'd only drawn his head and shoulders, and he was beautifully attired in coat and cravat. She'd never seen him nude. She drew nakedness, of course, but only corpses.

"It must be obvious to anyone that I'm looking at you,"

Daniel said. "I'm lucky Horace hasn't knocked the daylights out of me a dozen times already."

"He only notices—"

"He's not blind." Daniel gestured at the drawing. "If that's not a man made insensible by love—"

"You are never anything but sensible," Nora teased, but Daniel ignored her.

"Just finish the darn thing, and if sometime next week you aren't sure how I feel about you—"

"It would take longer than a week, surely. Two or three?" Nora suggested, her eyes downcast.

"That's being generous." He leaned back onto the couch cushions. Nora sketched quicker, hoping to catch the serious, smiling lines around his eyes. "Marry me, and I'll stow away in your luggage. You don't need all those hats."

"I don't think so either, but I know better than to argue with Mrs. Phipps."

Daniel grimaced, shifting in his seat. "She won't like me keeping you up this late."

"I thought I was keeping you," Nora retorted. "Sit still. I'm not finished."

"And what will I have to remember you?"

"You said I'm unforgettable," Nora said, shading around the narrow bridge of his nose.

"If you get something to look at—"

"In a minute," Nora told him, sending a quelling glance.

His eyebrows lifted.

"Yes, I have a portrait for you. Wait."

"I am." He wasn't talking about now, she knew. He meant

the years it would take to study. The years until he could ask to marry her again, not in jest. When he'd proposed before, in earnest, she'd reluctantly insisted that no decisions could be made until she returned from Italy.

She finished blending color on his cheeks, set the drawing aside, and reached under the sofa. "Here," she said, holding out a parcel, her hands no longer steady.

Daniel untied the string and pushed back the paper, but said nothing for a long time.

"Well?" Nora finally asked.

"Your hair is lighter than this, but you have the thickness right. The weight of it..." He swallowed, hurrying on. "I can tell you were drawing yourself. See?" He traced the faint line between the eyebrows. "You also get this when you are reading."

"I tried to do a smiling one—"

"It's perfect." He leaned in to kiss her. "Until you return."

⁓

Clara coughed, and Nora's hand jerked on the paper, leaving a thick, dark line in the middle of Mrs. Phipps's intricately coiled hair. "I'm sorry, did you say something? Forgive me, Miss Parrish. My wits are wandering."

"I said you must miss him very much," Clara said, her plump face tilted in sympathy.

"Very much," Nora agreed, too pricked by memory to pretend otherwise. She'd crossed the sea for the open minds promised by Professor Perra, but lately she'd received nothing but opposition or open hostility. Not one man had been as willing to change his obstinate mind as Daniel.

The fierce sun made the white flowers in the grass glint like stars, and the lazy pipe of a bird traveled over the chattering group. If Daniel were here, he'd lay his head in her lap and she'd brush his hair from his forehead without even noticing she was doing it. Her fingers moved on their own accord, as if in hope of finding his face beneath their touch. "If someone will not marry you because you are learned, I wouldn't count him any loss," she murmured to Clara.

"I hope there are two men in the world like your doctor," she said, doubt tainting the words.

Nora smiled. *None exactly like him but…* "Two? There must be a few more than that."

The patient, a middle-aged sister from the Convento Padri Agostiniani, was miserable not only owing to her femoral hernia. Angry red and swollen to a full ten centimeters, the bulge must have been exquisitely tender, yet the poor woman seemed to shrink as much from the men around her as from actual pain. Dr. Barilli, who was conducting the demonstration, seemed blind to this.

"Because there are no clear signs of mortification, we will proceed with the taxis until it is no longer safe to resort to conservative measures," he went on, as the sister shivered on her bed. "It has only been a half hour, and a hernia this swollen can take up to two hours of sustained pressure before softening."

There were six of them gathered around the bed, including Nora. Unfortunately, it was impossible to treat the hernia and cover the woman's genitals, but… "Perhaps the good sister would like a blanket for her legs," Nora suggested. "There is a draft." Without waiting for Barilli's nod, she pushed past two other students and laid a sheet over the sister's extremities.

"Careful. Don't knock me," Umberto Sagese said. Barilli had chosen him to begin the taxis, a steady, firm squeezing that could eventually coax herniated intestines back into place.

Nora resisted the urge to clench her teeth. She hadn't touched him, but ever since the cesarean with Dr. Marenco, other students had taken every opportunity to needle her and call her clumsy. Sagese, brilliant, ambitious, and resentful of the opportunities her expertise with ether had provided, was one of the worst. She kept her attention on the patient. "Is that better, Sister?"

The woman nodded jerkily, then wet her pale lips, closing her eyes against the pain.

"You must be strong, Sister," Barilli told her, then turned to Sagese. "Consistent, equal pressure will gradually evacuate the blood vessels. Unskilled men will jab and poke about, but that does more harm than good. Gentle firmness is required, like wringing out a cloth. Is it softening yet?"

Sagese cleared the hair from his eyes with a flick of his head. "I can't say, Doctor Barilli. I'm afraid my hands have gone numb."

Taxis took a toll on surgeons, too. It generally required two or three men working in turn, so that pressure was maintained when one man's strength gave out.

"It's probably time for a change." Barilli scanned the group of students. Nora lifted her chin, striving to catch his eye. She was skilled at hernia reduction, often working alongside Horace and Daniel, squeezing for an hour at a time. The poor woman would be more at ease under another woman's hands, she was sure of it, but Barilli skimmed past her. "Pozzi, take over for Sagese, please."

Nora dropped her eyes. She didn't like being overlooked in favor of a gangly boy not even in his twenties. Unfortunately, nothing she did could convince Barilli to notice her. Since she'd joined his class a month ago, he'd not granted her a single direct word.

"Sagese, what are the signs of mortification?" Barilli asked, turning to his favorite, who was stretching his tired hands.

"Vomiting, fever, unconsciousness. Acute pain. A strangulated hernia will turn purple or black. I recently read a case in an English journal of a successful surgical reduction after taxis failed—"

"Yes, yes, I read it. An admirable result, but—" Barilli cast a worried look at the sister. "It would be a good case to discuss in tomorrow's lecture, perhaps. Menotti, you will take over in half an hour from Pozzi. For now, keep an eye on Sister Clara Cecilia's pulse. Sparano, ready an enema for after the hernia reduces."

"Is there anything for me to do, sir?" Nora asked.

Silence. The students looked at her, then away. Barilli smiled thinly. "Fetch the good sister another pillow." He looked down at the nun. For her, the smile became genuine. "I know you are uncomfortable, dear lady. Trust me. This too shall pass."

Stubbornness spurred Nora's tongue. "Dr. Barilli? That case you and Sagese mentioned. Was it in the *Provincial*?"

Irritation puckered his forehead. "Yes. I believe from a Dr. Gibson."

"I know him," Nora said. "He's Dr. Croft's—"

"We are waiting for that pillow, Signorina Beady," Dr. Barilli snapped as if offended by her mention of her famous mentor. "Please have the goodness not to put your own elevation above the comfort of our patient."

Speechless, with her mouth half-open and her cheeks flaming, Nora searched his face for sympathy and found none. Wheeling around, she stalked to the linen closet, where she dashed a hand across her burning eyes and cursed under her breath. Her pulse drummed in her ears, rallying her to challenge Barilli's unfairness and eviscerate Sagese, Pozzi, Menotti, and the rest of them for standing by, enjoying her humiliation.

Gradually, the scent of the herbs freshening the sheets stole into her awareness. Her breath slowed and the fight bled out through her loosening fingers. She knew very well that confronting Barilli wouldn't help her. She had to accept his disdain and wait for another chance. The animosity of fellow students— men who should be her colleagues—she must endure. Perhaps tomorrow, in lecture, she could reveal that the case Barilli admired in the *Provincial Medical and Surgical Journal* was *her* surgery. Dr. Gibson—Daniel—had operated on her suggestion, and he would never have managed it alone.

Barilli, Sagese, and the rest might topple over in surprise, but it would serve them right.

CHAPTER 3

NORA FOUND IT STRANGE, EVEN AFTER MORE THAN A YEAR in Bologna, to return home for the midday meal. Growing up in the home of Horace Croft, she almost never saw him set aside his work. Even when lured to the dinner table, if Dr. Croft wasn't talking over his last case or latest theory, it was because he was preoccupied with some specimen he had tucked into his pocket.

Lengthy pauses in the best part of the day—even if it was impossibly hot—interrupted her focus, so Nora usually contented herself with a roll eaten in the square or a cup of coffee in the nuns' sitting room as she pored over her notes. Today, with the sisters still buzzing about Dr. Marenco's return, Nora was eager to escape the hospital, certain the sympathetic smiles and quickly averted glances meant Dr. Marenco's first impression of her was widely known by now. Between that and the scorn of Barilli's students, she could not find a safe corner in the entire university. She preferred to salve her pride alone.

Nora tied on her bonnet and hurried out through the courtyard and the west door, blind to the faultless blue sky, her eyes on the dusty cobbles spanning Via Riva di Reno. She was used to carrying her bag—she liked the weight of it, liked what the triangular shape and shiny brown leather told the people walking by—but today there was a painful pull across her shoulders. Even though Professor Perra had pushed for her admission and supported her studies, it was hardly enough with everyone else against her.

Turning south, she passed a high-walled palazzo, crossed Via San Felice, and walked briskly into the first narrow passage leading south again. Laundry lines hung listlessly above her, and a tortoiseshell cat stretched across a dusty doorstep, languorously washing his paws. There were broader avenues than this choked little byway, but she'd rather be home faster, and this route was more direct.

Croft's voice surfaced from memory, chiding her not to be reckless with her safety, but he'd been referring to the dangers of the hospital wards: fever, fatigue, infection. Her lips twisted wryly. Croft was too preoccupied with medicine to consider the risks of shadowy, nearly deserted lanes. She often took this shortcut, in spite of the objections of Mrs. Phipps.

But this alley didn't feel dangerous. The ragged figures flitting further down the narrow recess were only children. Nora couldn't make herself fear them—foolish perhaps, given the plight of Bologna's tribe of beggars, but they looked so fragile and small, like the sparrows who came for the crumbs Mrs. Phipps scattered on her windowsill.

The lane widened, and Nora stepped into a sunlit square, her thoughts trailing backward to the hospital and how she'd failed to impress Dr. Marenco. A costly mistake, especially considering how great an advantage it would be to have Dr. Marenco on her side. After a year—after this week, especially— she was ready to give up on winning over Barilli, Venturoli, and the other professors. Her defeat with Dr. Marenco was harder to take. They were both women. They had to have experiences in common. But Dr. Marenco was commanding, competent, beautiful—all qualities Nora wanted, but apparently lacked.

How had Dr. Marenco won her place in the hospital? As Nora puzzled, a young man leered at her from a shadowed doorframe. She narrowed her eyes, warning he'd be in more danger than she if he approached. She wanted only an excuse to take out her temper on some ill-mannered man, and she certainly couldn't when it came to Barilli and Sagese.

The fellow stepped back, intending nothing more than to tease her with his eyes. Her thoughts twitched immediately back to Marenco. Medicine wasn't a path a woman could take alone; she must have had advocates, like Nora, who'd been taught from childhood by Horace and recruited to the University of Bologna by Professor Salvio Perra. Certainly Dr. Marenco's renowned father and mother must have given her a strong start. No woman made it far without powerful allies. Nora assumed their similar backgrounds should have bonded them, but Dr. Marenco obviously didn't feel so.

Usually Nora did better, even with the doctors who resented her. Horace's mercurial temper had taught her how to get on with nearly any disposition. The sisters certainly never complained about her performance. But they were nuns, not doctors and surgeons. However much Nora admired them, she wasn't one of them.

Nora wrinkled her nose and brow, realizing she'd come to a standstill under the trees valiantly maintaining a barricade against this dry summer's heat on the south end of the square.

Lost in thought as she was, the shade was too inviting to quit unconsciously, which must be why she was here, not walking east along the side of the Gothic basilica behind her. She should have turned a hundred yards back. Luncheon and her lecture notes were waiting.

Nora turned around, squinting against the sun as she retraced her steps in front of the basilica's cliff-like facade. A pink house with white shutters, facing the long side of Basilica di San Francesco, stood halfway down the street. Wedged between larger neighbors, only two windows wide, composed of three floors and an attic, it was indistinguishable from many houses in Bologna, save for the ragged-looking English roses Mrs. Phipps stubbornly insisted on cultivating on her balcony, next to pots of abundant Madonna lilies more suited to the local climate.

Newer than the medieval buildings skirted by Bologna's famous porticos, this house was clean, close to the anatomical theater and the hospital, and closer still to the grass and trees in the nearby square, a luxury Nora and Mrs. Phipps had both deemed essential. Like London, Bologna was inescapably dirty, crowded, even cold and wet in the winters—but London had parks. There was little greenery in the heart of this city except private courtyards or rooftop gardens, and no miles of paths to walk.

Nora missed Lincoln's Inn Fields and the gardens in Regent's Park, but the beauty of the red city and its arched porticos had grown on her. She liked walking beneath them, looking in the stalls and watching the people gathering to share news in the shade or out of reach of the winter rains.

Those freezing rains seemed as improbable as a fairy tale today. Nora dabbed the sweat from her forehead with her handkerchief and let herself inside. She was thinking of Marenco and Barilli again, despite her valiant attempts to put their snide faces from her mind.

"Nora? What is it?" Mrs. Phipps looked up from her jigsaw table. It was one of the few activities she could do with Signora Carnicelli without being frustrated by their language barrier.

Nora dashed a hand across her eyes. She meant to give a reassuring reply, but her lips wouldn't form a lie. "I'm not perfect," she said, attempting to make the words into a jest. "And I try so hard to be."

Signora Carnicelli didn't know what she'd said, but she understood the tears and frowned with sympathy.

Mrs. Phipps stood and came toward her, her hands extended. "Of course you're not." She frowned. She was never a woman to coddle. "Why should you have to be?"

It was an eminently sensible response, but in so many ways, perfection was necessary. Patients depended on her. Her professors and the doctors expected nothing less. "I can't afford mistakes," she said dully. Other students could, from time to time, but as the only female student…

"Perfection is an impossible standard," Mrs. Phipps said. "You ought to know better." Nora did, but she still sought it in the neatness of her sutures, in the precise lines of her notes. In her private diaries, she kept her own records, comparing her performance to that of the other members of her class. This month, Bartolomeo Pozzi had lost seven cases to sepsis compared to her four. But Umberto Sagese, lean-faced, quick-fingered, an artist with the knife and the needle, had lost only three.

Nora scratched her shoulder. Her dress was cut simply and not particularly well, leaving a red chafe mark over her left clavicle. "Take that thing off," Mrs. Phipps said. "You're all wrinkled."

Smelly too, though Mrs. Phipps was too kind to say so. Signora Carnicelli's expression made it plain as she leaned away from the offending odors.

"I'll wash and change," Nora said. "But I have to go back."

Nora disappeared into her bedchamber where she could attack her buttons alone. Agitation made her clumsy, and she struggled furiously with her tightly fastened cuffs. They'd always been just a bit too confining. Finally freed, she shucked off the dress and stood in her underclothes in the darkened room, breathing harder than necessary.

The air was still, inordinately heavy. Nora pushed back the shutters, banishing the dark, but the heat outside was just as thick as the air inside the room. She moved to the washstand, where at least the water was colder than her skin. Her arms, too pale and freckled to look well in Italian summer sun, prickled from the chill. As Nora patted her face dry with a lilac-scented towel, her eyes fell on the dressing table, where a folded letter was propped against her hairbrush on top of the mirror-bottomed tray.

The letter was smudged from travel, but Nora knew at once it was freshly arrived, placed here by Mrs. Phipps to surprise her where she could tear it open in privacy. A letter from Daniel—his slanting handwriting always ran smaller at the end of a line than at the beginning—was just the balm she needed today. Nora brought the paper to her lips, closed her eyes and breathed, but no smell of Daniel clung to it. Which was just as well, because after a day in the hospital or a stint in the dissection room, he would smell just as sour as she did.

Her thumb cracked the seal and she opened the folds.

O dainty duck, O deare! he wrote, and Nora smiled as the weight she'd been carrying drifted off her forehead and shoulders. In his letters, Daniel had proven unexpectedly romantic. He did not litter the page with endearments, but his greeting was always carefully chosen, and he never used the same one twice. This one, she suspected, was from a book or a play or a poem a literary reader would recognize. She was not a literary reader, but ignorance of the source didn't make her enjoyment any less. These sweet words, sometimes puzzling, often absurd, occasionally seductive enough to make her blush, were all treasured. How did he find time to hunt out all of them or remember, after a year's worth of letters, not to repeat any? More than any direct avowal, it told her she mattered to him.

I love you, she thought and, after registering the date in the top right-hand corner, she drank in the words of the letter.

Hot as blazes here this week. We were all glad for the rain to come today. I feel like I'm continually wilting, but then I think of you, cooking in the Italian sun, and feel ashamed of myself. Have you gotten any rain? When you told me it had been more than a fortnight, it was hard to imagine... I removed an enormous bladder stone from a patient today. We attempted a variation on the usual procedure, sounding the stone with the patient sedated...

She read on.

His news, whether medically detailed or quite ordinary, transported her to Great Queen Street, where Daniel and Horace worked, argued, and slept in fits and starts, but more often spent late hours carving out secrets from clandestinely acquired corpses night after night. She missed the wet afternoons in London, the stink of the river, the brisk rattle of English voices, the proper making of a savory pie. Little things, but they meant home and the men she'd pulled together into her own version of a family.

Her lip wobbled. The sting of failure was gone now, replaced by a bone-deep ache. Nora sank her head to her hands and took long, low breaths. If she cried, Mrs. Phipps might hear her.

A moment's pause, then her eyes were clear enough to read again.

In short—Can I say that at the end of a four-page letter? Probably not. Forgive my stupidity—I keep terrifically busy. It's the only way I know not to perish from want of you. Horace will never admit it but his angina is growing worse so I feel I must guard him from overwork. An almost impossible task, but it keeps me occupied enough to sometimes dull the ache of being parted from you. Keep steady on and good luck with Professor Barilli's course. Send me useful notes.

All my love,
Daniel

Hands and letter dropped to her lap; Nora sighed, recognizing a little ruefully that she'd become a cliché. Next she'd be pounding her heart and groping for a handkerchief.

No, she wasn't quite that foolish, thank heavens. She was homesick. Though Daniel tried to make it sound innocuous, any mention of Horace's heart sent her stomach plummeting. Forgetting her luncheon, she went to her writing desk and filled three sheets for her "Dear Daniel," enumerating the humiliations suffered in Dr. Barilli's hernia demonstration, her infuriating awkwardness during the surgery with Dr. Marenco, and the tantalizing opportunity of learning to do such a procedure herself.

You and I have often worried whether I can find an English guild that will license me so I can legally work. But I imagine many English women would prefer a female doctor attending their births, which could sway a college or guild in my favor. This could be the right work for me, if I can convince Dr. Marenco to like me enough to spare the time to teach me. I'm as anxious about her as I am about Professor Barilli's class and will need all the luck you can send me. Thank you for caring for Horace in my absence. Mrs. Phipps is uneasy being away. She's grown used to mothering him and misses London more than I do, if that's possible.

Writing was helpful in soothing her pride, but the more she wrote, the more Nora longed for Daniel and home. In moments like this, her loneliness was as blinding as a migraine.

The reassurances she repeated like a catechism—another year isn't long, he misses you too, you'll be home before you know it—only helped so much.

A year *wasn't* long, but it felt like a lifetime, and her carefully rationed determination was fading fast. But she was here for a reason. She must earn her degree.

But—

There was no requirement of how much time students needed to spend at the university. Only that they finished their classes and practicals.

She set down her pen to toy with this new idea. Already her professors kept her at a frenetic pace. Lopping months off her course of study seemed brazenly overconfident. She already drew attention as the only woman in her class.

So why not draw a little more? the bolder, braver part of her questioned. *You could do it if it speeds you on your way home.*

Some might be afraid of the workload and schedule, but hadn't she been raised by Horace Croft, a man who considered the need for sleep an inconvenient weakness? If anyone was trained for long hours, she was.

A current passed over her skin, as it always did when she faced a challenge. She looked down at her hands. Steady. She pulled in a breath. If she could convince herself, perhaps there was a chance she could convince the people who mattered.

CHAPTER 4

DANIEL STRODE DOWN THE LONG FIRST-FLOOR CORRIDOR at St. Bartholomew's Hospital, London, acknowledging a passing student's deferential nod with one of his own and pairing it with a friendly smile. He knew the value of those better than most. A year and a half ago, he hadn't been welcome here, dismissed and disgraced after countermanding an order from the chief of surgery. Now he was responsible for his own ward, forty beds in two long rows reserved for children—not the most coveted assignment, but Daniel counted himself lucky to be back. A surgeon's reputation suffered if he wasn't affiliated with a hospital, no matter what he achieved in his private practice.

He went into the ward, circling his neck and rubbing a painful knot in his left trapezius. Coddling tired muscles would have to wait because his young wound dresser was already hurrying toward him. "What have we today?" Daniel asked, shrugging out of his coat. He'd intended to arrive more than an hour ago, but a kidney stone removal at the clinic at home had taken longer than expected.

"A case of the croup," Jeffers responded in his transatlantic Boston drawl. "Arrived this afternoon and doing very poorly. I wondered—"

That was the trouble with Jeffers. Too deferential, even after months as one of Daniel's three wound dressers. "Show me," Daniel interrupted, wincing at the pinch in his neck as he hung his coat on the rack.

Every bed in the ward was full. "She's on a cot at the end," Jeffers said, pointing to a hastily erected screen. Daniel raised a questioning eyebrow.

"A great deal of coughing," Jeffers explained. "But there's an orderly watching her. She's not alone."

"Let me take a look." Halfway down the ward, Daniel heard rasping barks, three in succession, followed by a high, thin wheeze. The coughs were typical of croup or laryngitis, but the wheeze—"Was stridor present before?" Daniel asked.

"Not this loud," Jeffers admitted.

Daniel abandoned his brisk walk for a run. Rounding the screen, bag in hand, he found a young girl with sweat-soaked plaits, sitting in the bed, fighting for breath between rib-cracking coughs as the frantic orderly waved spirits of ammonia beneath her nose.

"Her color—" Daniel broke off, for he'd seen cases like this before. Dyspnea came on fast. Jeffers couldn't be expected to know. Still… "You should have sent for me," Daniel growled, rifling through his bag.

"You were operating on Mr. Cavendish," Jeffers said. "I didn't want to—"

Daniel cursed under his breath. Though Jeffers lacked experience, he knew the business of medicine well enough. A surgeon's paying patients came first. God help the man who tried to live off a hospital salary.

"Someone else could have supervised Cavendish's recovery," Daniel muttered, to himself as much as Jeffers. "Move aside, please."

The orderly removed the vinaigrette. Daniel bent over with his wooden stethoscope, but a new fit of coughing obscured anything he hoped to hear. "It's fine, you'll be all right," he said, smiling at the girl with a certainty he didn't feel, hoping to alleviate the terror in her glassy eyes. Her face was purple, every breath a battle. She couldn't be more than seven or eight, and her checks were full, her limbs well formed. Before this illness, she'd been healthy.

"Where is her mother?" he asked, painfully aware of the empty silence where there should have been pleading, desperation.

"She's from the textile mill. No parents."

No payment for treatment. That explained why she'd been left for last.

Daniel waited until her coughing paused and sounded from the top of her lungs to her chin, his own throat clenching at the high, tight sound of air looking for an almost nonexistent passage.

"Don't give up," he told her.

"Do you want me to fetch more menthol?" Jeffers asked.

Daniel shook his head as his hand closed around a fine scalpel. Too late for inhalants. The child was dying from lack of air. "Be ready with a cannula."

Jeffers obeyed at once, extracting the steel breathing tube, hovering at Daniel's side.

While a student in Paris, one of Daniel's teachers had

attempted this numerous times during a particularly vicious outbreak of upper respiratory disease among the city's children. All twenty had perished.

From fever, not suffocation, Daniel reminded himself, though that was true in only twelve of the cases. Too many had expired during or just after the procedure. He himself had maintained artificial respiration for thirty minutes on a six-year-old boy, hoping to revive him after they'd cleared his trachea of mucus and pseudomembrane and inserted the steel breathing cannula in place.

"Keep breathing," he told the girl, while a quick tilt of his head warned the orderly and Jeffers that he was counting on them to hold her still. Noting her corded neck muscles, turgid veins, darkening color, and heaving chest, Daniel forced her chin back, pinching a fold of skin and dividing it lengthwise with a quick swipe of the scalpel. The girl bucked and thrashed, but by now another orderly had come running and flung himself atop her legs before she could do more than shove Daniel back half a foot. He stepped forward again, keeping his hands steady and lengthening the incision.

"Upper ring to the top of the sternum," he said, between clenched teeth, for Jeffers's benefit, "exposing the ringed trachea... Sponge, please." Daniel probed, the cartilage resisting his touch before marking the correct spot where the soft tissue yielded. He pressed down and punctured it with the slightest pressure of his scalpel. At the Sorbonne, the doctors had made every hole in the trachea with their fingers, puncturing the tissue as easily as a thin slice of beef, but the holes were imprecise, unpredictable. Instantly the girl's chest inflated like a great, rising sea, and he slid the cannula in place.

The girl stopped kicking and opened her mouth, unaware the air she was gulping was now entering through her neck. "Once her color's better, we'll clear the obstructing secretions," Daniel said, wiping the sweat off his forehead. "At the moment we must ensure she doesn't try to pull the cannula out. Bandage the skin surrounding it so none of the blood soaks into the opening and starts up a case of pneumonia."

Jeffers nodded, his eyes wide. "How…" He blinked and tried again. "That was so fast, Dr. Gibson." Realizing he sounded like a first-year on his first day, he swallowed, his cheeks flaming.

"With a tracheotomy, every second counts," Daniel said. "Once you've seen it done a few times and practiced yourself—" He couldn't say more, not with the girl lying between them, the orderlies still restraining her. He directed his words to her. "We can let go if you give me your word to not thrash about or disturb your neck," he told her. "I know that was frightening but it was the only way to let you breathe. Rest a few moments." He gave a quick squeeze to her hand. Tears were still slipping down her face, but she'd finished crying, too relieved to have air in her lungs once more. Daniel nodded to the orderlies to release her.

He wouldn't mind trying ether to stop her from struggling when they attempted the unpleasant task of clearing her throat of whatever prurient mass was currently obstructing it, but unless he removed the inhaler's mask and fitted the tubing to the tracheotomy cannula—two different diameters—*and* stopped her mouth and nose so the ether would be forced into her lungs instead of escaping into the surrounding air…

"We'll have to be quick clearing the secretions," he said, shaking his head. Last week a wound dresser had collapsed beside the table from inhaling ether that had escaped from a patient's poorly fitting mask. Improvising on the fly—when it wasn't strictly necessary—wasn't a sound idea.

He drew out his watch, counting seconds and watching the changing tints in the girl's round cheeks. "When did she fall ill?"

"She turned feverish two days ago but didn't begin coughing until midway through the night. When it turned to croup, they brought her in," Jeffers said.

Daniel frowned. Croup and laryngitis were common. He bent over the child with his stethoscope. She flinched at first, then relaxed once she realized he wasn't holding anything sharp. With her coughs and struggles alleviated, it was easy to tell that the lungs themselves were clear. "I don't hear any pneumonia," Daniel said. Jeffers smiled, so Daniel didn't tell him the lack of fluid in the lungs only increased his misgivings.

Wise doctors didn't alarm their colleagues or their patients with guesses.

But a quarter of an hour later, when the orderlies once again held the child down, and Daniel's forceps probed a gray pseudomembrane adhering to the weeping child's throat, Daniel knew his suspicion was right.

"Is that—?"

Daniel nodded. In spite of the overly deferential manner that handicapped him, Jeffers was remarkably well read for a second-year student. "My French professors called the croup that produces this type of gray pseudomembrane *diphtérite*." Diphtheria.

Jeffers's eyes were too wide to open any farther. He swallowed. "I've heard of the condition—also called malignant croup?" He lowered his voice. "The disease they call the child strangler."

Daniel darted his eyes to the patient, lying easy once again now that they were finished meddling with her. For the time being.

"It might be scarlet fever," Jeffers said hopefully.

"I don't see a rash," Daniel said quietly. They would, of course, check her, but—

Jeffers spoke again, this time in a softer voice. "I saw records of an epidemic of malignant croup over a hundred years ago in New England."

Daniel hadn't read them, or heard of the epidemic, but he understood why Jeffers continued in a whisper, why sweat was breaking on his pale forehead. "The reports indicated a forty percent mortality rate. They told of families losing three or four children—or all."

Daniel nodded. He didn't mention the twenty cases in Paris.

Nora walked down the corridor, her portfolio clutched to her chest. She'd never seen the great English universities, but it was hard to imagine they could rival this. The red-and-gray-checked floor tiles stretched for an immense length before her. The walls and the arched ceiling were ornamented with plaques, shields, and paintings, all gilded and brightly colored. With most teachers and students still enjoying the *pausa pranzo*, or midday break, the place was nearly deserted. One professor, his university gown accentuating the stoop of his shoulders, passed her on his way into the library, and then she was alone.

It does no harm to ask, she reminded herself.

She made her way to the anatomical theater, where, as she'd hoped, Professor Perra was preparing for his afternoon lecture under the watching eyes of the *spellatti*—the dark wood statues of skinless men posed at the end of the room. Perra was intent on a preserved lung specimen but the student beside him looked up at her entrance.

Nora dipped her chin in greeting. "Good afternoon, Professor. Good afternoon, Pozzi." Most medical students called each other by their last names, but after a year she remained Signorina Beady to all of them. That didn't stop her from using the informal address. They might not see her as one of them, but she was all the same—and stubborn enough to keep pushing for it.

Pozzi, long-limbed and perpetually uneasy, bowed as he would to a lady of his acquaintance. Nora's smile turned rigid but softened again when Perra acknowledged her with a more collegial nod. "Eleanora, what brings you so early?"

"I was hoping to speak to you."

They'd shared a ship from London, and since then, he'd developed a habit of using her Christian name. Since it was well known he'd supported her admission, no one seemed too surprised, assuming he must be a friend of her family's—like a de facto uncle, Nora supposed. More than once, she'd noticed Sagese's lip curling when Perra called on her in lectures or during hospital rounds. "If it's not inconvenient, sir," she added. Being careful with the courtesies due a professor might prevent Pozzi from passing on stories of Perra's supposed favoritism.

"Not at all." Perra turned to Pozzi. "I must excuse you for

now, Bartolomeo. I will finish my explanation in lecture. Study the chambers of the heart before you come."

"Yes, Professor." Pozzi's dark, wavy hair needed trimming and his eyes were shadowed. Some students said he might lose his scholarship and have to quit. Nora waited until he'd walked up the stairs, along the length of the spectator's railing, and out the door.

"I—"

Perra was shaking his head. "That boy could do well, but he's lost confidence in himself."

"It's easy to do when so much hangs in the balance, sir," Nora said.

"True." Perra assessed her with a tiny smile. "What is it that troubles you?"

He was always kind to her. He might refuse her request, but he wouldn't look down his nose in the condescending way Dr. Magdalena Marenco did. "It's about my examination," Nora said, clasping her hands in front of her to keep from fidgeting with her dark-blue skirt.

"You're worrying prematurely," Perra said. "And I've heard good reports from your teachers. When the time comes—"

"That's what I want to speak about," Nora said, blushing from the determination required to interrupt him. "I'd like to face my examination early."

He picked up one of his pins, marking a discoloration on the surface of the lung. It looked eerily like the black lung of British miners.

"Your eagerness is a double-edged sword." He frowned as he carefully adhered a square of white paper to a second discoloration. "It shows passion, but too much haste is foolish. You don't want to rush your education. The professors won't make your examination easy."

Nora nodded. No student looked forward to defending their thesis in front of the professors, answering any and all questions on every conceivable subject. And the last time a woman had earned her degree, she'd been pelted with questions for an hour longer than any student in living memory, passing only by the skin of her teeth.

"You can't afford to fail, Eleanora," Perra said. "You are judged more harshly than most."

"I know," Nora conceded, her eyes fixed on the white paper against the purple-gray flesh. She was tempted to tell him of the ache she felt when she thought of home, but he'd think her weak and sentimental.

Perra's inscrutable eyes trailed over her face. "This is not such a poor place to be, no? You've done very well here. Better than many." His eyes flashed to the doorway, and she knew he was thinking of Pozzi.

"He's not yet twenty," she said.

Perra shrugged. "This is his time to learn. And yours. I wouldn't think you would treat it so lightly." He turned his eyes away from her. "I admit I'm disappointed."

Her chest constricted, as if trying to make her disappear altogether. She stammered, the words hot on her heavy tongue. "I'm sorry, sir. I never meant to make you think—"

Nora pushed back against an invading memory of Daniel gently adjusting her fingers to demonstrate the best angle to expose the subcostal nerve. She clenched her hands to clear the tingle from her fingertips. How she longed for an ally now. "I thought you might believe I could do it." Nora's voice was small, aimed at the floor, but embellished with a hint of petulance that made her blush. "I've done well in my classes. I've taken extra lessons from Doctor Venturoli and Sister Madonna Agnes." The sister, known for her work at the orphanage apothecary, hadn't been offered a position at the university, but she was licensed by them to dispense within the orphanage and her expertise brought her a number of private students.

"You are doing remarkably well," Perra admitted. "And the demonstrations you've offered to me and my colleagues with ether generate a good deal of interest."

"I've been assisting with dissections since I was hardly more than a child. I helped in the clinic from the age of fourteen." Some of her fellow students came to the university having never held a scalpel or stethoscope. "I won't risk my chance to earn a degree," Nora assured him. "It's too important to me. But if I work hard, I think I can be ready in another six months."

He narrowed his eyes, considering. "For your degree, yes. But of course you'll need to stay at least another year to gain your practical experience. Only then can you join the list of physicians and surgeons licensed to practice in Bologna."

She didn't answer, her chest so tight it pulled like a newly wound clock, and his frown deepened. When he spoke, his voice was low and somber. "But I suppose you intend to go back to your young man and that deplorable English climate."

Nora squirmed, the mortification of letting down the one professor who believed in her almost enough to make her withdraw her request. "It would be an honor to practice beside you, but Dr. Croft expects me back."

"He thinks the other English doctors will allow you to use your degree?"

"We hope so. Once I'm qualified, there's no logical reason why I shouldn't—" Nora broke off. Logic had little to do with English medical regulations.

Perra studied her a moment, then gave her a perfunctory smile that only emphasized the sadness in his eyes. "If you are determined, I cannot stop you from trying. But you'll need to meet with me regularly for private lessons—like Pozzi. Every week."

"You would do that for me?" Nora asked, finally daring to look him full in the face.

"I recommended you for study here, and I won't see you fail." He laid a linen cloth over the shrunken lungs and turned as if he wanted to say more but finished with only a careless "Good," said absently and without conviction. When he added nothing more and kept his back turned, she backed silently from the room, her pleasure at his permission tempered by the unease smoldering like a spent fire in her stomach.

When darkness finally fell that night—it was not only the long summer twilight, but a burnished full moon that made the lectures extend long into the evening—Nora retired to her room for a rare moment of privacy to review her letter to Daniel while Mrs. Phipps conversed with the landlady on the balcony. Nora could hear their stilted conversation through the thin walls as they exchanged a day's worth of gossip, something Signora Carnicelli always had in abundance. Mrs. Phipps had painfully accrued enough Italian to be dangerous, and their awkward conversations were usually punctuated with Signora's laughter and corrections. Nora smiled as she reread a line and imagined Daniel rummaging through his Italian dictionary to discover the translation of *languire di desiderio*, and how he would blush when he saw it meant longing.

She tapped the page absently. There was room at the bottom for a brief postscript. If she told him she was accelerating her studies, he and Horace would count her early return as a surety. In six months, if she failed her examination or was forced to postpone, the defeat would be much worse, knowing she had disappointed them as well.

The pen in the inkstand seemed to taunt her. Did she truly believe she could do this if she couldn't record her decision on paper?

Telling Daniel has nothing to do with it, she told herself. She'd persuaded Perra to let her try. That was enough. Confiding in Daniel now felt unlucky. Better to surprise him with good news than let him down with bad.

She pushed her loose hair off her face, pressed the pen to the paper, and added only one sentence. *Give Horace a drachm of salicin at the first sign of angina and sit him down with an interesting specimen to keep him still for a couple of hours.*

She sealed the letter and put it in her bag to post on her walk to the hospital tomorrow.

CHAPTER 5

WHEN NORA ARRIVED AT THE HOSPITAL IN THE MORNing, she went directly to the women's ward to check again on Lucia, the cesarean patient, as she had for the last five days. Each morning she found her alive was another small miracle. The sisters had already opened the window shutters, so Nora saw, all the way from the other end of the ward, that someone else was already there with her patients. Her lips tightened under her narrowed eyes. She hadn't done so badly last week—not enough for Dr. Marenco to assign Lucia's care to someone else.

Theoretically, an attending physician could make any changes he—or she, Nora added stubbornly—wished at any time, but most respected the custom of allowing the student who was first on the scene to see a case to completion. Perra, currently serving as president of the hospital, staunchly advocated such an approach as beneficial to students and patients. Every doctor had favorites, of course, but most were tolerant enough to give every student a chance.

Replacing Nora with another student, almost a week into the patient's recovery, was a stinging and unfair rebuke, made worse coming from a woman who might have been a natural ally.

"Did you forget your way, Eleanora?" Sister Maria Celeste smiled gently at her, and Nora realized her feet had turned to ballast blocks. She was standing like an unwanted guest between the rows of beds, blocking Maria Celeste and her heavily laden tray.

"No, I—" Nora broke off, tearing her eyes away from the man bending over Lucia Sarni. With his back to her, she couldn't see his face. "I can help with the patients' breakfasts," she offered.

"That is very kind of you," Sister Maria Celeste said. "We're busy already this morning. Perhaps first you could assist Signora Langone in bed number five? Dr. Bertocchi ordered a warm-water enema."

Dr. Bertocchi never administered his own enemas. "Certainly," Nora said, and started for the cupboard to fetch the necessary supplies.

She was halfway down the ward when the man at Lucia Sarni's bedside turned. Nora missed a step. This wasn't Umberto Sagese, the darling of all the professors. Marenco had replaced her with Pozzi, who was always bottom of the class. Wooden-faced, Nora swallowed the searing insult and marched the rest of the way to the cupboard.

Nora was not so ambitious or hardened to feel any vindication when, two days later, it became clear Lucia was dying. Though Nora rated her skills above Bartolomeo Pozzi's, she wasn't vain enough to assume her efforts would have yielded any better outcome, and Dr. Marenco had made it clear Nora's assistance wasn't wanted. She stayed away, but her eyes were frequently drawn to Lucia's bed.

She was sounding a teenage girl's distended abdomen when

a priest came and walked solemnly to Lucia's bedside. Nora's eyes traveled like magnets to the scene, no matter how often she pulled them away. Lucia's yellow face had collapsed like the tip of a spent candle, her eyes no longer registering the people around her. Two nuns flanked the priest, their heads bowed, their vestures forming a black wall that hid the deathbed. Nora made certain none of them noticed her and the awkward way her hands jerked as regret tightened her joints. It was just as well she wasn't wanted there. She could not bear to think Lucia might, in some final flash of cognizance, recognize her and remember her foolish promise that Lucia would recover.

Nora straightened and put away her stethoscope, turning her full attention back to her own patient. *Ascites.* One of the students had mistaken the round, swollen belly as pregnancy, but the girl swore it would have to be an immaculate conception. She was telling the truth. Nora gave the girl a tender look. "It is fluid in your abdomen and can be easily fixed. It is not very painful." The girl's anxious eyes flinched. *Very* was a relative term. "One of the doctors will drain the swelling," Nora told her, unwilling to say more.

Even when Professor Perra arrived and confirmed Nora's theory, complimenting her percussion technique, she felt little satisfaction.

"You will help me drain this tomorrow," Perra said, at last capturing Nora's attention. "It will be a useful demonstration for your classmates."

Nora's head jumped up, checking his face for sarcasm. He smiled kindly, his eyes also traveling to the grim huddle around Lucia's bed.

"Yes, sir. I'd be honored." She'd been invited to demonstrate ether in small groups, but never to assist in a public surgery. She had only a day to prepare. Her eyes flew down to her skirt. She'd need a fresh apron pressed tonight.

"We will schedule it after *pausa pranzo* at four o'clock," he told her before leaving her to digest the good news.

"Will it hurt?" the teenaged girl whispered from the bed.

Nora shook her head. "When we finish, you'll be much more comfortable." The procedure wouldn't require ether or even a scalpel and was one of the simplest ways a surgeon could help. Nora reassured the girl with a smile instead of specific words, distracted by the drama of Lucia's death playing out only a few beds away.

Nora replaced her pen in her brown kit bag, but instead of leaving the ward, she approached Sister Maria Celeste.

"Isn't there something we can do for her?" she asked, tilting her head in Lucia's direction.

Maria Celeste shook her head. "Dr. Marenco says the organs are inflamed already. Tonight I'll take her other children to the orphanage."

"But her husband—" Nora said, appalled. She had seen the orphanages.

"Cannot care for the younger ones while he works. He begs half the time as it is."

Nora released her bottom lip. She'd been chewing it. "I told her she would be all right."

Sister Maria Celeste smiled. She had a round face with colorless brows and eyelashes. Some of the students called her "the dumpling," but the name seemed ill-fitting now. She was completely serene and confident. "Lucia has received absolution. She will be."

Nora's mouth twisted and she looked away.

"Have faith. You won't despair so much," Maria Celeste said and walked away after giving Nora a pat on the arm.

Horace had taught her how to fight for a patient, but never how to make peace with God when she lost the battle. Nora pulled in a bitter breath, certain she could feel the heat of Lucia's fever from across the room.

After supper, Nora stole back to the ward, her heartbeats pausing as she glanced through the shadows of the evening. A reassuring mound of blankets told her Lucia's bed was not empty yet. Nothing was so scarring a sight as a clean, smooth blanket where a patient once lay. Nora made her way quietly down the rows of beds, her boots muffled on the tiled floor. In the gloom she could see the eyes of the patients who were still awake trailing her.

Nora reached for Lucia's chart, brought it beside her candle, and scanned the dismal notes from earlier in the day, then the days before, a reverse sequence of Lucia's progression from dire to weak to merely weary as she flipped the pages.

17 Aug. One p.m.—*Dyspnea. Pulse sinking. Administered 10 minims aromatic spirit of ammonia.*

"It won't be much longer," said a bitter voice.

Nora turned. Bartolomeo Pozzi stood behind her, his arms folded, a scowl on his face.

"I know." She'd witnessed enough death to be sure of that. Lucia was thin, wasted, her pale face glazed with sweat. Her open eyes were unfocused and dull. She hadn't reacted to Pozzi's voice.

"Another black mark for me. You won't lose any points for this one." The disgust in his voice stung.

She paused, remembering how Daniel had turned into a mere husk of himself after one of his patients died of a blood infection following a minor finger amputation. "The best doctors I know hate to lose their patients, but they still do it often enough."

"Spare me. I know I won't make it through. The sooner I leave, the better for everyone." His thin shoulders hitched a little higher, accentuating the lopsidedness of his cravat.

Nora licked her lips. "This isn't your fault."

He laughed. "I'm not so arrogant as that. But if I had any promise, they'd trust me with patients who at least have an even chance." His eyes didn't leave Lucia. "I've signed eighteen death certificates this month."

Nora wasn't friends with any of her classmates, and Pozzi was normally as awkward around her as the rest of them, but his confession made her stomach twist with pity. No one could be expected to bear up under such heavy defeats, certainly not a boy as young as he.

"You have promise. You won a scholarship," she said, hoping he hadn't just lost it after yesterday's test in microscopy.

Pozzi grimaced. "His Grace, the Duke of Modena, sent me here as a kindness to my family. When my father died—" He broke off. "I'm the eldest and the only bookish one, except for my sister," he finished miserably.

"You aren't going to fail," Nora said, hoping wildly that this wasn't another of her predictions that would soon be proven wrong. "Your family is counting on you, no?" Barely waiting for his guilty nod, she went on. "Of course it's harder for some of us. I've spent almost a decade studying anatomy. Umberto Sagese has been mentored by his uncle. Your father—"

"Was a clerk," Pozzi filled in. "I'd never seen a scalpel, let alone held one. And then—" He ducked his chin. He'd fainted twice in their first week of anatomy lectures, but that was almost a year ago; he'd since grown quite a tolerance. "Well, you remember. I know you keep track of every mistake I make."

She blanched. "Not that *you* make. I record the results of every case, including my own. How did you know I've been tracking fatalities?" Nora asked, wanting to turn the subject from his failures. She'd drawn satisfaction from her tally, but the exercise felt petty now.

Pozzi glanced at her. "Sagese saw it in your notes. You left them beside your bag during Lucia's surgery."

"He searched my notes?"

"He doesn't want you to beat him," Pozzi said.

Nora grunted. She wouldn't. Enough professors disliked female students to make sure of that. Still… "He's that worried?"

"They're all worried," Pozzi said. "You've done more dissections than anyone. When Perra awards his book prize—"

"The other professors would never agree to give it to me, and I couldn't afford to accept it in any case. I get enough accusations of favoritism already," Nora said. After a pause, she added, "I wish we could help Lucia."

The woman's chin quivered and her head rolled feebly to one side.

"Her husband came earlier. She was quieter then. I fear her pain is escalating," Pozzi said. "That's why I'm still here. I've tried twice to give her opium so she could at least pass comfortably, but she vomited both times."

Then Pozzi, on his own, must have changed her into a fresh nightdress and sheets.

"I could give her a small dose of ether," Nora said. Four minutes with the vaporizer would be enough to ease any pain and allow her sleep. "Will you help me?"

Some of the tension left his face. "Most gratefully, Signorina—"

"Just call me Beady," Nora said quickly. "I'd rather be addressed like the others."

He made a face. "Beady is—"

"Or Eleanora." Perra used it, so maybe she could persuade Pozzi, too. This was a hospital, not a dinner party. Daniel and Horace didn't trivialize her with obstructive courtesy, and she missed that, though not nearly as much as she missed them.

"Eleanora." Pozzi nodded. "It's a beautiful name."

It wasn't Nora, but it was close enough.

CHAPTER 6

EXPRESS THE BULB SLOWLY AND TRY TO AVOID ACTIVATING the gag reflex," Daniel instructed Jeffers, guiding the student's hand slightly to the right in the child's throat.

"Isn't there some way to cut away the membrane?" Jeffers looked down the blocked airway with the same helpless frustration Daniel felt. On the bed, the infant tried to cry but lacked the air to finish the task.

"You must avoid even touching it. It won't remove and the slightest agitation can cause profuse bleeding into the lungs."

Jeffers withdrew the bulb syringe and leaned away from the patient. "Then what can we do?" he demanded.

"You can apply poultices to the neck and rotate the patients to their stomachs to bring the mucus forward." The authoritative voice rang from behind them, and Daniel took a breath before turning. But Silas Vickery, chair of surgery, continued, his volume swelling. "You do not put them in a ward to infect other children, and you do not slit their throats and ram cannulas down their trachea, which will only clog with further mucus."

Daniel bit back a retort and smiled reassuringly at the baby's mother, who was stationed at the other side of the bed, frozen, though she had been rubbing soothing circles on a chubby palm. Her eyes flicked anxiously between him and Vickery.

"We're nearly done, Mrs. Thompkins," Daniel said, smiling reassuringly. "Bear with us a moment longer. Your boy will breathe so long as we keep this tube clear, but I'm afraid that means he'll have to endure the restraints." Taking the syringe from Jeffers, he positioned it once more into the throat, but this time only drew up half a cubic centimeter of mucus. Expelling it into the nearby dish, he used his free hand to run a cool cloth over the baby's forehead. "He'll pull out the tube if we free his arms."

"I expect an answer, Gibson," Vickery snapped.

"And you shall have one," Daniel returned evenly, still looking at his patient. "Later. At present, my full concentration is required."

He swabbed the baby's neck, checking the bandages that held the cannula in place, though behind him, Vickery's rage charged the air like a gathering storm cloud. "Watch those thumbs," Daniel warned as Jeffers gingerly applied more bandages.

"The tissues are so much smaller in children," Jeffers said as a bead of sweat rolled down his forehead.

"But you've done well," Daniel told him. "And learned, I think, the importance of possessing cannulae and syringes in a variety of sizes." He transferred his attention back to the troubled mother. "We've done the right thing. We'll check his throat again in an hour. Keep him as calm as you can."

She barely nodded, quelled by Vickery's disapproving frown. "Thank you, Doctor," she whispered.

Daniel smiled thinly, knowing her thanks—and the child's restored, even breathing—would win him no points from

Vickery. Still wiping his hands, he turned from the bed, hoping to make it a few paces away before confronting the angry chief of surgery, but Vickery was at him at once, practically standing on his toes.

"We can talk in my office," Daniel said quietly. "I don't allow raised voices on my ward. It's bad for the patients."

For a moment, he didn't think Vickery would let him move. The chief of surgery was a giant of a man, a good three or four inches taller than Daniel. He'd always used his size to his advantage, towering over other physicians and surgeons, but as Daniel braced his feet and clenched his teeth, preparing for the inevitable, Vickery wheeled around and stalked to the office.

Daniel let out a breath—it was all he had time for—and followed, closing the office door.

"You have a concern, sir?"

"Yes, I have a concern," Vickery spat out. "Is it you I have to thank for these two children dying with metal tubes in their necks? And the other brought in with scarlet fever who now is also showing symptoms of diphtheria?"

"We separated those two children from the others with screens. What more could we do?" Daniel had learned over the years that handling Vickery took a delicate balance of assertiveness and pretended deference, though he wanted to swear at him like a sailor. "The girl with the tracheotomy has survived the night and is still breathing. She would have already died of suffocation. So will the baby you just saw if we cannot keep his pharynx clear."

Vickery's nostrils flexed, catching the scent of insubordination mingled with the odors of sweat and urine that hovered over the wards. "You cannot admit diphtheria patients. They must be treated at home, away from our doctors and other patients. The risk of contagion is too great."

"You know that they live in rooms that are packed like cattle stalls. The disease would fly through families, neighborhoods."

"Better that than my hospital," Vickery growled.

"What do you suggest?" Daniel asked. "I cannot send them home like this. When they arrived, they were taken for cases of croup. We only discovered the membranes after the tracheotomies. Are you going to forbid anyone with a cough from coming into this place? Without treatment, these children will die."

"Prolonging their deaths with a tracheotomy—and mark my words, that's all you're doing—just keeps them lingering in the wards, expelling contagion and adding to the general miasma."

"So I should have let them suffocate?"

Vickery leveled his voice to a grave pronouncement. "They will still suffocate. Case after case shows that you cannot keep the cannulas clear of mucus. If it had been a piece of food or an obstruction, I would have done the procedure myself, but you are delaying the inevitable. They will suffocate on mucus in the cannula or in their tracheas. The death is the same." He gestured fiercely at the ward beyond the closed door. "Only now it is spreading and there will be more."

"I could not have foreseen that. I had to investigate the cause—"

"Investigate in the morgue. They won't infect anyone there," Vickery snarled.

"Forgive me, Dr. Vickery." Jeffers slid into the room.

"Send him out," Vickery said, not taking his eyes from Daniel.

"I'm sorry, but I couldn't help overhearing. I'm the one who admitted the patient, not Dr. Gibson," Jeffers inserted, not daring to look at Vickery, but not willing to back down, either.

Before Daniel could intervene, Vickery swiveled his attention to the wound dresser. "And?"

Jeffers shrank.

Daniel sighed. "We've put up screens," he repeated. "If additional children fall ill, we'll put up more. We can't let—"

Vickery turned back to Daniel and stepped closer, lowering his voice. "Get them out of this hospital now. And the tracheotomies stop."

"Just where do I take them?" Daniel persisted, through clenched teeth.

"To your clinic if you prefer. Let your patients die of this disease, but not mine." As Vickery stalked to the door, he sent Jeffers a scorching, contemptuous glance. "Beware attaching yourself to Dr. Gibson," Vickery said. "His days at this hospital are numbered."

Biting down the humiliation of the scene, Daniel brushed his unsteady fingers against the wool of his coat and watched Vickery retreat. "I appreciate your loyalty, Jeffers, but you should be careful. I understand if—"

"Why does Dr. Vickery dislike you so much?"

"We need to keep a constant monitor on the cannula patients. Every hour won't be enough anymore," Daniel said. "Especially now that Vickery's watching." He ran a hand through his hair and stared, unseeing, at the stack of papers on his desk. There was an empty bed in the clinic at home on Great Queen Street, but that would be needed for Mr. Clayton, who was scheduled for surgery to remove an axillary tumor in three days' time. There wasn't room for both children or the ones who'd also need care in the days ahead. Vickery was right in one thing—diphtheria spread like grass fires.

"Sir, about Vickery..."

Daniel collected himself with a mechanical smile. Jeffers wanted to know, and it wasn't fair not to tell him, especially since he seemed likely—for now—to back Daniel against all comers. "You weren't here when everything happened. I suppose the simplest answer is because I work with Horace Croft. Started here intending to be one of Vickery's dressers, in fact, but I switched loyalties the first time I heard Dr. Croft lecture."

Four years ago, but it seemed longer, with everything that had happened.

"But other doctors who support Dr. Croft don't draw his fire."

Other doctors hadn't been invited to join Croft's busy private practice. Daniel had, and the overture had given him a dose of confidence like no other achievement in his young career. Other than infrequent demonstrations, Croft hadn't welcomed any wound dressers, trainee doctors, or surgical apprentices into his practice for years, preferring to work on his own.

Or so Daniel had thought.

He must have seemed insufferably arrogant presenting himself at Croft's clinic. He'd been so proud at being chosen, when in truth, Croft already had a protégé—the ward Daniel had often seen at the hospital delivering Croft's lunches, case notes, and forgotten overcoat. He'd taken Nora merely as the helper she pretended to be, not realizing it was impossible for Croft to do all the dissections, experiments, successful treatments, and late-night birthings that were credited to him.

When Daniel remembered his horror at discovering the truth, her force when standing up to him...

"When Vickery gives orders, he expects everyone to comply. One time I didn't, and a patient died. Vickery had me dismissed," Daniel said, hoping this would suffice.

"But you—" Jeffers frowned, then began again in a quieter voice. "Patients die. Half the time people blame the doctor. They're not always wrong."

"Don't let your colleagues hear you say heresies like that," Daniel said, only half joking. "Working for me, you already have enemies enough."

"I'd rather work for you than Vickery."

"That's kind of you, but you should still be careful," Daniel said. "It doesn't hurt to take a leaf from Dr. Adams's book. Diplomacy," he added to clear Jeffers's momentary confusion.

"Is that how you got your job here back?" Jeffers asked, smiling skeptically.

"No."

"Then how?" Jeffers pressed.

"Dr. Croft and I—" Daniel broke off. He fixed his eyes on Jeffers, who straightened his shoulders just slightly. "What do you know of Miss Beady, Dr. Croft's ward?"

Jeffers blushed. "I read the papers from a year ago but figured... I figured it would be better to get the truth from you." He finished in a rush, his eyes on Daniel's waistcoat, as if expecting a rebuke.

"She and Dr. Croft and I—" Daniel smiled as recollections flooded over him. Telling it without including her name hadn't felt right. She was key to the story. "We were experimenting with ether. One night a man arrived on the doorstep of our clinic with an obstructed bowel. A strangulated hernia, which before had always been successfully reduced. Untangling the hernia surgically was his only hope, but Horace was out of town.

"Miss Beady is a skilled anatomist. I had no one else to help. She suggested we put Prescott to sleep with ether since it was impossible for the two of us to operate if we had to restrain him. I was going to resect the bowel—"

Jeffers blanched, as well he might. Tracheotomies were child's play in comparison.

"But once we opened him, Miss Beady was able to free the bowel and restore the blood flow."

"And Prescott survived," Jeffers filled in, excitement pinking his cheeks now. His words accelerated. "I read the case."

Daniel nodded, grimacing. "The case, once it was written up, brought more than a share of celebrity and notoriety." Celebrity for him, notoriety for her, once Vickery had exposed the truth that she'd performed the surgery with Daniel. It was criminally unfair that she'd become a pariah, fleeing London for Bologna, while here he was, two years later, on the receiving end of a worshipful glow in Jeffers's eyes. Daniel cleared his throat and straightened his cuffs.

Jeffers sighed. "I wish I could have seen it. How did she think of it?"

Daniel's grimace relaxed into a smile. "She's patient and thoughtful. I was ready to cut in a panic, but she followed Croft's advice and advanced quietly. Someday, you can ask her to tell the story, once she gets back from her studies in Italy. For now, will you check on our two patients? I need to make arrangements to move them."

A doctor's life, it often seemed, was a series of gambles mixed alternately with unsolvable and unnecessary problems.

"Of course, Dr. Gibson." Jeffers paused at the office door, grinning. "I'd like to meet Miss Beady once she's back, very much. Don't forget, because I'll hold you to it."

Once Jeffers had closed the door, Daniel sat down at his desk, letting out a rueful huff. Jeffers would just have to remind him, because he already had a long list of things to do with Nora once she was back. Parading her in front of admiring medical students, no matter how deserved such admiration might be, wasn't first, second, or even fifteenth.

Sorry, Jeffers.

Telling her about Jeffers would be an amusing anecdote for his next letter, the thought of which quieted the discomfort of missing her for a moment. He drew out a sheet of paper. Not to write Nora, because he couldn't write to her until he sent a message to Great Queen Street. Horace needed to know about the two diphtheria patients he might have to bring home at the end of his shift, thanks to Silas Vickery.

CHAPTER 7

THE CROWD GATHERED IN THE ANATOMICAL THEATER for Professor Perra's demonstration was larger than usual. Students from all classes crowded behind the rails separating the standing gallery that lined the sides of the room. Six professors occupied the raised bench facing the table. There was the usual selection of interested strangers, some of whom had managed to beat the students to prime places with unobstructed views. There was also, Nora noted, a woman in the gallery, noticeable because of her claret silk dress and matching velvet bonnet. When she turned her head, Nora recognized her. It was Dr. Marenco.

Nora met her eyes, then resumed her preparations on the marble-topped table: a blanket, then a sheet, so the patient wouldn't feel too cold or uncomfortable, two more sheets to use as drapes to protect her modesty, a tray with rubber tubing and a syringe ready. She glanced again to the gallery, past Dr. Marenco to—"Pozzi."

He looked away from the classmate at his elbow, his eyebrows lifting as Nora motioned with a tilt of her head for him to join her. The murmur in the room rose as he descended the wooden steps and let himself through the gate in the railing surrounding the demonstration table. He came so reluctantly he reminded her of a Christian stumbling into the Colosseum.

"What is it?" he hissed amid the rising murmurs of the spectators.

"I think I can get you a better view," Nora whispered back. "You have a syringe?"

"Not with me," he said, his eyes widening.

"Well, I want another. That's my excuse for asking you down. Find one, will you, before Professor Perra arrives?"

He stared at her with his fragile-looking black eyes, as horrified as if she'd asked him to bring her a beating heart, then sprinted from the theater. Hoping she wasn't making a mistake, Nora resumed her work. She wasn't sure she'd brought a large enough basin. Overnight, the patient—that teenaged girl she'd assessed yesterday—had swelled further, to the point that when sitting, her navel reached halfway to her knees.

Pozzi returned, bearing a syringe in each hand.

"You don't mind setting them up for me? I'm going to get another basin." Nora walked away without waiting for a response. If he couldn't prepare a syringe, he was beyond her help, and she rather thought he wouldn't appreciate it if she only asked him to fetch and carry for her. If his confidence and his reputation at the university were to be redeemed, he needed to be seen working.

When she brought back the second enamel basin, both syringes were ready. Pozzi fidgeted beside the table. "Does Professor Perra—"

"No," Nora said. "But I'll suggest to him—quietly—when he arrives with the patient that you help with the procedure. Have you percussed an abdomen with ascites before?"

Pozzi shook his head. His eyes were so wide she was fairly

sure he had no idea what she meant. Quickly, quietly, Nora rehearsed what would happen.

"The patient will lie on her back. You'll tap the abdomen, moving out from the navel, listening for the change between tympanic sound and dull sound. That's where gas bloating ends and the accumulated fluid begins. Mark that line." She flicked a finger surreptitiously at the stick of charcoal she'd left on the instrument tray. "Then we're going to rotate the patient onto her side. You'll repeat the percussion. This time, the dullness will shift. Mark that line. Shifting dullness means there's moving fluid in the abdomen. Fluid we can drain away. If there's no dullness, if it's all tympanic sound, the enlargement is gas. If the dullness doesn't move, there might be constipation, or a tumor or—"

"Yes. I know."

"Good. Perra and I both detected shifting dullness yesterday. This won't be hard. Can you do it?"

His eyes darted to the crowded gallery. He licked his lips. "Yes."

"Good," Nora said again. "Have you done a paracentesis?"

"No. But that's why you want the syringes. To drain the fluid away."

Nora nodded. "With three syringes, we can take turns readying them and passing them to Perra—though he may ask us to take a turn extracting the fluid."

"I don't know if I can," Pozzi whispered. "What if I—"

"If you truly can't do it, you should go home," Nora said. "But this is no harder than the treatments you did for Lucia. Think of it as the opposite of an enema."

Pozzi swallowed, his nervous gaze traveling the gallery again.

"Change their minds," Nora told him. "You'll find a place here if you fight for it."

His finely shaped mouth twitched. "Like you did."

"Like I do," Nora told him. "Sounding abdomens and learning surgical procedures is the easy part."

Pozzi looked more confident until Perra arrived, with the patient borne ahead of him by two orderlies on a stretcher. The poor girl was in considerable pain, whimpering softly and clutching her distended belly. Nora understood the confusion diagnosing her. The shape and size of the swelling looked exactly like a woman six months along.

"This won't take more than a few minutes," Perra assured the girl. His eyes lingered a moment on Pozzi, but if he was surprised to see him there, he gave no sign.

Nora and Pozzi moved to either side of Perra as the orderlies helped the girl onto the table. Her lank hair half hid her trembling chin but could not obscure her wide, frightened eyes. She took in the rows of stern and curious men circled around her and seemed to shrink beneath the thin blanket, as if the wool had soaked up the chill of the cold marble table.

Perra smoothed his hair, straightened his coat, and addressed the audience. "Welcome, gentlemen. The patient before us today is Signorina Fanto, age eighteen. She has a history of constipation and abdominal pain but no palpable masses." The patient ran her hand over her distended stomach, as if ashamed of it. "Last week, she began experiencing progressively increasing abdominal swelling. Yesterday she presented herself to this hospital. Since that time, in spite of a purging diet and voiding the bowels, the swelling has increased in girth a further five centimeters. I believe this is a case of ascites and will demonstrate the method of diagnosis and treatment to you today."

As he spoke, he prepared the patient, gently peeling back her bedgown while deftly draping a sheet. The girl flinched at his touch and cowered beneath the thin covering. Above them, pencils scribbled furiously. Even the normally languid-looking Umberto Sagese, blessed with a prodigious memory, was frowning and taking notes.

"Signorina Beady will demonstrate the percussion."

Nora moved forward, taking her gaze off the suspicious dark eyes surrounding her to meet the wide, anxious ones peeking out from thick tangles of hair. "This will not hurt," she promised. "We are all here to help you." She began tapping over the grotesquely enlarged belly, working sideways from the navel, all the while murmuring to Signorina Fanto as if they were the only two in the room. With yesterday's successful examination behind her, she had no anxieties in front of the crowd today. She wished she could say the same for Pozzi, whose face had already grown three shades paler.

Nora tipped her face close to the patient and whispered, "Some of them are more afraid of you than you are of them," and signaled with her eyes toward Pozzi.

The girl produced her first smile.

"Here is where I detect the shift in sound from tympanic to dull," Nora announced, making her voice carry. She reached for the charcoal and drew a line down the patient's flank.

"Pozzi, if you and Signorina Beady will help the patient

turn… Forgive us, Signorina Fanto, we won't be much longer." Perra had noticed Nora's gentle encouragements and copied them with his usual charm.

When the girl was arranged on her side, Nora tapped again. "The sound shift is here." This time, the line she drew was several inches closer to the navel.

"Before attempting to drain the fluid, it is best to make sure," Perra said to the audience. "You do no good if what you are trying to drain away is in fact a tumor or impacted feces from severe constipation. Pozzi will repeat the procedure."

Pozzi circled the table. His hands were shaking, and his progress was slower as he tapped his way down her side, bent over the wooden stethoscope. "Here," he said on his second pass, sounding more certain than he looked.

Perra bent his ear and listened. "Nicely done. Now turn the patient."

Again, the point where the sound changed moved.

"The evidence argues persuasively for paracentesis," Perra announced. "We proceed as follows—" As he talked, he reached for the syringe, easing it smoothly into the taut skin and matter-of-factly withdrawing the first twenty cubic centimeters of fluid and ejecting it into the basin. The girl let out a breath. "Straw-colored and frothy," he observed with satisfaction. "Both characteristics of ascites fluid." He reattached the syringe to the cannula he'd left in the patient's abdomen and drew away another twenty cc's, then passed the empty syringe to Pozzi. "You and Signorina Beady will finish for me," he said.

"Yes, sir."

Nora was pleased to see that, after the first syringe full, Pozzi's hands didn't shake once.

———

"This is good, Eleanora." Perra set down her pages and folded his hands in his lap. "Very comprehensive."

"Thank you." Nora blushed with pleasure. "But I'm no closer to explaining why ether fails with some patients. Some breathe for ten minutes without falling asleep and others succumb almost immediately. Some hallucinate in terror while others thank me for the best sleep of their life."

This was her second tutorial with Perra since asking to accelerate her course. Pozzi had begged her permission to join the moment he'd heard of her extra sessions. Now, seeing the black sky outside the window and hearing the scolding church bells ringing eleven, Nora was grateful Pozzi had asked. His presence put Mrs. Phipps's objections about the propriety of spending long hours with Professor Perra to rest.

"It helps that Dr. Croft and Dr. Gibson send you their findings from London," Perra said.

"Yes, and they have good results—"

"Like you," Perra interpolated.

"But I'm hearing of more and more failed cases," Nora finished. "Some doctors undoubtedly struggle with the apparatus. It takes patience to master. In their frustration, they fall back to the easier method of applying a handkerchief, a sponge, or a paper cone. But so long as I use the vaporizer and dose exactly according to the table we developed, I have never suffered a crisis. Much better if a patient wakes during surgery, awful as that may be, than not wake at all."

"More study will be necessary if you want to persuade your examiners." Perra leaned forward in his chair. "Are you both spending ample time with the microscopes?"

"I went to the laboratory three times this week," Pozzi said. "The drawings of my specimens are just here—" He reached down and riffled through his portfolio. "I wanted to ask you about a cyst I helped Dr. Papania remove this week."

Perra reached for the papers. "And you, Eleanora?"

She dipped her head, unwilling to see Perra's searching eyes.

"I only went once," she admitted. "And I didn't examine any of my own specimens."

"But your specimens and drawings last week got Barilli's attention," Pozzi interjected. "He showed the entire room."

Nora flashed him a grin, grateful for his attempt to temper her failings.

"Still, you'll need to devote more time," Perra said.

He was right, but Nora wasn't sure where she'd find it between working on her thesis, lectures, and her hours at the hospital.

"You also need extra obstetrics instruction if you wish to succeed with your mad plan," Perra told her. A smile flickered, but whether meant to mock or encourage, she didn't know. "The easiest place for you to practice is teaching midwifery. Ask Dr. Marenco to tutor you."

"I don't think she'll agree, sir." Nora licked her lips. "She doesn't like me."

"Don't be silly," Perra said. "Liking has nothing to do with it."

"I could ask Dr. Zabbia," Nora suggested.

"He doesn't have half her skill," Perra said. "Magdalena can be prickly, but if you want to face examination in six months, you need someone of her caliber. Charm her. Get her on your side."

Nora conceded with a nod, keeping back a sigh. She'd learned many skills over the years, but she wasn't sure charm was one of them.

CHAPTER 8

DANIEL CONSULTED HIS WATCH AS HE WALKED DOWN THE stairs, unconsciously skipping the third tread above the landing, which creaked. Quarter to seven. He'd check the patients downstairs—they'd rigged up space for the Thompkins baby on the surgical table in a laundry basket—and still arrive early at St. Bart's, with plenty of time to—

The sound of silver on china arrested him midstride and he peered into the dining room, where Horace was skimming through a letter, his forkful of poached egg stalled in midair.

"You were up past two helping me with our new patients," Daniel said, wishing his scolds were half as effective as Nora's. Horace should be resting, not breakfasting this early.

"I was asleep before you were," Horace retorted. "I woke early to check on the girl." He grimaced. "Her fever's still rising."

Daniel slumped into a chair. Horace, eyes still on his letter, reached over to pour Daniel a cup of tea, which would have been disastrous, had Daniel not slid his cup hurriedly an inch to the right. The new housekeeper Mrs. Phipps had secured was a tartar. "Let me," he said to Horace, who had set down the pot and was groping blindly for the sugar. It had been a long night. Daniel gave himself three lumps.

"I'm afraid we'll have more," he said.

"Undoubtedly," Horace said.

"You don't think we could find a way..." Daniel sighed, knowing it was useless to suggest that either of them could persuade Vickery to do anything. Since their friend, Dr. Thompson, had retired from St. Bart's, Daniel's position over the children's ward was increasingly difficult. He and Dr. Croft would have to treat the children with diphtheria in their own, crowded homes or here.

"We don't have room," Horace said quietly.

Daniel sighed again and shook his head. "Vickery is denying care to children, simply to spite me—"

Horace's eyes rose from his letter. "Not only to spite you."

"You own a hearty share of his dislike, it's true." Daniel hadn't meant to eat, but he'd somehow begun spreading jam automatically onto two corners of toast, and three small, perfectly crisp sausages had found their way onto his plate. One had a bite out of it already.

"That wasn't what I meant." Horace set down his letter and wiped the largest crumbs from his beard with a napkin. "Vickery isn't sensible when it comes to diphtheria. I suppose one can't really blame him."

"Oh?" Daniel raised his eyebrows, the piece of toast suspended six inches from his mouth. Horace was not one to defend such a bitter rival.

Horace gulped from his own cup of tea. "Yes. Years ago—I was in the navy then, and he was in his early thirties—there was a rash of cases in Lambeth, and some came to St. Bart's. He was tending them. A fortnight later his children fell ill. Twin boys. Killed both of them."

Daniel replaced his toast on the plate. "I didn't know."

"He doesn't talk about it. Only the older ones of us would know or remember."

A shadowy vision of Silas Vickery huddled over his dying children rose like smoke, obscuring the image of the vicious, stalking surgeon Daniel knew. It was the first time he fully realized Vickery had chosen the same path of science and mercy that had called Daniel from the gentlemanly pursuits his parents would have preferred.

"You never told me."

Horace gave an impatient shrug. "If the losses had given him the least sympathetic impulse I would pity him, but—" The paper drew his eyes back like a magnet before he finished talking. Daniel took a bite, waiting for him to continue, but the letter engrossed Horace completely.

"Good news or bad?" Daniel asked, wary now.

Horace looked up, a grin punctuating his calculating face. "I've figured out a solution for both our problems."

"What problems would those be?" Daniel asked, unsure if the topic would veer to missing scalpels or the quality of cadavers or what to order for supper.

"What we've been discussing," Horace said impatiently. "Room. We've run out of room."

Daniel's forehead creased. "What do you mean? There's only two of us in this large home."

"I'm not talking about the size of the drawing room," Horace dismissed impatiently. "Space to practice. I'm trying to convince our misguided colleagues not to give up on ether, and you need a place to treat contagious patients without Vickery's interference."

Daniel craned his neck to steal a view of the writing on the paper. "What's in that letter?"

"Another request for private classes on the art of administering ether. This one is from a doctor from Holland. I've a pile of them upstairs. All willing to pay handsomely. If we had more room for lectures and patients, the sum we'd earn would be considerable. For both of us." Horace leaned back, his eyes focused and waiting for Daniel's reply.

It was flattering and intriguing, but... "The two of us can't run a practice that size by ourselves."

Horace took up his butter knife, balancing it like a scalpel across his thumb. "Nora will be back in another year or two. If she manages to bring back a degree, there is no one here who will let her use it except us. If we have a reputable facility, we can give her a place to practice."

Daniel's eyes drifted to the bushes outside the window, wilting in the summer heat. The truth of Nora's prospects scratched at him like a poorly turned shirt seam. "We have a reputable practice already. What will she say if she comes back and her only home has been abandoned in her absence?"

"I hope she'll say we've built a practice she's proud of." Horace's blue eyes flashed with defiance.

Daniel decided to avoid a debate on practicalities and cut to the quick. "What do you propose?"

Croft slapped the table and stood, making the saltshaker tremble. "We must move at once."

"Horace—" Daniel laid his bread down and twisted to try to catch the doctor's attention before he fled. "Move where? A London property like this one that doubles as a surgery and

clinic is no easy find." When Daniel had first presented himself here at 43 Great Queen Street, he'd been amazed at the
clever fittings in the surgery, the conveniently located alleyway
allowing covert deliveries from the gravediggers, the serviceable
downstairs clinic and slightly fancier upstairs consulting room.
True, the chaotic assortment of specimens and the disrepair of
the upholstery and plaster had appalled him, but he was used
to those now. He and Dr. Croft had everything they needed to
work.

"And consider..." Daniel's voice was placating, appealing.
"There are easier solutions. We could lease a hall or something
less drastic to accommodate lectures and our temporary influx
of patients. Perhaps rent a small second home close by."

Horace paused, stroking his beard, giving Daniel hope his
words had lessened the force of this particular storm of inspi-
ration. "You're right. Nora has roots here. We don't want her
to come home and miss everything familiar. She seems rather
sensitive that way." He nodded at Daniel approvingly. "We'll
need to expand this house instead. More rooms to hold our
patients. Put in another theater for my ether demonstrations
and for surgeries, with an observatory dome to let in light but
keep passersby from glimpsing our anatomical lectures."

Daniel coughed on the toast crumbs that had lodged in his
throat. "That's not at all what I said."

"Nora and Phipps will want more space—their own wing—
and we'll augment the clinic and add a lecture hall." Horace
patted his pockets, looking for a pencil. "Nora should sketch it
out. When the devil does she get home?"

Daniel pulled the napkin from his collar where he'd tucked

it and stood. When indeed? "And I need a chest of gold and a flying carpet. You cannot make it appear because it is wanted."

Croft pshawed and waved his hand. "I told you, there are scores of doctors and students eager to pay, not to mention our private patients."

Daniel raised his eyebrows. "You know the charity clinic often costs us more than we collect."

Horace hurried on, unwilling to concede that the pay-what-you-can system often yielded red-ink accounts. "If not for the poor, we'd have no one to study and no new discoveries or expertise to draw in the private patients."

Daniel bridled his frustration, forcing his words out slowly and distinctly. "You're describing an entire hospital, Horace. Clinics and dissections and surgeries need nurses, orderlies, attendants, cooks, maids. You haven't considered the full scope or cost. Even if we built out your entire garden, there would be no room for the additions you're wanting."

"You're right. I need my solicitor. Send for him at once. I'll be back in an hour and we can work out everything." Horace stuffed the letter into his waistcoat pocket. "I'm late and—" His voice broke off as a new thought took hold of him. "I'd like a lawn for cages if we take on animals to study."

Before Daniel could answer, Horace was gone, leaving only the reverberations of the hastily closed door.

"Animals?" Daniel scanned the empty room, the abandoned plate, his half-eaten toast that had lost all appeal. "Who's your solicitor?"

On the opposite wall, the mute portrait of Sir Francis Drake stared back and offered no assistance at all.

CHAPTER 9

A WEEK AFTER PERRA'S INSTRUCTION, NORA STILL HADN'T found a way to approach Dr. Marenco and was starting to think the doctor was actively avoiding her. How else to explain how quickly Dr. Marenco busied herself—or left—whenever Nora appeared on the scene? It was practically a miracle, how little they saw of each other.

Finally, after three evenings in a row of going back to the hospital, Nora cornered her in the women's ward. Marenco was donning her coat, preparing to leave after changing a dressing.

"Dr. Marenco—"

"I'd like to go home now," Marenco said. She looked tired. "But if you need help—"

"I wanted a chance to speak to you." As the days passed, Nora had become almost desperate. If she didn't persuade Dr. Marenco to tutor her, Perra wouldn't let her speed up her studies. "Could you spare a moment?"

Dr. Marenco grimaced and glanced at the gold watch on her wrist. It was a pretty thing, small and delicate, easier to consult than the timepiece Nora wore pinned at her waist.

Difficult to keep clean, though, Nora thought.

"I'm very busy, but we can talk if you insist," Dr. Marenco said.

Nora was tired, too, after working until lunch at the hospital, spending the afternoon standing in Dr. Zabbia's lecture, and skipping her dinner to return to the hospital to track down Marenco. "Thank you," Nora said. "I appreciate you being so generous with your time."

Dr. Marenco shifted her weight impatiently, as if her feet wished to leave without her. "Quite so. Now, what did you wish to say to me?"

"Will you take me on as a student?" The question tumbled out, rough as a rockfall.

"I already have a full complement," Dr. Marenco said. "I take five at a time and a class of twenty midwives. Come to me in January."

"I won't be here," Nora said. "By then I'll be back in London." She didn't add *This is my only chance*, but Dr. Marenco must have sensed it anyway.

Dr. Marenco raked an exacting gaze over Nora. "You're not finishing your studies?" she asked, her words dripping with derision.

Nora hugged her notebook tight to her chest. "I am forced to accelerate my studies and return home." Let her think it was money or conditions she could not control. Nora would never admit sentiments to this unmovable woman. "I intend to return with my degree."

Some hint of stubborn pride leaked into Nora's last declaration, and Dr. Marenco's lips lifted at the corners. "The students I tutor now started two weeks ago. You'll have to ask one of them to help you catch up. I don't do any review. And I tutor on Wednesdays. Starting at eight. You'll have to reschedule your sessions with Professor Perra."

"He told you?" Nora asked, taken aback. If Perra had bothered to discuss her, why hadn't he simply asked Marenco on her behalf?

"No. It was young Bartolomeo who told me. I asked him yesterday about his studies. He said they are much better now you've befriended him."

"I didn't—"

"I saw you invite him to assist with Perra's demonstration."

"Professor Perra was already tutoring him," Nora said.

"I like that you asked him. He needs friends." Her eyes softened. "He sometimes has the look of my own son. Like the world is too big for him."

Nora, rapidly calculating—*Marenco was her parents' name. How could she be married?*—was too late formulating a reply.

Marenco sighed. "Well, if I'm going to teach you, I must make a few things clear first."

"Yes. Your fees—"

"A British pound a week," Marenco said, waving impatiently. "But we need to talk. Not here. This isn't the place and I'm too tired. Tuesday afternoon before my next lecture. During the *pausa pranzo*, meet me at Santa Maria della Vita."

"The church?" Nora said, astonished.

"The church," Marenco affirmed. "Good night."

"Wait! I have another question," Nora said before Dr. Marenco could turn and go. It might not be too late to create a better impression. "Lucia Sarni's passing put me in mind of it." To Nora's frustration, no autopsy had been possible—in Bologna, the church and university only authorized dissections during winter. "I searched your book, but I couldn't find any postmortem examinations of your successful cesarean surgeries."

"Because they were successful," Marenco said tersely, her face darkening.

"Yes, but I thought perhaps you might have followed them over the years and—"

Dr. Marenco gave a brittle smile. "I'm not a vulture, Signorina Beady. I'm more concerned with the living. My mother might have tried it—she and my father shared a private laboratory in Bagnacavallo—but the university still won't allow me to use their laboratories. I'm not an official lecturer and I have no facilities of my own. Corpses are expensive."

Nora dropped her gaze from Marenco's flashing eyes. Just a moment ago she had been sure the woman was pleased with her, and now it was quite the opposite. "Of course. I hadn't thought—"

"Yes. You seem prone to that with distressing regularity."

"I'm sorry," Nora said. "I can't help wondering what a post-mortem examination might reveal."

"Three years ago I performed a cesarean on a thirty-six-year-old washerwoman living on Via de' Pepoli in the Quadrilatero," Marenco snapped. "I passed her in the street a week ago. If it's important to you, stay in Bologna. You shouldn't have to wait too many years for your chance. Washerwomen tend not to live long." She marched off in a swirl of skirts. Nora didn't follow or ask if she'd changed her mind about Wednesday's class. She'd show up at Santa Maria della Vita on Tuesday. If Marenco wasn't there, she'd go to Marenco's house for the Wednesday tutorial, hold out her money, and refuse to leave.

CHAPTER 10

I F ONLY THEY COULD SLEEP, DANIEL THOUGHT AS HE LOOKED at his three diphtheria patients, who he'd diagnosed with croup to keep them in the hospital until more beds came available at Great Queen Street. He'd pushed them into a far corner, trusting screens and burning pastilles to protect the other patients. Vickery would catch on soon enough, but if Daniel and his students were discreet, he could buy his little sufferers a bit more time.

The morning light was harsh in the ward, falling stark on the wooden planks of the floors and across the puffy, miserable faces, revealing the damage of another fitful night. The girl sent over from the textile factory had no family, no one to mark with anxiety the relentless swelling of her neck or the darkening shadows under her eyes. Disease had won a small battle since he saw her yesterday evening, the desperate light in her eye extinguished now by a grim, accepting dread.

Daniel ground his teeth together, trying not to show his doubts when he checked in her mouth. When Nora nearly died of cholera as a child, she must have looked as frail as this.

"Can you breathe well enough, Letty?" he asked her. She only stared, her brown eyes retreating to a place from which he was seldom able to recall patients. "If you can be strong for another few days," he coaxed her.

Fevers, for all their suffering, at least allowed a patient to escape into syncope or delirium. Diphtheria kept the children awake, aware of every terrible moment as death tightened its grip slowly around their fragile necks.

Daniel advanced to the next bed. A new boy had come in just an hour ago. At thirteen years he was older than the others, which had given Daniel some hope, but he was thin and small for his age. Not a good sign for a large airway, but sometimes the body surprised you. The boy squirmed under his sheet, his chin jutting forward, searching for a position that eased his breathing.

"Isaac?" Daniel asked as he approached. "May I have a look?"

The boy sat up in his narrow cot, his face obedient and frightened.

The mucus running from his nose was dark gray like a coal miner's or a chimney sweep's, but Isaac was neither. Daniel handed him a clean handkerchief. "Keep it with you. I'll make sure we bring an extra pillow to prop you upright."

The boy swallowed violently, his Adam's apple seizing and jumping. Daniel recognized the attempt to dislodge mucus in the throat. "Let me see," he said gently, tilting Isaac's head back to catch more light. The leathery tissue had amassed on only one side of his uvula. As it thickened, it agitated his gag reflex, causing his stilted swallowing and the frantic gleam in his eye. It was like trying to breathe with a small rodent burrowed in the back of one's throat.

"We'll keep using hot compresses to thin the mucus and use a rubber bulb—"

"This one of your croup patients?" Horace appeared at Daniel's shoulder, his lips pinched in assessment.

"I thought you were heading home for lunch," Daniel answered and stepped aside to give Horace a better view.

"Wanted to see your patients first." He tipped Isaac's head to the side with a finger on his chin, examining each side of the neck. "Not swollen. Would you open your mouth as wide as you are able?" he asked the boy.

Isaac complied, coughing at the change in position.

"There. Did you see on that laryngeal spasm? A piece of the membrane is dangling right over the trachea." Daniel could see no such thing from three feet back, but Horace continued. "You cannot remove the membrane. It adheres to the tissues and causes bleeding and inflammation, but occasionally flakes of it break off when they cough. This piece could be removed safely. Get the thinnest, longest blunt forceps you can find."

Daniel retreated into the depths of his bag, searching for a pair he knew would be perfect. He'd used them to remove an obstructing piece of steak from a man's throat just last week.

Horace took the forceps with an approving nod. "Ether would be helpful, but since Vickery has cleared it from the dispensary and only allows it for approved surgeries, we'll have to manage without." He scrambled in his own bag for wooden wedges used to force the mouth open to unnatural dimensions. He pushed the blocks far into Isaac's molars, stretching the fragile skin at the corner of the lips drum-tight.

"Wait, Horace." Daniel laid a hand over the forceps. "Even blunt ones can puncture the soft tissues if he moves. We can take him to our clinic and use ether there—"

Horace waved Daniel and his protest back.

"Stick out your tongue as far as you can," Horace instructed

Isaac, whose body tensed at the sight of the long silver forceps poised above his open throat. His eyes swiveled in panic. There was a flash of silver, a brief struggle as Daniel pushed down Isaac's shoulders, a sound of painful gagging and Horace held the forceps aloft, brandishing what looked like a piece of gray skin from a body too long dead. "If this had gone down the windpipe, we'd have lost him," Horace said, assessing the size and thickness of the membrane.

"I was just examining him. How did you see it?" Daniel asked, alarmed by his near miss.

Horace shrugged. "I've seen a great many coughs and I knew where to look. But if he hadn't coughed at precisely the right time—"

"Dr. Gibson!" One of the orderlies, usually as stoic as men come, appeared in the door, flushed with running. "I reckon your students are about to get themselves killed."

Horace raised his eyebrows. "I'll finish this," he promised.

With a rushed apology to the boy, Daniel hurried to the hall to follow the orderly. "What's this about?"

"Your dressers are doing their best, sir, but they're trying to stitch up a drunk man and he's three times their size. He's causing a stir in the surgery. I wanted you to help them before Dr. Vickery—"

Enough said. Daniel took the stairs two at a time and arrived at a scene straight from Bedlam. His students' patient looked like an overfed gladiator fresh from battle, a wash of blood running rivulets down his snarling face. Jeffers was slight and too brave for his own good, trying to make his way toward this giant of a man. Stoddard was larger, but the only dresser who looked like he knew anything about defending himself was Girard, a rough-edged boy from Paris who spoke English in a distinct growl. His tight shirt concealed tough and stringy muscles.

"Look out," Daniel warned as the patient lashed out and unleashed a torrent of foreign words. "What the hell is going on?" he asked his students.

Girard didn't shift his eyes from the attacker and answered calmly, "Italian sailor. He was in a fight at a pub and took a bottle to the head. He won't let us touch him, and none of us can talk to him."

"Then why the hell did he come?" Daniel cursed as the man's fist connected with Jeffers's chin. Jeffers cried out, grabbed his face, and fell back, knocking over a metal bowl that crashed to the floor. Picking himself up, he advanced again. Something to be said for Yankee stubbornness.

"They brought him in still unconscious," Girard said, shifting his weight as if expecting he'd have to take a swing soon. "He woke when we started the sutures, but his shipmates were gone by then."

"That's bloody perfect," Daniel muttered. "Jeffers, get me some ether. There's no time to set up the inhaler. Bring a rag."

Daniel sized up the man, who halted, his chest heaving like a street organ. Trying to smother him with a handkerchief of ether would be near impossible. Shards of glass glinted from his half-stitched wound.

Jeffers returned and pushed a pungent ether-soaked rag into Daniel's hand. Wary of moving close, Daniel pulled out his own handkerchief and mimed wiping his head and face and then pointed to the patient's face and held out the ether rag. Miming and smiling, Daniel inched closer. With exaggerated movements he tossed the rag to the man who caught it instinctively. Daniel demonstrated again by wiping his own face. The Italian raised the rag and wiped his eyes, bellowing as the fumes hit them.

"Damn," Daniel spat out. He hadn't counted on that.

Interpreting his burning eyes as another attack, the man lunged forward and tackled Daniel, pinning him to the nearby bed. Daniel tried to free his arms, but they were clamped beneath the greasy sailor.

"A bit of help, please," he commanded through gritted teeth.

The students rushed forward but this only made the man scream louder. "It's like fighting an ox," Jeffers grunted as he locked his arms around the man's shoulders.

"Italians," Daniel growled under his breath as he tried to pull his face out of the mattress.

He heard the patient's knee make contact with Jeffers, who grunted and doubled, but heroically kept hold of the brute.

Daniel twisted, almost slipping free, but the next second found his head buried in the suffocating armpit of the impossibly muscular man. Behind him glass shattered, most likely one of the new flasks.

Footsteps pounded behind him, and Daniel heard the table groan as a new man leaped into the fray with the force of a battering ram.

"I doan know what you've been drinking, but you'll let the doctor go if you want to leave here with yer bloody head." Daniel knew Harry Trimble's Scottish brogue at once. It was more pronounced than ever in desperate moments, and this certainly qualified. A burly shoulder knocked Daniel sideways, freeing him. He staggered away just in time to see Harry's fist smash into the man's jaw. The patient went slack and moaned.

"You're not out cold yet, but I can give you another if you request it." Harry shook the man, his red fist inches from his nose. "You're under my care now."

The man blinked stunned eyes, unable to assess this new threat. "He's drunk and probably concussed," Daniel warned. *Probably twice concussed after your blow.* Daniel felt unsteady himself. Harry's sudden appearance dazed him more than the wrestling match.

"You start the sutures," Harry ordered. "I'll manage him. Give me the ether rag."

Girard handed it over, clearly confused but unwilling to protest the newcomer's assumption of authority. Daniel wasn't that much better informed himself. Last he'd heard of his one-time friend, Harry had taken over a practice in Cornwall. What was he doing, charging into a surgery theater here in St. Bart's?

Don't look a gift horse in the mouth, Daniel told himself, gritting his teeth as he flushed the wound with water to dislodge another shard of glass.

Harry growled as the man struggled against the cloth pressed to his mouth. "Finish fast."

Daniel's eyes flicked from the bloody scalp to the man's face. He would normally do at least twenty sutures but if he spaced them farther... Swearing, Daniel closed the wound as the man grew quieter, his muscles loosening.

"That was too exciting," Daniel muttered. "Someone wipe

the blood off him. And for now, gentlemen, I believe we need not tell anyone we were all flattened by one Italian. We have our pride." He gave them a look and hoped they knew he was speaking less of their national reputations and more of what Silas Vickery would do with such a story.

They nodded, catching the subtext, and Daniel watched the three dressers gingerly wheel the stretcher with the subdued man from the room.

The crisis had ended so abruptly—like a curtain swung closed on a busy stage—that it took Daniel a moment to realize he was standing alone with Harry. He inhaled and searched for words.

As always, Harry beat him to it. "That was one for the books."

"Thank you for rushing in. He had me fast and it didn't smell good."

Harry laughed away some of the tension. "I wish you could have seen it. What I'd give for a picture! I had no idea who he had." He looked at the floor. "Did he hurt you? You've blood on your face."

"Not mine. He only squeezed me. Like getting hugged to death by a bear." Despite himself, Daniel's mouth twitched with a grin. "I'm not sure the medical papers would recommend fisticuffs to anesthetize a patient."

"Then I should write a paper on its efficacy." Harry dropped the curved suture needle into a cup of water to rinse off the blood. "You had three other men in here. What kind of useless students are they sending us now?"

"Perhaps you need to recruit us a few more navy men." It

was the first time they had seen each other in over a year. "I didn't know you were back in London."

"Truro was too quiet for me. I finished my locum and came back just this week." Harry's lip twitched and indecision marred his carefully set expression. "My wife prefers it here, as well."

"Wife?" Stunned surprise warded off Daniel's searing guilt for only the shortest moment. It rose hot as he looked into Harry's ginger-stubbled face.

"I always thought I'd resist domestic bliss longer than you, but she is…" Harry failed to find a word but the softening in his eyes told Daniel she was something spectacular.

"Congratulations." He slapped Harry on the arm, then realized what a paltry thing this was from a friend who should have known and stood beside him at the altar. Daniel shifted his feet. "When did you—"

"Just last month. We should have you over. Our rooms are small and nothing impressive, but…" Harry paused, his smile faltering.

Daniel nodded awkwardly, thinking of Isaac's throat upstairs. "I want to hear more, but I was in the middle of a case when I was called down." Harry flinched so swiftly it was easily missed, but Daniel caught it nonetheless. "Thank you again for stopping."

"Give your students a lesson in boxing. They'll need it again at some point." Harry tugged his coat straight and slid back into the hallway.

The room felt so empty after his departure that Daniel nearly called him back, but everything he thought to say involved their days as medical students in Paris and cases from their past. After the furious words that parted them a year ago, there was no bridge left to carry them into the future. Horace had sworn never to forgive Harry, and Daniel's loyalty to him made the regret for his former friend sour in his mouth.

Harry could have prevented it all. Instead of coming to him and Nora and Horace and telling them the trouble he was in two summers ago, he'd sold their secret to Vickery and let them walk into a trap. The memory of Vickery's jubilant sneer as he declared it was impossible for Daniel to have completed his celebrated hernia surgery—since Harry Trimble, the coauthor of the paper hadn't even been with him that night—turned Daniel's stomach. He'd counted on Harry and found himself helpless in front of an unforgiving audience, without a reliable friend in sight.

Except for Nora. She'd stood up for him, admitting the truth, that she was his partner in the surgery. Their discovery, and his reputation, had been more important than her own. It was brave and bold and she hadn't known how viciously the world would turn on her.

If not for Harry, Nora would be here today, quietly working alongside Daniel in the clinic and surgery at Great Queen Street. They would be married now, if Daniel had any say in it, and he would have been the one making happy confessions with soft eyes.

Daniel pulled out his watch and sighed. He'd been battered enough for three days, and he hadn't yet been at work for forty-five minutes.

Jeffers appeared at the threshold, the first signs of a bruise blooming on his sharp chin. "Dr. Gibson, I know you're busy with *croup* patients"—he leaned on the word—"but can you help us with one more here before you return?"

"What is it?" Daniel asked warily.

"A prostitute. She says her weeping arm wound is keeping customers away."

Daniel ran a hand through his hair, ignoring the pain in his shoulder. "God help us."

CHAPTER 11

NORA CHECKED ON HER PATIENTS, THEN LEFT THE WARD in the care of an orderly, but she went for the records room, not the cloakroom. Dr. Marenco's rebuke—*I'm not a vulture, Signorina Beady. I'm more concerned with the living*—made it impossible to focus on the studies awaiting her at home, and she felt the need to prove her point. Postmortem examinations of successful cesarean cases would help doctors refine their technique. Horace completed as many postmortems as possible, often paying gravediggers to steal bodies of his former patients. It was, Nora believed, a necessary evil. But here in Italy, under the eye of the Catholic church, dissections were rare and never clandestine.

Dr. Marenco's book had several accounts of cesarean section. A thorough recorder, she'd provided the patients' names, the dates of the surgeries, and the timelines of recovery, and though it was likely these women had been seen outside the hospital, it was possible they had received other treatment here. There was no harm in searching the records for their names and finding out where they lived—if they were still living.

Unfortunately, the records were patchy and organized chronologically, not alphabetically, making it impossible to search by name. With a sigh of disappointment, Nora closed her book and stretched in her chair. A glance at her watch told her it was nearly eight. She should have returned home hours ago. Hopefully Mrs. Phipps was eating instead of waiting for her.

Nora replaced the books and left, exiting the hospital by way of the children's ward just to ensure they were all sleeping peacefully.

"Eleanora. You're not on duty tonight."

Nora spun around, flinching like a guilty child.

"Doctor Salamone is covering this floor," Professor Perra said.

"He is, but I was searching the records. By the time I finished, it was so late I thought I may as well walk once more through the wards."

Perra shook his head. "If you don't pace yourself, you'll never last."

"I don't do this often," Nora protested. "And if Salamone is watching, why are you here? You work all hours. I'm sure you hardly ever see your family—"

"That is no impediment," Perra said cryptically as he looked across the dark room. Turning back to her with a worried arch to his brow, he added, "And I can leave at any hour, without risking my safety. I'm afraid I can't say the same for you. It's all right for students like Pozzi to stay late and walk home in the dark—"

"I can always stay here overnight if I need to. There's a soft chair in the sisters' sitting room. No need to worry, sir," Nora said.

"Dozing in an armchair is no way for you to—"

"I'm fine. Truly."

Perra put a hand on her arm. "You need a real bed. Let me drive you home."

A touch from anyone was rare enough that Nora had no desire to argue. Perra's grip was kind, unexpectedly welcome. She felt the frustrations of the day fall on her in a heap as weariness overcame her. There was no harm allowing someone else to make such small decisions.

She was familiar with Perra's plain black carriage and the sturdy pair of horses that drove him about in all kinds of weather. She didn't expect the pile of medical journals on the seat. "Forgive me," Perra said, sliding them onto his lap. "I read whenever I can. It's too dark now, but when I'm called out, I like to have something on hand. The trouble is, I forget to put them away."

Nora smiled. There were at least a dozen periodicals here. "Don't apologize. You've seen Doctor Croft's home. Journals and specimens everywhere—"

"I envy him that," Perra said, with a chuckle. "I'm not allowed to keep specimens at home. Once I left a drawing of the spleen in the parlor. I'd been summoned away in a hurry." He shrugged, as if she knew the end of his tale. "So I leave my journals here, and now I'm embarrassed because I've left you no place to sit."

"There's plenty of room," Nora said, for there certainly was, yet it felt different sitting here with him, his knees grazing her skirts with each jolt. "Thank you for driving me." She turned her attention to the gleam of black lacquer and the soft leather seats. "It's very comfortable."

"It has to be, when I read and sleep and sometimes even change my clothes in here." He grinned. "I am not supposed to arrive home smelling of hospital, but I won't trade my coat and trousers until you're gone."

Nora's cheeks heated; she stammered, "You smell perfectly normal to me."

"Because you smell the same way. Trust me, there's a smell. We just don't notice it."

"You're right, of course," Nora said. "But I grew up in Dr. Croft's clinic, and Mrs. Phipps never complains."

"She is an excellent woman," Perra conceded. He fell quiet as they drove, smiling, his eyes resting easily on the scenes passing in the window. It was tempting to relax herself, but somehow conversation felt safer than the tense closeness of silence.

"I heard you speaking to one of the students in French today. I didn't know you were a master of that language as well," Nora said. A sincere compliment seemed a safe topic.

"I grew up around so many tongues. It was unavoidable," he said, switching his focus from the window to her. "You've done very well here, studying in a foreign language. I've heard you speak to Madame Bouchard. Your French is very good, too."

Nora smiled. "My French is tolerable, but I'll never sound like you." He slipped from one tongue to another like a bird diving from air to sea, flawless and impeccable, so it was absurd of him to compliment her functional but stiffly accented Italian or her workaday French.

"You worked hard to master them," he reminded her. "You should be proud, but you have that failing I see in some of my students. You can't admit when you excel at something. Of course, there are some who think they are good at everything, which almost invariably leads to disaster, but I'll never have to worry about that with you. It's almost embarrassing to watch you receive a compliment." He cocked his head at her, the shadows from the lit windows outside playing with his face. "Have they really been so scarce that you are this unused to them?"

"I expect it's just the English way," Nora said quickly.

"It will be good for you to study with Magdalena," he said. "She'll teach you confidence."

Nora gave a derisive laugh and then blushed at her boldness. "She has nothing but criticism for me. And I never know what to say to her," she confessed more humbly. "She has such a mercurial temper."

"You are much more sanguine, I admit. Your levelheadedness will serve you well."

"Have you known Dr. Marenco long?" Nora asked.

"We were students together. Good friends. I'm happy she's returned in such good health."

"I'd never have guessed she'd been ill."

"It was good for her to go away. She has a tendency to overwork." He saw Nora's smile before she could hide it and grinned in response. "Don't say it. Your face makes it all too obvious."

"You know, we have a saying at home, about pots calling kettles—"

"Black. I know. But really, Eleanora, isn't overwork in the nature of our calling? The best doctors are not comfortable men."

Nora smiled, thinking of Daniel, fighting sleep in the library with a book in his lap after a long day at St. Bart's. Or

Horace pacing through slums in search of disease while other men relaxed in front of their fires reading classics and smoking pipes.

"Or women," Perra added with a grin.

"I suppose not," Nora said, and before she could frame her next thought, the carriage stopped.

Perra offered his hand. "Here we are."

Nora looked outside the window, perplexed by the large house beside them. "This isn't my street." She'd been too lost in conversation to pay attention.

"No. It is mine. You are drooping from hunger. A meal and then I will take you home."

The house faced a square with a fountain, splashing softly in the dim evening light. Sparrows swooped between the roof-tops, and a group of three handsome women passed by, taking the decorous late-evening stroll Italians called the passeggiata. A flock of English women would never think of roaming down Great Queen Street at night, but this was not London. Nora smiled. "It's very quiet here."

"Yes," Perra agreed. "Too quiet. You know I'd rather be busy." A flat note of bitterness struck a strange discord in his voice.

Nora studied the scene, searching for any reason he might be dissatisfied. This was a good place to bring up children, she thought. The trees were tall and broad, and the air was sweet.

"Come inside." Perra led her past a butler and through a bright and beautifully appointed hall. She followed him into his library, a room plush and exquisite in its details of burnished wood and embroidered silk, and seated her while he ordered a tray of food to be brought. The down pillows were fluffed

on the chairs, the books artfully arranged, and—Nora saw as
she trailed her eyes along the shelves—the issues of his journals beautifully bound: green for a decade's worth of the *Annali
Universali*, navy blue for *Bollettino delle Scienze Mediche*, and foreign publications in light brown. The curio cabinet contained a
collection of exotic birds, stuffed in various poses from nesting
to midflight. There were no specimens, no clutter, no drawings
of organs or botanicals, no sign of use, almost. Perra sank into
a chair, reached into a pocket for his pipe, and as if reading her
mind said, "Welcome to my home away from home."

Nora chuckled. It was a common joke at the hospital that
Perra lived at the university. "The back issues of *Lo Sperimentale*
are just there, if you are interested." Perra pointed with his pipe.
"You don't mind if I—?"

"I miss the smell of it," Nora said, smitten by a pang of
acute homesickness for evenings with Daniel and the smell of
his pipe. "Don't worry about me." She moved to the shelves,
disoriented by a home library so ordered. She didn't have
time to do more than leaf through one journal when a maid
appeared with a tray of meats and cheeses topped with olives.
Nora's stomach made itself known immediately and she abandoned her search.

She put a small pile on her dish and made herself wait for
Perra to do the same before sampling the spiced meat. Bent
over her plate, she picked her next slice of bresaola and listened
to his description of the orchards and olive groves outside the
city.

"South toward Brento there is a family farm that produces
the best oil I've ever had." Perra held out a small dish for her to

sample when a fusillade of rapid footsteps in the hall made him set it down, tumbling a few silky drops onto the tray.

"Excuse me a moment," he murmured.

He barely made it out the door before a haughty, unpleasant voice hissed in the hallway. "I thought I heard your carriage." Nora looked to the door, alarmed by the vibrating anger in the woman's words. "You missed Rosalia's dinner party. Just one more humiliation, Salvio."

If he'd answered, Nora couldn't hear it beneath the torrent of accusing words. "Your daughter was expecting you. As usual, her uncle came to the rescue, but he shouldn't have to. If you can't even show a particle of consideration—"

"I'm sorry. I must have mistaken the day," he said firmly.

"Oh, you were mistaken. As you always are," Signora Perra seethed, so quietly Nora wasn't sure she'd caught the right words. "I'd like to lock you out, but Rosalia shouldn't have to face the shame of a father sent from his home."

"Fina—"

"The poor girl has enough to contend with without you embarrassing her by your neglect. You smell like the hospital."

The footsteps resumed, until obliterated by the sound of a slamming door.

Nora sat poised with her plate in her lap, wishing to evaporate. When Perra returned, he glanced sheepishly at her. "I'm sorry you had to hear that. Clearly my wife doesn't know you're here. Let's get you away quietly so she's not embarrassed."

It was far too late for any of them to escape embarrassment. Nora put down her plate as the food in her stomach turned to a nauseating lump.

Perra rang, and whispered commands to a housemaid to summon the carriage to drive Nora home, while she gathered up an armful of books. "I'll take excellent care of them," she promised. "And I'll return them as soon as I can."

"Take all the time you need," he said. Beneath the drooping, half-hearted smile, he looked exhausted.

"You're not to blame," he said.

"Are you?" she asked, then bit her tongue as she balanced a periodical atop a thick stack of books. *Stupid, stupid question.* Yet it was hard to believe such violent anger could come from nothing.

He took the journals from her arms and led her into the hallway, Nora's eyes scanning for the woman she hoped would not reappear. "To hear my wife tell it, certainly. We liked each other well enough when we married, but it was almost twenty years ago. We were especially young and wealthy enough to have nothing to do but look for a handsome partner. It seems beauty is not all a marriage needs after all." He gave a wry, mirthless smile that hurt Nora's chest.

She dropped her chin, unable to meet his eyes. "I shouldn't have asked."

"It's no great secret."

"Still…" Nora paused, waiting for the footman to open the front door. She'd observed Perra's long working days; now she understood the reason for them. But she had expected to find only chilliness in his home and marriage, not blazing hatred. Perra was so easy in his manners, so genial and well spoken. His wife seemed an utter termagant. "I'm sorry. I'd always imagined…" She stopped, unable to express her pity.

"Thank you," he said mildly, his hand atop hers, as if he guessed her sympathetic feelings. "I am touched by your concern. Come, let's get you away from here."

CHAPTER 12

DANIEL PULLED ON HIS KNEES LIKE A MARIONETTE FORC-ing his weary legs up the stairs two at a time. He'd sent Horace to bed an hour ago, but now he needed the man's help, and—Daniel paused outside the bedroom door—his lights were still burning.

"Horace?"

"What?"

Daniel smiled at the unmannerly response, which would have put his mother in a twist but was so characteristic of Horace. "I need you. Jimmy Thompkins."

In a blink, Horace had joined him in the hall, still in his jacket and trousers. He'd not even undressed, so he must have still been working. Daniel wouldn't chide him, not now, but— "You still have a letter in your hand."

"Ah. Another development, but it will wait." Horace shoved the paper into his waistcoat pocket on his way to the stairs.

Daniel followed, talking in a low voice. "I need you to help with his mother."

Horace lifted an eyebrow. "That bad?"

Daniel nodded. "It's not his breathing, so there's no point in reintroducing the cannula, which is still free of secretions. He's—" Daniel broke off, shaking his head.

They had five young patients in two of the rooms downstairs. Letty, the first one they'd brought home from St. Bart's, had succumbed first, and it was doubtful whether any of these children would outlast the week, though up until a few hours ago, Daniel had hoped to save Jimmy. Cool sheets and ice had checked his initial fever. Mucus secretions had decreased enough to remove his breathing cannula, but then the fever returned.

"I can't break his fever. The tongue is dry and cracked. He's had one seizure already, but it was half an hour ago, while his mother was asleep. If you can convince her to come upstairs—"

Horace pulled on his lower lip.

"She's scarcely left him," Daniel went on. "I don't want her to see—"

Horace slapped his shoulder. "Of course. I'll make her eat something. Then, if the poor mite is quieter, I'll bring her back."

Daniel nodded. It wasn't the outcome he wanted, but in this case, it was the best he could do, though it tore at him to admit it.

Downstairs, Mrs. Thompkins stood over her restless baby, fretting with the ice compresses and a rag dipped in broth. The sweat ringing her face twisted her stray strands of hair into unruly curls.

"Let Daniel relieve you a little while," Horace said gently. "You've had nothing to eat or drink yourself and—"

"I can't leave him," she said, her voice high and strained. "What if—" She set her jaw. "He should be with someone who loves him."

Over the slipshod bun in her hair, Horace met Daniel's eyes. *You can't fool this one.*

Daniel's shoulders slumped. He turned away, walked to the basin of ice water, and dipped in a new length of cotton toweling. "I care deeply—" he began, throat tight. "I also care about you, and you'll ruin your health if you don't take better care of yourself."

"I can't," she choked.

Daniel faced the bed and found her closer than expected, confronting him.

"Mrs. Thompkins—" Horace said.

She scrubbed her cheek with a fist. "Give me that."

Daniel surrendered the dripping towel.

She laid it over her baby. "I know you are trying to help, but this…this time has to be mine. You care, but I…" She swiped at the tears again. "The time to love him will last just a little longer. I deserve to have all of it."

Daniel rubbed his gritty eyes, his unshaven chin, unable to reply.

"And your husband?" Horace asked, sending Daniel's stomach into a steep dive.

"Dead. Before he was born." She didn't have to meet their eyes for Daniel to see the red heat of anguish burning around her lashes.

"We understand," Horace said, and poured out a cup of broth from the pot above the spirit lamp. "Drink this though, please. To keep up your strength. As Dr. Gibson says, Jimmy is not the only one here who needs tending."

"We'll stay here with you," Daniel said and picked up a fan to move cool air over the stricken child.

"Wake up."

Daniel jerked in his chair, glancing wildly about the room before settling his eyes on Horace. "Is it—" His voice, rough from sleep, cracked and broke. Not another setback. It would kill Mrs. Thompson.

"No, no, the baby's still fine," Horace said, spreading his hands placatingly. "While you slept, he took half a cup of broth."

Daniel collapsed against the cushions, relieved his guesses were wrong once again. The past two days hadn't been easy. After a second seizure, baby Jimmy's fever had suddenly broken, subsiding only to climb again, though this time ice compresses, willow-bark tea, and steadily plying him with fluids had kept his temperature from spiking. Daniel had left mother and baby to Horace in order to claim a short nap, so he could face an afternoon of scheduled surgeries and an evening shift at St. Bart's.

"He's asleep," Horace said. "So's his mother. I've ordered John to keep watch over them both."

Daniel rubbed his eyes and sat up again, slowly this time. Horace wouldn't trust Jimmy or his mother to an orderly's care if he believed there was any immediate danger. "So I'm awake right now for what reason?"

Horace beamed and rocked on his heels, his thumbs hooked in his waistcoat pockets. "I should have let you rest, but I couldn't keep the news to myself."

"It's excellent." Daniel got to his feet and shrugged out of his coat, beating ineffectually at the creases. "But you could have told me Jimmy was improved after my nap." There was sunlight at the windows and the mantelpiece clock said quarter to one, which meant he had an hour before he needed to be at Bart's.

"Well, yes, but I wasn't actually referring to Jimmy Thompkins," Horace said. "Once he squeaked through the last crisis, I figured we had him safe."

Daniel sent Horace a puzzled look.

"I've just heard from my solicitor," Horace said, reaching into his pocket and brandishing a letter. "About our expansion. He's negotiated with the neighbors successfully. They'll move out at the end of the month. The builders will start work here on Monday."

"You can't be serious." Daniel snatched the paper from his hand. His eyes widened at the sum. "Horace, this is extortionate! You're overpaying for that tumbledown heap." They could have bought two houses at that price.

"We can only expand in one direction since we're at the end of the block," Horace said, maddeningly calm. "When you reminded me that Nora considers this her home, it didn't feel right to sell and find someplace else. And what about the charity patients? I've run the clinic here more than twenty years. There's no place else they can turn, not this close to St. Giles." A guilty light came into Horace's eyes, like a boy caught pilfering. "And they have the largest back garden."

Of course—animals. Daniel swallowed and handed the letter back. Horace was a wealthy man, for all he tried to hide it. "I hope you know what you're doing," he muttered.

"The plans are upstairs," Horace said. "Come and see."

Daniel rolled his eyes to the ceiling but stopped himself

before making the acid reply brewing on his tongue as he followed Horace up the staircase. Too many evenings in the clinic, too many disappointments, too many fireside hours spent alone: he was turning old before his time. If he didn't watch himself, he'd turn as sour as Vickery or as eccentric as Horace.

Never experienced at reading building plans, Daniel still surmised the scope of the project from the tiny notes adorning the plethora of intersecting lines and angles: surgery gas lamps and a concealed staircase entrance for deliveries, as well as a patient ward that held twenty beds.

Horace's project, when finished, would be remarkable, an ideal home and a fitting place to carry out more groundbreaking work. In a private hospital, no one could tell Nora what work was unfeminine and unsuitable or tell Daniel which patients he could or couldn't admit.

"I'm expecting nothing less than marvelous," Daniel warned, relaxing into a grin.

Horace practically bobbed on his toes. "Why would we bother with anything less?"

CHAPTER 13

NORA ADJUSTED THE RED SCARF AROUND HER SHOULDERS, thinking how poorly her Italian fashions would translate to London. She'd be mistaken for a Romani if she walked the sooty or snow-crusted streets of Marylebone in her loose blouses and thin, layered skirts, but she was dearly tempted to try it; the thought of wrestling herself into tiny gloves and tight cuffs held no appeal.

She threw her eyes to the clock tower and wondered again why Magdalena had asked to meet her here today instead of in the classroom.

"You look like a light-haired Sicilian," a familiar voice called out behind her.

Magdalena was striding toward her, her quick steps as determined when she crossed the piazza as when she crossed the patient wards.

Nora grinned nervously, hoping that was a compliment. "It's good to know I'm blending in."

Magdalena arched a haughty eyebrow. "But the freckles are ridiculous," she said with a concealed smile that made Nora think the woman was secretly fond of them.

"We cannot all be gifted with your Mediterranean skin," Nora lamented. Magdalena's full cheeks gave no hint of her age and glowed with the shine that Nora had grown accustomed to on the faces of the Bolognesi.

"Come. There are things you must see," Magdalena commanded, unable to shed the authority of the hospital even on an afternoon stroll. She led Nora to the square shadow thrown over a corner of the courtyard by the imposing Palazzo Comunale and pointed to the carved balcony where a bronze statue of Pope Gregory sat enthroned several stories above the milling people. His hand, heavy with jeweled rings, was raised in blessing, but his eyebrows clenched in a furious leer. Nora had never liked the artist's rendering. She had passed under it hundreds of times walking to and from the university and now stood with her nose wrinkled quizzically at the *dottoressa*, wondering why they were standing here.

"They say Michelangelo himself carved the eagle beneath his throne," she told Nora, squinting against the sharp burst of late sun shooting over the top of the building. She pointed to the stern statue. "He lords over the city, passing judgment and laws, overseeing the souls of everyone inside the walls. But she—" Magdalena nudged her gaze to the left and toward the roof where a smaller statue of the Madonna and her bambino resided, virtually camouflaged against the russet building.

The Madonna gazed down on them, her face almost cautious as she raised the Christ Child from her knee to look over the piazza, as if distrustful of the people below. The infant, however, scanned the scene with calm interest, his chubby hand extended in curiosity. Rays of carved light burst from behind the Madonna, imitating the setting sun in the sky behind her.

Dr. Marenco looked again from Pope Gregory to the

Madonna. "You see? In art, as in life, in the shadows, in the woman's realm—that is where life happens. He was born in a stable. I doubt Giuseppe, though a saint, was much of a midwife. I've often wondered who attended her." Magdalena's face was lost in abstraction, the spent light of the day reddening her to the same pink as the walls surrounding them. "God came through a woman's body. It is time a womb was given the respect it deserves."

"I agree." Nora's voice sounded even more ardent when using the Italian word, *certamente*. And she was glad of it.

"There are many who accuse me of trespassing on heaven when I open the womb with a knife. I prefer to think of it as visiting heaven. I believe I am invited." Magdalena directed her words to the statue of Mary, as if conversing with her. Nora kept still, unsure how to respond to such mystical declarations. Magdalena's voice traveled over the murmurs of the people passing in front of them. "Are *you* invited, Nora?"

"*Scusi?*"

Magdalena didn't repeat her question. She waited, her black eyes warmed to a coffee brown in the light.

"I don't know how to answer," Nora stammered, gazing at the Madonna for help.

"If you feel like a *trasgressore* inside others' bodies, you always will be." A wind swept through the piazza, pushing Magdalena's loose hair and voluminous skirts against her unyielding body. "But if you work as one invited, then you will have the authority to heal. Do you understand? Does it translate?"

Nora wrinkled her brow in thought, rolling the unfamiliar word through her mind. It scraped like sharp pebbles on tender feet. "Transgressor?" she asked in confusion. "Sinner?"

"No." Magdalena shook her head and blew out a frustrated breath. "*Trasgressore*. One not allowed to come to a house," she said in clumsy English.

Nora's face lit with understanding. "Trespasser, *naturalmente*."

"We are not the trespassers, Nora," Magdalena continued with an approving nod. "We know the stirring of the womb. It is the men who try to steal our place and push us away from the women we serve who are trespassing on sacred realms. They cannot know as we do." She gave a shrug, her face thoughtful. "As we cannot know the stirrings of the testicles."

Nora choked on the unexpected word, spoken too loudly and causing one man to turn with a hopeful grin in their direction.

"Dottoressa," she admonished in a whisper as a blush climbed her neck. "We are not in the hospital."

Magdalena scowled at the man who wagged his eyebrows and gestured rudely at them. She threw him a volley of fast threats and took Nora by the wrist. "We will go inside Santa Maria della Vita." She threw one last insult at the man and marched across the piazza to an alley at the east corner that held the ancient church. "Have you been inside?" she asked as she came to the heavy front door sandwiched tight between adjoining buildings.

"I've been in many churches here. I don't believe I've visited this one." She eyed the entrance nervously. She'd entered the cathedrals more in the interest of art than religion. She wondered now if Magdalena, who was colorful, outspoken, and as staunchly Catholic as the nuns, would expect a conversion. Though Nora had dutifully attended the parish church in London with Mrs. Phipps on many a Sunday, a road-to-Damascus experience seemed foreign, implausible, and completely beyond her.

"This way." Magdalena pulled her scarf over her thick hair as she entered the building, and Nora imitated her, feeling at once both mysterious beneath the drape of her red silk and an impostor. As they entered the nave, Nora's eyes lifted to the impossibly high dome, carved of white stone and adorned with billowing marble clouds where saints and angels reached out sculpted arms to the mortals below. She breathed carefully, as if the air were not hers to take. It was as beautiful a view of the heavens as she'd ever imagined, joyful souls climbing upward in weightless, colorless grandeur.

Beside her, Magdalena smiled smugly at Nora's reaction. "You think you work for a hospital, Nora, but you do not." She gestured to the sweeping stonework above them that arched its way to the apex of the sky. "You work at the Great Hospital of Life and Death. You cannot heal the human body until you acknowledge its purpose to house the soul. Follow me."

As they wove their way among the quiet worshippers and went deeper into the church, the ivory splendor of the entry gave way to baroque paintings, green marble, and gilded altars. Magdalena led her off to the side where several life-sized terra-cotta statues were grouped around a prone figure on the floor. "The scream of stone," Marenco murmured as they drew nearer.

Nora paused as she registered the scene before her. A figure of the dead Christ lay peacefully with his head on a pillow, but his respite from torture was bought at a steep price. The agony of the women running to his body stopped Nora's words, and she pushed her hand against her heart as she took in the clutching fingers, the wails of misery, the hopeless horror on the women's too-real faces.

"You have seen this, no?" Magdalena asked.

Nora gave a wooden nod. She'd never seen these statues, but that was not what Magdalena meant. The corded veins of pain threatening to burst through the skin, the arms thrown up as if to hold off the blow of death—she had witnessed it too often. The wails of despair torn from the patients of Croft's surgery rose like ghosts in the still air until Nora pressed her fingers to her ears.

"To stand at the gate of life and death is a calling, not a profession. If you accept the call, you will live where joy meets misery and ecstasy meets torment. You will walk between suffering and relief. You will grant life and destroy it."

"Destroy it?" Nora's eyes rose to the tortured face of the sculpted Mary Magdalene, for whom the doctor beside her was named. "I would never destroy it."

"When you tell a husband his wife is dead, or a mother that her child is lost, you will be the last thing they see and hear before their life descends into sorrow. It will destroy them. It will perhaps destroy you." Magdalena's blue scarf fluttered against her cheek as she spoke, throwing her smooth neck into shadow, so unlike her carved namesake. The sculpted Mary Magdalene opened her mouth in a shattering scream that surely tore her vocal chords, as her nostrils flared in some failed attempt to draw air into her faltering lungs.

A shiver shook the curve of Nora's spine. "Has it destroyed you?" she asked.

Magdalena's eyes rose as if listening to silent voices. "No. But I was called by these women. They told me, sinner though I may be, to attend Christ's children as they attended Christ. Do they call to you as well?"

Nora took in Jesus's lax hands and lifeless face. For a moment her mind held a faded picture, constructed more from Croft's accounts than remnants of her own memory, of the hollow faces of her dead mother and baby brother. She'd been the last to see them alive. Had she, in her illness, tried to nurse them before Horace found her, nearly dead, clutching a dipper beside an empty pail? She must have screamed like this, watching them go, even if the only sound fluttering from her dry throat was a cracked gasp. She wished she could remember.

Magdalena was waiting. "I think so. I would answer their call," Nora said in a tight whisper. "I think I already have."

"Good," Magdalena pronounced in no-nonsense accents, dissolving the image in Nora's mind. "Then you are not a waste of my time. Professor Perra said you want to accelerate your studies and so we shall. This was your first lesson." She faced Nora squarely, waiting until their eyes met beneath their loose veils. "Never give up your post at the crossroads of life and death. People will say you do not belong there because you are a woman. But look to the Sacred Mother. She screamed in agony to bring God into the world and screamed in agony when he was torn from it. She kept her post. Will you do the same, Eleanora? Or will you let someone or something drive you from your place of life and death?"

Nora's eyes traced the lines of pain that extended from Mary's anguished eyes to her moaning mouth. She knew the spot of the stomach that twisted and clenched to produce such a desperate groan. "No, Dottoressa, never."

Magdalena pressed her full lips together, a flash of determination igniting her eyes. "Then there is much work to do and no more time for philosophizing. I will see you at my house Wednesday evening. Until then, you must work!"

CHAPTER 14

Dr. Magdalena Marenco kept a house on Via della Cane, between the great Basilica di San Domenico and the smaller church of San Procolo. Nora arrived at quarter to eight on Wednesday evening and was admitted by a housekeeper who conducted her past a pile of trunks with labels indicating they must have recently returned from Dr. Marenco's African travels. Nora bit back a question. It was no business of hers what the boxes contained, though the house's eclectic furnishings—ornamental calligraphy framed on the walls, oddly shaped bronze lamps, a game of unusually marked ivory tiles on a side table instead of a chess set—sharpened her curiosity.

"In here," the housekeeper said, pointing to what must be the drawing room. The other students were already gathered, seated in a mismatched collection of Queen Anne chairs. Nora gave Pozzi a fast greeting with her eyes and took the chair closest to him, separated by an older man she didn't recognize and one of the sisters from hospital. The nun was young, hardly more than a child, and cast nervous glances at the men around her. Her lips parted with relief when Nora took a seat at her left.

Dr. Marenco swept in, her hospital clothes abandoned for an evening costume of woven silk. It was a deep-cut bodice embroidered with demure roses and vines of small blue flowers.

She had discarded the veil the Bolognese women wore to keep off the sun and dust, and her thick, black hair drifted like a cloud above her milky shoulders. Nora swept her gaze over her own wrinkled gray skirt, feeling more like the shy nun in the coarse serge habit than the elegant doctor.

Dr. Marenco launched into a description of fibrous tumors without any preamble, and Nora fumbled to find her notes as Italian medical terms flew past her, her mind clutching at them in fragments. Dr. Marenco was no Horace Croft when it came to teaching. Horace ambled through his lectures, amused by questions, seduced by tangents, often ending far from his original topic. Marenco kept to the point, a general leading a forced march in a straight, grueling line. Nora's mind panted to keep up.

When the lecture ended, she doubted more than ever her decision to leave Bologna early. Dr. Marenco, who she'd thought would be an ally, was quickly turning into her most formidable obstacle. Ignoring a knot of unease, Nora approached her teacher as the other students dispersed for the night.

"If you've come to ask me to slow down—" Dr. Marenco began.

Nora shook her head emphatically. "No, Dottoressa. I had a comment about the illustrations of the tumors."

Marenco's eyebrows raised and Nora hastened on. "I believe I could provide you better examples, easier to see the fibers and different structures."

"Some English book?" Dr. Marenco asked dismissively.

"No, Dottoressa. I study painting and have done many anatomical illustrations. I could provide one for your scrutiny."

Nora prayed her face did not flush and forced her chin up as if she were not trembling beneath it.

"Ah." Marenco gave an unexpected smile. "A Manzolini in our midst. Doctor and artist."

Nora opened her mouth to contradict the comparison to the university's legendary instructor, the famous Anna Manzolini, whose wax models known round the world had turned the working university into a museum of wonders. But Dr. Marenco allowed no reply.

"How long have you practiced medicine?" she asked.

For a second, Nora was taken aback. She'd never practiced, certainly not officially, and—

Dr. Marenco smiled. "Come now. The only students who have your kind of experience are the sons of doctors or surgeons. My father was a surgeon too, and in our town, when he was unavailable, I did the work myself. I learned from him and my mother. She received her license in Bologna, and they sent me here when I was eighteen, though of course there were fewer women than in my mother's time."

"I still think it's a miracle there are any of us at all," Nora said, and caught her lip in her teeth. Dr. Marenco might be offended by lumping them together, as if she thought herself equal to a mature and experienced doctor who'd wielded a scalpel almost as long as Nora had been alive.

Instead of bristling, Dr. Marenco smiled. "To an English girl, certainly. For me, it's sad to see fewer and fewer of us. In my mother's time, when Napoleon and the French occupiers were defeated, and women finally readmitted to the university... Did you know they'd all been dismissed?"

Nora shook her head.

"Yes. It was shameful, trying to destroy our long tradition of female scholars, but a greater tragedy has been happening since. Every decade of this century fewer women apply, fewer are admitted, fewer are licensed. Though I'm permitted to practice, I have to lecture privately, as the university won't hire women anymore. Their doors are slowly closing—and they will close if we capitulate. Always remember you are as able as your colleagues and better in some ways. You have smaller hands."

Nora glanced at her fingers, wishing her sleeve were as lovely as Marenco's instead of the bland, bleachable white linen. "You aren't the first to tell me that." Daniel had said the same thing about her hands, leaning over a dying man. Nora smoothed a wrinkle in her skirt, trying to brush away a pang of homesickness. "When I was orphaned, Horace Croft took me in and raised me. He taught me medicine at home, but I was never permitted in classrooms or lectures."

"Hid you well, did he?"

Remembering, Nora pressed her lips together. "Not well enough."

"Good. You shouldn't have to hide. Especially after apprenticing to such a redoubtable surgeon."

Nora's eyes flashed to Marenco's, searching for sarcasm, but she saw only briskness.

"And the ether—" Dr. Marenco moved aside a china elephant to set down her papers. "What can you teach me about that?"

Nora blinked. "Anything you like, Dottoressa."

"Good," Dr. Marenco said, her movements crisp and

efficient as she flipped through the stack of drawings she had shown during her lecture until she came to the one of fibrous tumors, studying it as she spoke. "In ether, I'm the student. I want you to teach me how it's done. The potential is too great to ignore, and you have more method in your technique than the others I've observed. I will forgo your fee and you will forgo mine. An even trade."

Nora drew in her breath. "I'd be honored, Dottoressa."

"Enough," Dr. Marenco exclaimed. "That word in your mouth grates on my nerves. It will be Magdalena for you. And do not think I will call you Beady. Hideous name." She thrust the tumor illustration at Nora. "Have your version here next week and I will compare."

Nora's automatic reply of *Yes, Dottoressa* was now forbidden so she nodded mutely. Though she'd been told to use Dr. Marenco's first name, she was not yet courageous enough to attempt it.

"Good night, Eleanora," Dr. Marenco said as she dropped onto the nearby couch, crossing her ankles and reaching for a book, as languid and lovely as the Venus in the painting behind her.

"Good night," Nora managed and clumsily gathered her papers and pencil into her bag. Her heart raced as she hurried from the house. She'd finally be able to impress Dr. Magdalena Marenco, no matter how long the drawing took.

CHAPTER 15

DANIEL SANK INTO THE WORN LEATHER CHAIR OF THE
United Service Club, burrowing his shoulders into the
softness while his ears reveled in the relative quiet. Though the
room buzzed with chatter, there was not a moan or scream to
be heard, and no builder's hammers, saws, or chisels, either. He
clenched a pipe in his mouth more to fend off conversation
than for the cherry tobacco. Since he rarely escaped work for
an evening, tonight he didn't mean to waste energy on unnecessary words. In a nearby armchair, Croft was mumbling on
about noncorroding metals, as he had been since leaving home,
but Daniel had long ago lost the thread. No matter. Horace
required no reply, only a warm body for his voice to bounce off.

And warm it was. Men filled every corner of the ample
room. Their sparkling glasses of amber liquors and fragrant
pipe smoke radiated a particular air of bonhomie on this black,
rainy evening. Lord Ashwell, one of the few peers to frequent
this club, dozed beside the fire, his white whiskers twitching as
he dreamed. He reminded Daniel of a cat, making him wish for
a mind untroubled enough to allow such placid slumber.

A group of surgeons from the University College Hospital
was gloomily watching two of their number muddle quietly
through a game of chess. After the accidental death of one of

their colleagues at the hasty hands of their famous head of surgery, Robert Liston, they had the look of deflated protégés, not at all anxious to return to work. Daniel couldn't blame them. The unfortunate student had lost his fingers and died of infection all because Liston was showing off the speed of his dissection knife.

"Silver sutures are being used, but is it an arbitrary use? Would copper be more malleable to the wound?" Horace stroked his beard, his lined face looking more deeply etched than usual in the room's low light. With four children now at Great Queen Street and two more, optimistically diagnosed with croup, in the ward at St. Bart's, both he and Daniel were working like demons. An hour at the club while John, the orderly, kept watch was a welcome respite.

Daniel responded to Horace's query with a polite sound of interest and refilled his pipe. Horace's mind ran faster than his own. Best to let him jog ahead, clear the road, and put up markers before attempting to follow. Daniel reached into his jacket pocket to put away his pouch of tobacco, paused, shifted in his chair, then gave sudden and undivided attention to his pipe.

Vickery had marched into the room, alongside a pair of younger doctors. One was his newest dresser, the other unfamiliar, perhaps a prospective student. From the corner of his eye, Daniel watched them greet the University Hospital doctors, but Vickery had little interest in chess. Smoothing an exceptionally tailored navy-blue coat, he sauntered to within a few yards of Horace's chair. Daniel had seen him use this sidling gait only once before—that dreadful symposium, where he, then Nora, had been practically put on trial before the London scientific community.

"That you, Silas?" Horace surprised Vickery—and Daniel—with a smooth greeting and a forced smile that sent a warning prickle up Daniel's neck. Daniel glanced around, but Lord Ashwell slept on, and anyone watching this unfolding scene was doing so discreetly.

"You must not have read my latest article, Croft. I'd expected some response from you by now," Vickery said.

"Dr. Gibson and I have been making a serious study of throat diseases in children and the lifesaving applications of the tracheotomy," Horace said. "So I haven't had time to read your treatise on the larynx, trachea, and esophagus of a dead Asiatic elephant."

Horace had an abiding fascination with comparative anatomy. His rooms were filled with specimens, including a collection of human and ape skulls with tabulated, point-by-point comparisons and a complete, wired skeleton of a pygmy shrew, no bigger than the end of Daniel's thumb, with bones as thin as a sheet of paper. If an elephant carcass had been available in London and gone to Vickery for study instead, it would explain Horace's icy courtesy, even without Vickery causing the influx of young patients at Great Queen Street.

"I heard you were interested in my elephant specimen."

"Not after I learned you'd outbid me for it," Horace said. "I saw your clumsy work with the bird from Iceland."

Daniel knew better than to reassure Horace that another elephant would come his way. There might not be another here in London for dissection in either of their lifetimes. And the great auk, a large, flightless bird native to Iceland, had long been a sore point with Horace, as the species was now considered extinct. Vickery had bought the bird right under Horace's nose, and Horace would never forgive him for it.

"I suppose you couldn't afford the elephant—not while undertaking your renovations. Do you think it wise? I fear you may be overextending yourself," Vickery said. "And it cannot be comfortable for you or your patients with so many builders about."

"You could relieve the patients, at least. Let them back into St. Bart's," Daniel said, more sharply than he intended. "Horace and I don't mind the hammering."

"And how are your human specimens faring?" Vickery asked, settling himself into a more relaxed posture as he towered over their chairs to let them know they'd not be rid of him easily.

"Don't see how it concerns you since you sent them into the streets to die." A storm was brewing on Horace's brow, pushing warning wrinkles around his eyes.

"Well, I told them to go to your house, but I agree that's hardly better than the streets. In the streets no one would slice open their throats as they die." Vickery's words were just light enough that a charitable-minded man could take them as a joke, but Daniel and Horace knew better. So did Vickery's new wound dresser, who grinned with anticipation, recognizing this for a shot across the bow.

Daniel took a wary inventory of the men scattered around the room. No one was paying attention. Yet.

"We are in the business of relieving suffering," Horace said in a voice so low Daniel worried it wouldn't reach Vickery. "I suggest you stop trying to hinder us in our mission."

"I am in the business of saving lives. And I'm afraid life is full of suffering. You have an unpleasant habit of relieving people of both pain and life." Vickery had no veiled courtesy now. His black eyes glinted like two dead stars.

"You blasted fool," Horace growled. "You ignorant, jealous, pompous, myopic—"

"Careful, Horace," Vickery interrupted. "I'm your head of surgery. I'd hate to dismiss you." The lie danced on his face.

"You're more the ass of surgery than the head!" Horace lurched to his feet, but Daniel, anticipating the move, grabbed the back of his coat, forcing him back into his chair.

"Are you a surgeon or a boxer?" Vickery asked derisively.

"Are you an imbecile or a ratbag?" Horace snapped, wrenching free and shoving to his feet. Sweat shone on his brow, and his hand was trembling.

"He's baiting you," Daniel warned Horace in a low whisper, afraid to meet the eyes he knew were watching from every corner of the room. "He wants you to make a spectacle while he stays calm."

"I'm happy to oblige." Horace stepped forward.

Daniel sensed another person approaching just as a hand landed on Horace's shoulder.

"I've just been hearing about your latest ether successes, Dr. Croft." Harry Trimble's voice ballooned with unnatural cheerfulness over the frozen scene. "It's all the doctors speak of in Truro."

Horace's eyes sliced to Harry's, hardly happier to see him than Silas. He glared back and forth between two men he hated, planting his feet as if he'd like to take them both.

"Don't put your nose in here, Trimble," Vickery warned. "I don't believe it went well for you last time."

Harry smiled, his teeth as tight as his calculating eyes. "I came out well enough."

Men were gravitating closer, their ears pricked. Vickery raised his voice for the benefit of any curious eavesdroppers. "Did you? I must have heard wrong," Vickery sneered. "The story I heard was that you ended up marrying the girl you operated on illegally. Seems strange, but I suppose if you were the one who put that baby in her—"

Harry lunged for him. Daniel grabbed and missed, but Horace was faster, reaching out with lightning instincts and snapping Harry painfully across the legs with his walking stick. Harry nearly fell to the floor, but Daniel's mind was reeling, too, grappling with Vickery's words as if turning them round or right side up would change their meaning.

It didn't. The truth was plain in Harry's furious face.

Daniel knew about the raped girl, the illegal abortion, and how knowledge of both had allowed Vickery to bribe and threaten Harry into recanting the claim that he'd taken Nora's place at that infamous hernia surgery. He hadn't known the girl was anything more than a patient to Harry.

It didn't matter. If he didn't get Harry and Horace out of here… "No," was all he had time to say, grabbing his friend's arm, Vickery's strident laugh still ringing in his ears. "We're leaving."

"That's what I was going to say." A new voice joined the fray, cold and authoritative. "Gentlemen—" Lord Ashwell, awake now, frowned reprovingly.

"Forgive me, my lord. We didn't mean to disturb you," Vickery said with a deferential nod.

"Surely there's no need to quarrel so vehemently. This isn't a political club," Ashwell chided, signaling for the club's waiters. Beneath Daniel's grip, Harry's muscled arm quivered, but the approaching attendants convinced Vickery to retreat a step.

He wiped down his vest with ostentatious dignity. "Not all professional men are gentlemen—" He stopped as Horace's walking stick clattered noisily against the table, upsetting a liquor tray on its way to the floor and cutting off his words with a crash.

An unnatural jerk of a limb tugged Daniel's gaze away from the spilled liquid and toppled glasses. Horace gasped, and by sheer instinct, Daniel caught him before he collapsed to the floor.

"Horace! Where's your medicine?" he demanded, appalled by the whiteness of Horace's face and his grimace of pain.

Unable to answer, Horace gestured wildly with his left arm.

"What is his medicine?" Harry asked urgently.

"Digitalis," Daniel said through clenched teeth as he struggled with Horace's collar, trying to loosen it while Horace groaned.

"Digitalis," Harry cried, glancing wildly about the room, which was peppered with physicians and surgeons. "Does anyone have some?"

An elderly doctor from University Hospital hurried forward, unstopping a black bottle he'd pulled from the pocket of his coat. "It's a high concentration. Start with just a few drops."

None of Horace's previous angina attacks had been this

dramatic or frightening. "Open your mouth," Daniel said and tried not to panic or lose count of the drops falling steadily onto Horace's outstretched tongue.

No one was seated any longer. Even ancient Lord Ashwell had hobbled forward in concern. Blurred murmurs accompanied the strained wait as Daniel watched for Horace's limbs to soften and his breathing to become less ragged.

"Here." Harry was behind them with an armchair. "Someone get a footstool."

"I'm fine," Horace said at last, wiping his mouth angrily. His hand released its fierce clutch on his chest. "Stop acting like a pack of old women!" He pulled away from Daniel and straightened his coat with sharp tugs, unable to hide his panting. "I don't need coddling—or needling from you, Silas. Your idiocy will be the death of me."

Harry laughed before he could stop himself. Several of the students hovering behind him did the same. Taking advantage of their distraction, Daniel commandeered Horace's hand to inspect his fingertips and nail beds despite Horace's resistance. Blood was finding its way back where it belonged.

"Are you better now?" the lender of the medicine asked.

"Fine, fine. I just need some air." Horace waved him away.

Before Daniel could think to ask, a waiter produced Horace's overcoat and hat. Behind him, another attendant offered Daniel's and Harry's as well. Daniel understood their impulse to diffuse the crowd. In any case, he wanted Horace at home, where he could check his reflexes and listen to his chest.

He watched the waiter help Horace into his coat before accepting his own. When he was sure Horace could walk, he followed him grimly from the club, pausing only to thank the doctor who provided the digitalis, even though it meant blandly enduring Vickery's smug smile.

"Daniel, wait!" Harry's voice arrested him on the staircase. "What was that? Is he all right?"

Daniel studied the worried lines around Harry's eyes. He'd aged since their Sorbonne days. Why hadn't he told Daniel he loved the girl who he'd saved?

Daniel sighed. "His angina's growing worse."

"Let me help see him home. I know he hates me but"—his eyes were brave and didn't glance away—"we can't lose him."

Grateful another person understood that truth, Daniel agreed with a one-shouldered shrug and led Harry outside.

It took them half a block to catch up to Horace.

"I don't want you, Trimble," Horace spat as soon as they drew near, the cold blasts of London air finally cooling his temper enough for speech.

"If your angina returns, Daniel won't be able to get you home on his own," Harry said between breaths.

Horace's lip curled like a baited cur.

"You nearly had yourself a match back there," Daniel said, directing the comment to neither and both of them. "I've never seen Vickery so close to a fistfight."

"I'd welcome it," Horace growled, successfully diverted. "Why did you stop me?"

"Because this was the first hour of peace I've had all week, and you've ruined it," Daniel said, trying for humor. "Now we have to trek all the way to Athenaeum club and hope they've forgotten my drunken scene last year."

Horace shook his head. "I'm not going anywhere with Trimble." He stopped walking, staring straight ahead as if Harry weren't there.

"I'm sorry—" Harry began, but Horace cut him off with a curse and stumped away down the pavement, Daniel and Harry following in his wake.

Daniel glanced sideways at his former friend. "Is what Vickery said true? You married the girl who needed that surgery?"

Harry's chin rose. "I married Julia Buchanan."

Daniel searched his memory and flinched. "Buchanan? Your old sailing master's daughter?"

Harry nodded.

"Find a pub if you like," Horace snarled. "I've no time for swapping reminiscences with cowardly traitors. I'm going home."

He stalked around the corner, his shadow veering maniacally in the lamplight.

"That went better than I expected," Harry mused.

Daniel gave a fleeting smile and dropped his voice. "I can't let him go on his own."

"Of course not. Watch him. Make sure he takes his drops," Harry said. "He should carry them with him."

Daniel nodded. "He'll have to from now on. It's getting worse." Horace was fading in the shadows as he drew farther ahead. Daniel looked back and forth between them.

"Go," Harry said. "I can explain it all later."

Relieved by the promise of a future conversation, Daniel bid his former friend good night.

"No need to run," he said once he'd caught up with Horace, forcibly taking the older man's arm. "Let me hail a hackney."

"I'd rather walk," Horace said. His color seemed improved, though temper poured almost visibly from his ears and nostrils, so Daniel let him march on, keeping pace at his side.

"This will just increase your odds of another episode," he said with a roll of his eyes.

"What do you know about Trimble's wife?" Horace demanded.

"Not enough," Daniel mumbled. "Only what Nora told me after the fiasco."

"So what happened?" Horace asked.

Daniel wet his lips. He didn't want to betray a confidence.

"You and I don't owe Trimble anything," Horace said. "And I deserve the truth. If Nora gave it to you, she should have given it to me as well."

"It's not a happy story," Daniel warned.

Horace snorted.

"Fine. When we get home. It's not a subject I want to bandy about in the street."

Surprisingly, Horace didn't protest and continued marching double time until they were safely ensconced in what passed now as their drawing room. The furniture was covered in dust sheets, and scaffolding obscured one wall where the plasterers had been working all day. Horace sat down in his favorite chair and propped his feet on a crate of books that had been moved here so the builders could enlarge the library and install display cases for Horace's specimens. "Well?"

Daniel's face twisted. The details were painful enough to

imagine on anyone, but he'd met Julia Buchanan, more than once. A beautiful girl, not even old enough to be out the last time he'd seen her, though perhaps she'd be close to twenty now. Recalling her bright, sparkling eyes, ready smile, and her fondness for her younger siblings and her father, Daniel didn't want to cast her as victim in the tale Nora had shared.

"Harry was tending an emergency of his own the night Nora and I did the hernia surgery," Daniel said flatly. "A girl who'd slashed open her wrists. Pregnant. A rape victim. At the father's suggestion, Harry performed an abortion. The father feared if they didn't, she'd attempt violence again. But she lost so much blood, Harry kept her at St. Bart's. He only made a record of the stitching he'd done on her arms, but Vickery examined her in the following days and guessed from the soiled sheets that wasn't all Harry'd done. When he read our paper on the hernia surgery, Vickery unfortunately realized we claimed Harry was operating on John Prescott the same night he was recorded in the hospital logs stitching up the girl. Vickery threatened Harry and the girl with exposure, and sweetened his offer with three hundred pounds."

Horace made a noise of disgust. Daniel couldn't tell if it was directed at Harry or Vickery. "Nora said she couldn't blame him for succumbing to that kind of pressure. I still think—" Daniel shook his head. He wasn't sure anymore. He'd thought at the time that Harry still harbored romantic feelings for Nora and acted from jealousy and spite, but if he'd been in love with Julia Buchanan, resisting Vickery would have been that much harder. What must it have been like for Harry, frantically sewing up her arms and trying to keep her secrets? Not to mention performing a surgery to save her that could have cost him his license? He'd been in as much danger as Nora that night.

Of course, Harry might not have been in love with Julia when it happened. The feeling could have taken root later. It was hard, sometimes, not to care too much for patients. Harry's marriage might well be a case of compassion gone too far.

But he seemed happy. The mere mention of her name by Vickery had made Harry see red.

"He should have told us," Horace said. "Just because another girl's name was at risk doesn't mean it was right to sacrifice Nora's."

Daniel nodded reflexively. And yet… "If the truth hadn't come out, Nora would still be here," he said quietly. "A happy outcome for you and me, but I'm not sure, in the end, if it would have been best." Much as he missed her, she needed Italy. She deserved the chance to qualify as a real physician, even if she was never granted the right to practice.

Horace fumbled with his daily paper, his eyes roaming the headlines. "You think this wife of Harry's is all right?"

Daniel cocked his head in question.

Horace wove his fingers together. "Violence leaves its mark. Sometimes I see patients afflicted with night terrors or melancholia even decades later." He frowned at the empty fireplace. "Not our concern, I suppose."

"No," Daniel agreed. He had no business speculating. Harry had shown he was quite capable of looking after his patients himself.

CHAPTER 16

Nora GRIPPED HER SCARF ONE-HANDED, FIGHTING THE boisterous wind and spatters of rain, her other hand clutching the portfolio of drawings close to her chest. Magdalena had paid her an incredible compliment by requesting instruction in ether, and their first session had gone well. Working in Nora's sitting room, Magdalena had spent hours practicing heating and cooling the vapor. Mrs. Phipps had adamantly refused to act as subject, but Pozzi had volunteered. Magdalena had sedated him without any difficulty, marveling at his response. She'd ordered a vaporizer of her own to Nora's specifications and copied out Nora's dosing tables. They would practice again on Sunday, but this visit wasn't about ether. Nora had slaved over the university microscopes late at night so she could present these drawings to Magdalena before class on Wednesday, determined to impress her.

And the drawings were good. Perra had provided two uterine tumor samples from the specimens in his office and found another three from his colleagues. The resulting folio of drawings was, if not as large as Dr. Marenco's current collection, of superior quality. Nora had exerted all her skill with tint and brush to capture every detail at two different magnifications. She sounded the knocker, smiling as she imagined Magdalena's response.

Magdalena answered the door herself. "Eleanora. Thank the Blessed Mother you're here." She crossed herself quickly, then swept aside her untidy hair. She wore a cloak.

"Is anything the matter?"

"I need your help. Your coming now is nothing short of a miracle." Magdalena picked up her bag from its resting place on the chair by the door. "A boy's just come saying there is a woman in terrible labor. She's in the care of a competent midwife so it must be urgent. Do you have your vaporizer?"

Nora shook her head. She'd set out with only the drawings and left her bag at home.

"Damn!" Magdalena spat. "Mine is not finished yet." Her face twisted with fury and decision. "There's no time, but I have ether at least. You said you know how to use a handkerchief."

"Yes, but it's so imprecise…" Nora began.

"Perhaps we won't need it," Magdalena said. "Here is my coach."

Nora set down the drawings against the floral-papered wall. There'd be time for them later. She jumped into the carriage a second ahead of Magdalena, who shouted at the driver to hurry.

"Have you treated this woman before?" Nora asked. She hated stumbling into a case deaf and blind. Any information helped.

"Never. But she's in the Quadrilatero and the message came from Nicolina Dragna, who's been tending to births for decades. She's come to me for medical training and she's adept. If she says it's an emergency, you can be sure." Magdalena pushed a fallen lock of hair behind her ear and rubbed her hands together as if limbering her fingers for the work ahead.

Outside, it was beginning to rain. Nora swayed with the coach, her hands clasped around her knees, her knuckles white.

When the driver pulled up to the street, they disembarked, heedless of the quickly forming puddles that seeped up the hems of their skirts. The driver pointed them through a narrow gap between two buildings and assured them it would open into a courtyard. The home they wanted would be on the southern side.

Nora thanked him and hurried to catch Magdalena before she disappeared in the maze of tenements. As soon as they emerged into the courtyard, a young boy bounded toward them. "*Rapido!*" he ordered and pointed them up an exterior staircase where several women had gathered despite the rain, looking with worried eyes to a second-story flat. Their whispered prayers rushed over Nora like a wind as she pressed through the wet huddle.

Anguished panting greeted their ears as soon as they opened the door of the dim apartment. Following the sound, they found a bedroom where a swollen woman crouched on all fours contorted in pain; another woman, doused in sweat, gray hair plastered to her distraught face, knelt beside her, her arm lodged in the birth canal. Magdalena jumped to her side, pushing up her sleeves.

The midwife's breaths were almost as labored as the patient's when she spoke. "Transverse, laying right on the cord. I've been trying to hold the baby off the cord, fighting the contractions, but I cannot turn it. I've done everything and there is no room to work and the contractions are too strong."

The woman screamed and dipped her back as a contraction with the force of a gale pounded her body. Magdalena traded places, pushing the baby against the muscles shoving it down. "I feel the spine. The waters have come away. It's too dry. We have to cut the baby out. Get the ether. Nicolina, get her on her back and keep the baby off the cord!"

Nora barely heard over the mother's screams, but she had already grabbed Magdalena's bottle of ether. She poured it onto a cloth and waved it to disperse the most pungent fumes before pressing it to the woman's face. Her eyes rolled toward Nora and widened in terror.

"It's medicine to make the pain stop. Breathe and it will put you to sleep and you will be free—" The patient's fist collided with her ribs and Nora gasped, but she tightened her grip over the woman's face. The woman needed to inhale for at least one minute for the ether to calm her. In her excited state she wouldn't go quietly.

A powerful sputtering broke from the woman's mouth, followed by the worst laryngeal spasms Nora had ever heard. A breathless, ceaseless coughing rattled her body.

"She's choking!" the midwife cried.

Magdalena looked up from the scalpel she had pulled from her bag.

"It's the first stage of ether." Nora tried not to show her doubt. "It can cause spasms of the larynx. If she keeps inhaling, the throat muscles will relax."

Instead of inhaling, the woman held her breath and lashed out at Nora again, clawing at her hand holding the ether rag.

"Can you get her to be still?" Magdalena said between clenched teeth as she ripped the clothing from the woman's body to reveal the abdomen.

"I'm trying. What's her name?" she asked the midwife.

"Paola."

Nora brought her head down to the patient's face and forced her to meet her gaze. Paola's eyes were a flashing brown, animal-like in their panic. "Paola, this medicine is from the Mother Mary. It is blessed by the priests to take away pain. I know it smells strange and makes you cough but if you breathe slowly, all of your pain will go away."

She could feel Magdalena's eyes boring holes in her back as she lied, but she'd long ago learned that in this city, no one doubted the supremacy and miracles of the Blessed Mother Mary. Judging by the size of the crucifix hanging from Paola's neck, she would be much more prone to listen if Nora invoked her faith rather than her intellect.

Nora flinched when a high keening accompanied the rattles of Paola's throat. She braced for another scream but the sound mounted into a note of song. Paola was singing as she gasped.

"What in the lakes of hell?" Magdalena hissed.

"She's delirious," Nora said.

"Tie her down," Magdalena shouted, but Nora's hands were engaged in the struggle to keep the ether rag over Paola's face, and Nicolina couldn't move her arm from holding the baby off the cord. With a cry of frustration Magdalena put down the scalpel and began binding the woman's arms to her sides using the clothing she'd just cut away. The unsettling song continued, broken by racking coughs.

"It will take three more minutes," Nora said, only guessing. She'd never had a patient react so violently. But then she'd rarely applied ether using just a rag. She and Daniel and Horace had begun experimenting with vaporizers almost immediately.

"Can't wait," Magdalena said, snatching her scalpel.

Nora cursed and poured more ether onto the rag, hoping to speed the reaction. Paola's movements grew sloppier. "You can't cut when's she's fighting you. One more minute!" Nora's voice rose as the midwife groaned. Another contraction was forcing the baby down, and she could not hold him.

"Now!" Magdalena swiped the scalpel down the midsection before Nora could open her mouth to object. A fountain of blood spilled from the wound. With breathless speed, Magdalena pulled the thick skin away. "Nora! Come quick!"

Nora left the rag on Paola's face and jumped to Magdalena's side to swab the incision.

"No time for that. I'll hold. You cut," Magdalena ordered.

Nora snatched up one of the scalpels. Magdalena had drilled her sufficiently on procedure that her movements felt automatic, though this was frighteningly new.

Don't think of that, Nora told herself. She took one breath as she ran her finger over the uterus, feeling the hard shape of the baby's limbs. With caution, she pushed the scalpel in, praying she did not cut the child. Magdalena handed her scissors and Nora cut downward until a dark-colored fist no bigger than a blackberry bloomed from the incision. Magdalena plunged her arm into the cavity.

"Fundal pressure!" she snapped and Nora obeyed, dropping the scissors and pushing the baby away from the birth canal toward the open uterus.

"That's me," Nicolina cried in relief as Magdalena's fingers met hers and she handed off the baby.

Nicolina fell backward onto her seat, rubbing her arm. Nora took the limp baby. A girl. Dusky and purple. She wasn't stirring and her eyes were swollen closed.

Nora threw a glance to the mother, relieved she was sleeping and unable to see the specter of her bloated and discolored daughter.

"Why isn't it crying?" Magdalena asked as she dropped the placenta into a water pail on the floor.

"No life yet," Nicolina said as she recovered her feet and took the child, vigorously rubbing the gray body.

Nora's hands shook as she pulled out two threaded suture needles and handed one to Magdalena who began stitching up the uterus. Nora followed behind, tying strong knots in the dissected abdominal muscles. The goal now was to close as fast as possible. Lost in the task, Nora only faintly heard the midwife muttering frantically as she worked on the child.

"Your first cesarean operation," Magdalena murmured as they closed.

"Mine?" Nora asked in shock.

"You opened the uterus. Yes. It is yours." Their eyes met momentarily, Magdalena's dark and serious and grim and... proud. "How is the patient?"

Nora jumped. In her single focus of helping Magdalena she'd been unable to monitor Paola. The soaked rag was still covering her face, and beneath it the skin was a pale blue. Nora yanked the rag off to reveal Paola's jaw open and sunken at such a strange angle she hardly recognized the screaming, singing woman of five minutes ago. She prodded a half-opened eyelid, eliciting no flinch or movement. Nora pressed her ear to Paola's lips, relieved to feel a warm, slow breath pass over her skin. She fumbled at her neck to finally find a weak pulse, the heart thudding reluctantly after long pauses.

"Nora?" Magdalena asked again.

"Pulse 48. Breathing quiet, but faint."

"Reaction to stimulus?" Magdalena asked as she tugged at the strands of catgut trailing her needle.

"No," Nora whispered. There was no reaction of any kind. This was the fifth stage. The one from which the rats and chickens rarely woke. The one they never reached when they used the vaporizer. Nora took a cup of water, wet her hands, and began patting Paola's cheeks, her motions growing in speed and intensity as Paola's face wobbled lifelessly.

"Paola," she whispered. "It's time to wake up. All the pain is over, just as we promised." Nora pushed the eyelids open again, but the pupils did not contract. She rubbed Paola's neck, gritting her teeth when the woman's head flopped like a corpse against the heavy chain of her crucifix. Nora pressed her hands above Paola's heart and gave a mighty heave as she had seen Horace do to patients with a failing pulse.

"Her skin is getting darker," Magdalena pointed out. Paola's face was morphing from a sickly blue tinge to a dusky purple like her daughter.

The thought made Nora turn to the midwife who was also using water and smacking the child, still with no results.

As Nicolina pleaded with the baby and Magdalena tried to close the gaping wound, the small room blurred before Nora's eyes and she swayed, clenching her fists and fighting the darkness. A new and unwelcome impulse overpowered her:

flight—to desert her post at the crossroads of life and death as blood dripped to the floor and a macabre silence filled the stuffy, windowless room. Nora closed her eyes, and with the same moan mounting in her that she had seen in the faces of the terra-cotta women, she grasped Paola's slack hand and tried to call her back from the depths.

"Paola? Paola…"

Half an hour later, as they left the house, Magdalena dropped a defeated but comforting hand on Nora's shoulder. Nora flinched.

"Sometimes—"

"Their deaths are my fault. I should never have used a rag."

"Eleanora—"

Nora turned her face away and stepped out of the sheltering portico into the now abandoned courtyard and the rain. It was sharper and colder than an hour ago and stung like needles on her face. "I'm sorry. I need to be alone." Without waiting for an answer, she turned and walked blindly into the street, her breath a fog around her face.

CHAPTER 17

T HE CONTRACTION OF THE FLEXOR MUSCLE," NORA mumbled in answer to the professor's question as he stared pointedly down his broad nose at her. Gone was the fast whip of her head when her name was called, the pride that accompanied a correct answer even when she struggled with slippery Italian words. She had been replaced with an automaton, efficient, silent, adept at blending into the fringes of a pack of students.

From several feet away, Pozzi caught her eye—a difficult feat these days—and his dark eyes narrowed with confusion. Nora dipped her head once more, angry she'd let herself interact with anyone, even through a glance. As soon as the lecture was over, she escaped to the side courtyard. It wasn't landscaped or tended, so few people bothered to visit the pebbly, neglected spot. She had an hour before she needed to be at the hospital, and the walk from the university was only fifteen minutes. Plenty of time, then, to sit and be alone.

She ensured her privacy before she leaned against the red stone wall and let it catch the exhaustion throbbing in her spine—the same exhaustion that had plagued her ever since Paola and her unnamed daughter died. She closed her eyes, refusing to acknowledge the heat in her throat or the moisture behind her eyelids. She must be like Horace—focused, unflappable, callous.

"Nora?"

Her eyes flew open. Pozzi was ten feet away, approaching carefully.

"I'm just resting," she said, letting her words leak with annoyance at being caught out.

His squinting gaze didn't register her words at all. He continued forward. "You're not well."

Nora glared in disagreement.

As if reading her thoughts, he continued. "Your heart is not well. Right now, you want to weep." He was only an arm's length away. She'd managed to keep even Mrs. Phipps at bay for the last week, and she'd already forgotten how to be this close to someone.

"There is a huge difference between killing someone and not being able to save them," he continued. "You didn't kill Signora Napoli. You couldn't save her."

Gravity amplified, pulling Nora down, off of her trembling feet. She let herself take a seat on the uneven ground, adjusting herself to avoid a rock digging into her hip. Pozzi sat beside her. She wanted to answer him, but at the sound of the woman's name, the weight, the heat, the moisture of the pain building in her chest was too much. It condensed into swollen tears that fought their way past her restraint. She swiped at the traitors.

"No," Pozzi said in thick English, digging for his handkerchief. "Let them."

"If I had the vaporizer that day—" The words were as hollow as the empty chasm beneath her ribs.

"*If* is a terrible word." He cut her off. "Let's not use it." His cheek lifted into the beginning of an encouraging grin.

Nora swallowed down all her unspoken words. His squinting eyes were welcoming. After sharing tutorials with Perra and Magdalena's classes, he was the closest thing she had to a friend. Unlike the other students, he no longer ignored her, but complimented her openly and often saved her a place beside him. "When pretty girls cry, they get even lovelier," he said with a warm smile. "Why do you English try so hard to hide it?" His own eyes were growing pink and glossy as he gazed at her. Her breaths grew heavier with anxiety. If this boy wept... "I wanted to give you time to grieve, but you aren't doing it right, Nora. You've barely spoken in days."

"Doing it right?" she stammered.

He nodded. "You must let the pain out, not hold it in. My mother says—"

She shook her head. "It's all too much." The words came out in English, and she didn't care if he understood. She needed to throw her complaint to heaven in her own language. She turned to him, needing someone to witness the truth that burned holes through her chest until she couldn't breathe at night. "The baby at least should have lived!"

His smile melted away, leaving a tangle of distressed creases around his eyes. He wrapped his hand over hers, clasping her fingers in a tight grip. "*Should* is often worse than *if*." He sighed and stroked her wrist. "I know what medicine you need." He leaned his head against the building, the black waves of his hair pressed flat against the dull stones. "Let's walk tonight. We'll leave the city and go to my favorite vineyard and drink until we can't see straight and forget this world"—he gestured to the university buildings and the students walking across the lane in the distance—"for an evening."

There was nothing she wanted more than oblivion—to forget and escape—but when she turned to him, she saw more than concern in his eager expression. She had little experience with men, but could not miss the gravity in his eyes as they lingered on her face. His hope filled her bones with indescribable weariness.

"No, Pozzi. I think I should spend the evening resting. And right now I am expected at the Grand Hospital of Life and Death," she said bitterly, heaving reluctantly to her feet, thrown off-balance by his unexpected tug on her hand.

"Nora," he said with a strange expression lighting his face, "I could make it better for you. At least for one night." He rose to full height, which brought them eye to eye. At age twenty, he looked more child than man. His touch was more hopeful now, his gaze more fervent. She shook her head. Better to pluck the small splinter of desire out of him now before it burrowed any deeper. "Pozzi, you need to study. You didn't know which nerves supply which fingers when Professor Perra called on you this morning."

She looked away so she wouldn't see him deflate.

Drunken oblivion was tempting, but drinking with Pozzi would be a mistake. "Let's study tomorrow," she called over her shoulder as she left him in the dirty side yard of the lecture hall.

"Anna Grey's wound is granulating nicely. I changed the dressing and gave her Warburg's tincture for the fever," Jeffers reported. "Unfortunately, Tommy Benson's fever hasn't abated, and he vomited—"

"Give him a menthol rub and cool him with wet sheets and ice," Daniel said curtly, having just spied the hallboy from 43 Great Queen Street loitering outside the door. Jeffers could be trusted to see to Tommy Benson. "Excuse me."

Daniel hurried into the corridor, unease lapping at his heels. "What is it, Peter?" A doctor soon became accustomed to urgent summonses and bad news, but Daniel didn't want either coming from the hallboy. "Is it Dr. Croft?"

"No, sir!" Peter shook his head and smiled apologetically. "I didn't mean for you to worry. A letter came for you in the morning post but you was already gone to hospital."

Daniel ignored the note of reproach in the boy's voice, echoed, no doubt, from Mrs. Crawford the housekeeper. Daniel had stopped breakfasting at home three days ago, since the current level of chaos wreaked by Horace's horde of workmen defied belief. Compared to the ruckus at home, St. Bart's was a haven of peace.

"Mrs. Crawford said you'd want it straightaway."

"I do. Thank her for me." Sometimes Nora's letters came a day or two early, thanks to the vagaries of the post, and sometimes she wrote twice instead of once a week. Whether this was an extra or an early letter, he wanted her news now more than ever. Her words would carry him back to ordinary times, when the house was haphazard instead of outright hazardous, the scene of study and surgery, not a demolition experiment.

He sent the hallboy home and found himself a quiet corner

in an unused surgery. It was too windy today to take the letter outside.

Her words took him away, but not, as he'd expected, to a pleasanter place. As he read over the terse and clinical account of her cesarean surgery, his heart slowed, and he grew cold, numb, and heavy, as if he too were succumbing to death by ether. There were dimples in the paper where the ink ran, places where her tears had splashed the page.

What terrifies me most is knowing these moments will come again. I will make more mistakes because I can't help it. I don't know if I have the heart for such a cruel profession. Artists and anatomists don't kill.

Daniel folded the letter and wiped his eyes, but he didn't get up, though work was waiting. He hoped Mrs. Phipps or some friend had comforted her by now. These were heavy burdens to shoulder alone, and the comforting words he had for her wouldn't arrive for another fortnight. Daniel returned to the ward and spoke to Jeffers and Stoddard, instructing them to carry on without him for the rest of the afternoon.

At home, closeted in the temporary quarters assigned to him while his former bedchamber was converted into a gallery to display Horace's collection of anatomical curiosities, Daniel did his best to shut out the sawing and hammering shaking the house.

You are a wonderful artist and anatomist, but your drawings and dissections don't save anyone, not directly at least. You wanted more. You can do more. If you have changed your mind, so be it, but please consider the balance.

He tapped the pen against the edge of the desk, his mind traveling over his own ledgers of life and death: the patients who died from postsurgical infections when all indications had been good, the ones who lingered for weeks on the brink of death, then surprised everyone by recovering.

Accounting is dismal at the best of times and especially now, but your sound decisions will always outweigh your mistakes. Even those will not always be fatal. Yes, the profession can be cruel, as you know. What I know is: you'll learn fortitude without staining your soul. I love you.

If she still needed words when these came, he hoped he'd chosen the right ones, ones that would be enough. It was a great deal to expect from a letter, but he could do nothing else.

CHAPTER 18

"PROFESSOR?" NORA PEEKED HER HEAD IN THE SURGICAL room. The light from the gas torches fell over the lifeless body of a young woman. Her dark, coarse hair fell over one side of the table.

Professor Perra looked up from the woman's open abdomen and set down his syringe. With some corpses, it was necessary to inject saline to counteract the withering of the organs. "You got my note." He smiled and gestured her in. "It's not a perfect specimen. She died yesterday but when I was certifying her death, I found she was roughly five months pregnant. We rarely ever have a *prima gravid* to work with. But we must be quick. The body won't last in the heat."

"And the other students?" She was never lucky enough to be the first one at a demonstration.

"This woman is only for you. I will be assisting."

Nora looked down at the corpse's rigid jaw. It gaped open to reveal a mouth punctuated with missing teeth.

Nora's eyes flashed upward in time to see Perra's repressed smile. It flicked at the edges of his mouth, tilting his black mustache.

"This body wasn't purchased by the university. I secured it myself. For you." He forced his lips back into a serious line, but his cheeks were flushed.

"You shouldn't have." A body like this was extremely expensive, never mind Nora's present reluctance to take up the knife. For anything. "Won't you get in trouble? This body isn't sanctioned by the authorities, is it?"

"Your Dr. Croft is not the only man who can find ways around restrictions. We'll be quiet about this one."

In spite of herself, Nora edged closer to inspect the opening. He'd already removed the obstructive organs and placed pins to mark the bulging uterus and ovaries. Nora rocked back on her heels, putting distance between herself and the two bodies on the table. She couldn't...

"You think your fire is doused," Perra said, his soft voice sympathetic. "You are choking on the smoke."

Nora still didn't understand all of the Italian idioms, but she agreed she was choking on something. Her throat was hot and painful as she looked at the round womb that had turned into a sepulchre. "A month ago you would have rushed past me and started working already." Perra moved to her side of the table, approaching cautiously. "You've let misfortune crush your spirit. Magdalena assured me that the surgery had little chance of any success. The cord was collapsed. The mother was already dying."

The corners of Nora's eyes burned. Her breaths came faster.

"If you quit now, Eleanora, you will waste their deaths. What you learned will be for nothing. You will leave others to repeat your mistakes. And they will."

He was only a foot away, his soft words falling on her hair as she dipped her head.

"I understand now why Dr. Croft allowed you in his

anatomical room since childhood," Perra continued, and a pang of homesickness wrenched her. "Your work is tireless and astoundingly accurate. You have the gift of healing."

Nora only realized he was speaking to her in English when he switched to his rolling Italian. "*Me fa male qui*," he said, placing his hand over his chest. *It hurts here.* One of the most common phrases heard in hospital. "You cannot give up. This is my gift." He passed his open hand over the body.

Nora's hand shook against the table. She pressed her fingers to still them. "*Grazie, Professore*," she whispered, fighting the tightness in her stomach. "How did this woman die?"

"Treatment." His answer came fast and final. "The pains of a poorly set broken leg caused her a great dependency on opium these last four years. She was found dead after a large dose. No husband or children." He set the scalpel down next to Nora's hand, close enough that the warm metal handle brushed the side of her little finger.

She wasn't ready to see another tiny, lifeless fist. She closed her eyes, searching for an excuse to leave. The only one she found was cowardice, so she picked up the knife.

"Are you ready?" Perra asked.

She reached forward and the trembling in her fingers amplified, spreading up her arms. She stopped and shook her head, too weak to navigate this body.

Fingers closed over her own. "*Assieme*." *Together.*

He took her hand with the scalpel and guided it to the cold skin. She pressed her thumb to the woman's stiff side to test the rigidity of the corpse and inhaled. *A body like all of the others.*

She let her eyes sweep over Perra's preparations. His

methods were different from Dr. Croft's. He'd made clearer demarcations between the tissues and organs, while Croft tried not to disturb the natural, more confusing appearance of the inner body, but the work was just as meticulous.

Perra let go of her hand, took a white cloth, and covered the woman's face reverently. "I've already prayed for her soul. You may begin."

Nora blew out an anxious breath and rolled her shoulders before picking up the scalpel. "What first?" she asked.

Perra smiled. "She is yours. You say what is first."

Nora's eyes went longingly toward the lungs. They were always fascinating, and these ones in front of her were not riddled with tuberculosis. She sighed as her hand curved reluctantly toward the uterus. "I made the incision here," she said, pressing the razor to the thickened tissue in the same spot where she had opened Paola's uterus. A flood of images swallowed her, and for a moment all she saw was Paola's face. She heard the strange combination of choking and singing. The smell of ether rushed back so quickly she almost gagged.

"Nora?" Professor Perra asked.

She looked up from the spot where she had frozen, her blade immobile. "*Mi dispiace.*" *I'm sorry.* Her eyes pleaded with him.

He met her gaze, unflinching and waiting. There was no escaping his kindness.

Nora pressed the steel tip into the stiff flesh, leveraging her fingers back to make sure the cut went no farther than the uterine wall. "Blunt scissors, *per favore*," she murmured. She could feel the angles of limbs and a tiny body as she cut her way carefully across the organ. With no contractions pushing the baby, no tiny hands or feet appeared. She would have to coax and ease the fragile body out. She sensed movement behind her and glanced at Professor Perra, who was almost sound-lessly muttering a prayer. Nora slipped a slender finger inside the uterus and found a limber leg, hardly more than a hairpin between her fingers.

"Dio Padre," she whispered her own two-word plea. It had never been this difficult before. Pretending the dissection was a true operation, she didn't expand the incision, but instead strug-gled to locate the smooth, round head. She managed to grip the back of the neck and gently tugged, the tiny skull cradled like a stone in her palm. When the body emerged, the translucent skin was a heartrending crimson, and the child fit in her palm except for the limp legs draping over her wrist. Minute fingers and toes grazed her skin lighter than a housefly.

"A girl." Nora's wooden voice didn't even make it to Perra's ears. The eyes were fused shut and the lips not yet parted. She held a clay sculpture, rough and rudimentary, not yet crafted into the fine details of eyelashes and dimples. "I don't feel well," Nora said, unable to set the fetus down or turn away. Already the tiny features were collapsing, losing their distinction and delicacy.

Perra's wide hand cupped hers, bore up her failing palm as the dead child burdened it with its horrible weightlessness. "Before you panic," he murmured in her ear, making the hair on her neck rise, "*look*." His little finger skimmed the child's head. "The ear, perfectly formed. The shape of the clavicle. There is no horror here, Eleanora."

Nora took a shuddering breath, grateful for the warmth and strength of his hand beneath hers. She turned her head so her tear would not splash the child. It landed on Perra's arm instead.

He made a sound of sympathy and stepped closer. She smelled the smoke of his pipe woven into his jacket. "If you look, it will no longer horrify you. You will see a miracle."

"I can't," Nora stuttered on the words. "I killed Paola and her daughter."

"Shh." A comforting hand landed on her shoulder and Nora closed her eyes, overwhelmed by the desire to see Horace's face and hear him snap at her to be reasonable and get back to work.

She forced herself to turn back to the fetus and take in the threadlike veins glistening beneath the clear skin, the minute ribs more delicate than a row of fish bones, and the tiny nose nestled above the waxy lips.

"Let me take her for you." Professor Perra lowered the feeble corpse into a silk handkerchief and laid it beside the mother's covered face. "We will return her to her mother before we bury her, but first, you must finish. You have more to learn."

He stroked the uterus with reverence. "Before pregnancy it is only the size of a dormouse and yet, here we come to the great mystery of life. In Catholicism we call this the holy of holies. The place beyond the veil where God is manifest." Nora looked up and his eyes glinted in the steady light. Perra's scalpel movements were small and clipped, notching his way carefully inside the uterus to reveal the placenta. Horace always wielded his scalpel in fluid, unbroken strokes that made his students gasp in admiration, but Perra's way yielded the same impressive result in the end. He lifted the uterus free after several minutes and laid it between them. "Eleanora, you have begun to unwrap the mysteries of anatomy, but there are many mysteries of life you have ignored. You still think that a scalpel gives you charge. You can surgically deliver a baby from its mother's womb, but you know nothing of the love that put it there."

Instinctively, Nora turned to the open door, hoping the sight of a passing nun would make her sudden discomfort disappear. But it was late at night, and the nuns never frequented the cadaver rooms. Their concern lay wholly with the living.

"Too many physicians think their foe is death," Perra went on, and Nora's tension softened slightly. He wasn't troubled. It was only her, bristling like a cat at words like love and mystery.

"Can't you see the mercy in it?" he asked.

The lantern closest to her let off a thin ribbon of sable smoke. She tightened her brow as she watched it curl through the light and shadow. "You think it better that these women and babies die?"

Perra's hand caught her arm gently. "No. I will do all I can to spare them. But if they pass, I will not beat my breast. I will pray for them and commend them into another Healer's hands."

Her lips parted, desolate for words. Perra continued. "English doctors teach their patients how to live at any cost. We must also teach them how to die in peace. It is the most important part of our work."

She looked down where he touched her, a smear of blood across her arm. "You must learn more than muscle structures and sutures. I can teach you more than these things."

"I know. But in England—"

"You are here." He consulted his watch. "I must go. My family is expecting me. But I will return in the morning so you can show me what you've found."

He patted her arm kindly as he left. Only in the privacy of the dim room did the tight ache of anxiety in her head begin to melt into the familiar focus of discovery. As her fingers smoothed over muscles and organs, Nora let go of Paola's sobbing song and the purple baby. They were swept away by the unexpected discovery of a missing kidney. With no other students or doctors to compete with, Nora spread her arms, loosened her elbows as she worked, and lingered over the details.

CHAPTER 19

D ANIEL'S EYES SLEWED SIDEWAYS ONCE MORE, TAKING IN Horace's embroidered vest and monogrammed cuff links. He'd even ordered out his dusty carriage, which he normally refused if any destination was less than an hour's walk, and was humming quietly in his seat beside Daniel.

"Are you going to explain this elaborate theatrical? Or keep up the pretense that you had a sudden fit of sociality?" It was Daniel's last chance to ask. They had already passed the park and the homes were growing more imposing, which meant they were almost there.

Horace's eyes wandered outside the window to the tired horse passing in the opposite direction, the smell of its sweaty hide drifting faintly on the air. "It's more than dinner. You are to bring up your diphtheria patients," he instructed as he turned his attention to the crease in his trousers. "Speak of them as if you flowed with pity instead of blood."

"I do pity them—"

"This is not a medical audience. Hide the case details. Mention the mothers."

Daniel stiffened. *The mothers.* He'd thought of little else the past week. The crisis with Jimmy and Mrs. Thompkins had taken the starch out of him, and though the baby boy was improving daily, that harrowing night would haunt him for a good while yet. Two other mothers hadn't been so lucky. One, whose eight-year-old son had expired midway through a tracheotomy, had nearly choked herself on sobs, pressing shaking hands to her chest, and expelled her grief on the floor of the charity clinic. Cruel agony had expanded until it left no room for breath. Usually steady, Daniel's voice had trembled as he lowered himself to the floor and pleaded with her to take deep breaths and live for the sake of her other children.

Horace might think the gory details were in the cups of mucus or the steel glinting from the children's closing throats, but the mothers' sufferings were just as excruciating...

Horace was still murmuring instructions but Daniel only collected half of what he said. *Funds for the building... Philanthropist...*

He heard enough to understand their mission. Impress. Engage their sympathies. Collect money to equip the new clinic they'd started building with every modern advancement. Somehow Daniel must make them feel the horrors of diphtheria without upsetting their evening party. It was a familiar performance he'd grown accustomed to in his parents' home growing up: interesting gossip, some righteous indignation for Parliament's latest escapades, and perhaps a mention of Turner's newest work of art. Only this time he must sprinkle in news of the wounded and dying and appeal to their charitable inclinations.

When they were ushered into Lady Stephenson's drawing room, Daniel's quick survey identified only a few familiar faces.

Lord Ashwell, from Horace's club, stood by the window, nodding at intervals at a rather vehement speech from their host, Sir George. A cluster of ladies gathered around a framed case of tropical birds.

Lady Stephenson smiled in welcome, tilting her head apologetically to indicate that she would join them later. The gentleman half-concealing her from view was discoursing energetically. One woman's eyes were quite glazed over, and the young lady next to her... Daniel's gaze halted on a familiar pearl-drop earring dangling beneath a wing of dark hair.

"Champagne's this way," Horace whispered, jogging Daniel's elbow. Daniel nodded mechanically, his brain numbed by an icy flood, each thought shoving forward awkwardly like limbs underwater.

Mae Edwards.

Daniel took an involuntary step of retreat, accidentally jostling Horace.

"This was a bad idea," he murmured.

Horace's arm halted an inch from the tray, and he grunted an abbreviated demand for explanation, just as he would over the dissection table.

Daniel forced a smile, warning Horace there was no time to say more. Mae was turning—fortunately, away from their corner of the room, giving him a few more moments. He inhaled sharply. This would be damned awkward. He hadn't seen Mae since she'd broken off their engagement, two and a half years ago on February nineteenth. He remembered the crisp feel of her letter in his hand, the sharp, tight lines of her usually languid script, warning him something was wrong before he'd read a single word. He hadn't thought of that slog home in the rain for years, but it needled him now as if it were new. Her rejection, following right after Vickery dismissed him from St. Bart's, had been a double betrayal.

Next to him, Horace swore under his breath.

Daniel's eyes tightened in confusion. He agreed with the sentiment, but Horace had never met Mae. He couldn't have recognized her.

"Hell and damnation," Horace muttered again. "I need a stronger drink."

Worried now, Daniel watched as Horace gulped at a glass practically snatched from the tray.

"I told her not to risk it," Horace muttered in a voice burned husky with irritation.

"Risk what? You know Miss Edwards?" Daniel asked.

"Edwards? Who is Miss Edwards?" Horace demanded, his voice pitched a little too loud. Daniel swiveled into the shadow of a large, potted Boston fern, fearing she'd overheard her name. He wasn't keen to be spotted until he'd decided on an approach. At that moment Sir George, their host, advanced on them with outstretched arms.

"Dr. Gibson! Dr. Croft! Well met, gentlemen. It is a pleasure to see you again."

"It's most kind of you to invite us," Daniel said hastily. If Mae hadn't heard her name, she'd surely heard his. A hot burn crept up his neck. To Sir George's inquiries, he offered a selection of bland, amiable remarks so he wouldn't have to think too much about the mystery of Horace's muttering or that other guest in the same room. He felt like a fish swimming around in a jar. At some point he and Mae must acknowledge each other, but until he knew what had overset Horace…

"What's the matter?" Daniel whispered when they finally found a moment of relative privacy. Mae was less than ten feet away, still with Lady Stephenson. A man Daniel hadn't noticed before crossed the room and wandered to Mae's side. His fingers grazed along her lower back and she turned, tilting her face up to his, bestowing him with her gentle, secretive smile.

Daniel inhaled, bracing against the falling sensation that came with his memory of Nora smiling at him in public, her eyes teasing him with kisses she could not give in company. No one had looked at him with secret promises in so long.

So Mae had an admirer. That would help. Daniel would not be expected to stumble through a lengthy conversation if she was occupied elsewhere. The man's fingers continued to trace her lower back, sweeping discreetly from side to side, barely touching. Mae had turned away and was speaking as if she didn't notice, but she must. It was the exact thing he would have done to tease Nora, testing if she could keep up her conversation without being distracted by their silent exchange. Heaven knew he always fumbled and lost his place before she did.

"Didn't you see Lady Woodbine?" Horace hissed through tight lips, jerking his head toward Mae's circle of women.

On Mae's other side, turned partly away from him but talking animatedly and flushed in the lamplight, Lady Woodbine's youthful face glowed rose gold. Daniel hadn't recognized her as quickly as Horace, but she'd never been his patient. Her cheeks were rounder than he remembered. He'd spoken to her only once, when he'd doctored her husband. She was an intelligent woman, who'd taken it upon herself to question him on the dose of camphor he'd prescribed Lord Woodbine a year ago; an unusual experience, but one he'd enjoyed, because it reminded him of Nora.

"Not at her face," Horace growled. "Look down."

Cheeks reddening, Daniel complied. A quick glance reassured him this wasn't ogling. The telltale bulge, camouflaged by the best attempts of Lady Woodbine's dressmaker, couldn't entirely escape notice. "She must be pleased. They've been married for years." And still no children.

"Damn fool," Horace spat out, his face darkening like a looming storm. "I told her... I told him..."

"Let's have some punch," Daniel said, turning Horace away by the elbow and steering him across the room. "You can't look at her like that," he muttered, once he was satisfied they were out of earshot. "You're all thunder and brimstone. What could she possibly have done to upset you?"

Horace drew a deep breath and resettled his shoulders. "I suppose it's not my concern." The lines about his eyes sagged. "Such a pity. I liked her."

"What do you mean 'liked'?" Daniel's pitch sharpened, but he kept his tone low, not wanting to risk being overheard. The footman with the tray was close as a shadow.

Horace waited until he passed, then murmured around the rim of his glass, "Her first pregnancy killed the child and nearly her as well. She won't survive this one."

Daniel's face slackened with shock. "I didn't know."

"You wouldn't," Horace warned, cutting off as Lady Stephenson's brother approached. Horace extended his hand, as smiling and affable as if his anger had never been.

Best let him get on with his charming charade. Daniel turned around and caught Mae gazing at him. He thought she would startle or pink when their eyes met, but her serious face only twitched with the hint of a smile. She dipped her chin minutely in greeting.

Daniel swallowed. It would be fine as long as—

"Dr. Gibson?" Lady Stephenson beckoned to him, the gossamer feathers in her hair dancing above her brow with her smallest movement. Daniel advanced, surprised that his legs worked so smoothly.

"I didn't know if you'd seen Miss Edwards or been introduced to her fiancé, Mr. Murrell," Lady Stephenson said, pleasant without a hint of irony. "I understand you and Miss Edwards are acquainted."

Daniel kept his expression mild. Their engagement had been common knowledge. The break would be well known, too. He doubted Lady Stephenson would try to humiliate him in front of Mae's new companion at her own dinner party, but Daniel had never plumbed the depths of the motives of society women.

The only thing he needed to be was polite, and that he could do. "Miss Edwards. Lady Stephenson. Lady Woodbine. How lovely to see you." He smiled—the practiced, bland one he used with Silas Vickery. He allowed himself his first full look at Murrell: thin face, pale hair, a sharp chin. "And Mr. Murrell, it's a pleasure to meet you."

"It's nice to see you again, D—Dr. Gibson." Mae's lips stumbled on his formal name. She pinked at her mistake, made under the double gaze of Daniel and her betrothed.

Mr. Murrell's face didn't hint at the slightest animosity or jealousy. *Perhaps he didn't know?* Daniel accepted the offered hand hesitantly.

"I'm so pleased to see you, Dr. Gibson." Lady Woodbine spoke up, allowing Daniel a reprieve as he turned his attention to her. "You came tonight with Dr. Croft? I've the best news for him."

"I believe I can surmise what it is," Daniel said with a forced grin.

Lady Woodbine lowered her eyes modestly, but her pride showed in the intentional strum of her fingers over her bulge. Daniel cleared his throat, searching for some bridge between this sensitive news and his dying patients.

"I've had young children very much on my mind at present. I'm treating several urgent, precarious cases." Seeing the women lean closer, he tried one of Horace's favorite tricks. "But it's too heartrending to speak of at such an elegant party. I saw you were taken with Lord Stephenson's collection of exotic birds—"

"But the children?" Lady Woodbine asked. "Are they in danger?"

"Mortal, I'm afraid. But, ladies—"

And from that moment, they begged for increasingly disturbing details. The more he tried to conceal the plight of his patients, the more they pleaded to know.

"I cannot tell you of the mothers," Daniel insisted. "Not with Lady Woodbine in such a condition."

"Are the mothers ill also?" Mae asked, her hand tightening on Mr. Murrell's arm.

"Only with despair." Daniel didn't need to pretend to catch

his breath. His eyes were hot on their own accord. He cut his answer short, and the circle stood in appalled silence.

"What can be done?" Lady Stephenson asked, her eyes narrowed, as if squinting might bring Daniel's private thoughts into focus.

"What indeed? There are remedies Dr. Croft and I are attempting for these children, whom the hospitals won't admit, but the costs are considerable. Dr. Croft has mortgaged his home to try and build a more effective hospital to save them." Their rapt eyes swiveled to Horace, standing by the window. Daniel dropped his tone to quiet sorrow. "But I'm afraid we haven't the funds to manage all that we hoped."

"Did you know my own Dorothy survived diphtheria?" Lady Stephenson asked, not looking at any of them.

It made sense now. Horace would have known about Lady Stephenson's daughter. Perhaps treated her himself. "That's remarkable!" Daniel murmured. "You must have a great talent for nursing for her to have come through such an ordeal. The young lady is very accomplished. An ornament to society."

Too much? He watched anxiously for a clue that he'd overdone his praise. But no. Lady Stephenson's eyes were damp and distant. *Proceed delicately.* He must separate these wealthy patrons from their pounds and guineas with as much skill and patience as he coaxed muscle from bone, fascia from organ.

Mr. Murrell straightened, surveying the distressed faces of the women around him. "Perhaps it *is* too distressing. Such recollections are painful and Lady Woodbine—" he trailed off, at a loss for how to proceed. The rules for referring to pregnant women were ill-defined and fraught with peril. He tightened his hold on Mae's arm. "Come, dear. Don't lose your appetite."

He didn't wait for her reply but led her away, unaware, or ignoring the way her feet lingered until the last second as she cast apologetic glances at the other women and at Daniel. His chin was too rigid for Daniel's liking, his nose too pinched in what looked like disdain.

Mae, her stiff shoulders expressing mute displeasure at being manhandled away from the conversation, was steered nevertheless into Lord Stephenson's orbit.

"What sum is needed, Dr. Gibson?" Lady Stephenson had caught him staring, and her question came out clipped and demanding.

"That... I..." He looked to Horace, who thankfully was watching. "I don't know if Dr. Croft is too proud to accept funds. If anyone can charm and persuade him..." He gave Lady Woodbine a pleading look. "I wish you luck."

He let out a silent breath as Horace approached with greetings and expertly feigned surprise at the topic of conversation. Daniel only needed to nod in sympathy and agreement as Horace played his part masterfully—first the faint outrage at being asked if he needed money, then the polite refusal, followed by his accounts of diphtheria.

Across the room, Mae was no longer being fondly caressed. Mr. Murrell's hand hovered at her back like a shepherd's crook to deter wandering.

It was not a foreign experience, watching Mae from across the room at a party. Being six years older, Daniel had perfected it after returning from medical school in France when she was still a year away from coming out, but old enough to cause a restless stir among the young men in their families' set. She'd agreed to marry him when she was eighteen, even knowing he could not wed her for another three years. And then, six months before the wedding was to be set—Nora.

Daniel stared into the clear liquid of his glass, schooling the tinge of shame that stained his thoughts. He'd been faithful, entirely proper, but dishonest. Once he discovered Horace's best kept secret—the beautiful ward with the hands of a surgeon—he'd neglected his letters to Mae, telling her nothing of his reluctant interest and fascination for this strange young woman. And Mae had never been a *bad* fit for him. Her lack of interest in his career was balanced by his lack of interest in French fashion. Like most successful couples, their relationship would have sufficed—but never satisfied. He understood that now. It had taken the revelatory experience of discovering what it was to share intellectual passions as well as romance.

He had failed Mae, just as surely as she had failed him when she dropped him at his lowest hour. And now she was being guarded jealously by a stranger, and Nora was separated from him by seas and mountains, as well as years. Daniel chewed the inside of his cheek and watched the ripples of his champagne reverberate against the clear wall of his glass. It seemed neither he nor Mae had followed the script they'd written as children. As he listened to Lady Stephenson promise a formidable sum, he couldn't avoid a faint twinge of relief. Of course he couldn't speak for Mae, but he thought—hoped—they'd each be happier with futures they'd chosen rather than the ones they'd learned to expect.

Daniel caught Horace's dimple—the one that appeared only when he felt particularly triumphant—and returned his smile.

He would be happier, so long as Nora came back.

CHAPTER 20

Nora peered up as Magdalena adjusted the tiny
eyepiece.

"This is a lucernal microscope," Magdalena said—Nora had
finally grown used to referring to her by her Christian name. "It
was my mother's."

Nora had never seen such a piece. It was not a brass, upright
tube like Horace's, but a heavy wooden box with fragile mirrors
and lenses protruding from the top.

"Italian design for viewing and drawing specimens,"
Magdalena added. "Now we are just waiting for this evening's
specimen to be delivered."

"What is the specimen?" Nora asked, heady with the honor
of a private evening with the doctor.

"Patience," Magdalena said as she straightened from her
crouch before the instrument. Nora swept admiring eyes over
Magdalena's dress. She wore a wrap of midnight blue woven
with sapphire and gold. Her ruffled, cageless petticoats showed
at the front, and the effect was hypnotic when Magdalena
walked, the soft skirts flowing with her. But then Nora found
everything in Magdalena's home hypnotic: the dim lights of the
green glass hurricane lamps, the tapestries that didn't feature
Roman fables, but strange tribal markings, and the statues of

exotic animals marching across the mantelpiece. On the wall there was a framed painting of a stern-mouthed woman and, under that, a dark oil portrait of a young boy. Nora's eyes must have lingered.

"Nicolina Marenco, my mother," Magdalena said curtly, fishing in a drawer for something and coming out with a small brass screwdriver. "There is a better portrait of her at my ancestral home in Bagnacavallo, where my brother lives." Magdalena stared at the portrait as if noticing it for the first time in years. "That is the face she gave the world, but not us. You should have seen her eyes when she looked through this." She used the screwdriver to adjust one of the brass fittings.

Nora settled into the horsehair sofa, her body relaxing against her loose stays and unbuttoned sleeves. Nora had never had friends to share gossip with, and the novelty of spending an evening with a like-minded woman made her almost giddy.

Magdalena's young servant stepped into the room. "A delivery, Dottoressa," she said softly as she held out a small, corked bottle. The dark cobalt glass hid the contents. Magdalena's skirts glided silently as she swept over, taking the bottle and thanking Maria.

"Let's be quick," she said to Nora as she pulled a glass slide and a dropper from the cabinet of the microscope. Nora joined her at the desk, and Magdalena withdrew a dropperful of a cloudy white substance Nora didn't recognize.

Magdalena placed the slide carefully beneath the lens and motioned to Nora. "Line your eye up with the target hole and adjust it until the image is sharp." Magdalena turned up a lamp, and Nora felt the heat of it on her cheek as she aligned her pupil to the pinpoint hole. The fuzzy shadows honed into an image of small tadpole-like creatures.

"What are they?" Nora asked, her smile involuntary as it always was when she intruded on the invisible world. "They're not fish embryos."

"No. Not fish. Human," Magdalena said. "They're spermatozoa."

"Magdalena!" she spluttered. Whipping her eyes back to the slide, she watched one swing its long tail and whisk out of sight. "But this is fresh," Nora gasped, unable to hide the hint of horror in her voice. "Who brought it?"

"Ask me no questions and I'll tell you no lies. But it is not so very difficult to find men at the university willing to participate in extra experiments." Magdalena gave a puckish grin and looked out the window across the russet sky. The sun had sunk beneath the horizon but left a red tinge to the gathering twilight.

She couldn't possibly mean one of Nora's fellow students... What if the donor knew she was the one studying tonight? Or, heaven help her, a professor?

In order to hide her dismay, Nora turned back to the microscope. The spermatozoa quivered impatiently. "I told you I was curious to see it. I just never thought—"

Magdalena laughed. "You think too little of me, then." She gave Nora an appraising look, stepping closer. "I've wondered if you are as innocent as you seem. You never cringe at a naked body, but when I mention the sexual act—"

Nora's face flamed and Magdalena didn't need to continue. "Ah," her mentor said in knowing tones.

"I'm not married," Nora mumbled.

Magdalena's lips pressed together but did not hide her amusement. "That has nothing to do with our discussion. My son is proof of that."

Now Nora knew she was being teased. "You seem happy with your life," she replied neatly. "I'm sure your son is lovely."

"An English answer!" Magdalena laughed. "Yes, I love my son, Lisandro. A beautiful boy who lives with his father and lets me spoil him when I'm able." She pointed to the portrait of the young boy beneath her mother's, his skin milk white against the smudged black background, his eyes large and serious. "He does not inhibit me at all."

Nora's chest constricted and she held her breath, unwilling to look at either her mentor or the frantic spermatozoa. Her eyes fell on the inlaid tabletop.

"So, even this Dr. Gibson you have mentioned?" Magdalena pressed. "Nothing?"

Nora shook her head firmly, all her concentration on the gold leaf pressed into the exotic wood. *No one in England speaks like this.*

"Well, that explains other things," Magdalena said softly with a note of condescension.

Nora's head snapped up. "What other things?"

Magdalena peered at her, as if deciding whether to answer. "Your naivete with Dr. Perra. Do you have no interest in him? He is wealthy and powerful, not to mention kind." Magdalena sat, her heavy brows lifted in curiosity as she studied Nora's face.

"Do you mean as a lover?" Nora balked and scooted backward. "No! Certainly not. Why—"

Magdalena's brow flexed with amused pity. "You could have him if you wanted him. You've caught his attention."

Nora was sorry she hadn't worn her high-necked blouse. Red heat surged up her chest, and Magdalena would see it even in this dim light. She was beginning to understand why she never spent hours in drawing rooms with gossiping women. "Professor Perra would be mortified if he—"

Magdalena silenced her with a lazy sweep of her hand. "Salvio would confess if he heard me. You can be as blind as you please, but I give you this advice—watch yourself."

Nora thought of Perra's gentle eyes as he spoke to her during their recent dissection. He'd made no brazen gestures when they were alone, even late at night. It was like saying Horace was in love with her. "I think you're mistaken," she said, her mouth stern even though the words quivered.

"On your head be it." Magdalena shrugged. "Personally, I think it an advantageous liaison. Salvio is an enjoyable companion." She held out her hands in a dismissive gesture. "What an unexpected girl you are—of no birth or money, yet able to place yourself at the sides of gifted and powerful men." She tilted her head as if detecting something new in Nora's face.

Nora steeled her jaw, the room cold against her searing skin. "Horace Croft carried me home on the brink of death as a child. I did not *place* myself. And I—"

Magdalena put a strong hand on Nora's arm, cutting off the torrent just beginning to pour from her mouth. The room fell silent, and Magdalena's face softened. "Don't get in a temper. I was only making conversation. But I see now there is no use.

You're a lamb in the lion's den." Magdalena gave her a wistful, pitying frown. "My warning stands. Be careful."

Nora's chin shook from the protests she'd checked when Magdalena interrupted her. She swallowed them, and straightening her shoulders, she turned back to the microscope and pretended to look, seeing only blurred shapes. The gas lamp hissed quietly beside her.

"And don't worry about the sample," Magdalena said after a quiet moment. Nora glanced up from the spermatozoa to see Magdalena watching her from the brocade chair. "It's not Salvio's."

CHAPTER 21

Horace's side of the hall table bore the usual heap of letters this morning; Daniel noticed two on the opposite end, waiting for him. He smiled, though he'd been up much of the night with his patients (three cases of diphtheria from a single family and a woman who'd mangled her arm in an accident in a shoe factory) and he had four calls to make in the West End before an afternoon at St. Bart's. He smiled because today was Tuesday, when he usually received a letter from Nora.

Looping his paisley scarf around his throat one-handed, he swept up the letters with his other on his way out the door and tore hers open while waving abstractedly for a hackney.

My Dear Daniel,

Another evening in the hospital pharmacy with Sister Madonna Agnes. She is the quietest, most unassuming woman I've ever met, but what a genius with her medicines! I don't think half the doctors realize how lucky they are. I've never concocted such precise tinctures or rendered salves as pleasant and sweet smelling. Her knowledge of botanicals—

"You want a ride or not?" An irate driver, perched on the box of a dusty coach, waved to catch Daniel's attention.

Daniel looked up, still rooted to his spot on the sidewalk. "Yes, forgive me. Number thirteen, Russell Square."

Had he packed a new roll of gauze? Daniel opened his bag to check. Yes, it was there, next to his instrument case.

"And you're wanting to go today, sir?" the driver asked with exaggerated courtesy.

"Yes," Daniel said, ignoring the driver's impatience. He swung inside the carriage and immediately returned his attention to the letter. As she often did, Nora had included a sketch: this time one of her and a plump-faced nun, enveloped in thick aprons and laboring over a complex distilling apparatus, surrounded by clouds of steam. Nora had clearly intended to make him smile, the way the sister's raisin eyes and dumpling face conveyed such fierce attention. Her own hair was drawn springing up into curls and corkscrewing every which way. She hadn't colored the drawing—it was done only in pencil—but it was no work at all to imagine the flushed tint in her cheeks and the pale glow of her blond hair. Her brows, unusually dark for such light coloring and a little too thick for fashion, were bent in the familiar way—indicating not only complete absorption but also that she was probably working out which patients to try out the medicine with first.

He could imagine himself beside her, practically smell the crushed leaves heaped on the table in the drawing. The women almost seemed to move, with Nora just ready to turn down the flame, and the sister reaching for a pipette without breaking her scrutiny of the liquid collecting in a round flask.

He wanted to be there, scrubbing used glassware, stripping leaves from stems, unpicking the knot at Nora's waist when it was time to remove her apron. He loved his work, make no mistake, but—

My day will be mere sloggery without you, he wanted to write in response. *What were you and the sister brewing?*

If she sent him Madonna Agnes's recipe, and he tried it, would it soothe his lack of her or make her absence worse? No matter how faithfully he reproduced the formula, it wouldn't be the same as actually sharing the experience like in days before, and—please, God—the years ahead of them.

Even if he whipped out his diary right now and penned a quick response, his letter wouldn't reach her for another two weeks. Still, the urge to answer back as if she was nearby, waiting to hear what he said, was foremost in his thoughts, though in just a few minutes, he'd arrive in Russell Square, where Mrs. Lytton-White was expecting him to painlessly cut out her corns, thanks to the ether inhaler tucked at his side.

Reluctantly, Daniel folded Nora's letter away—he always had at least one tucked in his breast pocket—and glanced into his bag to check his supplies again, where he rediscovered the other letter from the tray, still unopened and crumpled beneath his stethoscope. He took it out and smoothed it against his knee. It was from Lady Stephenson.

Daniel cracked the seal, smiling again, because her generosity would make a world of difference for his patients. Already Horace had ordered new mattresses, linen, and iron bedsteads to fill the rooms of their expanding house. He was interviewing new orderlies, reviewing plans for a new model of ether inhaler—

Beneath the courteous greeting on the second line, Daniel stopped, his heart accelerating. He went back to the beginning, reading word by word.

My husband, Sir George, was pleased to hear of my interest in sponsoring your new hospital but happened to mention the matter yesterday to Dr. Silas Vickery. Dr. Vickery assured him the best way to help your work was to divert the money to improving existing facilities, and Sir George is nothing if not economical. I hope you will not be overly disappointed, but I'm afraid my husband has decided that the sum I promised must be used to forward your excellent work at St. Bart's. Dr. Vickery has assured me that, as the physician responsible for the children's ward, you will be able to spend the money at your discretion, so I imagine it will be every bit as helpful to you, though it comes differently than I originally planned.

"Sir? We've arrived, sir." Daniel looked up and saw he was stopped in front of the Lytton-Whites'. Rushing to the hospital and demanding answers from Vickery—blast him—would have to wait.

~

By the time Daniel arrived at St. Bart's, his smoldering temper was throwing sparks. Collecting Horace from the hospital surgery with an angry jerk of his head—judging by his tools, he was tidying up after removing stones from some poor fellow's bladder—Daniel gripped Horace's arm and stalked with him down the hall. "This time I might just murder him," Daniel growled.

"Vickery?" Horace nodded sagely. "Yes, it's a trifle unfair."

Daniel stopped. "Did Lady Stephenson write you, too?" How on earth was he so calm?

Horace looked perplexed. "Lady Stephenson? What has she to do with this? Even though your new appointment is technically an advance, one can hardly—"

Daniel cut him off. "What are you talking about?"

"Vickery. He's promoted you. Taken you away from the children and given you wards three and four."

Daniel swallowed the fire in his throat. There were no curses strong enough for this moment, so, wordlessly, he handed Horace the letter.

Horace read, his brow creasing. "But...she promised! Vickery can't—"

"He has," Daniel muttered, glaring at a passing orderly so that he veered as far as he could to the opposite side of the hall. "And if her husband has decided to send her money here, there's nothing she can do about it. Who—" Daniel broke off, too angry to speak. No doubt the physician newly in charge of the children's ward would have full discretion to spend Lady Stephenson's two hundred and fifty pound gift. He would also be able to admit whomever he liked onto the ward, if he even thought about it, which Daniel doubted, because his replacement was surely one of Vickery's lackeys.

"I'm going to knock him flat on his arse," Horace growled.

Daniel laid a hand on the man's shoulder, alarmed by the crimson surging into his face. He patted his pockets with his free hand, searching for the extra bottle of drops he'd carried since Horace's spell at the United Service Club.

"I have my own here," Horace grumbled, and downed an indeterminate number of drops in one quick motion.

Daniel raised his eyebrows.

"Don't lecture me about dosages," Horace snapped. "I've been doing this since before you wore trousers."

"We'll speak to Vickery, for all the good it will do," Daniel said, calmer now, and thankful for it. Vickery was probably counting on an angry outburst—a perfect excuse to sack Daniel and, if he was lucky, dismiss Horace as well. "If we storm in there and yell at him—"

"He can't move you from the children's ward. You must refuse," Horace said. "Taking orders from that pestilent boil, that waste of skin and bone—"

"Strategy. I'm sure he has one," Daniel said quietly. "What's ours?"

Horace was still muttering under his breath when they presented themself at the chief of surgery's office, but he managed a terrifying smile that made the young dispensary assistant, currently taking notes from Dr. Vickery, blanch.

"Dr. Gibson! Dr. Croft! You must be here to thank me," Vickery said, spreading his fingers on the desk blotter and pushing smoothly to his feet.

"Excuse your assistant, Silas." Horace stood motionless, waves of authority breaking off him as if he were a lone boulder in the raging Atlantic.

"I've no intention of taking orders—"

"Go," Horace whispered quietly. The young man gave

Daniel a questioning glance, then fled. The smile immediately dropped off Vickery's face.

"I'm not changing wards." Daniel decided it was better to begin with a statement rather than an argument.

Vickery flicked his hand as if he could sweep Daniel away as easily as a gnat. "I offer you the honor of a promotion to head surgeon of the women's wards and you come to complain?"

"You only did it to keep me from my patients and the money I secured for them."

"I cannot have you sabotaging our work here for private projects or stealing patients from this hospital."

Daniel groaned. "What an asinine… You know there are more sick than every hospital and doctor could possibly tend."

"Nonetheless, this institution's reputation—"

"You stole our money," Horace interrupted, banging his hand on Vickery's desk. "It wouldn't shock me at all if it were mine, but this was for diphtheria patients you refuse to treat!"

Vickery stiffened. "Consider the appointment rescinded, Gibson. You may continue as dresser to Dr. Wilmott, and Dr. Croft may resign."

"Resign?" Horace echoed. "How would that look for you, Silas? How would that look for this hospital once I explain the entire sordid business to the papers? Or send off a missive to the princess?" Horace ground the last words between his teeth, demolishing them before they dropped like coal dust in the charged air.

Vickery's eyes narrowed and his mouth curled into a chilling smile.

"I would hate to tell her of your progressing senility. You

grow more erratic by the day, Croft. Word of your eccentricities and exorbitant spending are reaching the upper circles. Did you truly mortgage everything to build a hospital for the poor who cannot pay? After sending that hussy you call your ward alone to Italy in hopeless search of a medical degree? What must that cost on top of all else?"

Daniel twitched forward but Horace moved faster, hurling a cut-glass inkwell against the wall. It spewed black stain on the white walls and bounced to the floor, unbroken. Daniel caught Horace's arm before any more of Vickery's possessions fell victim. "No," he whispered, giving an infinitesimal shake of his head.

Vickery, who'd ducked, was straightening to his full height. He smoothed back a hank of pomaded black and gray-streaked hair that had flopped onto his forehead. "Thank you for proving my point and leaving evidence. Your days are numbered here. You will end up poor, obscure, and pitied."

Horace jerked, but Daniel didn't loosen his grip. Impossible to appeal to public opinion—or Princess Augusta—now. Vickery's accusation was too dangerous, especially with splashed ink bearing witness on the walls.

"What if we could have saved your children?" Horace demanded. "Would you send these away then? Tell your colleagues to confine their practice to failing measures?"

Vickery might as well have been carved from ice, not deigning to blink, let alone answer. "I will send word to Dr. Wilmott of your new assignment," he told Daniel.

"How lucky your children died." Horace's eyes narrowed to a razor point, flashing as sharp and dangerous as a scalpel. "If they saw you now, they'd be ashamed."

Vickery's control broke. He slammed his hands onto the desk as if he meant to vault over it. "Croft—"

"You brought up Dr. Croft's family first," Daniel said, angling himself between the doctors. "Unless you intend to apologize for your slander, don't mention Miss Beady." Daniel glanced left at Horace, assessing the sweat gathering on his forehead, the invisible quivering detectable only through Daniel's grip on his arm. "As the chief of surgery at this hospital, you have authority to assign me wards three and four, but I'll be no one's dresser," he finished firmly as he steered Horace through the door.

Returning to the hall was like surfacing after a dive underwater. They both inhaled greedily. "In here," Daniel said, at the first empty room, a pathology laboratory with a barricade of books round the walls and twin microscopes resting on the soapstone counter.

Horace took no coaxing to sit. Daniel found his own chair and loosened his collar. One button snapped loose and tumbled across the floor in his haste. Mrs. Phipps had always reinforced his and Horace's buttons to withstand the coming of the Lord, but today Daniel was glad it gave quickly. He needed to breathe.

"Perhaps if we speak to Lady Stephenson—" he finally suggested.

"She has no say in it." Horace knuckled his sternum.

That was only too true. Daniel's lungs deflated. Lady Stephenson was an imposing woman, but if it came down to a financial battle between herself and her husband, she'd lose. She'd signed her fortune into his hands the day she took his title and name.

"Then I will speak to Lord Stephenson. That should sort it out. Is your pain fading yet?"

"Not yet." Horace gasped, his brow glazed with perspiration.

What would Nora do? He imagined her turning to assess Horace with a cool, critical frown, her head tilted, her light hair loose on her shoulder. *Elevate his feet. Mention the ocean. Put friction on his shoulder to stimulate blood flow.*

Daniel dragged over a crate full of new books, the box scraping and grinding against the flagged floor. "Put your feet up, Horace," he said, lifting the man's legs for him and positioning them firmly. "We need to get to the seaside, escape Vickery and Bart's for a spell. Nora keeps saying she longs to do the same thing but is too occupied with classes." He remembered his third task and knelt beside Horace, rubbing his flat hand vigorously against the front of the man's bulky shoulder. "Is it relaxing at all?" he asked.

"It's beginning to." It was rare for Horace to accept nursing of any kind, but he breathed out and closed his eyes as Daniel worked. When he spoke, his words were smaller than usual, his voice tired. "We must get that money back, Daniel. I've already spent it."

Daniel watched the pale face in front of him fold into a rare bout of humility and worry. He didn't like it at all. "I know. Don't worry about it now. We'll go to another party and sort it out." Lady Stephenson wasn't the only benevolent woman in London.

CHAPTER 22

Nora and Pozzi were breathless when they reached the hospital after a half mile of brisk walking from the university's library. Nora had a partially eaten pear in her hand. She took one last bite, wiped the juice from her lips with the back of her wrist, and tossed the rest away. Pozzi, who was holding the door for her, caught her glance as she hurried inside. Reading the censure in his face, she rolled her eyes at him.

"I've eaten," she said.

"Yes, like it's your duty," he said.

"Why is it you think you need to take care of me?" Nora asked as they climbed up the stairs.

"Well, you're very pretty," Pozzi said matter-of-factly. "Also, I think it's because you don't want me to, which makes attempting it irresistible."

"I should never have made friends with you," Nora said.

"Like you have so many others to choose from. You're lucky to keep me when you act so prickly," Pozzi retorted, smiling.

"Isn't there someone else—?" The blush mounting in her cheeks made it impossible to finish, so she gestured helplessly. He understood.

"There might be someone." He grinned. "Soon. But it doesn't stop me from admiring you."

She tsked at him, a noise she'd learned from Magdalena.

"I'm sure your man in England has many excellent qualities," Pozzi said. "But he is there, and I am here."

"And what about this girl of yours?" Nora demanded.

"Who says there is only one?"

Nora arched her eyebrows. "If that's so, you can hardly have room for me."

He laid a hand on his heart. "There is always room for you—" He ducked out of the way because she'd swung her bag at him.

They reached the wards, and there was no more time for talk. But toward the end of the day, when Nora was tiredly accounting for the stores she'd used in Sister Madonna Agnes's ledgers, the sister and Pozzi found her.

"A boy's just come in with a broken arm. Compound fracture," Pozzi said. "And Doctor Marenco has left already."

"What about Dr. Venturoli?"

"He's with the burn patient that came in yesterday," Sister Madonna Agnes said.

"It will have to come off," Pozzi said. "It's—"

"Show me," Nora said, already pushing away from the desk.

Pozzi led her to the ward across the hall where the boy cowered in a bed, sweating and pale, his eyes dilated. His father stood beside him, his face as twisted in worry as the hat he tortured by wringing it to a pulp. Nora steeled herself as she approached, gathering details like the streaks of tears down the father's dusty face and the size of the boy. He looked ten years old, but in the poorer class he could be as old as fourteen. They grew slowly on their infrequent meals. He cradled a left arm hidden beneath a shirt that had been wrapped around it and was now red with blood. The father looked at Nora in confusion as she approached.

"I am a student of medicine," she said briskly, hoping to sweep away time-wasting arguments. "I can help your son."

The father nodded woodenly, his eyes back on the boy. "He fell off a cart and the wheel rolled over him. Luckily the cart was empty, but—"

Pozzi gingerly undid the bloody wrap, revealing a hole over the humerus. No garish bone protruded, but mud clung to the lip of the wound. "Where is the bone?" Nora asked, bending forward as the boy sent up a fresh cry.

"I looked at it before I found you." Pozzi spoke low and fast. "At first I thought I could splint it on my own, but when I probed, I thought the fragments were too small to have any hope of mending. And I don't think all the bone is there. You see where the skin broke? The pressure from the wagon wheel would have—"

"Yes, I see," Nora said, understanding perfectly and cutting him off. Professor Venturoli insisted they give no gruesome descriptions to the patients, but that they speak simply and comfortingly, always hiding the seriousness of a case to allay fear.

"I believe we should relieve his pain quickly," Pozzi added, giving the father a sympathetic look.

Amputations were relatively straightforward, and Pozzi was strong and quick. Nora was about to suggest that she fetch the vaporizer when—"Let me give the ether," Pozzi said. "I want the practice."

Nora nodded, glad that he, unlike other students, didn't shy away from letting her handle the saw. Sister Madonna Agnes's whispered prayers made a low, comforting hum amid the boy's whimpers. "'I am the resurrection and the life,'" she murmured, one hand clutched over her crucifix, the other pressed to the boy's head.

Nora dropped her eyes and turned to her bag. At least this surgery was uncomplicated. There was enough arm left to make a serviceable stump. She pushed up the boy's filthy, blood-soaked sleeve and fastened the tourniquet, keeping an eye on Pozzi's preparations with the vaporizer. "We have ether, which I'm sure you've heard of," she explained to the boy and his father. "It will put—" she hesitated. "What is his name, sir?" she asked softly.

"Aldo," the father answered. The boy was too occupied with his pain to hear her.

"The medicine we have is miraculous. He will smell its fumes and fall into a sleep. He will feel nothing."

Pozzi explained to Aldo as he placed the rubber inhaler over his mouth and nose, patiently waiting for the ether to warm atop the flame. The boy did not sputter or fight. His eyes grew heavy and his limbs slackened. She watched his chest rise and fall, counting his breaths.

Sister Madonna Agnes led the protesting father away from Aldo's side. "Just to the next room. You can hear if he cries out for you," she promised. "You do not want to see his arm taken off." Fresh tears wet the father's gray face as he submitted to the nun's instructions and left the room.

"I'll probe," Nora said at last, and stuck a finger into the wound. The boy stirred but didn't make a sound. "I feel the pieces. You're right. Best to take the arm off." Even if he survived with it, the arm would be crippled.

"I was thinking about ten centimeters proximal to the wound," Pozzi said, and Nora smiled, thinking of the indecision and lack of confidence he'd showed just months earlier.

"Yes, that's a likely spot. The vessels will be easy to find there."

She cut and tied and stitched, as Pozzi worked deftly around her, passing knives and saw and needles. Minutes later, they were done, the mangled arm in a basket full of sawdust, ready to deliver to the anatomy lab.

"We did some good work there," Pozzi said, as the orderlies carried the boy away to the recovery ward.

"It's a pity he had to lose the arm." Nora moved the basin and poured out some water to wash her hands. When Pozzi joined her, she stepped aside and dried her hands on a clean spot on her apron. "The ether couldn't have gone any better," she said.

Pozzi beamed as he took up the soap to scrub away the dried blood. "I thought if we started with hardly any ether and gradually increased—like the frog in boiling water. It worked." He gave his attention to his cleaning, picking at crusted bits of skin.

After gathering her scalpels, Nora turned back to him. "How did it feel?"

"Better at this end of the table." He smiled, his thin face crinkled with humor. "Better with you. If all surgeons were like you, I could do this all day. Venturoli would have screamed at me until the last stitch."

"Remember that when you're the mentor and you get some poor apprentice." She waited until he finished washing his hands and threw him a snowy towel. He lingered over the task, drying each knuckle, as if too absorbed in his own skin to meet her eyes again.

"You're optimistic," is all the reply he gave.

That night, Nora let him walk her home. He was more talkative than ever tonight, and after rehashing the surgery, he moved on to the subject of his family. As they milled beneath the porticos, they passed the robed Sisters of the Sacred Lamb, who were busily handing out brown loaves and rough woolen blankets to the beggars with nowhere to go for the night. Gesturing animatedly, Pozzi spoke of his eleven brothers and sisters. As with most families, death had whittled their numbers. The ones who survived counted on Pozzi's career to support them now that their father had died.

Nora tried hard to listen to his stories, but she was imagining the arduous years ahead of him. Her eyes traced his narrow shoulders, his slight build, his anxious face, so unlike the other surgeons she'd known. Of all the degrees at university, who had selected medicine for him? Nora gave the anonymous fool an imaginary shake of her head while calling up a smile for Pozzi, encouraging him to continue. He needed to talk, and she was happy to listen.

CHAPTER 23

"Another case of septicemia," Professor Venturoli murmured to the small knot of students as they approached the next patient. As always, he spoke away from the patients. Why burden the sick with the sad truth? Nora recognized the patient in the bed they approached, an elderly man who'd had a painful carbuncle drained on the side of his knee. She'd administered his ether. "If we may look at your surgical site, Mr. Gazzola?" Professor Venturoli asked, keeping up a kindly dialogue as he lifted the sheets and undid the bandaging.

She was not prepared for the red stripe running up his great saphenous vein, as if painted with rouge. One of the students touched it, but Nora knew already what it would feel like—warm, turgid, but not the rock-hard vein of phlebitis. Pozzi rolled his shoulders beside her and arched his back as if searching for a more comfortable position for sore muscles as he tried to see over Sagese's head.

Venturoli let them all have a good look before offering reassurances to Mr. Gazzola and leading them away to confer privately.

"Mr. Pozzi," the professor asked, and Pozzi snapped straighter beside her. "What is your diagnosis and course of treatment?"

Pozzi swallowed and shifted his weight. "Septicemia certainly. It has attacked the popliteal vein—"

Nora closed her eyes, willing him to correct himself.

"The location of the infection was more anterior to the knee," Venturoli said with a worried frown. "The great saphenous vein. It is making its way to the heart. What do you believe we should do?"

Pozzi's face was red, his eyes slightly unfocused. This flustering wasn't like him. Months ago, perhaps, but not now. "We must amputate before it reaches the hip socket," he answered and Nora released her held breath.

Before she realized she was doing it, she pressed the back of her hand to Pozzi's forehead. Her strange action halted Venturoli's reply and caused one of the students to glare.

"He's hot," Nora said in alarm. It was not a flushed warmth from embarrassment or an overwarm ward. His skin was dry and burning. She hadn't realized she suspected anything until she'd touched him.

Pozzi's eyes widened and he put his own hand to his face at the same time Venturoli did.

"Signorina Beady is right," the professor agreed. "Mr. Pozzi, how long have you felt unwell?"

"I don't. I'm just tired," Pozzi insisted.

"That's good news," Venturoli said, though he still frowned. "Miss Beady, take him to the sisters and give him a quiet bed where it can pass. I am glad you recognized the symptoms."

Nora's cheek flexed but she couldn't manage a smile. The heat still singed the back of her hand where she'd touched her friend.

"Show-off," Pozzi whispered as she accompanied him slowly downstairs to the convalescing rooms. "You had to know my own symptoms better than I did."

Nora gave a weak laugh. She hadn't seen him the previous day. How long had he been like this?

Sister Benedetta gave him a bed with curtains for privacy and shooed Nora back to work. "He's in God's generous care and my capable hands," she said as she poured him a glass of weak wine. "Come back later and he will be much improved."

Pozzi had closed his eyes as if in pain when his head sank into the feather pillow, but there was a smile of satisfaction on his lips as he sipped the wine she held to his lips. He did not look worried and neither did the nun. Perhaps a fast fever would do him good and allow him a much needed rest.

"Don't get too lazy down here eating the sister's good food and drinking her wine and lying about all day," Nora teased.

He smiled and opened his eyes, but weariness pulled them down again. "I'll try," he murmured.

———

Nora was reviewing her day's notes in the study room when Magdalena entered and approached quietly, uncharacteristic for her.

"Yes?" Nora asked, hoping it wasn't a difficult birth just beginning. She was longing for a quiet evening with Mrs. Phipps and as much tortellini as she could hold. She hadn't eaten since morning.

"Pozzi," Magdalena said, her lips stiff.

"Yes?" Nora repeated. Though still tired and feverish, he was doing well after three days in Sister Benedetta's care. Nora had seen him only an hour earlier when he admitted that *lumaca* was not the word for a card used to brush wool, as he'd told her, but slug. Nora now understood the strange looks she'd gotten from her female patient with the sprained wrist.

Magdalena didn't answer, and Nora put down her quill. She hadn't noticed how dim the room had grown until she tried to read the tight lines of Magdalena's face in the shadows. Magdalena opened her mouth but closed it, changing her mind.

"Now you're frightening me," Nora said, but Magdalena didn't refute her as she expected. Nora's smile fell away into her sinking stomach.

"He has tetanus, Eleanora."

Nora's smile returned as she gave a sigh of relief. "No." It wasn't a desperate cry of denial, but a firm rebuttal. *Magdalena was mistaken.* Nora stood, more irritated at the sloppy diagnosis than frightened. "If you'd seen him an hour ago, his jaw was flapping just fine."

"Eleanora—"

"No tightness. No spasms. What made you think—"

"Sister Benedetta just found me. His arm has begun to spasm." Magdalena's tired eyes shone with reluctance. "She had already begun to suspect."

"One cramp of the arm?" Nora's incredulity gave way to disappointment. Magdalena should know better. "He's been in bed for three days. He probably slept on it wrong. He's had a sore back—" Nora's words plummeted to silence as if they'd stepped off a cliff.

He'd begged her to rub his shoulders every time she visited

him. Her fingers had worked their way over his corded muscles while she laughed at him for overwork and letting his back get to such a state. *You'll be a hunchback by thirty*, she'd chided.

"He didn't present in typical fashion," Magdalena soothed. "And it wasn't one spasm. He's had three since you left him after dinner. But I cannot find any cut on him. Do you know of any recent wounds?"

Nora couldn't answer, and the room blurred as her eyes refused to focus. She reached out reflexively to her medical bag and fumbled to put her notes away. A memory tugged at her brain, shy, as if trying to spare her the discomfort of remembering.

"No." She turned to Magdalena. "Last week we amputated an arm. I think that was the last surgery he did. He would have told me if he cut himself."

"The thirteen-year-old amputee who died of tetanus?" Magdalena's words were heavy and exhausted, too heartbroken for shock.

Nora shook her head. She'd been the one cutting. Pozzi had only held the vaporizer. It couldn't be. But then, he'd probed the wound before she even got there. The evidence rolled together, like a stone over the door of a tomb.

Magdalena grabbed Nora's bag from her hand. "I know," she agreed with Nora's unspoken disbelief as she guided her forward. "We must be quick and aggressive. I want him moved to my home immediately before it worsens. It will be quieter and we can stay with him. One of the sisters will come and help if I ask."

Nora nodded again, her mouth working as slowly as her

brain. "We have to let his family know." She pictured his brothers and sisters, all of them balanced at the precipice of poverty, waiting for his salary. Inexplicably, she hated them for needing his money, forcing him to wade into the perilous world of medicine.

"There is a wagon waiting. Sister Benedetta is having a mattress placed in it so we can move him without making him sit up. I don't want to do anything to bring on more seizures." Magdalena's plum-colored skirt spilled down the stairs as she hurried.

"Does he know?" Nora asked, her foot frozen midstep.

Magdalena's boots stopped echoing on the stone stairs. She turned slowly. "I haven't told him."

"Don't," Nora said, the word suspended between them. She could feel Horace's reproachful glare from across the ocean. This time she agreed with Venturoli. Knowing would only add to Pozzi's suffering. "We should pretend not to know."

Magdalena's thin mouth revealed nothing, and her stern eyes kept their steady hold on Nora's. "For now," she agreed. "We may yet pull him through if the case is mild."

Nora said a clumsy prayer with every step, knowing from Magdalena's set jaw and moving lips that she was not the only one.

Midnight was not an appalling hour. Daniel was awake at this time more often than not, studying, dissecting, or simply lying awake hoping he was not hoping alone. He'd sketched out so many scenes in his mind for the future, as richly detailed as if

Nora had drawn them herself. Sometimes they felt more real than the time he was passing, waiting.

"Done for the night?" Horace looked up from his stack of bills.

Nodding, Daniel stifled a yawn and slid the clinic ledger into a shallow drawer. Like all the new cabinetry, it glided shut with scarcely a sound. But even that deepened his frown. How much had that fine drawer cost them?

"You and I will demonstrate on Mr. Cripp's axillary tumor tomorrow evening," Horace reminded him, as he stacked his papers together.

Daniel nodded, only half attending. He wasn't sure these late-night lectures were healthy for Horace's condition, though the effect on his spirits was miraculous. After his spell in the pathology room, Horace had endured two fretful days at home, while Daniel suffered through the cheerful congratulations for his new promotion. Now Horace was working more ardently than ever, and the short rest seemed to have worked the magic for which Daniel had hoped. There'd been no more chest clutching, no more spasming attacks. Yet.

"I'm looking forward to working under the new lighting," Daniel said, trying to draw his mind back to Mr. Cripp's upcoming surgery. It was like driving a carriage through sludge.

Though construction continued on the upper floors and conservatory, and the patient ward was still in shambles, tomorrow's demonstration would be the first in the new lecture theater, and Horace's anticipation was acute. All day he'd paced the halls, mumbling to himself, lamenting the fact that the wooden trim was not quite completed. Astonishing from a man who never noticed whether his waistcoat matched his trousers or if he'd remembered to tie his cravat. From his refurbished rooms, Daniel had even heard Horace practicing his lines in the new water closet.

The lectures collected ten pounds a week, nearly a year's salary for child laborers, but far short of the amount needed to appease the creditors. Daniel sighed. Even after his promotion, he received only a pittance from St. Bart's. Hopefully, the prestige of the appointment would nourish the growth of his private practice, but so far, with him and Horace practically at daggers drawn with Vickery, they were attracting more raised eyebrows than wealthy patients.

"You're overtired. Perhaps a pipeful of cannabis?" Horace suggested, stowing away the bills and closing the cupboard.

Daniel wavered a moment, then shook his head. "I've a letter to write. Which, by the way, so do you. She's complaining about your lack of letters."

"I need some decent food first." Horace insisted. "Mrs. Crawford still treats me like I'm about to melt. I'm not an invalid."

"The lighter diet seems to have helped," Daniel reminded him. "I hope you'll continue. I haven't told Nora about your attacks, and I know you haven't. If something were to happen to you—"

Horace snorted. "Nothing will happen. And what would be the point of telling her? She'd only worry. She's got enough to fill her head as it is."

"I agree," Daniel said, talking over Horace so he couldn't start up again. She hadn't written again about the patient who'd died during the cesarean, but her recent letters were shorter and more subdued. "But if something did—"

"Something could happen to any of us," Horace argued, refusing to be silenced. "At any time. We know that better than the philosophers. Let's not pretend otherwise." Horace raised a finger as he always did when he thought he'd found a winning point. "Furthermore, I don't write because I'm occupied with this house, which will mean much more to her than a letter." He swept his hand over the corner of the new desk where Daniel sat. It fit beautifully into the alcove beneath the window. "We've done more than even I envisioned. No one in London has better facilities. When Nora comes home—" He brushed at the front of his coat. "She'll have a place to work suitable for her talents. She'll want more than charity work, if I know her."

"Do you ever think"—the question was halfway out before Daniel could stop it—"she might prefer to stay in Bologna?"

Horace considered. "I'm not saying I'd like it there. My French is better, but I suppose I could manage in Italian if I had to. You'd do all right. You speak Italian like—"

"A boy forced to study by an overbearing mother," Daniel said, smiling in spite of himself. Horace assumed she'd want them both to join her if she stayed, but time changed people. Changed hearts.

"And when she sees all this—" Horace gestured at the lecture room and shook his head with a smile. "No one in their right mind would give this up."

Daniel was quiet because he'd seen the sketch she'd sent of the Teatro Anatomico at the university, a room similar to this in purpose, but otherwise as unlike it as a cathedral is to a cotton mill. In Bologna, Nora worked in a hospital. In Bologna, she could become a full-fledged lecturer. She had friends there now: Magdalena Marenco, a fellow student called Pozzi, and of course, Salvio Perra, a man too charming for Daniel to contemplate in comfort tonight.

"No one in their right mind would give up working with you." Daniel smiled, because it didn't help to brood. "They wouldn't dare to."

"I suppose it's easy for you to worry." Horace patted Daniel on the arm. "With her so clever and pretty and surrounded all day by Italian men. I did consider that when she asked me to send her, and I concluded—"

"Horace."

For once, Daniel's tone made him pause.

"Stop talking," Daniel ordered.

"Quite right. It's getting late." Horace wandered into the unfinished hallway, crunching on the discarded papers and plasters as he made his way upstairs.

Daniel rubbed the back of his neck and sighed. Lingering on thoughts of Nora raked his stomach with longing but the moment he stopped, he was assailed with thoughts of the ledger. The plasterers alone were waiting for thirty-five pounds that currently did not exist, and the upholsterer had sent two notices.

His chest tightened and he rolled his shoulders back before he extinguished the lamp and stood a moment in the black room, hoping the darkness would erase his thoughts, rub out his fears like a piece of Nora's charcoal scoring away a failed drawing. But when he left the room he carried his troubles with him, like children borne away to their cradles for the night.

CHAPTER 24

THERE WAS NO HARROWING WAIT TO SEE IF POZZI'S symptoms would grow into a serious case. As if trying to spare them the suspense, Pozzi's spasms began that night, pulling his right hand into an anguished claw and forcing him to double over as pain racked his abdomen. Nora and Magdalena sat on the bed next to him, taking turns stifling tears and retrieving useless medicines.

Late in the night, Nora watched her mentor smooth the hair from Pozzi's brow, her wavering profile painted on the wall by the lone candle. Her lips moved, whispering prayers that were probably as familiar as nursery songs to the boy who grimaced even in his sleep. "Lisandro had measles as an infant. I did not sleep for two nights except when I napped with him in my arms." Magdalena said, her low voice carrying in the silence. "I think we should send for his mother."

The words shook Nora from her stupor, and she pulled her head off the arm of her chair where it had fallen. "I'll send for her tomorrow, but there is still hope. I've seen plenty of cases recover." It was an overstatement. She'd seen three. All treated by Horace. "I'm going to put more belladonna on his throat," Nora said, rifling through the jars and glasses of medicine.

"Belladonna, theriac," Magdalena said, pacing to the black

window, "calomel, opium, turpentine. Bleed him, pass his urine. If he cannot eat or breathe, he will die."

"He can breathe," Nora insisted as she opened the belladonna. The dark green-black liquid pooled in her palm as she poured, the grapelike scent expanding into the air. She let it drip across his throat, careful to keep any poisonous drop far from his lips. Less than a minute later another spasm woke him. Pozzi's head pulled back, his mouth drawn down in a frown so unlike him Nora had to turn away.

His tongue pushed against his teeth, his arms gripping his stomach. "The abdomen is hard as brick," Nora said, trying to tamp down her panic.

"That's to be expected," Magdalena said calmly, meeting Pozzi's stare as his eyes widened in pain. "It's uncomfortable but will pass in a minute."

It was the longest minute Nora had ever known. When Pozzi's body relaxed, she noticed a tear collect in the corner of his eye. "Tetanus," he gasped, his lips barely opening.

Nora's hands flew to his jaw. It was already tightening like an overwound clock. Her fingers traced his chin down to the tender hollow below his tongue. His chin pointed to the dark ceiling from the pull of the muscles. The symptoms couldn't be advancing this quickly.

"Pozzi," Nora asked, taking his hand in the dark, "did you have spasms before today?"

A matching tear gathered in his other eye and slid down his cheek. He blinked and Nora knew that was his answer.

"Why didn't you tell us?" she demanded, clenching his fingers.

"Venturoli." His voice was slurred from the rigid muscles of his neck, but Nora understood.

"*Lo stupido!*" Nora cried, standing above him, her voice shaking. "He says doctors must protect patients, not patients protect doctors! We could have—"

"What?" Pozzi asked, and the room fell back into predawn silence and chill.

"We could have fetched your mother." Magdalena's voice was firm and steady as it marched across the room. The candle guttered.

"I don't want her to see," Pozzi stated simply. He looked at both of them, lucid, but not fearful. "I'm sorry you have to see. Maybe you should go, Eleanora."

Nora shook her head. There was still time. "We can fight this. Can you swallow?"

He blinked another yes. That meant nodding was no longer possible. He needed wine while he could still take it, but when they tried, he sputtered and knocked the tumbler from her hand. It spilled red against Magdalena's expensive linens. The movement brought on another spasm.

Magdalena brought the candle closer. His tongue was pushed so hard against his teeth, it protruded in the tiny openings between them, lacerating against the points and edges. Pink froth, a mix of blood and spit, gathered on his fixed lips as his face turned red, then purple, then almost black. Guttural sounds rattled in his throat and his back arched. Nora hid her face, clamping her lips together to stop her scream.

"Where's your vaporizer?" she cried, turning to Magdalena. "Ether relaxes muscles. He needs ether!"

"We can try it," Magdalena said and darted from the room.

Nora snatched the vaporizer the instant she returned and pieced it together, cursing when she fumbled. "All we have to do is keep him breathing. His own body will do the rest. He can heal himself if he has time to do it."

"Quickly, then," Magdalena said.

"Hold on, Pozzi," Nora said, clamping the mask down. Magdalena turned the valve. Nora counted seconds, trembling with relief as his body went slack. "That's enough," she said after one minute.

Pozzi was limp and still, not asleep, but not fully aware. Nora passed his wrist to Magdalena. "I feel his pulse, but I'm too shaky to count it," she confessed.

"Sit down," Magdalena ordered. They watched him in silence. "How long do you think it will last?"

"I don't know," Nora said. She prayed the respite would be enough.

———

Nora woke fully dressed in an unfamiliar bed with no memory of sleeping. Images of Pozzi flooded her, and slowly she pieced together the room. This was Magdalena's bedchamber, now bathed in morning light with the branches of a stone pine tree visible through the window. Nora pushed back the covers and clambered to her feet, reaching for memories of how she had come here when Pozzi—

She flew down the corridor to the guest room. Pozzi was there, sleeping, his head anchored back by his muscles as if pulled by unrelenting ropes, his shoulders barely touching the bed. Professor Perra sat beside Magdalena, speaking in a low murmur.

"When did I fall asleep?" Nora asked. "How did I get to bed?"

"You didn't go to sleep until five thirty. I led you like a child," Magdalena answered.

Nora remembered none of it. "What time is it now?"

"Not yet nine. I sent for Salvio and wrote to Pozzi's mother. The other students are being told this morning."

"Told what?" Nora asked, her eyes flashing a challenge.

"Eleanora." Professor Perra's tone was precisely modulated, as if she were a child. "It will likely be today."

"No," she insisted.

"We believe he broke ribs this morning," Magdalena said. "He won't take deep breaths anymore." As if answering a summons, his body gave a heave, and a spasm arched his back from the bed.

"Dose him again," Nora said. "Why aren't you giving more ether? He just needs time."

Perra took her hand. "He may not wake if we do. And his mother will be here within the hour. I sent my carriage for her during the night. We must give her the chance to say goodbye."

"He doesn't want her to see him like this." They couldn't give up yet. "I'll give the smallest amount," she begged.

"I'll get more water for the vaporizer," Magdalena said with a sigh, and Perra didn't argue.

Pozzi's body was so rigid now during spasms that Nora had to tent the mask with paper in case an attack seized him mid-dose. She prayed and counted seconds, watching his body sink into a more natural position, counting his pulse with reckless relief.

"You cannot keep him on ether for days at a time," Perra pointed out, his pity sad and quiet.

Nora couldn't contemplate what lay ahead—only this moment when Pozzi's face was less morphed into a leer by the unforgiving muscles. But one hour later he had the largest spasm yet, as if his body had saved the torment it wished to mete out to him and doubled it as punishment for daring to seek reprieve.

When Pozzi's mother arrived, she was white-faced and red-eyed. She came timidly into the house as if unused to the luxuries surrounding her and confused to find her dying son in such a place. Perra led her to her son's bedside, explaining all they were doing to keep him comfortable and ease his suffering. She nodded as if she understood, but when she saw him, stiff and arched, his lips pulled back and his purple tongue bleeding, she let out a shriek and fell at his side, touching his face as if looking for confirmation the distorted body before her was her boy. Nora turned to the wall. Turned to stone.

At four o'clock, after a dose of ether, Pozzi was able to pant out words of love and apology to his mother. Perra wrapped his arm around Nora as she wept in the corner of the room where Pozzi could not see her distress. She submitted to his arms, feeling no comfort, but grateful to lean against something that could bear her up. She half listened to the priest who came to bless Pozzi and promise him eternal life, unsure why his gentle words made her angry. At seven, the spasms stopped coming and going. Pozzi's body shook without respite for over an hour. One leg went slack and Perra recognized his spine had broken under the relentless pressure. Pozzi's mother clung to Magdalena and let out a wail, now as torn as the rest of them between wanting the pain to stop and wanting Pozzi to live.

Just after eight, when the bells of San Domenico were echoing through the red city's thin, cold air, Pozzi's purple face collapsed and his shaking stilled. His eyes were half-open, his limbs rigid even in death. His mother screamed and cradled his head against her breast, her words racked with pleas for her son's soul. Magdalena, though her face was stricken, kept her post at the crossroads of death and held Signora Pozzi, absorbing her cries.

Unable to watch, Nora fled the room, her own chest so tight she felt like the disease had jumped from Pozzi to her. She could not manage a deep breath with the pain bending her down. Perra found her and gripped her arms, not letting her turn away or fall to the floor, waiting for her to find her breath again.

"Do you want me to take you home?" he asked, his eyes red and wet.

The word was strange in her ears. It meant nothing. The tall, rented house beside the basilica? Or across the Mediterranean in London? She met his eyes, perplexed, as if he spoke a language she'd never heard.

"No. I—" She firmed her lips. "First I must write up my notes."

"Eleanora—" Perra cast a worried look over her as if he thought the last two days had broken her sanity.

The work of a surgeon was cruel. Hadn't she whined that a lifetime ago? But there was a new understanding unfurling its agonizing tendrils in her mind. *Dosages.* Did she give Pozzi enough ether? *Predictions.* What if she had begun before the muscles stiffened? She wanted to scream and wail and rant at Professor Venturoli. Ignorance didn't protect anyone. Better skills, better treatments could.

"This cannot happen again. Never—" Her throat clenched. The heat in her chest was unbearable. She gasped for breath, and Perra enfolded her, pressing his lips to the top of her head.

"Poor girl," he said. "You need to go home to your Mrs. Phipps and be nursed yourself."

Nora bristled. Her back straightened, her teeth clamped tight. He didn't understand, but Mrs. Phipps would leave her in peace to study even when sobs racked her in the middle of the night. Mrs. Phipps would stroke her head without taking away her notebook, even if it was dotted with tears. Mrs. Phipps would understand that if Nora didn't learn more, Pozzi would die again, thousands of times over in thousands of corners of the world.

"Yes, please. Home." In her mind she saw Horace, his eyes defeated and tired, his collar limp and his cravat askew. *The only thing for it is work.*

⁓

When Mrs. Phipps nudged her awake, the room was dark, the woman's worried face distorted by candlelight.

"What is it?" Nora asked, stretching out her hand for her kit, for her book, for her notes.

Mrs. Phipps shushed her and took Nora's outreached hand. "You were crying in your sleep, dear," she whispered. Her frown deepened as she helped Nora into a seated position. "You're still dressed. At least let me help you take your stays off and get you into a nightgown." Her strong, wiry fingers lifted Nora's blouse over her head and began unlacing her corset, just like she'd done when Nora was small. Nora submitted to the tender touch, feeling the wrinkled hands brushing her skin like an anointing. Fresh tears welled. So it was real? How could she ever sleep again, if every waking was only a fresh reminder that Pozzi would not?

Mrs. Phipps finished and slipped a crisp nightgown around Nora's shoulders. As Nora pulled her arms into the sleeves, Mrs. Phipps waited, watching her every move for clues. Nora pulled off her skirt and sat back down on the bed, the cold cotton of the nightdress sloughing some of the tension from her skin. When her eyes met Mrs. Phipps, one tear wrestled free and dropped to her lap.

Nora opened her mouth, tested the words briefly in her mind before releasing them. "I want to go home."

CHAPTER 25

DANIEL EXTENDED HIS ELBOWS AND STRETCHED HIS arms, signaling the other doctors and students back. In their excitement they'd drawn too close, as they often did when Horace worked, and he was testier than usual today. Better to give him a wide berth. He'd already snapped at a student for not handing him the scalpel he wanted, though it was the one for which he'd asked. When Horace barked that the ether mask was fitted wrong to the patient's face, Daniel told the operator to open the vent at the front a little wider to allow a greater mix of oxygen and smiled placatingly, silently reminding the other doctor that a soft center did exist beneath Horace's salty crust.

The tumors across the bottom of this patient's foot were some of the largest Daniel had seen on a man still working and going about his daily tasks. Six uniform, round balls protruded like marbles encased under the skin. Horace took up his fountain pen and drew an ellipsis that would make an anatomical artist like Nora proud. He had no drawing skill, but when it came to marking flesh, his lines were precise as a surveyor's. Horace finished marking the tumors and held out his hand for the small surgical scissors which Daniel passed to him. As Horace cut, his expression softened with inner focus, like a mother lost in the face of her child.

"You must be careful not to rupture or cut into the sac of a soft tumor such as this," Horace said as he swept his scalpel through the skin. "If it bursts during surgery, you risk infection, and it makes it much harder to remove it completely." His deft movements were always misleading. Watching him, a student would believe that parting a razor-thin sheath of skin from a glossy white tumor without tearing either was easy. Daniel smiled when he saw one of the lean, rangy students twitch forward, hungry to feel the easy slice of skin beneath his hands.

Wait for it, Daniel thought, knowing the students were about to see something they would write home about. Daniel flexed the patient's foot to give Horace more room as he cut into the fourth tumor protruding from the side of the heel. As the cutting bent Horace's right hand in an unnatural angle, he shifted the scissors to his left with hardly a hitch in the rhythm of the procedure. He could cut with equal skill in either hand. After two years Daniel was still making progress in the technique, but his left-handed attempts were amateur compared to Horace's.

Murmurs rippled through the crowd and heads nodded with admiration. Horace's coarse beard did not hide his small smile when Dr. Black swore in admiration and said, "Liston can't even do that."

Daniel turned his head to grin in agreement when Dr. Black's face melted with shock. Daniel whipped his attention back to the surgery and saw Horace frozen, the scissors hanging askew from his fingers, a slice of skin hanging beside a trickle of thick white pus. He'd pierced the largest tumor.

No one spoke. Horace looked at his own hand in disgust.

Daniel recovered and shot forward, catching the remnants of the burst tumor with a cloth. "Bad angle?" he asked in low tones.

Horace's lips bristled and he flexed his hand to reposition the scissors but they trembled and fell with an appalling clatter. Around him, the students were paralyzed, blank fear evident in the way they leaned back as if preparing to bolt.

Laugh, Horace. Bring it off with a joke. Daniel's desperate wish went unheeded. Instead, Horace's face grew red and he reached for the scissors with his right hand, swinging them in a circle around his finger, testing the balance and reaction. He calmed a little as they landed back in his expert palm with a satisfying clap of metal on skin.

"Shall I?" Daniel offered.

Horace glared and put the scissors back in his right hand. "My assistant moved the foot," he said, leaning his head toward Daniel. "I got complacent. Even under the sleep of ether, the doctor must always be prepared for unexpected movement and adapt to it."

Daniel did not allow his face the smallest reaction. He'd not moved the foot a millimeter, but the important thing was to diffuse the tension.

"Now," Horace continued, "We'll reposition the foot and continue. Like so." He reached for the foot with his left hand to show Daniel how he wanted it angled, but his fingers clutched at the air an inch away and he lost balance and fell forward. The razor-tipped scissors fell alarmingly close to Daniel's arm.

Dr. Cole, never on cordial terms with Horace, spoke up from the back. "Has the doctor been drinking?"

Jeffers whipped around with a scowl and clenched hands.

Before his favorite student did something regrettable, Daniel interjected smoothly. "Gentlemen, this is my fault. Dr. Croft has been treating diphtheria patients round the clock as well as keeping up his surgical schedule. I suspected he had a fever this morning, but didn't dare suggest he miss a surgery. Dr. Cole, you are well qualified to continue. I'd like to examine Dr. Croft. The queen will never forgive us if we lose one of her favorite surgeons." His last words wiped some of the smugness from Cole's face.

"Fever, my—" Horace broke off when Daniel clamped his hand in a viselike grip.

"Stoddard, assist Dr. Cole, please, and Girard, you monitor the ether. Jeffers—" Daniel motioned briskly to the doorway and pushed Horace onward, hoping the doctors didn't hear Horace's muttered curses as he was pushed out the door.

Horace's muscles rippled beneath his grip. Daniel strong-armed him against the wall before he twisted loose. "Howl like a hound all you like once we're alone, but you will walk silently with me to your office. Vickery has eyes and ears at every corner in this hospital, and the last thing we need is that fool breathing down our necks."

A doctor turned the corner and narrowed his eyes at the strange scene, but kept walking, just as Jeffers joined them, silent and obedient despite the questions shouted by his eyes. He was loyal, which was why Daniel had requested him. Safe from unfriendly eyes, Daniel released Horace's arms and prodded him forward, thanking heaven and the saints above that Horace's office was only two turns away. Daniel bolted the door behind them as soon as they were inside.

"Before you lose your temper—" Daniel never saw the fist until it collided with his chin. Stumbling backward, he just managed to fall into the chair instead of to the floor, his hands cradling his stinging face.

"You interrupted my surgery!" Horace bellowed.

Jeffers let out a yelp and leapt between them, stopping when Daniel held up his hand.

"Horace, you dropped your scissors and miscut. We've been together for years, and I've never seen you slip." Daniel pressed his tongue to his tender lip. "And now you've hit me."

"I didn't drop the scissors!" Horace roared.

"You didn't drop the scissors. You didn't drop your dinner knife the other day or collapse from chest pain at the club." Daniel stood, feeling too vulnerable with Horace towering above him.

"You think I'm a doddering fool," Horace hissed, advancing.

The unusual angle of his eyebrows caught Daniel's focus. Horace's left eye was too soft. He was trying to glare, but the lid muscles weren't contracting even though rigid veins marred his temples.

"Horace," he whispered. "You're having an apoplexy." His eyes swung to Jeffers. "Get an invalid carriage ready. We need to lay him down and transport him. We might need a trustworthy stretcher bearer to help us. No one else is to know."

Jeffers nodded and was gone.

"You take that," Horace yelled.

"Take what?" Daniel asked, confused and trying to think of some way to calm him. "Horace, I don't think this is a simple attack of angina."

"My snuffbox. Stuffbox. Snuff."

"Snuffbox?" Daniel tried to put firm hands on top of Horace's but was pushed away. "Is that where your digitalis is?" The door handle turned and shook against the dead bolt. "Daniel?" Harry's voice filtered through the door. "Jeffers said you needed some muscle."

Daniel went for the door, blessing Jeffers's choice. He opened cautiously and motioned Harry inside, flinching when Horace knocked a stack of books to the floor. "Careful. He hit me already."

Harry turned to Horace and the two Scotsmen sized each other up. They were well matched. What Horace lacked in youth, he'd gained in fury.

"I'm afraid he's having an apoplexy," Daniel said, trying to think of how to subdue the man without hurting him. He felt like a naturalist trying to cage a rhinoceros. "He cut into a tumor and dropped his scissors in the middle of surgery, and now he's not making sense."

"He never makes sense," Harry reminded him.

Horace bellowed and charged, ramming the empty chair toward them, but Harry seized the wooden back, throwing it aside, sending Horace off-balance.

"Don't hurt him!" Daniel snapped.

"Wouldn't dream of it," Harry grunted as he seized Horace, pinning his arms. "What's the plan now?"

"We need to get him home. I'm worried he'll work himself into a grand seizure."

Harry struggled to maintain his grasp on the older surgeon. "Get some restraints—"

Daniel flinched at the idea and instead caught Horace's face between his hands. "We need to treat you. If we lose you, we lose every person you could save. We're going home."

Horace shook his head, but his struggles were growing weaker. His eyes roamed the room, too blank. Daniel's stomach twisted with panic. He didn't need to find Horace's digitalis now that he always carried his own. He pulled the small bottle from his vest pocket and, cupping Horace's chin, let loose several drops inside his slack lips. Within seconds Horace bent double, his knees hovering between standing and kneeling.

"Horace?" Daniel asked. The man remained hunched, and a high-pitched groan squeaked from his mouth.

"Give him room," Harry snapped. "Can you breathe?" he asked, trying to help Daniel guide Horace to the floor.

"No," Horace gasped, lurching away from them, groping at the desk for support.

"Lie down, man!" Daniel's voice, always calm with his patients, swelled as Harry snatched the toppled chair and rammed it into the back of Horace's legs, forcing him to collapse into it.

Teeth clenched, Daniel loosened Horace's collar. The old man's forehead was spotted with beads of sweat. "We need cold water for his face, Harry. Go mix a drachm of alum and a drachm of silver nitrate in a cup of water."

Daniel fanned Horace and checked his pulse—sluggish. He was growing quieter, which worried Daniel more than his temper.

"Haven't you any names to call me? Here I am cradling you like a helpless invalid after pushing you out of your surgery. Surely you can come up with an insult for that."

Horace's eyes fixed on the ceiling and Daniel, ignoring his training and giving into alarm, shook him. "Horace," he snapped, just as Harry returned and knelt beside them, briskly rubbing Horace's face with a cold rag.

"Jeffers will bring the nitrate and water. How are his pupils?" Harry asked.

Daniel clapped a hand over one of Horace's eyes, counting out the time it would take for a normal eye to adjust to the darkness. He didn't get to fifteen before Jeffers appeared, holding a tin cup. Daniel removed his hand, grateful to see the pupil swollen in size.

"Give it to him," he instructed the dresser, who obeyed with shaking hands, some of the liquid running from one side of Horace's mouth. Harry slapped the side of his neck to encourage swallowing.

"There's a stretcher in the hallway and a carriage waiting at the side entrance. But the only thing available was the ice wagon," Jeffers apologized.

Daniel could have kissed him. "That's perfect. We can put Horace in there, limp as he is, without drawing any attention." The hospital regularly delivered bodies for families in enclosed wagons, laid on ice to transport to homes or funeral parlors.

"But are you sure you should move him? We're already here." Harry pointed out.

"I need him home. I may have to tend to him round the clock."

Harry nodded. "Get the stretcher and throw a sheet over him. You two take his head and I'll take his feet." Horace's left foot dragged, the toes catching the floor, but he said nothing when they covered his face with the sheet. Harry peered outside, waiting until the hallway was empty before gesturing them forward. Between them, they managed to bear him out of the hospital and onto the street where the wagon waited, the back doors open to slide in the stretcher.

"I need you to cover for us here," Daniel told Jeffers. "Rumors will spread fast. Try to keep them quiet. Just say he had a fever and muscle aches and went home to rest. No one will come nosing around Great Queen Street if they think he has flu." They'd gain some time—hopefully enough for Horace to recover. Daniel hit the side of the wagon, signaling the driver to hurry.

"Thanks, Jeffers," Harry said as he slammed the door.

Horace stirred beneath the sheet, spewing a rebuke that came out garbled and unintelligible. Harry rubbed a hand over his forehead. "This isn't heart congestion. He's confused."

Daniel pressed his lips together, unwilling to nod, though he couldn't deny or disagree with Harry's assessment. "I thought he was recovering." Horace had been so much better. The lowering diet, the extra rest… "Vickery driving him to the brink of bankruptcy and his lecture schedule—" Daniel swore quietly and leaned against the seat, too weary to hold himself up any longer. Meaningful words no longer fit through his throat.

"We'll put him right again." Harry took Horace's wrist in his hand.

"We'd better," Daniel choked.

CHAPTER 26

After Pozzi's death, the university turned black. When Nora entered the anatomy building, the students were knotted in dark, colorless masses, voices hushed, faces turned toward the polished floors. Even young men she'd thought too arrogant and heartless to care were dressed in honor of Pozzi. She weaved among them, aware of the empty space at her elbow where Pozzi usually chattered, grateful for their sable jackets and sober faces. She couldn't keep on, not without these visible demarcations between Now and Before.

In her pharmaceutical lecture, Sister Madonna Agnes, usually curt and phlegmatic, stood silent before them, eyes glossy, before clearing her throat and beginning.

Nora was undone. She dipped her head and watched tears blur her notes on cannabis and amyl nitrate. When the church bells rang for *pausa pranzo*, Nora stumbled into the corridor, numb and stiff, half-blinded by her stinging eyes.

"Eleanora." Perra's voice curled warm around her neck, and she felt the weight of her books lifted from her arms. "We will leave these in my office and go for a drive."

She meant to answer, certain there were words to collect and organize into a reply, but they disbanded before she could marshal them into any kind of order.

"Your Dr. Croft prescribes daily walks to almost all of your patients, no?"

Nora nodded. How she longed for her Dr. Croft, as Perra put it. If she were with Horace, she would be with Daniel and could weep openly and press her pain into his strong heartbeat. He would have liked Pozzi. The momentary thought made her breath stab with fresh agony.

Perra passed off her books to another student with directions to deliver them to his office, and he took her arm, guiding her outside to his carriage. She entered it, grateful for the shadowed recesses and the anonymity. No passersby would see her distress.

"The funeral was difficult for you yesterday," Perra stated baldly as the carriage moved forward. "It is not like your English arrangements."

A scoffing laugh escaped despite her misery. In England, women seldom went to funerals. Here she'd gone to church and witnessed Pozzi's mother wailing and rocking, his sister grabbing at her face and no one hushing them. No one informed them such grief is private, too sacred to share.

"There are things we know that your people do not," Perra continued, his voice nudging softly. "That funeral was one of your best educations thus far. Every pain must be felt, Eleanora."

Her pink-rimmed eyes raised to his, curious but certain she already hated what he would say.

"You may cage the pain, postpone it, let it settle in the joints as arthritis or fill the arteries of the heart, but the moment of attack will come. The pain will be felt in its full power, no matter how long you have kept it at bay." His hands, the only part of him she could bear to look at, opened in appeal, the fingers coaxing.

She heard Pozzi, saw his earnest eyes as he gazed at her. *You're doing it wrong.*

If she spoke, if she moved, the veneer would shatter. She would have to raise her head up and scream like Pozzi's sister, and that would only amplify the anguish. They rode in silence, Nora rocking with the jolts of the carriage because she refused to grab the handle or the strap. No, she needed her arms pinned tight to her torso to hold herself together. She watched the scenery pass by in a blur, only vaguely aware that she was going somewhere and not at all caring where it might be. When the carriage stopped, she saw only a hill, the grasses tinged yellow by the November chill.

"A walk, signorina." Perra took her hand and pried her from the darkness of the carriage. The breeze blew free over the hilltop, and the touch of it, wrapping her wool skirts close to her legs, felt like a passing embrace. Keeping her arm, Perra led her through the long grasses. Below, far in the distance, a cluster of stone houses studded a road and roan cows grazed in the fields. To their right a scraggly vineyard crossed the landscape, the vines haphazard on the ropes strung to support them.

Nora shuddered at a memory. "Pozzi said he wanted to take me to a vineyard when I lost my cesarean patient." She tested her voice, grateful it didn't quiver, though it was flat and lifeless. "He said it was in the country, and we could get drunk and forget everything. I told him no."

Perra grinned fondly, his eyes set on a distant point. "Why didn't you take him up on his offer?"

No. That was for her alone to know. She kept silent, her teeth biting into her cheek.

"He loved you," Perra stated when she refused to answer.

"He might have thought so," she admitted as a grasshopper, frightened by their footsteps, leaped to her skirt and clung there.

"Of course he did." The wry amusement in Perra's voice made Nora look up, but he kept his eyes on the village, the wind moving his hair off his forehead as his eyes contracted in thought. He led her past the stiff remains of yellow flowers, their stalks dried, their colors faded. "Did you love him at all in return?"

"I adored Pozzi. I thought of him as a brother."

Perra shuddered. "How dreadful for him."

Nora's chest contracted and she stopped walking. "I was helping him in every class. I nursed him when—" She cut off, damming the images of his last hours. "I never led him on."

Perra stopped yards ahead of her, his back turned so she couldn't see his expression. "No. His foolishness was his own fault entirely." His words were more forlorn than the wind clawing over the bent grasses.

"Sir?" Nora approached but did not draw level, warned off by the hollow, bitter edge in his voice.

They were near the middle of the hill, where centuries of relentless wind had swept away enough soil to reveal the rocky boulders beneath. Perra perched on one of them. "Do you still insist on sitting your exam early? Six weeks is not far away."

"Yes." Her crossed arms relaxed a degree, grateful for the change of subject.

"Eleanora." His voice was tender and coaxing, full of sympathy. "Why are you rushing? You are grieving now, in no state to perform as you must. But more to the point, what must be said to convince you Bologna holds more promise and possibility for you than England?"

She was grateful for the wind on her face, dabbing her eyes dry. "Sir, I—"

"Do not call me 'sir' today. It is Salvio. There are days only Christian names will do. Do not be heartless and forget I am grieving as well."

Nora dipped her head. Somehow she had hurt him. "I'm sorry."

He had asked her something. It took her a moment to recollect, distracted as she was by the pinching of his eyes, the flex of a muscle in his cheek—the symptoms of a patient trying not to noise his pain.

"I miss the comfort of my family." She flinched as soon as she spoke, recalling that Perra had no such comfort in his life, and hurried along, anxious to put more words between her and the blunder. "I've Mrs. Phipps, of course, and sorely need her, but Croft is like my father and—" Daniel's pale face and dark, serious eyes came so clearly to her mind she almost stumbled.

"And?" Perra pressed.

"I have commitments there. And I am sick with longing to be back." The wind did a fast turn and tugged strands of her hair free, leaving it to snap like a flag of surrender before her face.

"*You* are sick with longing?" There was a hint of acerbity that made Nora inspect his face and find a humorless smirk marring his usually calm expression.

"Sir?"

His face darkened. "Salvio."

"Salvio," she repeated, a thrum in her chest.

"What are you longing for?" he asked, his eyes fixed on her face.

Nora rubbed one hand to her sternum, the part her corset didn't reach and bind together like a bandage for her broken heart. "Familiarity," she said at last, seeing in her mind's eye the fire in the study, Horace's scattered books, her watercolors spread across her desk, Daniel searching through the journals while Horace snored in his chair. However long she lived in a place, it would never have the same broken-in feeling as that room. When she came back from her imagining, the field before her looked too immense and empty.

Perra stood. "Then why do you reject what you long for?" His gaze raised the hairs on her neck. "I've lowered all pretense, given you allowance to call me by my name as a friend, as your doctors do in London. I could be familiar."

Nora nodded in agreement. "I am so grateful. I—"

"I don't want your gratitude."

Nora frowned, lost.

"I want your comfort. I want your success. I want to work beside you in the years to come and not lose you to a country that refuses to acknowledge your talent." Spots of pink rose in his cheeks as his words grew more adamant.

"But I can't stay here."

"What would change your mind? Do you need a patron? I could provide anything your salary does not." He stepped closer, blocking some of the wind. Her hair, released by the breeze, fell against her cheek.

"That is beyond generous, but I am motivated by family ties, not a salary."

"They are not your family, Eleanora." His voice barely rose above the wind. "They found you. As did I."

"I don't understand." She didn't wish to.

"I don't mean to make it a contest. I ask only that you open your eyes and see how freely I acknowledged your talents from our first meeting. How I pressed for your advancement. How they tried to bar your way and only parted reluctantly."

Now the words rankled. "Because they love me and didn't want to lose me, even for a time. It had nothing to do with not wanting me to study. They've always wanted that."

His smile was full of doubt and pity. "They do love you, in their English way. But theirs is not the only love in the world."

He took her hand, making her startle from the strange touch. His fingers were as hot and dry as a fever when he pressed his thumb into the softness of her palm. "What if I loved you like family? Claimed you like family?" His eyes searched hers, intent on every detail of her expression.

"I don't understand," she insisted, afraid to reveal the wrong emotion. "You can't."

"You don't want to understand."

She recognized the voice he used in his lectures, the tone he employed when guiding students to conclusions they couldn't make alone. "Are you so ignorant of the offer before you? Or do you plead ignorance to avoid discomfort, as you did with Pozzi?"

The name plucked her nerves and she flinched. "Pozzi was barely more than a boy. Four years my junior. Calf love."

"And I am a professor, sixteen years your senior. What is mine?"

Nora froze, her mouth still parted to speak, her breath crystallized in her throat. "Sir?"

"Salvio." His eyes were as distant as the night sky and as unfathomable. "Don't say you don't understand. Be as kind to me as you were to poor Pozzi and do not mislead me."

"You're married." Her weak words didn't trouble him.

"In name only. A souvenir of my youth. Fina hates me and carries on with her own *chère ami*. I am free to do the same." His face hardened as he spoke, twenty years of frustration pushing its way to the surface.

"But I'm not," Nora reminded him, testing if he would release her hand, but he retained it. "I promised Daniel—"

Perra's fingers ran up hers, questing each one. "I see no ring," he said as her stomach plummeted with the movement. She'd not been caressed in almost two years.

Pushing away the swelling under her ribs, she took up his other hand. His eyes lit, until he felt her trace his wedding band. "Here's one," she said, dropping his hands at once.

"Eleanora, you must know—"

"Don't burden me with declarations you can't honor."

"I *can* honor them," he fought back, his face gleaming with the effort to make her see. "I can secure you a place as a surgeon and a lecturer. I can give you a home. I could come home to you every night instead of my small palace of miseries."

His pain was overwhelming, and the picture he'd drawn just before… "Stop, Salvio."

"You think you love another," he pressed. "But he only found you first. You haven't tested your heart with anyone else."

"Love isn't an experiment."

"We are both scientists. An experiment is always recommended," he said. The wind tugged at his coat and his disheveled hair. Nora tried not to look at his lips but failed. "Kiss me once, Eleanora, and then I will accept your answer."

A thrill of panic ran under her skin. "That's a terrible idea," she scoffed, but she was in his short midday shadow, and his arm had found her back.

He closed his lips over hers before she could process the movement, and her breath was lost in his mouth. Weakness emptied her. She felt her ribs fall away, her spine disappear, until she was left with only her starched dress as a frail exoskeleton. She trembled as he explored her lips and shuddered when his mouth slowly released hers. He pressed his forehead to hers the same way Daniel used to.

Tears stung her eyes and she stepped back, unable to control the shaking of her limbs. She wanted to crumple to the safe dirt beneath her and weep with her head in the grass. Not because the kiss had been awful, but because it had moved her, however unwanted it had been. She wanted leaving Bologna—leaving grief—to be easy, unentangled. She lowered herself to the rocky ground, her feet unable to hold her. He knelt beside her, clutching her hand. "Eleanora, you need not look frightened of me." His voice was above her, falling on her bent head. The sky swam with dark spots. She could not answer.

"You're white as a sheet," he said and put a supportive arm around her back. "Lean on me. I won't kiss you again. I wanted you only to see the possibility—"

Her swollen eyes met his, and she gripped her black skirt in her fist. "It's not possible."

"Eleanora," he pleaded, his jaw flexing with worry.

"I've given my love away already. I want to go home." Not just to her apartment and Mrs. Phipps. To London, where her people were waiting for her.

CHAPTER 27

I'LL HELP ANY WAY I CAN," HARRY SPOKE FROM THE CORNER of Horace's bedroom. Daniel hadn't heard him return.

"I can't thank you enough," Daniel said, taking the glass of brandy Harry held out to him. "I'll stay the night," Harry offered. "Horace wouldn't like it, but he won't know."

Daniel looked at the sleeping face, the body lying flat and still on the mattress. He paused, unsure how to proceed. "What about your wife? She won't like being deprived of her husband."

"Julia's quite all right on her own and used to me being gone all hours with patients," Harry said, deaf to Daniel's soft-footed approach to the subject of his wife. "But as it happens, she's visiting her mother today and will be glad to spend the night with her family. We have an obnoxious upstairs neighbor, and the rented rooms I can afford for us are nothing wonderful, believe me. I've sent a message already." As he finished, the floor shook from an echoing crash downstairs as some wall or other came down. They both jumped.

"Accommodation here is nothing wonderful just now, either," Daniel said wryly.

"I don't think all this noise is good for Horace," Harry said, shaking his head. "Those workmen are brutal. I've been in navy battles that sounded less alarming."

"I could try to send them home for a few days, but that would surely set him off," Daniel said. "He's entirely caught up in finishing the house, and I don't know where else to take him. I can't leave London."

"I know. Can't be helped. It was just a thought." Harry sighed. "The Crawford woman told me I was to make sure you ate your supper. She's a brawny one."

Daniel sputtered in his drink. Harry had used the same term for ardent Frenchwomen he couldn't handle in medical school, and the memory made him laugh and choke at the same time. As he coughed, he managed to get out words. "She managed an asylum before Mrs. Phipps hired her. I can't think of a more fitting qualification."

Harry laughed. "Well, then do as she says. I'm sure she has tricks up her sleeves."

"I will," Daniel promised. "I'll bring in some cards after we eat, and you can beat me out of some of my hard-earned money."

It was now or never. Daniel pushed the words from his brain to his tongue. "I'm sorry I haven't come to meet your wife."

"You've met her before. Years ago. When we had dinner with—"

Daniel shook his head. "She was a child and a stranger. But now you are a family, and I haven't—"

Harry seemed to catch the heaviness resettling on Daniel's shoulders and smiled. "Why apologize? I never invited you. How do you know you were wanted?"

A grin escaped Daniel. He checked Horace's face, knowing there would be no change. He gave Horace's hand a gentle tug to check muscle tone, wishing for a wound he could treat, a tumor he could cut away, a fever he could bring down with ice and herbs. Horace lay like a boulder fallen from a mountain. Mute, immobile, inscrutable.

Apoplexy of the heart could stop blood flow to the brain. But this looked more like a grand seizure. Either way, another spell could end him.

As if he'd read Daniel's thoughts, Harry dropped the humor from his voice. "When does Nora come home?"

Daniel drew in a breath. *Not soon enough.*

"I haven't told her," he murmured quietly. "About Horace. About any of his attacks." He waited for a response, but finally had to look at Harry to gather his silent reaction.

His worried frown managed to scold and pity Daniel simultaneously.

"I was stupid, Harry," he admitted, returning his gaze to the motionless man before him. "I didn't think it would come to this. I didn't want to worry her—" He broke off, remembering her brokenhearted letter after losing Paola, the cesarean patient, and more recently, a missive weighted with anxiety over the health of her friend and fellow student Pozzi. "Do you think he'll wake?" His voice faded away.

"He will," Harry said, infusing Daniel with some courage. It was short-lived, as Harry added reluctantly, confirming Daniel's worst fear, "But I don't know if he'll be himself. He may be damaged permanently."

Daniel closed his eyes, feeling the room lean in the darkness.

Harry's voice reached him in his misery. "I'll watch him while you write her," he offered. "You need to get a letter off today."

Standing was a feat, considering the load of exhaustion and worry Daniel had to lift to push himself upright. He dragged his feet to Horace's desk, knowing if he went to his own room he'd pace and never begin. Listening with half an ear to Harry's quiet conversation with his unconscious mentor, Daniel dipped a pen and tapped it against the rim of the ink bottle.

He had no poetic endearments for Nora today, only her name, and a reluctant account of medical details he was loath to share. He'd never imagined writing up this case this way.

We were in surgery at St. Bart's when a seizure took his hand, causing him to fumble with the scissors… I'm afraid it's not the first sign of trouble. I mentioned his angina but held back the rest. There have been several smaller attacks.

He kept on, knowing he owed these words to her, that he'd miscalculated, perhaps catastrophically, by keeping them. If he'd told her when Horace's angina worsened, she might be home by now. Instead, he'd chosen to prioritize her training because he assumed that was what she would want. Suppose he'd assumed wrong?

I should have told you sooner, but I didn't want to burden you with additional worries. I'd increased his dose of digitalis, and Mrs. Crawford and I have been moderating his diet and sleep habits. I thought he was getting better. I wanted all your news from home to be encouraging. You've been so hard on yourself of late.

Daniel grimaced. Perhaps he'd inadvertently push her out of her depression. Once she knew he'd hidden Horace's ailing health, the blame and failure she'd been fastening onto herself might direct itself to him. It couldn't be helped now. He waffled, biting the end of his pen as he considered whether to confess the details of Vickery's treachery and the financial woes, but Horace clinging to life seemed plenty enough to burden her with.

I will do everything I can for him. You must choose whatever you think is best, but Horace would not want you to sacrifice anything on his account.

He left a last promise of love, hoping it was reciprocal, before he signed and sealed the letter, found the hallboy downstairs, and instructed him to send it off express. With heavy footsteps, he returned to Horace's bedside.

Harry had finished speaking to him and was sitting quietly, gazing out the window. "You told her?" he asked as Daniel entered.

Daniel nodded and took up the stethoscope. He checked the heart and lung sounds again and then sat, settling in for the long wait.

The walk back to Salvio's brougham—Nora tested his name in her mind as they walked, only it sounded like an indictment, not a greeting—was silent but for the rustle of the grasses and dead wildflower stalks that crunched underfoot. The wind was at their back now, pushing her home, bearing her up. She did not glance behind, wanting neither to see how he felt, nor for him to see her. She let the driver help her inside because he had dismounted and was standing beside the door. Salvio followed and took the seat opposite, his misery palpable. As soon as the carriage moved, he leaned forward. "Eleanora, please. Speak to me."

"Of course I will speak to you." She obliged, her voice indifferent.

"You cannot be so ignorant or childlike. There is no harm in a kiss." His voice was begging, not scolding, pleading with her to agree with him.

"Then no harm is done," she replied as stiff as the gust of wind that shook the carriage.

He reached across the space between them and snatched up the hand she had foolishly left in her lap. "Did you feel nothing?"

Her face heated with a rush of blood under her skin. She felt such a barrage of things that his question mocked her and turned her tongue to flint. She wanted her hand back to press it protectively against her complaining heart.

"You said you would speak to me," he reminded when her silence became too much for him.

If she opened her mouth, she would berate him. The words quivered on the edge of her mind, begging for release. Shame bloomed in the pit of her stomach every time her skin reacted to his touch. *How dare she think his lips soft and masterful? How dare he force her to know it? How stupid to be alone with him in this empty countryside when he looked so famished.*

She pulled her hand back and wrapped it around herself. He was still waiting for her to speak, but if she rebuffed him, he would argue with her. If she was kind, he would advance again. "I love Daniel Gibson," she managed to say, though his name almost doubled her pain.

"Why?" Perra demanded before she even finished.

Her irate eyes met his, steady this time. "That is not a fair question. One cannot express—"

"*Nonsenso*! Poets have been expressing every detail of human love for millennia. Tell me why you love him." His worry had turned to agitation. She must not rile him further.

"He is kind. He sees me as his equal. He is gentle." She meant the last descriptor as a rebuke, but Perra flicked it away.

She leaned back. "I don't want to discuss it any further. You performed your experiment, and I still love Dr. Gibson." She had spent her strength. Fresh tears made her chin tremble and she needed the safety of her bed, a place to lie and let the anguish seep from her eyes.

"He can offer you a fraction of what I can. *Per favore*, Eleanora. Forget him. He's nothing but a dream to you already."

The more she resisted, the more desperate he became. Perhaps he had imagined he would wrap her in his arms and kiss her and she would submit willingly, even gratefully.

"You are clinging to a young girl's dream," he added. "Everyone experiences calf love. You. Pozzi. Me, once upon a time, and you know how that has worked for me."

"Daniel and I are not the same as you and Fina," Nora spat out. "And Pozzi…" It felt wrong to speak of him now.

"How do you know?" Perra challenged.

She struggled within herself.

"Eleanora, I love you." His voice broke her already fractured reasoning. "It began on the ship journey here, and I determined to hide it. But my feelings have only grown. I cannot lose you."

She turned away, making a sacred meditation of the passing buildings, her whole soul absorbed in the carved pediments and corbels, willing her mind to think of nothing but the chips in the stone and the color of the weathered bricks.

"I cannot believe our kiss didn't stir you," Perra said.

It was not our kiss. She clenched her jaw, trying to stop her teeth chattering. "Pozzi never pushed when I refused."

"Pozzi was a child with the first pangs of fondness. I am a man in love who knows a singular opportunity when it comes. We will never find happiness like this again."

Nora's brow lowered under the weight of her incredulity. *What happiness was he speaking of?* Her chest was a ravaged ruin where her heart used to be.

The vehicle stopped at the beginning of her street, and Nora's hand flew to the handle.

"Eleanora?" Perra's voice followed her out the door and she felt his hand graze her sleeve, but she had gained the light of the street and the noise of shoppers under the porticos. She did not look back as she hurried for the shelter of her rooms.

CHAPTER 28

Years as an asylum matron had made Mrs. Crawford adept at moving silently into a room, yet Daniel heard her. He didn't turn around in his chair. "He's sleeping," he said quietly. "But you can leave the tray." And pray that when—if—Horace waked, he'd be well enough to take some nourishment.

"There's broth and milk for him," Mrs. Crawford said.

Daniel thanked her with a nod, still unable to look away from Horace's gaunt face, more weathered than ever beside the crisp sheets. The left side still sagged. Sometimes the effects of an attack weren't permanent, but it had been almost two days. Not a promising sign, and Daniel wasn't sure, in the past two hours, if it had been right to give Horace laudanum to settle him. Once Horace regained some clumsy movement, his frantic struggles to speak and climb out of bed had been terrible to watch, and Daniel feared the excitement might kill him—never mind what injuries he might do to himself. He'd flailed like a drunken man, only far, far worse. Drunkenness was temporary.

The hall clock had struck midnight only moments ago, and Daniel glanced at another half-finished letter on the table beside his chair. He'd believed so fervently that today's report would be better. Instead, the truth came out cringing and painful. *Dearest Nora, please forgive me. I must give you more disturbing news...* How could such neat script contain such a mess of a situation?

He should have held Horace back. Stood firm. Make him moderate the burdens he put on himself, even a little. "You're resting now, stubborn fool," Daniel whispered with a sad rub of his eyes. All the lectures were canceled for the present. Already twenty pounds lost since yesterday. Harry had visited both Daniel's and Horace's patients today and helped with three of the diphtheria children, but he couldn't keep such a schedule; certainly not unpaid, as he was at present. With a sigh, Daniel took Horace's pulse and checked a pupil and heart sounds one more time before he pulled the crocheted blanket off the back of his chair and fell asleep to the reassuring sound of Horace's steady breaths.

Someone scratched at the door, and Daniel's eyes shot open, then instantly closed again. The sharp light of day had broken into the room like a thief and assaulted him.

"Come!" he meant to call, but his dry throat seemed lined with sawdust. Only a rasp came out.

Mrs. Crawford bustled in.

"You needn't worry," she said briskly. "Dr. Trimble looked after the patients at morning clinic. He'll see to the most urgent cases in a round of afternoon calls if you visit Dr. Croft's society patients. Neither of you are expected at St. Bart's."

"Sounds like he has everything in hand," Daniel said, trying to convince himself that he must make some attempts to carry on. The world wouldn't wait for anyone, even Horace Croft. "He's not supposed to see Lady Stephenson today, is he?"

"No. But Lady Woodbine has requested a consultation. I have her letter—"

Daniel scanned it. "We can put her off, just for a day or two. I imagine she wishes to consult him about her pregnancy." Horace had already made his thoughts clear on the subject weeks ago, saying he wanted nothing to do with the ill-fated endeavor, but perhaps Lady Woodbine wished to contribute to their work with the children—

That thought cleared his mind of the lingering sleep. Daniel rose. He'd attend her and see if he could summon up enough charm to… Daniel grimaced. Plotting his course around wishes was like venturing into the Sahara without a map. Short of an unforeseen savior, he must find a way to resolve these financial problems on his own.

"I'll write today to set an appointment with her," Daniel said.

"An excellent idea, Doctor."

"I must get to work." He pushed out of the chair, wincing when his back protested. "Will you be able to sit with him today?"

"Certainly, but I'm afraid I didn't come here just to check on you. There's a visitor." Mrs. Crawford's pinched lips told him it was not a pleasant caller. "He insists on seeing you."

Daniel frowned. "I haven't washed. Or changed."

"I'm very sorry. I explained you couldn't come but he won't leave," Mrs. Crawford said. "He said to tell you it's important." She held out a card. It read: James Holwell, Arbuthnot Latham Bank.

Daniel stared at the card, then at Mrs. Crawford. He swallowed. "I'll need at least ten minutes."

And a shave. A fresh shirt.

Horace was incapacitated and wholly unable to advise. He'd borrowed for the new house and the subsequent improvements based on his income, and Daniel knew too little of his personal finances.

"I'll bring him some refreshments."

"Thank you, Mrs. Crawford." Daniel sped to his own room. He wouldn't reassure any bankers looking like this.

Knowing the interview needed to come off well, Daniel combed his hair, shaved, and brushed his teeth before descending to the parlor, where he found Mr. Holwell looking about critically as if appraising the furnishings. Daniel was tempted to explain that these had come with the house, but confined himself to a clipped greeting, "May I help you?" And then adding with a bit more iron, "I was with a patient and I've not breakfasted yet."

"Dr. Gibson. I very much regret—"

Holwell looked like a banker, Daniel thought. Cautious, dry, exceedingly polite, but implacable as a case of rabies.

After a brief compression of his lips, more suggestive of disapproval than regret, Holwell continued. "We missed the last payments on Dr. Croft's mortgages."

Daniel clenched his teeth, annoyed that such a detail couldn't be settled by the sending of a note. "I'm very sorry. He's been exceedingly busy, and now, just a trifle unwell."

"So we heard." The banker turned expressionless eyes from the window back to Daniel.

"Pardon?" Daniel snapped. No one at 43 Great Queen Street had spoken with the bank.

"He left the hospital days ago in a compromised state and no one has heard of him since," the banker continued, refusing to be silenced by Daniel's glare. "I'm afraid we were informed by his employer that he most likely will not recover, and we feel it best to recoup assets now..."

His voice trailed off as Daniel stalked closer, his jaw clenched. "What employer?"

"Dr. Vickery, head of surgery," Holwell said with a sniff.

"He is Dr. Croft's fellow surgeon, not employer," Daniel said as he schooled his face to modulate disgust. Horace had turned down Silas's position repeatedly, convinced managing other physicians would keep him from research in his clinic. "I'm afraid Dr. Vickery hasn't seen Dr. Croft and is mistaken in the information he gave you. It is difficult to predict recovery after an illness," Daniel said evenly. "But I hope for the best."

"As do I," Mr. Holwell agreed. "As do I. Unfortunately, bankers are not much in the business of hoping."

"I'll look over our records and make sure you receive payment right away," Daniel said. "Thank you for coming to inform me of the oversight."

The banker didn't move when Daniel pointed him to the door. "But Mr. Gibson, I'm afraid there is a buyer offering more for the property and the bank feels, in light of the missed payments, our interests are best served—"

"Another buyer?" Daniel's neck prickled. "What buyer?"

Mr. Holwell clutched his cane as if fearing he'd have to use it. "Another doctor wishing to secure the premises."

All pretense fell away. Daniel gritted his teeth as he hissed the words. "What doctor?"

The man stuttered. "I don't know if it's confidential." Though he spoke with a superior voice, his shoulders cowered. "We've been assured Dr. Croft is on the brink of bankruptcy by reliable sources at St. Bartholomew's."

Daniel blew out a hot breath like a volcano leaking steam. He only knew one man unscrupulous enough to seize Horace's home and clinic while he lay helpless. "There is no risk of bankruptcy. Can a man not catch the flu without jealous colleagues ripping away his home? There will be no sale! You will have your money, every farthing of it!" Daniel snapped.

"What's this?" Harry asked, and Daniel snapped his head around. He hadn't noticed Harry enter the foyer until that moment.

"Mr. Holwell from the bank, trying to foreclose on this house and hand it to Vickery!"

Harry's face blanched. "You can't be serious."

"In cases of nonpayment, the terms of the mortgage allow the bank to sell. If the proceeds from that sale provide more than is owed us, the surplus naturally will go to Dr. Croft. And there will be a surplus, I am happy to say. We've been presented with a very attractive offer. Dr. Croft may counter, of course, if he wishes to retain the property, but he will need to rectify the late payments first." Holwell broke off as Daniel's face darkened. "I will give your solicitor until the end of next week."

"That's only eight days." Harry screwed his eyes in frustration.

"My sympathies for Dr. Croft. Good day, gentlemen." Mr.

Holwell tipped his hat and advanced backward out the front door, like a man unwilling to show a tiger the back of his neck.

"Oh, he'll not think me gentle—" Harry began.

"Eight days," Daniel repeated, a sudden weariness smothering him.

"Then we can't waste a minute," Harry goaded, not allowing any sympathy for Daniel's slumping shoulders. "Go see the solicitor now. Horace was so distracted before he was ill it's no wonder he's gotten careless with payments. He's a wealthy man. You can soon put things right."

Nothing would be served by contradicting him. Daniel smothered his unease, for he was not nearly as confident as Harry. "But to pay more for a house he bought fairly, only because Vickery wants to take it." The words stuck like sand in Daniel's throat, hot and scraping.

"If only I hadn't promised not to kill anyone when I became a doctor." Harry shook his head with regret. "See if the solicitor can fight it."

"That will be another bill." Daniel rubbed his forehead wearily. Horace was in no condition to explain his finances. They were completely dependent on the solicitor.

"Can I help?" Harry asked.

Daniel shook his head quickly. Any help Harry could give would be far too small to cover the yawning debt Horace was carrying. "I'll find a way to manage. It's just handling the patients while looking after Horace that will be difficult."

Harry squinted in sympathy. "I'll close clinic early and watch Horace. I can stay for weeks if you want. Go now," Harry insisted again.

"What about your wife? I can't claim you for days at a time, let alone weeks."

"She'll understand why I need to help. If she wants company—" Harry broke off, shrugging rather helplessly. "She can visit her family again."

"No. She can stay here." Daniel spoke automatically, his mind too tangled in the thorny mess of finances to know what he was saying. The idea cleared as he continued. "We've plenty of bedrooms and no one to fill them. Bring her here and you can take a suite in the addition."

Harry frowned. "It would be nicer than our Lambeth flat, but removing completely would... Perhaps we should wait and see if—" He looked ashamed of himself.

"He'll survive," Daniel said in a dead monotone before he wandered like a blind man up the stairs to look in on Horace—thankfully, still sleeping—then began excavating the financial papers from Horace's desk. As he rifled through the heap, his eyes caught his half-finished letter to Nora and he groaned. This was a postscript he couldn't bear to write.

CHAPTER 29

"WHERE IS YOUR FOCUS?" MAGDALENA HISSED AT HER ear as they made their way down the ward to their last patient of the morning. She spoke softly enough the student following behind them wouldn't overhear.

Nora shook her head as if to wake herself. "I'm sorry. I've not slept well."

Magdalena made a scornful noise. "Pozzi wouldn't want you to ruin your studies over grief."

Nora nodded, ashamed because she had not thought of Pozzi at all that day.

"Our next patient, Dottoressa?" Umberto Sagese, sallow and wearing his usual scornfully curled mouth, had caught up to them. Magdalena gave a brief case history while they walked. The woman in question was forty-three and pregnant for only the third time. Her abdomen was too small and her limbs too swollen. She had the indefinable features of poverty, a dull look to the eyes that betrayed a lean life with no comforts.

It was Sagese's turn to perform the exam, but his questions were overloud and he rolled his eyes when the woman did not understand what he meant by menses. Nora's spine tensed. This gray-haired woman with missing teeth was something between an animal and a person to him, too poor and stupid for sympathy. Nora waited for Magdalena to censure him, but she was scanning another chart, engrossed in a different case.

When he finished, Magdalena led them from the ward, too distracted to notice Nora's indignant frown and narrow looks at Sagese. "I've a meeting with Dr. Alessi to discuss funds for my class of midwives and I'm running late. I'll expect your notes tomorrow on the cases and your diagnoses." Her look warned Nora that her notes had better be more impressive than her performance today. Nora pinked as she watched Magdalena hurry down the empty hall.

She waited until they were alone to round on Sagese.

"What did you mean by treating Signora Territo that way?"

"What are you talking about?" Sagese's eyebrows lifted. He spoke in the drawl of his southern town.

"You showed neither courtesy nor respect, addressing her like a farmer berating a cow. If Dr. Marenco hadn't been so preoccupied—"

Sagese twitched his narrow, high-bridged nose to a sneer. "I won't be lectured by *you*."

Nora rolled her eyes, the rebuke too trite to pierce her. "Yes, I know; I'm a woman. Or is it my being English that bothers you?"

Sagese looked up and down the corridor to ensure they were still alone and wiped his hair from his forehead. "You act like you are top of every class, but everyone knows you cheat."

Nora snapped to attention, her blood rising. "I've never cheated on anything!"

Sagese looked more bored than anything. "What do you call it when a student makes love to a professor?"

Nora froze, the words like ice water in her ears. "What?" she whispered.

Sagese rolled his pencil through his fingers. "Your overnight dissections. Your late-night rides in dark carriages. His arms around you. Did you think no one would discover you?" Sagese shook his head, his green eyes narrowing with frustration. "Not that it matters. No one can touch Perra. He can have whatever favors he wants. But don't pretend you are better than me. I certainly can't seduce Dr. Barilli when my grades fall."

Nora's lips fell open but the retort that came was childish, unconvincing even to her ears. "I never! Why would you think—"

Sagese only scoffed. "Even the doctors are tired of it. Haven't you noticed how they look at you? I think Barilli is jealous. If he'd known you were available, he'd have enjoyed you first."

Nora's fingers curled into a furious knot. "You're disgusting. You've no right to slander me with insulting lies. I ought to report you."

"To Perra?" Sagese smirked.

No. Not him. "Dr. Marenco," Nora said evenly.

"She's no saint," Sagese said. "Naturally you would conspire with her. Stay out of my way. And save your lectures for someone who cares."

Nora watched him retreat, her stomach threatening to return her breakfast. In the ward behind her, someone broke into a coughing fit. She looked at the wall opposite, seeing nothing. Her mind wheeled through pictures of every interaction with Professor Perra: his dark library, the untidy interior of his carriage, their knees grazing as he rode with her through the moonless streets. She felt his hot kiss on her numb lips. *But no one had been there. How could they know?* Nora stumbled to the coughing patient to rub camphor on her chest with shaking fingers.

"Dottoressa? Are you well?" the patient rasped.

"I'm only a student," Nora said. "And I'm fine."

———

"This is bad. Very bad." Herbert Jamison, Horace's solicitor, shook his head and turned over another of the pages Daniel had liberated from the chaos in Horace's study. "I warned him not to borrow from Arbuthnot Latham Bank, but they offered a lower rate of interest and Dr. Croft wouldn't be dissuaded."

"They can't sell the property to Vickery," Daniel said.

"It's an unusual step for a couple of missed payments, but—"

"Delayed," Daniel said. Before leaving Great Queen Street, he'd dispatched a draft from his own bank with the missing funds.

"I will certainly argue against such a drastic step," Jamison said. "But the simplest way around it is to offer more money to cover the difference between Vickery's offer and the amount Dr. Croft negotiated. Unfortunately—" He frowned at the untidy ledger, full of scraps of paper tucked between pages detailing expenses not yet recorded: the lease of Nora's apartment in Bologna, her tuition fees, the new wallpaper, the furnishings, and an astounding sum to the firm of builders who'd orchestrated the work on the newly enlarged house. "There is not a great deal of liquidity at present."

Daniel's head rose. *Not a great deal* was at least something to start with. "How much?"

The solicitor's dark eyes tightened. "I should have been clearer. There is no liquidity whatsoever. Quite the opposite. How has he managed to spend it all?"

Daniel exhaled. "You know Horace; he never lets money get in the way of science."

"I don't suppose you can make it up from patient fees?"

Daniel rubbed his face, hiding the despair in his eyes behind his fingers. Horace wasn't working. "We can last a month, maybe two, on my savings and my income," Daniel said. "But not if we have to buy off Horace's bankers. I have no access to my inheritance; I have only my own earned money, which is scant in the first years of practice, I'm afraid."

Jamison pressed his palms together and tapped his two forefingers against closed lips. "Normally I would not advise depleting your own funds. But in this circumstance…" He coughed. "I am familiar with Horace's feud with Dr. Vickery. I will negotiate with the mortgage holders at Arbuthnot Latham, but I fear they will require at least an additional two hundred pounds within days. The creditors"—he shuffled papers—"cabinet makers, painters, and the like will need at least that much as well."

The sum Jamison was suggesting wasn't impossible, not if Horace returned to work in a couple of months and Daniel borrowed money from his sister, Joan. She was not a rich woman, but comfortable, and levelheaded enough to have something stashed away. They could continue writing the household accounts with red ink for a time, if they knew they could right things before too long. But Daniel couldn't even predict if Horace would live out the next six months, let alone work in them. "What of Horace's investments?" Daniel asked.

"He had some losses in the past few months. He was heavily invested in railway bonds," Jamison said. "And he's been making large withdrawals for Miss Beady's expenses and his building project. His illness has come at a most unfortunate time."

Did all lawyers possess such a spectacular ability for understatement? Daniel relaxed his jaw and took a deep breath. "Talk to the mortgage holders. Negotiate the best deal you can."

He wasn't giving up Horace's dream or Nora's home, certainly not because of Vickery. "I'll find the money to see us through."

London treated him to a day as dreary as his mood as he walked home. The sky was nothing but an oppressive sheet of white and the city beneath it a huddled lump of gray. Approaching home, he spotted a large coach waiting outside and the driver helping Harry inside with several heavy trunks. A young girl stood nervously at the front door, her face obscured in a fur hood.

"Daniel, come meet Mrs. Julia Trimble," Harry said, sliding the trunk beside the umbrella stand and shutting the front door against the cold.

The girl removed her hood, and though her teeth chattered, she managed a nervous smile, her cheeks bitten with chill. She was as pretty as Daniel remembered from their meeting years ago, her blue eyes wide and bright, her blond curls thick and heavy.

"How do you do, Mrs. Trimble. Welcome." Daniel took her hand.

"Thank you for having us, Dr. Gibson. Your home is most impressive." Her eyes roved over the massive entry as she shivered.

"Into the drawing room," Daniel insisted. "There's always a fire and it's too drafty in here." He took her arm and led her on as Harry paid the driver. "So you've tamed my wildest friend into a domesticated animal?" Daniel asked as he settled her into the armchair closest to the flames. She leaned away from the stuffed boar with intimidating tusks perched beside her seat.

She laughed. "Don't be deceived by appearances. Harry still barks and growls. Unlike this poor fellow."

Daniel didn't believe her for a moment. Harry always went from a lion to a kitten in the presence of ladies.

"I appreciate you being willing to come and stay. I'm in a tight corner at present with Horace ill and Nora away." Thoughts of the solicitor's words gave his stomach a sick turn. "Without Harry I couldn't keep our patients or run clinic."

"He'd walk the earth for you," she stated simply. "And if he would, I would." She stretched her fingers toward the fire, gathering the warmth through her gloves, and praised one of Nora's watercolors on the mantel as if this was merely an afternoon call, but Daniel had a hot lump in his throat. He blinked hard and turned away when Harry entered the room.

"So?" Harry asked, his smile bent and mischievous. "Do you blame me now for forsaking bachelorhood?"

"Not in the slightest," Daniel admitted.

Harry gave one of Julia's curls an affectionate tweak as he passed her.

"I do, however," Daniel continued, "blame her. Why did you ever condescend to a man like Harry?"

Julia laughed. "Careful, Dr. Gibson. I'm quite savage when defending people I love."

Daniel tried to imagine her face distorted by anything other than contentment. "I'm sure you're terrifying," he teased.

Again she laughed, the sound so strange in the large house that he realized it had hardly been heard since Nora left. His heart seized with a pang as Harry folded his rough hand around Julia's. He hadn't given a single thought to what it would be like to be exposed to their honeymoon happiness—how long had they been married?—when he suggested this arrangement. He'd have to school his heart not to complain.

"I've told Julia all about the wonders of this house," Harry announced. "I'd like to show her around so she can acclimate. Let me show you the surgical theater. It's spectacular."

Julia clenched Harry's hand. The other lingered at her throat.

"It's not for everyone," Daniel said. "You'll like the leopard skeleton. Horace finished it and put it on display in the conservatory. And there are some fine paintings in the dining room and the crystal sent from the King of Holland." A set worth, at a guess, fifty pounds. Daniel grimaced, for his next move was becoming clear, though Julia could enjoy the glassware for a few days, at least.

"You received crystal from King William?" she asked, her head perking with interest.

"Not I," Daniel corrected. "Dr. Croft nursed their ambassador to London through a nearly fatal fever a few years ago. They sent the crystal in thanks to our queen, but she had it delivered to the man who earned it. Along with an invitation to knighthood," he couldn't help adding, though he wouldn't have dared if Horace had been present.

"Dr. Croft is a knight?" Her blue eyes sparked with disbelief.

"Turned it down with grace and humility so as not to offend Her Majesty." Daniel straightened a china bird he'd carelessly moved aside yesterday when he needed a place to put down his heavy stack of books. He'd have to change his habits with Julia Trimble about. "Horace came into the world a poor, untitled boy and has no ambition for what he calls empty honors."

Julia blinked. "Harry, if you are ever so fortunate to receive such an honor—"

Harry snorted. "I love you for thinking it, but I promise, that situation will never arise."

"And you refuse, I will murder you." Julia finished, with a winning smile.

"I'm quite safe, my dear." Harry grinned. "Horace is an original. Hates me, but I think he'll fancy you all right."

"He's sleeping now," Daniel said. It would be sometime before the laudanum wore off. "But I will introduce him to you later. For now, Mrs. Crawford will see to your things, and Harry can show you the curiosities."

Someone should enjoy them, while they still graced the library and drawing room. But how much would he be able to sell without drawing unwelcome attention? And would it bring in enough?

CHAPTER 30

D R. ALESSI WAS SLIGHTLY DEAF AND WEDDED TO OLD-fashioned treatments, regularly stating his opinion that anesthesia was contrary to the will of God. Still, trailing him around was better than being near Perra, so Nora had taken to following him during hospital rounds. She kept her lips closed (Alessi wasn't interested in hearing from the university's female student) and told herself the sideways looks that followed her were just her imagination.

She was perched beside a patient, watching her sleep off the ether required for debridement of a scalded arm and reviewing her thesis notes, when a rustle of sound drifted through the ward. Her fellow students abandoned their work and hurried to the door.

"What is it?" Nora called to them. Only one obliged, throwing an answer over his shoulder without slowing down. "Emergency appendectomy in the theater."

She piled her notes together, stuffed them under one arm, and hastened after him, joining the throng filling the corridor. By the time she squeezed through the theater door, it was too late to find space anywhere but at the back, and she had to set her notebooks on the floor and stand on them to gain enough inches to see over the shoulders hedging around her.

A pallid-looking patient, curled up in pain, was whimpering on the table. A student from Ravenna readied the instruments, and Romolo Mondelli, who shared her classes with Dr. Marenco, was measuring out drachms of ether. The presiding surgeon wasn't in sight. "Who's demonstrating?" she asked to no one in particular.

"It's Perra," someone muttered, just as she spotted the professor walking toward the table. Sagese was beside him, tying Perra's apron as the professor rolled up his sleeves.

For a moment, Nora was too stunned to react. Then she swallowed. She had studied appendectomies and ether more than any student in the university, and while she expected distance and awkwardness after rejecting Perra, seeing Sagese in her place cut too deep.

"You're not administering the ether for him?" the student beside her asked.

Obviously not. She choked back a retort and kept her face smooth. "I was busy in the wards," Nora murmured, but the words seemed to seep around her like ink soaking into linen, and she feared that everyone heard. No one said anything.

"She's young," Nora said quietly, nodding in the direction of the patient, whose lids fluttered and subsided under the fumes of the inhaler. "Looks otherwise healthy. Unless the appendix has ruptured, she has a good chance of recovery."

She was talking to distract herself, and though two of the men beside her nodded, their measuring glances made her think they'd rather distance themselves. She pressed her lips together and turned her eyes to the scalpel Perra held aloft.

"Shall we?" he asked the crowd, and Nora shifted behind the tall shoulder in front of her. She didn't need to see.

⁓

On Friday, Magdalena sent for her.

"What happened?" she demanded before Nora had time to divest herself of bonnet or bag. "With Salvio," she added, exasperated by Nora's confusion.

"What are people saying?" Nora said cautiously.

Magdalena gestured to the low ottoman beside her. "All sorts of rubbish, I'm sure. All I know is you two are no longer talking. Coffee?"

"Please," Nora said, sighing as if the drink were a cure.

It wasn't, of course, but she felt better with the hot liquid inside her, and better still once she yielded to Magdalena's persuasion and confessed the truth.

"I admire your independence," Magdalena said at last. "You are always your own woman, but you'd make a terrible general. No strategy at all. It would have been better to put him off or flirt with him, at least until your exam was over. He's a proud man, Nora."

"What about my pride?" Nora demanded, scowling into her empty cup. "The only good thing is his anger may silence these ridiculous rumors. No one will think we're lovers now."

"There's nothing to confirm a suspicion like a lovers' spat," Magdalena countered.

Nora lifted stricken eyes to her friend.

"The rumor I heard is that he ended your affair, and you aren't taking it well. Rumor is seldom kind to women," Magdalena said quietly.

Nora stiffened. "What do I do?"

"Carry on," Magdalena said. "Pretend not to hear it. If you cower now, everyone will think it is true."

"They already do."

Magdalena took her hands in a warm, firm clasp. "Make them doubt."

Nora left for home, still uneasy with Magdalena's encouragement to brazen it out. She was right—courage and a tough hide were essential for females who took any path other than the narrow ones society offered. But Nora had other considerations, chief of which was her examination, three weeks away. Perra had not so much as looked at her since their drive to the countryside, and even without eye contact, she felt a palpable frost in his vicinity. She'd counted on one ally at least when she faced the professors. Now, it seemed the best she could hope for was Perra ignoring her or feigning politeness. But he knew the weak spots in her thesis, the places during practice where she'd tripped on words or blundered. Neglect might not satisfy him, when sabotage was so easy.

Despite today's wind and chill, the streets bustled with people, but Nora had no eyes for the families out for their evening stroll, the vendors setting up stalls for the yearly Christmas market, or the tumblers drawing crowds in the squares. Her resentment built with every step. She'd done nothing wrong. Now, more than ever, she was confident rejecting him was the right choice, so why was she alone being punished? Why were his hints and insinuations—if he hadn't outright lied—so readily believed?

Hunching her shoulders, irked by the jollity filling the

square as thickly as the scents of fresh breads and coffee, Nora dragged her feet to the door of her boardinghouse, because scowling at strangers only made people look at her oddly. She had endured enough speculation already.

Breathless when she came to the top of the stairs, she trembled with anger as she let herself in the apartment. She fully intended to snap at or sob her way into the lap of Mrs. Phipps, but that lady greeted her with troubled eyes and a letter in her hands. It was still sealed.

"News from home?" Nora asked.

"Yes. An express." Mrs. Phipps paused as Nora froze. "Signora Carnicelli's nephew went looking for you, but… It's been here for hours now, but I couldn't open it. Not without you."

Nora wasn't fooled by Mrs. Phipps's precise posture and firm lips. She accepted the envelope gingerly, her pulse accelerating. Horace may have been overexcited about some discovery and paid the painfully exorbitant fee for an express letter, but this was Daniel's script and he'd never do something so impetuous unless necessary. Any express letter meant dire news.

"Sit down," Mrs. Phipps urged.

That was probably best. This news—whatever it was—was at least a week old, she reminded herself, but that didn't soften the roaring in her ears. She dropped onto the sofa and cracked the seal.

My Dear Nora—

She ought to read aloud, so that Mrs. Phipps could discover the news the same moment as her. Except speech was impossible and her eyes were already halfway down the sheet, picking up lone words like a starveling gathering crumbs.

"It's Horace," she said heavily.

"Is he—?" Mrs. Phipps wavered, unable to finish her question.

"Ill." Not dead, though that could have happened by now, in the days since Daniel had penned this letter. "He's suffered an apoplexy." Nora faltered, for the worn face in front of her—loved, lined, and normally so resolute—quivered and went slack. She dropped the letter and wrapped her arms around Mrs. Phipps's thin shoulders, as if her strength could keep the older woman from melting.

"That fool man!" Mrs. Phipps's voice, shaky and shrill, resonated through both of them. "I knew he'd wear himself to flinders. If I—"

The broken sentence cut, sharp as a shard of glass. They were here, instead of London, because of Nora.

"We can be home in three weeks," Nora said. "Two if we're lucky." Ships for England left almost daily from Venice.

"We cannot go," Mrs. Phipps said dully, extricating herself from Nora's arms and steadying herself with a ratcheting breath. "That would be nonsensical. It may not even matter." She pressed her lips together, but her chin wobbled with the strain. "You have your exam."

Weeks from now.

Moments ago, that had seemed woefully insufficient. Now, a single day's delay was excruciating. "I think they need us." Nora passed her the letter. Mrs. Phipps would not understand the significance of all the symptoms Daniel reported. He hadn't advanced any prognosis, and Nora could only guess at Horace's future and pray he had one. No matter what she did, Horace would live or die in the next two weeks without her. He might have died already. It was impractical to race home, instead of biding time and waiting for more news. Only a reckless gambler would stake so much on such uncertain odds.

A scientist wouldn't. But a surgeon would.

Nora rose. Her hand rested, momentarily, on Mrs. Phipps's shoulder. "Stay here. I'll arrange what I can and be back soon." She would at least try.

—

Nora stood in front of the knocker. The house was stately, almost a palazzo, and she'd stood here a full minute, wondering if she was mad to proceed. But it was useless to go to Perra. Even if he listened to her—doubtful—his advocacy would only feed rumors of a sordid affair between them. Even if she earned her degree, it would count for nothing, and stubbornly, she almost didn't want it if she only won it because of Perra's favor. It was daunting to face such a crisis without a friend, but Professor Barilli was not on speaking terms with Magdalena, and Pozzi, who might have bolstered her courage, was gone. She rapped the knocker, wishing it didn't sound so loud in the street.

"Eleanor Beady for Professor Barilli, please," she informed the butler when the door opened at last. The knocker had seemed too loud and now her voice seemed too small. "It's an emergency," she added in a stronger voice.

The servant bowed and withdrew. A minute later he returned. "I'm afraid the professor cannot see you now."

"He must." Nora swallowed. "I insist."

This man wasn't used to resistance. After a moment he

raised his voice. "Luca." Another manservant entered the corridor.

"You don't want a scene," Nora said, glancing between them as they approached her. "And if you throw me out, I swear I'll make one the neighbors will never forget."

They paused. Finally, "Watch her," the butler snapped, and vanished again. When he returned, Barilli was with him.

"What is it, signorina?" Usually he was only mildly irritated by her presence; if she followed him during his rounds, there was an extra crease in his forehead. If she sat too near the front of his lectures, his voice was a degree sharper. But this visit pushed him past irritation to agitation.

"I beg a favor," Nora said. "Please." He hadn't dismissed his servants and clearly had no intention of ushering her into a private parlor, so she rushed on, unwilling to miss her chance. "My exam is scheduled after the Christmas holiday, but I must go home to London at the first opportunity."

"Then go home, signorina." His face was unreadable, but he nodded to his servants who at last melted away.

"I cannot waste the chance Dr. Croft has given me," she said softly, repeating the phrase that had sustained her when her brain was too tired to learn, after Paola, after Pozzi, and now, under Barilli's glare. "I must at least try."

Barilli's closed expression cracked open at Horace's name. He was an ardent admirer. "I know of him," he said acidly. "But I see no reason why his achievements should propel yours. My opinion of females in the medical profession is well known, and this latest contretemps between you and Salvio Perra, a colleague I generally respect, only confirms—"

"He had an apoplexy," Nora murmured numbly. "He may have already died of it."

"Dr. Croft?" he demanded.

She nodded.

Barilli's face went slack for a moment, then anger gathered in the furrows on his brow. "I was never in favor of your accelerated schedule. Perra should never have indulged you. I doubt you will pass the exam in any case."

"Then what is the harm in failing tomorrow instead of in three weeks?" Nora asked. "Please, Professor."

"These are serious and solemn occasions," Barilli said. "Not to be rescheduled on a whim."

"Returning to nurse my guardian is not a whim," Nora said. "Last year, Efisio Scaturro's exam was moved so he could attend his brother's wedding."

"The request of the Count di Landino—"

"Is more important than mine," Nora finished.

"Naturally," Barilli said.

"What about the needs of Dr. Croft?" Nora asked. "We are one another's only family."

"Then I suggest you shouldn't have left him," Barilli said.

Nora flinched as if slapped, her eyes stinging. She wanted to howl, but filaments of steel held her straight and silent. She would not cry in front of this man.

"I will see you on December 29, as scheduled," he said and began to turn away.

"You might. But in the meantime, I will petition every professor. I'll petition the governors of the university and the duke," Nora said. "I'll—"

"A waste of time," he snarled.

"Yes," she returned levelly. "And if Dr. Croft lives, I will tell him how you denied me."

His eyes glittered. "You threaten me?"

"I beg you! I won't leave Bologna without the chance to earn what I came for. That's not what Horace taught me." Something changed in his face when her frantic voice twisted the word *beg*. It sent a chill across Nora's arms.

"And if you fail, you go home to him in disgrace due to your impatience."

"I'm not impatient, I'm compelled. A few weeks make no difference to you, Professor, but it could make a world of difference to Horace and me." She swallowed.

Barilli looked away. "Your affection for him does you credit," he admitted. "At least that feminine virtue is intact."

"Please, sir."

She could almost hear the wheels of his mind turning. "You'll have no friends judging your thesis," Barilli warned. "No professors in your pocket. After your recent behavior—"

"I've done nothing," Nora said. "Only study and work, but that doesn't matter. It was Perra—your colleague—who made a dishonorable offer and humiliated me when I refused him. But he has power and I have none."

"That's a bold accusation," Barilli said, and though he was not a tall man, Nora took a step back. "I may be able to persuade some of my colleagues to judge your thesis early. Not tomorrow. It's too late in the day to arrange now. But the day after. If—"

Nora nodded for him to go on.

"If you agree to submit to the examiners' judgment. Whoever they may be. You will not be able to appeal."

He was giving her a chance, but only one. If she failed, she couldn't rewrite in one or two year's time, not without weighty favors from someone, and she had no one to ask.

"Thank you, Professor." Nora bowed, briefly, as the male students did.

"If you're not ready—"

"I'm ready," Nora told him. She had no idea if she was lying or telling the truth.

CHAPTER 31

"WAIT. I NEED TO CHECK MY BAG," NORA SAID, STOPPING Magdalena on the stairs. She'd come this morning to escort Nora to the university.

"Again? I've seen you inventory it half a dozen times already." The wide sleeves of her red-hemmed academic gown flapped as she gestured impatiently. "They care what you know, not what order your papers are in."

Nora grimaced, resisting the urge to unbuckle the bag and smooth her hands over her thesis one more time. She'd spent the night pacing, dictating the conclusion to Mrs. Phipps. Hours of copying had left Nora unable to write.

"Don't plague yourself with worry," Mrs. Phipps advised, but the woman didn't follow her own advice. This morning she hadn't been able to swallow a mouthful of breakfast. Whatever facade Mrs. Phipps presented, Nora knew she was worried sick.

As Nora passed through the door into the street, Mrs. Phipps caught her hand and squeezed it. She might have murmured something, but Nora's heart was pounding too hard to hear.

This was the last time she'd walk to the university. The harsh sun made her eyes squint, even though the day was brisk and blustering. "We should have driven," Magdalena said as the wind tugged at the carelessly pinned strands of her hair.

"It's only a half mile," Nora said, almost smiling at how much she sounded like Horace. "I need to walk out my nerves."

In half an hour, she'd step into the *biblioteca comunale* and face Barilli and whatever accomplices he'd gathered to see her fail. She had her preferences of which professors she wanted to stand before but didn't dare hope.

Before the breeze and smell of midday fires could calm her jumping heart, they reached the courtyard of the Archiginnasio. The percussion of shoes and carts and hooves on the brick pavers—usually one of Nora's favorite sounds—didn't reach her ears. Above her, playful angels romped on the ceiling of the portico, laughing despite their naked state on a frosty day as students passed beneath them through the massive black doors of the library.

"Will we be in the anatomy theater?" Nora asked, suddenly realizing she didn't know where to proceed. She pictured herself standing alone in the sunken medieval theater as the benches rose in a ring around her, the professors scowling down at her from the lecturer's throne between the skinless *spellati* statues.

Magdalena shook her head and led her to the staircase of the artists, past the coat of arms honoring the great teachers of medicine and science to the floor above. "You'll be in the Stabat Mater Hall. I won't be able to observe."

Nora's bag dropped too low and thumped into a stone step, sending her off-balance for a moment. "They won't let you?"

"I didn't ask. I don't want you to look weak. You do not need a chaperone or a mother." Magdalena stopped at the top floor, well away from the open door of the imposing lecture hall so as not to be seen or heard. "Let me see who's in there." Magdalena moved her slippered feet with uncharacteristic stealth, daring a cautious look inside before hurrying back to Nora's side. "They didn't see me," she whispered. "You know Barilli is in there. He's vicious, but an admirer of Horace Croft. Mention your mentor's techniques often and perhaps he will forgive you for being a woman."

Nora's lip shook, but she nodded. "Who are the others?"

"Venturoli," Magdalena said in her clipped fashion.

The director of the surgical clinic. Nora let out a breath. *It could have been much worse.*

"He's a disciple of Tarsizio, as you know. He values the practical over the theoretical." As she spoke, Magdalena straightened Nora's cuffs and her belt. "And Fabbri's in there. He's fair. Admit your limitations and don't pretend to know more than you do. He talks slow. Wait patiently and whatever you do, don't babble."

Nora nodded again, her fingers twitching to write down every instruction. How would she remember with her ears thundering so? There was a tightness in Magdalena's eyes, and she was avoiding Nora's gaze.

"And?" Nora asked reluctantly.

"Perra," Magdalena whispered.

Nora closed her eyes in a wordless prayer as the ground lurched beneath her.

"Be careful with him," Magdalena instructed. "He's like a bear, dangerous when wounded. Don't provoke him further."

Nora's eyes flashed down the hallway, her stomach cold and constricted. She'd never *provoked* him in the first place.

Magdalena patted her cheeks with unexpected roughness.

"You look like you're going to faint. Don't lock your knees. You need your blood today."

Nora backed away. She didn't want to look too flushed, either, as if she'd run to get here. "Will you be out here, in case?" she asked.

Magdalena scoffed. "Do you think I have nothing to do for hours? There are patients to tend. Go do your job and I will do mine."

And with that, she nudged Nora forward. Nora sucked in a breath that didn't seem to reach her lungs and forced her feet to the open door.

The room, christened in memory of Rossini's famous libretto performed there, looked larger than Nora remembered. The lectures she'd attended here were accompanied by buzzing voices with swarming bodies filling the empty space; today only a single chair perched ten feet in front of the massive teacher's desk. The four seated professors conversed in dull tones and looked up as she approached.

Nora moved toward them, alarmed that her steps didn't seem to bring her any closer. She was a satellite suspended alone in the void of the hall. The double-headed eagle on the wall to her left peered fiercely over the flock of crests gathered under its wings. The walls were crammed with imposing coats of arms of the university's most successful alumni, their vibrant, busy colors clashing in the rosy light spilling through the red curtains.

Professor Fabbri cleared his throat. His hair had long ago receded, but his bushy eyebrows and mustache were still black as pitch despite his age. Venturoli's stiff collar reached almost to his lips, and his soft white hair landed haphazardly on his lean face. Barilli was handsome, clean-shaven and middle-aged with a cravat tied in a casual knot, but Nora knew his pleasant face hid a hostile smugness. Nora slid her eyes to the side to assess Perra. Seated on Barilli's right, he was examining the papers she'd submitted by messenger at half past four this morning and refusing to look up. His posture was unnaturally stiff, his jaw tight. A jolt of panic electrified her nerves.

She wished she could have done this two weeks ago when she had Perra's support.

"Thank you for this opportunity, gentlemen," she said as soon as she believed her voice strong enough to reach them. She must put anger and hurt behind her and pretend an imperviousness she didn't feel.

"Signorina Beady." Professor Fabbri nodded at her, but Venturoli's stare skimmed over her to the ceiling. He chewed the inside of his cheek, lost in thought, probably ruminating on the cardinal's latest attack of gastroenteritis because he was his consulate surgeon.

She looked at Barilli. She didn't dare appeal to Perra. Barilli did not respect her, but Magdalena was right, he followed Horace's discoveries with interest. What Magdalena didn't know was that Nora had appealed to him using Horace once already. His admiration of Horace had never encouraged him to be more tolerant of her in lectures or at the hospital. While appealing in Croft's name had convinced Barilli to reschedule her examination, it seemed unlikely to win her the favor she would need today. Barilli narrowed his eyes and folded his hands together on the table, leaning forward. "Shall we proceed?"

The other doctors nodded and made soft concurring sounds. Barilli gave her a dangerous grin. "You have been quite the spectacle for the past year and a half, Miss Beady," he said in the most rolling, accented Italian. He would challenge her language acquisition as well as everything else. "An English girl convicted of practicing medicine illegally seeking sanctuary in our ancient walls."

Her hot throat contracted. She must force the words. "I was not convicted by law, sir. Only by popular opinion. And I hope I have not been a spectacle, but a student. I came only to learn."

"While your knowledge is extensive, your motivations are suspect." Dr. Barilli's smile had slipped into a stern line. "When a woman travels so far outside of the realm sanctioned by Almighty God, there is a great deal of curiosity."

Perra's eyes flicked up but stopped short of her face. Without Perra's advocacy, there was little chance these men would pass her, but she was here, and she refused to make it easy for any of them. They were obliged to listen for a least a few hours.

Nora dug her fingernails into her hand, looking for something to hold as she stood on exhibit before her judges. She'd hoped they'd at least begin with a pretense of fairness. "With all respect, I do not believe I stepped outside of my sanctioned realm." Professor Fabbri pinched his lips and adjusted his spectacles. "Women are givers and nurturers of life. I can think of no pursuit more suited to our strengths than preserving the life we create. Your esteemed Dr. Marenco has taught me it is the duty of women to stand at the post of life and death, something I discuss at length in the last half of my thesis concerning the philosophy of medicine."

Professor Perra bent his head back down to leaf through the pages.

"You are no doubt aware of my interest in anesthesia," Nora began. "And more recently, in surgical remedies for the complications of childbirth. My research has identified a number of useful principles to guide surgeons and physicians. I have also made a study of the philosophical pillars that should support them."

Venturoli flipped through the thesis, scanning it. Had he even read it?

"While the physical properties of anesthesia continue to be documented, the moral question of anesthesia is debated almost to the point of violence. And though cesarean surgeries can save lives, too many doctors are convinced these surgeries are an abomination. We must address not only the medical results of anesthesia, but the philosophical uncertainties as well."

"These are not new findings, Miss Beady," Professor Venturoli said, circling a hand impatiently. "This is not a first-year examination where we test your abilities to parrot known information."

"There were two cesareans performed in Bologna this year," Professor Barilli put in. "And three deaths, a 150 percent mortality rate. And yet you advocate the procedure?"

Nora clenched the pencil in her hand and beat back the specter of Paola and her dead child. "Yes. Unfortunately we lost both mothers and one child." The other doctors frowned and Venturoli looked ready to stand and leave. "But," Nora continued, "one child was dead before we began, and both children would surely have perished had we not intervened. We turned four deaths into three."

Professor Fabbri ruffled his black mustache. "You are racing ahead. We will discuss your thesis after a thorough examination of your medical knowledge."

The other doctors nodded and Nora swallowed. She was grateful they could not see her legs shake beneath her long skirts.

Fabbri stared at her as if assessing where to begin his interrogation. She was glad Magdalena had warned her to keep quiet because his words came at an achingly slow pace. He started questioning her on the pathology of the womb and continued with theories of the cesarean. She made sure to mention Tarsizio's tutoring of Maria Dalle Donne, the first and only female director of midwifery at the university. When Fabbri again fell into silence, Venturoli picked up the inquiry with his favorite subject, hernias. Here Nora had the advantage, being able to explain her successful hernia surgery in London—the one Sagese and Barilli had praised so many months before. Barilli's lips pressed together and Venturoli's turned up at the corners. She crossed her fingers, hoping she had at least won him over.

Barilli leaned hard into the lymphatic and nervous systems, and when he couldn't discourage her, he leaped without warning to the male reproductive system.

He wants me to squirm. Nora straightened her back to the point of pain and answered tersely, though her cheeks warmed as she stood alone before their critical eyes. Epididymis and vas deferens caused her no pain, but she forced herself not to stutter on the Italian words for scrotum, testicles, and erection— Barilli's attempt to make her look as brazen as the accusations swirling round her. She kept her eyes on the tabletop in front of the men, not daring to let her scorching face meet Perra's.

There was no clock on the wall. The curtains made it impossible to judge the movement of the sun across the sky. Nora only knew the passage of time by the sweat collecting in her palms and the ache in her feet and the back of her legs.

Perra had kept silent. The other doctors leaned forward in anticipation, scrutinizing his tone and posture, suspicion in their eyes. He raised his eyes from his paper. "Miss Beady, would you like to take a seat?"

She blinked, her heart falling as Barilli rolled his eyes theatrically. "No, Professor. I am used to standing for long periods." Her hips ached to lower onto the chair behind her but she didn't dare now he had offered.

"Suit yourself," he said and put his papers down. "What do you plan to do with a prestigious degree from the University of Bologna if it were granted to you?"

It wasn't a question of pathology or anatomy. The doctors grew still, their eyes focusing with new intensity on her face.

"I plan to honor it by practicing the art of medicine," she replied, trying to hide her unease.

Perra's black eyes had a gleam of pity, tinged with victory. "But, Miss Beady, this is not allowed where you live, correct?"

She breathed faster. "To my knowledge, no woman has tried to register yet."

He nodded as if amused by her naivete. "I fear that a degree in your hands would be fairy dust. You would sail away and it would dissolve to nothing before you touched the shores of England."

Fabbri was squinting in concentration. "We cannot award degrees based on where a student wants to practice—" he interrupted.

"No," Perra agreed, his gaze level and direct as he stared into Nora's eyes. "But I will not be made a joke. I will not award our degree to someone who wants only to play at medicine for a year or two."

She lifted one foot minutely to relieve her throbbing arch. "I have applied myself diligently to every study and class. I spent the first year attending lectures I could hardly understand, laboriously translating notes from fellow students—" *Like Pozzi.* Her breath hitched and she schooled the tremble in her chin.

She blinked and reset her shoulders. Unlike Pozzi, she had this chance, and no matter what happened, her result could not be as unfair as his. With fresh courage, she met Perra's eyes. "I came here at your encouragement, at Dr. Croft's expense, and at great personal sacrifice. I do not know if I will find a place to practice in England, but I mean to try. And if that door is closed to me, I will pry open another one elsewhere. Medicine is not a game to me. It is a calling."

"Very well," Perra murmured. "You will then enlighten us on the dosages and uses of hydrocyanic acid—"

After another long quizzing on botany and medications, Nora at last had to submit and accept the chair. Her feet were trembling with pain and her head was light.

"Shall we return to the thesis?" Barilli asked.

There was more? Nora's throat was so dry that she nodded and swallowed, feeling her tongue stick to the roof of her mouth.

Dr. Venturoli consulted his watch and sniffed. "I think it best we be concise. I am wanted by the cardinal this evening."

Nora sighed silently. For better or worse, let it end soon.

Barilli jumped straight to the attack. "Your table on page nineteen does not take into account the higher infection rate when dealing with the abdominal cavity."

Hiding her exhaustion, Nora explained she had little information to go on but found infection rates when opening the womb to be generally lower than when opening the stomach or bowels. After she'd placated him, she tried to quiet Fabbri's fears that cesareans resulted in delayed menstruations for the mother and poor respiratory health for the life of the child. Venturoli had to be painstakingly reassured that the absence of pain during surgery due to ether did not congest the nervous system and suppress the flow of blood after surgery, or keep a mother's milk from coming in.

The red light from the windows had darkened so gradually that Nora realized she could no longer read the papers in her lap, and Venturoli was making an exasperated show of lighting a lamp.

"One more question, Signorina Beady."

In the shadowy light, Perra's eyes had softened. Instead of studying her with indifference or dislike, she felt the pull of an unspoken plea. "What have you learned in Bologna that you could not learn in London?"

Her eyes widened. The other doctors disappeared from her view and mind. A tumult of images rushed her memory: Magdalena pointing to the screaming statues, Pozzi's trembling limbs, Paola's purple mouth, the orange sun fingering the

medieval alleys, the confused jumble of voices in her first lecture. She gave her head a small shake to make the pictures fall
into an intelligible order.

"I learned what it was to have the freedom to learn,
Professor. I may have been an oddity, but I was *allowed*, even
befriended by a few." She swallowed. "And I've assisted in surgeries never attempted in England. Twice! And in the lives of
Donne, and Manzolini, and Marenco, I discovered my own
possibilities. In London I learned techniques, pathology, and
anatomy from a truly great surgeon, for which I am thankful.
But I was a shadow there, working out of sight. In the Città
Rossa, I am not a phantom. I am real."

Nora looked up, not for the first time, at the fresco painted
high over the teacher's desk. The Virgin Mother peered down
at her, her hands clasped on the wriggling Christ Child who
was clutching her collar. The holy woman studied Nora, her
eyes expectant and serious. *Stand your post*, she seemed to say.

The men turned away from her and muttered in low voices
impossible for her exhausted mind to distinguish. As they con-
ferred, she kept her eyes on the only other woman in the room.

"Miss Beady—"

Nora snapped her attention back to the desk, her nerves
buzzing with a new surge of alertness. Perra was the one speaking, his lips unsteady with emotion. "After consultation, it is our
solemn responsibility and privilege to award you a doctorate of
the arts in medicine from the renowned University of Bologna
on this, Friday the twelfth of December, the year of our Lord
1847."

Nora's lungs refused to draw air. She struggled to her feet, her eyes stinging. They were waiting for her to say something, but Barilli's firm mouth warned her not to show too much emotion.

"*Grazie*," she choked out. "*Grazie mille.*"

She wanted to wring their hands and beg confirmation that she had heard correctly. Instead, she folded her fingers around the handle of her bag and waited for instruction.

"We fully expect your degree to be used to register you as a working doctor." Perra's stern words made her nod fervently.

"*Si, Professore,*" she promised.

Fabbri smiled at her and extended his hand. His black mustache ruffled good-naturedly. "*Congratulazioni,*" he cried as he folded her hand in his. He complimented her Italian and told her he would miss her in his classes.

Venturoli bowed a hasty acknowledgment as he gathered his things to make his appointment with the cardinal. Barilli's eyebrows knotted, and he approached reluctantly. "If I ever travel to London, I would very much like an introduction to Dr. Croft," he said. "Please relay to him my best wishes for a speedy recovery."

"It would be my honor," she answered, despite the cold fear in her stomach at the mention of Horace. *Let him be well.*

Professor Perra managed a crooked grin. "If I know my colleague, Magdalena will be waiting outside for you in a towering temper. You've been in here for six and half hours."

Nora balked. "Was it truly that long? She told me she wouldn't wait."

"Women tell people a great many things," he said, a bitter edge to his voice. "Congratulations." He slung his coat over his arm and left without a word, following the other professors out the door, their footsteps soon dwindling to silence.

Nora stepped forward, then stopped, turning her eyes up to the fresco of Mary. She'd never see it again. The woman smiled over the head of her child, like so many other women Nora had seen, carrying on conversations despite the infants venturing across their laps. Nora smiled back, then turned the wick knob of the oil lamp, plunging the room into darkness.

CHAPTER 32

I can't believe it," Nora said numbly when she staggered into the corridor and found Magdalena and Mrs. Phipps waiting for her. Magdalena was the first to embrace her.

"Try." Mrs. Phipps, never demonstrative, was a yard away, beaming fiercely.

"I can't believe I got any votes. Especially Perra's," she said quietly.

"He's angry, not a fool." Magdalena picked up Nora's hand and squeezed it. "I'm proud of you. Furious, but still proud."

Nora looked a question at her.

"Did you think I wouldn't hear?" Magdalena said quietly. "Your landlady is sad to be losing you. I know all about the traveling coach hired to take you to Venice and the berths booked on the London mail packet." She forced a grin. "I know Mrs. Phipps rolls your underclothes instead of folding them when she packs your trunks. Your landlady doesn't think that very wise."

Nora gathered her breath. It felt like her legs had been knocked clean away. She wasn't ready for this. "There seemed little point in saying anything. I might not have passed and—"

"You intended to sail anyway."

"I knew you wouldn't approve."

"Of you abandoning your studies? Certainly not. But even now I hate losing you." Magdalena swallowed and blinked her brimming eyes. "Either way, it isn't my place to tell you what to do. You are a grown woman. And you are a friend. I will miss you."

Nora couldn't speak. She reached for Magdalena and held her tight, the parchment slipping from her fingers and fluttering to the floor.

"Careful," Mrs. Phipps squeaked, and lunged after it, cradling it to her chest.

Magdalena laughed shakily. "I was angry for a very few minutes. I told myself not to say anything until you did, but—"

"I wouldn't have left without saying goodbye," Nora said, relaxing the embrace only enough to hold Magdalena at the elbows. "I swear."

"I know. But I decided to make it easier for you—"

"Impossible," Nora said. Her mouth crumpled, and she hid her face in Magdalena's shoulder. "But thank you."

"You are impossible," Magdalena said and sniffed. A patch of damp grew on Nora's right shoulder. "Don't ever stop. There aren't enough impossible women."

"I won't," Nora promised.

———

Nora was not asleep. The last few articles were packed, including her parchment, carefully stowed in an embossed leather folder. She'd gone to the hospital already and bid goodbye to as many of the sisters as she could find. With her thoughts full of them, of Magdalena and Pozzi, and so many others, she was too jittery to sleep.

She started when she heard someone pound at Signora Carnicelli's door but didn't rise. This noise couldn't have anything to do with her. She had no practice, no patients of her own. This wasn't even her house, just her last night in these rented rooms.

The hammering continued until Nora heard Signora Carnicelli rouse herself. Murmuring fretfully, she answered the door. All was quiet then, until Nora heard footsteps on the stairs.

Her door opened, and a shaft of candlelight fell across the floor. "Signorina Beady," the landlady hissed. "There is a doctor here for you."

Perra. It had to be. All this time, she'd been thinking so hard of everyone except him. She thought about sending him away, then rejected the idea. "Tell him to wait," Nora said, and dressed.

Signora Carnicelli had lit a lamp in the parlor, but the room was still dim. Perra was striding back and forth, but he stopped when he saw her, revealing a stricken face.

"Why are you here?" she asked.

"You are leaving?" he demanded bitterly.

"I told you I never meant to stay."

"And you got what you wanted." He laughed bitterly. "If I'd known it would mean your immediate departure, I wouldn't have voted for you. No matter how my colleagues disagreed."

Nora's eyes tightened. "I hope you don't mean that. I would have boarded the ship with or without my degree."

"Without a goodbye?" Perra opened his hands in supplication.

"Do you deserve one? What did you tell people? I could hardly get Barilli to speak to me."

"I told nothing!"

Nora raised her eyebrows.

"But I didn't contradict anything, either."

Nora turned away. Even with her eyes closed, even after long breaths, her voice was high and tight. "No, you didn't, and in the meantime I've been shunned, humiliated, and insulted."

Even Sister Madonna Agnes, so gentle and tolerant to everyone, had been guarded in her goodbyes. Nora had brushed away the pain of it, but it returned now with double force.

"Forgive me. I turned my back on you. I was hurt, jealous. Shamed. And even though you have decided, I must ask you again. Please, Eleanora. Don't leave. I can't—" He drew an unsteady breath. "Even if we only remain colleagues, I cannot lose you."

Nora's folded arms gripped tighter as the discomfort and shame she'd endured for weeks scorched her skin again. "I don't love you. Even if I had, how could I love you now?" Her voice broke and tears streaked down her cheeks. In spite of herself, she glanced back at him. "You left me to fight alone. You let me be punished for an affair that never happened. You pushed me aside and all the professors followed suit."

He flinched as if struck, his face crumpling. "I'm so sorry. Let me make it right."

Her mouth twisted. "But it's all done now. They already think me tainted."

"I'll kill any rumors," he promised, closing the space between them. "I've already told the professors. And I'll be content with whatever kindness you can give me. Let me be mentor. Let me be father or brother. I believe in time—"

Nora shook her head. "It's useless, Salvio. Magdalena is my mentor. My father is Horace Croft. I can't forget how you treated me, however much I would like to. Let this idea go. Let us part with your initial kindness intact, Salvio. You brought me here. Let me leave with your name a blessing on my lips and not a curse."

"You are sure that is all I can give you?"

Nora nodded, not trusting her voice.

He shuddered and reached for the pocket of his coat. "You are wrong, *cara mia*."

She smelled the inescapable scents of the hospital on his clothes as he reached toward her. She watched him warily.

"This is for you. I hoped to convince you, but I came prepared."

Nora looked. In his outstretched hand was a folded paper. He motioned with his eyes, telling her to read. Nora took the paper and angled it into the light.

Written in Latin, it said:

I, Dr. Salvio Perra, Professor at the University of Bologna, Chair of Anatomy, and President of the Grand Hospital of Life and Death, recommend Dr. E. Beady of London, England, without reservation. While completing studies in Bologna and working under the tutelage of myself and the noted obstetrician Dr. M. Marenco, Dr. Beady demonstrated skills, knowledge, and dedication of the highest caliber. Dr. Beady's expertise in anesthesia and obstetrics is

*unparalleled, and will be an asset to any hospital, patient,
or medical practice.*

> *Salvio Perra,*
>
> *Bologna, Italy,*
>
> *12 December 1847*

The letter trembled as she brought it to her chest like a child. "You didn't have to—"

"Yes, I did." His eyes were soft, tender. In one swift gesture he leaned forward and kissed her forehead, and then each cheek, his lips lingering against her wet skin.

"*Addio*," he breathed against her ear, using the Italian word for *goodbye forever*, instead of his usual *alla prossima*, or *at the next*.

Nora's stomach flexed as she leaned into an unexpected pain.

"*Addio*." The word broke on her lips. "*Grazie di cuore*."

Perra pressed his lips together, fighting for his last words. "*Voglio invecchiare con te*." *I want to grow old with you.* He cast one more glance, saw the pain on her face, and added, "But I see that is not to be."

He left, but a barren chill remained in the space where he'd stood, like the cool sea wind that would envelop her soon and carry her away.

CHAPTER 33

LONDON CAME INTO VIEW SLOWLY, THROUGH A VEIL OF stained fog and drizzle. The agonizing, yet entirely uneventful voyage was at last complete, but Nora stood on deck beneath her umbrella, trying to contain her impatience as the sailors shouted meaningless things about gangways and moorings.

Mrs. Phipps touched her arm. "Leave the baggage to me. You go on."

"Are you sure?"

Mrs. Phipps smiled. "You'll feel better once you see him."

Nora wasn't as certain. If anything, her confidence had eroded during their passage. She was afraid of not finding Horace at all, afraid of finding him broken beyond healing and repair, afraid of finding Daniel changed and remote or not as she remembered. And what would he think of her? Her hair was longer, her skin darker, and anxiety had left her thinner than ever. She'd kissed another man and become used to giving commands. All in all, she was everything a young lady ought not to be. Yet on the whole, she was satisfied with who she was. "I hope so," Nora said. "But if you'd rather go…"

Mrs. Phipps shook her head. "Go on. I would…" She drew a long breath and tried again. "I'd be grateful if you went first."

"Of course." Nora squeezed her hand, feeling stronger because they were both afraid. A minute later, she was in a hackney, the imaginary sway of the ocean still pulling her body as the horse slogged over muddy roads. She knit her fingers tightly together, her heart pounding jaggedly in her throat.

The city—her home—looked different. She'd forgotten, without realizing it, that London was the most populous city in the world and that poverty looked different here than in Bologna. Want had looked happier there, in a city where eating songbirds was a delicacy, not a sign of desperation, where fruit filled the markets year round and porticos sheltered everyone equally from wind and rain. The faces Nora saw through the carriage's grimy windows were white and pinched from the January cold.

She stared at her lap, counting the turns until Great Queen Street, when at last the house loomed into view. She frowned. The bronze plaque at the front door was gone, and the door itself—it used to be dull green—was now a glossy black, increasing her foreboding, though there was no funeral wreath and only the second-floor curtains were drawn.

They were not, she noted, the same curtains.

Daniel had apprised her of the changes but reading about the carpenters had not prepared her for the result of their work. Nora clambered from the coach before it had fully stopped and stared in amazement. All traces of soot on the stones were gone. The railings around the basement windows were newly painted and a stained-glass window had been installed above the front door showing a blue caduceus, the serpent-twined stick representing medicine. There were topiaries on the whitewashed steps that matched the ones in front of the house next door. Nora's feet veered closer because she didn't trust her eyes. Yes, the topiaries were the same and so was the black paint, and there was a second, larger window here with the same blue glass staff, this time surrounded by palm leaves in shades of green. She'd expected changes, but nothing like this.

Nora advanced on numb feet that barely managed to carry her back to her customary door. Instead of entering, she caught herself reaching for the knocker.

You're being ridiculous, she told herself, but when she extracted the key she'd kept so long and carefully, it no longer fit and she felt herself fighting tears.

Her desperate, peremptory rattling of the knocker had no immediate effect. She tried again and—

"Can I help you, madam—" John, the orderly, who never opened the front door, gaped at her, his eyes fighting between recognition and disbelief. "Miss Nora? It's really you?"

"It's me." Nora's eyes traveled behind him, collecting strange details: a marble entry, a missing wall where the dining room should be, and strangely enough, a flowered vase displayed beautifully on a column. "But I'm hardly certain I'm at the right house," she said as he hurried her inside and took her valise.

"It's a sight changed. As are you." Grinning broadly, he stuck his head out the door and looked down the street. "Where's Mrs. Phipps?"

"Following behind with our trunks." She could see into the drawing room and observed a lace doily laid across Horace's favorite chair. *Cosa in nome di Dio?*

God's name has nothing to do with any of this, Nora corrected herself silently, in English. Perhaps the temporary housekeeper had things more in hand than Nora imagined.

"John? Did you answer the door?" A musical voice, far unlike the tones she'd imagined for Mrs. Crawford, floated from the hallway. Nora turned in time to see a young woman appear, her aquamarine eyes the same color as the Italian lakes and her thick blond hair set in a becoming style. Their eyes met, mirroring equal surprise.

"Mrs. Trimble, this is the lady o' the house," John announced.

"Mrs. Trimble?" Nora repeated, fighting through confusion.

"Miss Nora?" The woman's face lit with comprehension, and Nora found her hand encased in small, soft fingers whose grip was surprisingly strong. "How can it be? From Italy! Are you well?" The woman was pulling Nora in, kissing her cheek.

Nora barely heard the questions over the working of her mind. "Mrs. Trimble?" she tried again. "Harry's wife?"

"Julia to you." The woman beamed, her face quick and bright and kind. "You'll turn them all on their heads when they know you're here."

"All of them?" Nora's eyes flicked over the strange foyer, looking for evidence of Horace. No discarded papers...or parts. Anxiety tightened Nora's face. She must ask but found her numb lips unwilling.

Julia Trimble frowned at the change in Nora's expression. As recognition dawned, her hand flew to her open mouth as if she'd made a terrible mistake. "I am so sorry. How terrible of me—"

Blackness gathered at the edges of Nora's mind, as sounds echoed hollowly in her ears. Julia was still speaking but a sick coolness was creeping over Nora's skin.

"I should have said first thing, but you surprised me so," Julia continued. "Dr. Croft is upstairs, convalescing."

Nora released her breath as if it had been punched from her, her eyes hot with tears. She must hear it again. She turned to John. "Is he?" she pleaded.

"He's past the worst danger, as Dr. Gibson puts it."

"Daniel?" Her ears collected only silence though she strained to hear his voice, his footfall on this new stone floor.

"He's making calls at present. He had no idea—"

"Where is Horace?" Nora cut John off before he finished.

"In his same room." Julia smiled and pointed up the stairs. "Don't wait another second, but if you shock him the way you shocked us—"

Nora didn't hear the rest over the pounding of blood in her ears and her boots on the stairs. A tear fell as she gained the second story. Mrs. Trimble was right, though; she must not fly at Horace. He wasn't ready for such shocks.

His door was open enough to peek inside. Horace sat by the window in a chair with a tray in front of him, struggling to cut a piece of chicken while an older woman who could only be Mrs. Crawford looked on.

Dear God. Nora exhaled. He was alive, but... She pushed open the door with shaking hands and stepped into the room.

The knife fell with a clatter. "Nora?"

Only faintly hearing the housekeeper's cry of surprise, Nora measured her steps, promising she wouldn't rush him, but found herself on her knees at his side. She didn't flinch at how awkwardly he caught her hands.

"My dear girl."

"You're here." Her eyes were leaking. "I was so afraid."

"I'm not made of glass," he grumbled. "Stand up, and let me up so I can see you properly." He wasn't exactly clumsy pushing out of his chair, but his left hand looked less willing than the rest of him. Mrs. Crawford offered an arm, but he waved her away.

"Is Phipps here?" he said, scouring the doorway with searching eyes.

"She's bringing the luggage behind me," Nora promised.

"Then you'll not be needed," he said to the housekeeper. "You are released at once."

The housekeeper didn't look nearly as horrified as Nora at this declaration. She rolled her eyes. "About the thanks I expected from a wart like you. And welcome home to you, miss. I'm anxious to see Alice. I'll leave you two to catch up." Her voice came out bored and phlegmatic despite Horace's abrupt termination of her employment. "Make sure he finishes his supper."

Nora waited until she heard the soft close of the door. That was different too—the effect of new carpets and hinges. "Looks like Mrs. Phipps knew exactly who could tame you," she teased, looking to the door Mrs. Crawford had just closed.

"Tamed!" Horace scoffed. "She's a tyrant. And stingy with cake!"

Nora laughed, her grateful tears dropping against smiling lips. "I've missed you so much," she said. And had been so afraid she'd not get the chance to tell him.

He gave an irritated wave of his hand that made her fear for his steadiness. "Daniel didn't tell me you were coming."

"Did you think I would stay in Italy when you weren't well? I rushed home."

Horace smiled weakly, disengaging, and sitting down heavily. "Of course I'm happy to see you, but eventually you'll have to go back and—Damn it all. Daniel shouldn't have frightened you." The fingers of his good hand drummed on the arm of his chair. "I'm flattered my dear, I truly am, but this flight back to England is unlike you. Didn't you consider the practicalities?" His words slurred when he tried to rush them, but his characteristic displeasure made her want to hug him and dance about the room. If he was only worried about her studies…

"Practicalities be damned," she whispered through her smile. "Stop looking like a thundercloud. Heaven knows I didn't expect an effusive homecoming, but this is awful even for you." She bent to peck his leathery cheek. "You are irreplaceable."

He huffed and told her to bring over a chair. Nora took the footstool instead, not wanting to move out of reach, even for a second. He smiled at this, but said nothing, tucking her hand in his. "I suppose we both are rather silly. Still, you shouldn't have left your studies early to come check on me," he insisted. "There's such a thing as postage."

"I didn't leave early, Horace." She clung to her secret a moment longer, because it was too delicious on her lips not to savor. "My degree is in my portfolio."

He stared, motionless, absorbing her words. "So soon?" he asked, his voice stunned and quiet. "You are a doctor?"

The whispered word falling from his lips and the flash of pride on his face choked her. She blinked, trying not to show weakness, and nodded instead.

He gave her arm several slow pats as he gazed over her head. "Less than two years."

"You didn't think it would take me the full three when I'd already spent ten years training with England's greatest surgeon?"

Horace's expression changed, fell into a blank gaze as he stared at his left hand resting in his lap. "Surgeon," he murmured. "At least one of us is, now."

The smile fell from her face; her stomach followed. "How bad is it, Horace?"

He frowned and allowed himself a sigh. "I can't grip well with my left hand and I've foot drop. No dorsiflexion. Perhaps some control will come back. Difficult to say."

She squeezed his hand. "I feared much worse."

"Your degree. Let me see it." Struggling up on his weak arm, he was halfway out of his chair before she could stop him.

"Stay here. I'll fetch it." Her bag was on the floor just inside the door. Thumbing past her instrument case (at some point she'd persuade Horace to let her examine him), she retrieved the folder with Perra's recommendation and her parchment.

Horace snatched the portfolio the moment she was within reach, attacking the ribbons that fastened it. He picked up the parchment and angled it into the window's gray light.

Nora knew every word by heart, but Horace stared at the Latin words so long it seemed he too was committing them to memory.

"Well done, my dear." When he looked up, the familiar twinkle was back in his eye. He patted her hand. "Is Barilli the same man who publishes on hernias?"

Barilli's scornful sneer glinted through the fog of her mind, muted by the cold London weather. "He's a singular man, self-serving, who didn't like me at all. But he was on my exam board and passed me. He expects special treatment from you, I'm afraid."

Horace flicked his mouth in resignation. "I'll send him some trinket. But not my bones from the Amazonian eel."

"You got one at last, did you?" Nora's eyes were searching through the droplets on the window for a carriage to halt and release Mrs. Phipps, but there was nothing to see except black-topped hackneys moving gloomily through the drizzle. "I think Barilli is more of a fountain-pen type of man."

From the look on Horace's face, that sank Barilli even lower in his regard. His eyes kept roaming to the doorway.

"Tell me how Daniel is before I see him."

"Not as changed as you," Horace said with a lifted eyebrow. Nora's stomach tumbled.

"Will he approve?" she asked jokingly, but not entirely so. Her tongue wanted to finish with one more question she could not bring herself to ask. *Do you?*

"I have a feeling he'll like the extra freckles." Horace scanned her like a specimen. "Your color is good. They didn't overfeed you, did they?"

Not exactly reassuring, but typical. She turned away to conceal the anxiety gripping her.

"Nora." Horace's voice was strange, almost scolding. "He'll be beside himself."

She dabbed at her eyes, schooling her breath. "The house is beautiful."

"Oh, the house!" he exclaimed. "You must see it at once."

Nora gave him a hand as he lurched to his feet.

"What *have* you done?" The voice from the threshold made them both turn. Mrs. Phipps was trying to cover her excitement behind a straight mouth that was not cooperating. "I can't even recognize the place. And that monstrosity in the library? Must you have the entire creature on display? Would not a head suffice?"

"It's an African zebra, as you well know. And you left me with a despot. If I put my work down, it disappears while my back is turned. At least this way she cannot carry it off and hide it."

Mrs. Phipps moved forward, her brow furrowed. "I hope by now Mrs. Crawford's trained you a bit better than I ever did." Her brisk facade faltered as pity softened her mouth. "Did you forget to take care of yourself?"

His nose lifted in distaste, but only one side, wrecking the full effect. "I'm in no danger. Except tedium. I can't cut."

That gave Mrs. Phipps an excuse to let a small laugh escape. Nora saw the way she clutched the pocket of her skirt and knew she was holding herself back from the embrace her arms wanted to give but her practical mind would never allow.

"Did you show him?" Mrs. Phipps asked her. There was so much to say and show that Nora didn't know at first—

"I saw it," Horace answered, glancing to the degree as if there were no other thing in existence. "She managed the impossible."

Mrs. Phipps flashed him a knowing smile, something

secret, as only passes between proud parents. Their mutual satisfaction traveled almost visibly round the room, striking Nora in its path. She took a small breath and blinked hard.

"Of course she did," Mrs. Phipps agreed.

CHAPTER 34

THE LIGHT WAS FADING WHEN NORA LEFT HORACE WITH Mrs. Phipps, who promised to watch him. Indeed, Mrs. Phipps seemed reluctant to cede his care to anyone else, even her old friend, Mrs. Crawford, and Horace had been more energetic in her company. All through the evening, he'd resisted returning to sleep, pressing them for stories. They'd obliged, but Nora kept dropping sentences when she thought she heard a sound downstairs, her nerves strained with the thought of Daniel returning home. When Mrs. Crawford and Julia brought in trays of tea and sandwiches, they were invited to stay and listen, and so the evening passed in a lighthearted way Nora had not experienced in months.

When Horace's eyes drifted closed in the middle of a description of Dr. Marenco's forceps delivery of a past-term baby girl, Nora extracted her hand from his, picked up the empty tea tray, and nodded conspiratorially at Mrs. Phipps. "I doubt anyone else is interested in what stitches I used," she whispered. "The hour is late. I'll tell you all good night." Mrs. Crawford protested and tried to take the tray, but Nora shook her head. "I'd like to stretch my legs," she insisted quietly, and tiptoed from the room.

The hall was dark and Nora moved slowly, her hand tracing

the unfamiliar texture of the new paper on the walls, feeling her way to the stairs. She could find her own way to the kitchen and was curious what the remodel had made of Cook's dank domain.

The door at the end of the downstairs hall was partly open. Nora nudged it aside with her hip. After she dealt with the tray, she'd rummage around for candles. For now, there was just enough light to locate the basin beneath the rain-washed window and see a glinting coal stove where the old Rumford range used to be. She poured out the dregs of tea and stacked the empty cups.

As she made her way back to the empty foyer, the front door swung slowly open, revealing a man's silhouette shaded against the gray dusk. Her heart stopped, but his sagging shoulders and automatic movements—unlacing, then toeing off his muddy shoes, setting them carefully just outside the door— meant he hadn't seen her. The hall was too dark, and she was in shadow. He stepped inside, his stocking feet leaving wet prints but making no sound. His hair, windblown, damp, and two weeks past the time for trimming, drooped across his brow.

"Daniel?" She didn't mean to whisper. Her voice had no strength for more.

His head snapped up like a man startled from sleep, searching until he found her in the shadows by the staircase.

"Nora?"

Her lips were numb. Her eyes, accustomed to the dark, traced the tired lines of his face, the weary shoulders. "I came home."

"How?" The lone word was rough, unsteady. "How are you here?" He was somehow several feet closer to her.

"On the mail packet from Venice. Then a hackney," she recited, knowing he wasn't asking for particulars. Her paralyzed brain couldn't come up with anything else. She felt the air between them as if it were a solid obstacle holding their years apart and all the anxiety of the future.

"I meant what miracle—" He stretched out both arms, drawing her like a comet, embracing her in a grip that dissolved her hesitation. Even when he released her, the feel of his arms lingered. His hands found her face and he pressed his cold fingers into her skin, as if convincing himself she was flesh, not phantom. She opened her mouth to answer, but he pressed her close and they spoke in kisses instead.

His lips traced hers, and she found the answer to her doubts in the supple corners of his mouth, replied in the broken breath of relief that escaped between her teeth.

He was not ravenous or scorching like Perra. He was solid and warm, a piano newly tuned with every note sounding joyfully. She couldn't bear to open her eyes. The swelling in her stomach and chest deserved concentration unbroken by sight or sound.

When he did release her, it was only inches, pressing her cheek to his own to exchange only the most necessary words. "Why didn't you tell me you were coming?"

"I did. Two days before we left, I sent an express. Our ship must have beat it here from Bologna."

"But your schooling…"

"I'm finished."

This time he positioned her far enough away to study her face in the faint light, his troubled eyes squinting. "You quit?"

She reached and covered his hand in her own. "No. I finished." Her smile broke into a shattered laugh. "I did it." He shook his head in disbelief as she continued. "I have my degree from the University of Bologna."

"No," he breathed in wonder.

Again he didn't wait for an answer, telling his feelings with kisses instead of words until, breathless, he paused and brushed back her hair with a curving finger, tucking it behind her ear. "You proved yourself. And you came home."

Did she imagine that there was more astonishment in his last words than the first?

"Of course." She searched his eyes. "Why do you seem surprised?"

He embraced her again. "Never mind. Have you been with Horace?"

"Yes." She held him back as he turned to the stairs. "He's fine. He's sleeping, but he should have some broth when he wakes. I was going to tell the maid." Nora grinned at him. "But perhaps she'll need to rescue your shoes first? I haven't seen rain or mud like this since I left."

He flicked her question away. "They can stay outside on the step. Both the cook and the maid are nursing family in town with diphtheria."

"Is it still very bad?" She measured him again with her eyes. "You look so tired."

"There are fewer cases now, but with Horace down I've had twice the load—"

"Sir, my apologies." John appeared in the hallway and hurried forward. "I had stepped out to fetch your dinner."

"Is there a plate for Miss Beady?" Daniel asked, submitting to the servant's attempts to help him out of his coat.

"Yes, sir, for both of you. Sandwiches and stew. And I'll fix your tea. It will be ready by the time you're in dry clothes." He disappeared into the kitchen.

"My coat took the worst of it," Daniel said. "I'm not letting you out of my sight now you're here. We both need to eat. I saw the way your eyes widened when John mentioned stew."

"I'm starving," Nora admitted. She'd had little appetite before, only picking at her food.

"Well, it won't be fancy, but I can feed you," Daniel said. "What did Horace say? How was the journey home? And your exams?"

Nora shook her head in a firm refusal. "Horace is tired from our long conversation and sleeping like a babe. You need to sit and rest and eat. You look ill, Daniel."

"Just tired, but I've forgotten all that already—" he broke off and grinned, but his eyes were solemn. "You are truly here?"

Nora shook her head, smiling like him, but with an earnest ache beneath. She pressed up onto her toes and kissed him. "Truly."

"Your voice sounds different," Daniel said, angling his head slightly. "I can hear the Italian lingering." He took her hand and led her into the sitting room where a fire burned in the grate. He went for the candles, but—

"I'll do that. Sit," Nora commanded.

Raising his hands in surrender—she'd forgotten how he used to do that—he fell into the sofa nearest the warmth of the fire, unable to hide the sigh that escaped, nor resist closing his eyes for a spell.

She sat by his side, taking up his limp hand, detecting no fever, just fatigue. "Tonight you must sleep. I can attend to Horace."

Daniel smiled as if she told a joke. "You just crossed the ocean, Nora. I imagine you need the rest more than I do." His hand found her head, and he stroked her hair as she laid her cheek against his shoulder. She tipped her chin up to see his face, but his smile was fleeting and quickly replaced by tight lines of pain thrown in relief by the orange light of the fire. "What is it, Daniel?"

Quickly his face smoothed and he patted her head. "I lost another child tonight. A beautiful infant girl."

Understanding filled the quiet. Daniel tugged her toward him, leading her to his lap where he gathered her close. "How can I be allowed such happiness when others are so tormented?"

"Perhaps we've had our own torments already," Nora offered, breathing in the scent of his shirt. "Perhaps now we are allowed to be happy."

Daniel's hold on her loosened a fraction as his face tightened. "I hope that's true." It sounded more lament than belief.

She pulled her head away from his chest and met his eyes. "What is it?"

"I would give anything to have good news for you right now, but besides his illness, Horace is in financial trouble," he said, the words measured. "Without his income, I don't know how we'll pay the debt on the house. He spends like a fiend when the mood's upon him."

"How bad?" Her voice sounded so calm, so reasonable, but her heart jumped tempo.

"I sold the antiques and the crystal. I'm trying to be discreet about it, but—"

Nora flinched. If the crystal was gone, they were desperate. "And I've been sending home bills from Italy," she whispered, guilt tightening her throat.

"It's not your fault—" Daniel began but Nora interrupted.

"How long do we have?"

"I've beat the creditors off for another month. Now that you're home, I could lecture again in the evenings while you see to Horace. I don't have his reputation, but some doctors will still be interested. Harry helps with the clinic and Horace's patients. Perhaps we'll get by."

Horace had insisted on tottering about the house this afternoon, showing her the new surgery and lecture theater. The laboratory and ice cellar. "Could we sell?" The words burned, causing her eyes to prick.

Daniel's face morphed into a mask of disgust, and he curled his lip. "Vickery went to the bank and tried to buy it out from under us when we missed a payment. I staved them off but Vickery knows we're still in trouble. The bank worries no one else would want such a large home with such unusual features. Vickery offered to take over the mortgage but not much more. If I can't keep up payments or sell for a decent price, Vickery will get Horace's life work for pennies on the pound."

"Vickery in our surgery?" Panic crept like a fog through her body.

"I've stopped him for now, but he can afford to wait. Once we default, he will simply buy it from the bankers." Daniel rubbed his eyes as if to scrub out the image.

"We won't let it happen." Nora's eyes wandered the room, the shadows changing with the jumping flames of the fire. "Did Horace truly spend it all?"

Daniel sighed. "The offer to knight him still stands. It is possible the title might spur some wealthy patron to give him a loan."

"Then he will be knighted," Nora said, her words steel.

"You know his opinions—"

"He will be knighted if I drag him there and push him to his knees. If he loses his surgery, it will kill him. His annoyance at being made a knight will only wound him."

"You could probably make him do it," Daniel said with a smile. "You know how he responds to my attempts at persuasion." His face was thinner than she remembered, and no wonder, given all he'd been contending with. Thank goodness he'd had help. She was more grateful than she could say that it had come from Harry and Julia.

"When did the Trimbles come?" Already she'd grasped that the vases of flowers, the doilies, the bowls of potpourri, even the neat loaves of bread cooling in the kitchen, were Julia's doing, not Mrs. Crawford's.

"For the past three weeks. Thank God. With so much diphtheria on top of everything else—"

The discussion turned to medicine and Harry and an exhaustive description of her exam, safer topics than longing and love and the size of the soft sofa, subjects that nudged persistently into the front of Nora's mind. "Have you seen your new rooms?" Daniel asked.

"They're beautiful. Mrs. Crawford did a lovely job."

Daniel's brow contracted. "I'll do everything I can to make sure you don't lose your home, Nora."

She kissed the worry on his forehead. "Don't think of it now. Tonight we should only be happy. Horace is recovering and we're together."

"Much more than I expected when I woke up this morning," he admitted, his cheeks creasing with a smile. "I suppose you're going to make us be proper and part for the night?"

An electrical current jolted her spine. Surely her everlastingly proper Daniel wasn't suggesting—

"I had hoped to sit here all night and not leave your side, but I'm selfish. You haven't slept in a real bed in weeks," he said.

No. He was proper still—though perhaps not quite so much as before. She'd been too long in Italy. Without hesitation she kissed him. "I'm the selfish one," she promised. "Given my way, I'd keep you here but you'll fall asleep in minutes and wake with a terrible crick in your neck. You'd best go. I'll see you tomorrow."

"If you're up early," he said as he stretched his long back. "I'll be leaving as soon as it's light."

Nora gave him a look. Had he forgotten? "I always beat you to the breakfast table."

Daniel grinned. "Still an early riser, then?" He kissed her cheek and the palm of her hand, turning it over to trace a triangle between three freckles dotting the back of her wrist. "These are new. I rather like them, but I like discovering other things haven't changed."

"Either way, I suppose I'm likely to surprise you," Nora said. "It's been a long time." She brushed the hair from his forehead.

"Before, I would have thought this wants cutting, but now I think it's dashing."

"Dashing?" He looked ready to laugh, but also pleased.

"Yes!" Nora said. If he stayed longer, she'd not be able to resist repeating their earlier kisses. Already this was too great a test for her endurance. "Best get out of here while you still can!"

He clambered off the couch. Heading to the door, in the loose-limbed walk she recognized, he glanced back. "That's new."

Pressing her lips together in a vain attempt to hide a ridiculous smile, Nora shook her head solemnly. "Not at all. You just didn't know it."

His eyebrows lifted, and he swayed where he stood, coming back toward her. "*Va via!*" Nora told him, shooing with both hands. "Go away! Good night!"

CHAPTER 35

DANIEL'S STEPS LAGGED AS HE REACHED THE FRONT stairs of 43 Great Queen Street. His face was deep in his collar, buried away from a blowing rain that just missed being classified as snow. It hit his skin as cold as the spray of the Arctic Ocean. He'd spent much of last night lying awake and staring at the ceiling, imagining Nora on the other side of the house. His decision to tackle errands instead of enjoying breakfast with her, watching the morning light illuminate her sunstreaked hair... Well, it had been tantamount to torture, but he'd done his duty, seen his patients and made the necessary call at the solicitor's office.

Daniel shook some of the wet from his sleeve and looked down the nearly empty street. If he were less greedy, he'd find some other errand to perform and postpone confessing today's failures. In spite of his best efforts and best arguments, he'd failed to find a new sponsor for the clinic and hospital at Great Queen Street.

But the frozen wind and his own impatience to be with Nora were too sharp to resist. He must see her face in the daylight and prove her impossible appearance last night had not been delirium. With his thoughts warring equally between eagerness and dread, he extracted his key from a damp coat pocket.

Laughter poured out at him the instant he opened the door. The hallboy hurried over to divest him of his sodden coat, hat, and umbrella. In the drawing room, Nora's voice mingled with Harry's brogue. Daniel followed it, drawn to the warmth of her happiness as much as the glow of the fireplace.

"Daniel!" She flew across the room and into his arms before he even realized he was reaching for her. His hands glided across her back, feeling the solid substance of her ribs, the weight of her arms around him. She was no spirit conjured by wishing.

"She's a witch, Daniel," Harry said, laughing. "Flew here on a broomstick last night and bursts in on me when I came back from hospital today with a 'Good morning, Harry' as if she were not gone this year and a half." Harry pointed to his shirt. "I'm wearing my coffee, thanks to her!"

Nora chuckled. "It will stain the new rug, and I still can't mind because I'll remember it all my life," she said. "I always told him not to sit balanced on two chair legs. He came down with such a crash Mrs. Crawford thought the builders had come back." She gestured to Julia who was wiping her eyes. "I couldn't have done it if Julia hadn't come up with the idea not to send word that I'd come home last night. You've met your match," Nora warned Harry.

Still shaking with suppressed amusement, she ran her hands over Daniel's frost-stung cheeks. "You're frozen," she murmured in a voice low enough to hook him by the belly. "And I'm just standing here laughing. To the fire," she ordered and pulled him close to the grate.

"Did you sneak out early to tend patients?" Julia asked.

Daniel shook his head but said nothing, not ready to break

the carefree mood. He cast his eyes over the scene, trying to paint it like a picture in his mind, but unable to ward off the fact that this fireplace, that sofa, the looking glass over the mantelpiece, the bed where Horace was convalescing, would all soon belong to Silas Vickery.

Thrown off by Daniel's quiet, Harry stopped laughing. "Did we lose another one?" he asked, his smile wiped away. "Is it Timothy Bevers?"

"No," Daniel assured him. "I've not seen Timothy today." He forced a smile. "It's this cold. I'd love to linger here by the fire, but Knowles's lecture is in an hour, and I had planned to go." The grin came easier when transferred to Nora. "Dr. Beady, you will join me?"

"Patrick Knowles?"

Harry nodded. "It's about time you attended a London lecture without hiding at the back. There are some decent minds in England, you know."

"I know that better than you," she retorted.

"We can introduce you as Dr. Beady." Harry's smile turned sly. "Or the future Mrs.—"

Daniel sent him a warning glance. No matter how glad he was to have Nora back, he was not ceding his proposal to a casual mention from Harry.

"Are you coming too, Harry?" Nora asked, and though her voice was steady, her cheeks flamed.

"He's not," Julia said, before Harry could answer. "I haven't seen him since yesterday, and—" She grinned. "Well, I'm sure adding a third to the party is quite unnecessary."

The surgical theater at St. Bartholomew's Hospital was as crowded and busy as Nora remembered it: high walls trapping the stuffy air and the rumbling conversations of doctors, surgeons, and students who jostled for better views of this afternoon's spectacle. Nora noted only one difference—her. Instead of sidling to the back, pretending she was taking notes for Dr. Croft, she had a place at the front tier of seats, supported by Daniel's arm. She appreciated his shielding her from the shifting crowd, but—"You won't be able to take any notes unless you let go of me," Nora whispered.

"The two of us can compare recollections later. I don't want to miss any part of Knowles's technique. Horace thinks him promising," Daniel said, adding with a murmur in her ear, "And I like being together, arm in arm."

The room quieted when Dr. Knowles and his assistant opened the leg of a young man whose bout with scarlet fever had left his tibia riddled with the disease. The sound of the chisel cracked violently in the room as he snapped off the infected portions, explaining that the remaining bone would create its own callus growth and strengthen over time. "It spares the limb," Dr. Knowles said with a grim frown. "Amputation is not a panacea."

He leaned into his work, and a piece of diseased bone broke free with a sound like a gunshot, making the man beside Daniel flinch. Perhaps to cover the start, he leaned close to Daniel and murmured, "So long as the sawed-up bone doesn't fill with more infection." Nora nearly answered with a clipped *Amputated bones fill with infection as well*, but she was not in Bologna. A second later, she regretted biting her tongue. She must begin as she meant to go on, and that didn't involve silence and deference. Caution and diplomacy, yes, but not timidity.

Afterward, when the patient was borne away, Daniel led Nora down to the table, where the doctor was wiping his ivory-handled tools and returning them to their nesting places in his velvet-lined case. "He has progressive views," Daniel whispered. "I think you should meet him."

"Dr. Knowles." Daniel extended his hand. "We are most impressed. That was a tidy bit of work."

Knowles smiled at Daniel and brushed off the compliment. Only then did he glance Nora's way. Hoping to win him over with her interest, she stepped closer. "I had a clear view of the bone, but I wasn't near enough to see how you selected where to cut." The man smiled indulgently. "It comes through years of study. I hope you don't feel too faint after my demonstration." He eyed Daniel, a reproof in his raised eyebrow.

Consciously maintaining her smile, Nora persisted. "I was curious if you were selecting your surgical margin through discoloring of the periosteum or if the infection had progressed to bony growths."

From the corner of her eye she caught the flicker of Daniel's mouth and knew his dark eyes would be dancing, however bland his expression.

Dr. Knowles fumbled the carved forceps that he was trying to put away. "What did you say?" He frowned at her as if she'd begun speaking gibberish.

"You have just met Dr. Beady, sir," Daniel explained. "I

know Horace has told you about his bright ward who studies medicine."

Dr. Knowles did not return Daniel's smile. He looked like the dumbfounded victim of a card trick. "I suppose that is why you brought her," Dr. Knowles said, speaking over Nora's head. "I was going to speak to you privately about her taking a place that might be filled by one of our young students, but—"

"I'm sorry for the misunderstanding, Dr. Knowles," Nora said. "Of course you want serious students in your lecture. I assure you, I am. I've a medical degree, like most of the others."

His eyebrows hitched even higher, and he mumbled something as he replaced his remaining tools into his kit. "I'm sure you have considerable intelligence. However, the practice of surgery also requires iron nerves and tremendous physical strength. You might be able to manage minor things such as the closing stitches. Many women are skilled with the needle, but toiling with the saw and chisel..." He chuckled. "You say you are qualified, but I'm afraid I can't imagine it. Of course, if you studied abroad, say in America—"

"My degree is from the University of Bologna," she informed him with some asperity. "A medical college older than any English university."

"How interesting," Dr. Knowles said, closing the buckles of his bag. "Well, if you want more details of this procedure, I am working on a monograph. No doubt you will see it once it is published. Excuse me, I'm afraid I must go."

He strode away quickly, vanishing into a crowd of men that somehow always remained a yard away from her.

"Pompous ass," Daniel muttered.

"You don't need to make enemies because of me," Nora said. "I saw the surgery at least. You and I can practice it next time we have a suitable body."

"You'll do it neater than Knowles," Daniel said.

"He'll never think so." Nora sighed. "Doesn't matter. I knew how it would be. Thank you for bringing me. Even with my degree, I couldn't have waded in here alone."

"Give them time to get used to you. Once they see you're on their side—" Daniel started.

"In science, yes. In sex, never. I can't be on their side." Nora scanned the room and watched as eyes darted away from her as if they hadn't been staring when her back was turned.

"They needn't embrace me," she mumbled to Daniel. "If they could just find me less an object of disdain, I'd be happy."

"Perhaps they stare because you are beautiful," he said in an undertone. "I do."

Before she could answer, a knot of students passed them on the way out of the theater, talking loudly and looking at each other so that they almost ran into Daniel and Nora. Halting feet away, their laughter cut off as if guillotined. "Dr. Gibson," one student said, apologizing for nearly running into him. He looked at Nora, his face pale. "Miss," he said.

She waited until she and Daniel gained the corridor and were out of earshot. "It's so easy to say we're ready to face them." Nora leaned against the iron stair rail, her voice as distant as the echoes of footsteps hurrying across the ward above them. "But when they stop in their tracks and stare like I'm an aberration, I always feel like I've swallowed a lead bar. I hate making you a spectacle as well."

She looked away from Daniel but his firm hand found her elbow, turning her, his body as close as her thick skirt and the public space allowed.

"When I feel I've swallowed lead, I simply imagine these small-minded men at home with their wives, if they are so fortunate to find one, being chided for working late or ruining another shirt with bloodstains. I compare that grim picture to my future life, working at your side, you wrinkling your nose as we discuss suture needles and tonics." He touched the tip of her nose and smiled when she flinched. "I think they are mad with envy, so they must imagine reasons to disapprove."

"Envy?" Nora raised her eyebrows, unconvinced.

He nodded. "Unfortunate, but unavoidable, from any man with eyes and sense."

"That's the problem, then," Nora said, smiling in spite of herself. "Most men have the first and completely lack the other."

"I have too much sense to argue with that," Daniel said, and grinned as he ushered her out the door.

CHAPTER 36

THE FRONT BELL SOUNDED A SHORT AND TIMID RING JUST
as Nora laid out her paints in the conservatory. Though
a deformed leg bone posed patiently on a white cloth on the
table, well lit by the soaring windows, the picture in her mind
was of red buildings and twisted alleys full of flapping linens.
Perhaps she could paint that, too. Later. Recollecting that Mrs.
Phipps was out and Mrs. Crawford was in the kitchen, Nora
gathered her skirts and hurried to the door, opening it gingerly.

A woman with a nervous frown stood on the doorstep,
wearing an elaborate silk dress that inadequately concealed her
heavy pregnancy. Her maid was at her elbow, in a dress more
simple but still finer than many of Nora's.

"Is Dr. Croft in?" When Nora hesitated, the woman pressed
on more defiantly. "I've written two letters but had no reply."

"Dr. Croft hasn't been well, my lady," Nora said placatingly,
guessing at the correct style of address. The woman didn't blink
at the title, so perhaps Nora had guessed right. "He hasn't seen
any patients for weeks."

The woman's face turned contrite. "I hope it's nothing too
serious."

"He's recovering at an encouraging pace. Please come in,"
Nora urged, hoping from the size of the rubies dangling from

the woman's ears, they might at least keep her business. "Perhaps one of the other doctors can help."

The woman crossed the threshold as quickly as a cat, and Nora nearly betrayed her astonishment by blinking.

"Are you the ward I've heard him talk about?" the elegant woman asked.

"I am. Miss Beady."

"From Italy?"

"I was there, yes. How—"

"He talked about you at Lady Stephenson's party. The guests were most interested." Words fell from the woman in a rush. "If he isn't able to see me, perhaps you—?" She glanced to the side again, as if fearing scrutiny, though the hall was empty but for them and the door to the street shut. "Would you speak to him? I fear he's displeased with me."

"I can't imagine that," Nora began. Horace had strong opinions, certainly, but he understood the necessity of diplomacy with wealthy patients. "Come into the parlor," she said. "I'll send for some refreshment." *And tease out your story in an order that makes sense.*

On entering the bright room, the lady relaxed visibly, no doubt soothed by the familiarity of a tasteful seating arrangement in richly patterned chintzes. Nothing medical intruded here, save the bone on the table in view of Nora's easel and paints, and Nora covered it quickly with a corner of the sheet.

"At Lady Stephenson's dinner, Dr. Croft and Dr. Gibson said—" The woman licked her lips and dropped her voice. "They said you were earning your degree as a doctor."

"Yes. I did." Nora smiled disarmingly, in case confirming this whispered suspicion alarmed the lady.

She didn't seem discomfited. She simply smiled and said on a sigh, "I do love Italy. Did you visit Venice?"

"Yes. It was quite remarkable." Nora had passed through in less than a day on her journey home but had spent three days there on the way to Bologna, with Salvio acting as tour guide to her and Mrs. Phipps. The memories weren't as pleasant now, knowing he'd harbored romantic hopes. "But I'm very happy to be home," she added.

The tea tray came before Nora could steer the conversation to the lady's concerns, but this was just as well. The familiar ritual of doling out cups and slices of lemon seemed to put her even more at ease. She leaned back on the sofa, cradling her cup. Her eyes were deeply shadowed, and the maid's protective gaze never left her.

"May we start from the beginning?" Nora asked. "Might I have your name?"

The lady laughed. "Forgive me. I've been so rattled. It's Rawlston. Athena Rawlston. My husband is Lord Woodbine." She moved her spoon through the tea slowly, correctly, not clinking against the cup.

"It's an honor to meet you, Lady Woodbine," Nora returned. "You are a patient of Dr. Croft's?"

"I was." She frowned uncertainly. "He attended me last year through a difficult miscarriage at about the sixth month. He was of the opinion that my husband and I shouldn't try for more children. He said it would be too dangerous."

"Did he say why?" Horace would have been entirely frank

on the subject, and resolute in his opinion since he'd decided to offer it. Lady Woodbine ran a covert finger against the side of her swollen belly. Clearly his instructions hadn't been heeded.

"When the baby died—" Her mouth twitched, and she took a sip of tea before carrying on. "Though she was small and stillborn, my labor was protracted and my husband sent for Dr. Croft when our usual doctor floundered." The cup shook in her hand, and she reached forward to set it on the table.

"Fearing for my life, he…he took out the baby."

She said nothing more, but Nora needed no details. He must have had to extract the child in pieces. A craniotomy. "I'm so sorry," Nora said.

"He said not to risk having another, that my bones are badly formed for childbearing."

That sounded like Horace—to assume a simple directive could surmount the eternal longing for love and children, and the expectation to provide an heir, at any cost.

"I—" Lady Woodbine brushed a hand over her skirts, her fingers tightening around her knee. "You can see I wasn't compliant. I sought other opinions. Dr. Sympington, who attended Lady Marlowe, was hopeful I could deliver a child safely. Now he is less certain. He and two other doctors advised me to end my pregnancy." She swallowed. "That was two months ago."

Though always dangerous, two months ago, a craniotomy would have been reasonably straightforward. Now, unfortunately, it was not.

"How far along are you?" Nora asked. It was not hard to guess, having seen the woman's walk. Still, Nora's heart sank at the answer.

"I believe eight months." Lady Woodbine met Nora's gaze. "I will not kill my child, whatever the result. I allowed Dr. Croft to intervene before because he and the other doctors assured me my child was already dead. It had been days since I'd felt her moving. This baby"—her hand fluttered again over her rounded abdomen—"is alive." Her lip trembled and Nora knew she didn't need a lecture on the likely outcome. "My husband I are Catholic," she explained with an iron glint in her eye, as if daring Nora to disapprove.

"I understand." Nora took a sip of tea while choosing a response. "Does your husband know you are here?"

"He knows I've written to Dr. Croft. He wrote himself first."

"He doesn't know you are consulting me."

The lady smiled. "Miss Beady, I didn't know I would be consulting you. But you answered the door, and I confess that it is much easier to talk with you than with a gentleman. I have prayed and prayed for months that all would be well... I suppose you think that was foolish."

Nora shook her head, remembering the faith of Magdalena and the nuns. While she couldn't claim their certainty, she was inspired by it. Within her, she knew she hoped.

"It's harder to reassure myself now. I remember what it was like when my daughter died and—" She picked up the cup and composed herself by swallowing a sip of tea. "I'm terribly afraid."

Lady Woodbine's maid concealed her dismayed frown with a lace-edged handkerchief, but Nora caught the distress in her eyes.

Nora set down her cup. "I would like to put some questions to Dr. Croft. He's recovering still, but perfectly capable of advising." He was also registered with the college, and she was not, still uncertain of the best way to apply. Presenting herself in person would only invite rejection.

But Lord Woodbine had written to Horace, so arguably he'd agreed to his wife seeking Horace's advice—just not Nora's. Helping Lady Woodbine was not like working with London's poor, and instinct warned her to be careful. "Would you mind if he joins us?"

Lady Woodbine stiffened slightly about the mouth. "If he refuses again—"

"His only aim is your well-being, I assure you. But your condition sounds serious. I need more information about your first pregnancy if I am to determine whether we have options—"

"You can help?" The question escaped quicker than a mouse fleeing a broom, exposing the fear beneath Lady Woodbine's carefully guarded expression.

Nora added a lump of sugar to her tea. *Don't make any promises*, she told herself. "Perhaps. There is a high level of risk, and I need to speak to Dr. Croft. I learned techniques in Italy that are not yet accepted here." Nora gave her a knowing grin. "They are all Catholic there."

A shadow of mirth crossed Lady Woodbine's face and then faded to mist. "I don't expect to live, Miss Beady." Her solemn voice fell to the floor. "I hope to, but you would not be blamed if I did not."

Nora wished she could be as confident.

"But if you could save my child—" Her fingers closed

around a small rosary clutched in her hand. "That would be enough."

Nora shook her head. "Your church insists there must be a reasonable chance of saving both of you. You are asking for a cesarean section, yes?" Without thinking, her words came out ordered like Magdalena's.

Lady Woodbine spoke to her lap. "When the doctors told me to end the pregnancy, I found a book on difficult confinements. I read Italian, so—"

"*Theses on Anatomy and Physiology*? Written by M. Marenco?"

"You know it?" Lady Woodbine's face lifted eagerly. "He says there are women and babies who survive."

Nora smiled. "Dr. Marenco was my tutor. *She* is the best doctor of obstetrics I have ever seen."

"She?" The frown on Lady Woodbine's forehead deepened and then released into a smile. "You can't mean—"

"Magdalena Marenco. Brilliant and talented. She performed two cesarean operations when I was in Bologna. I was at her side for both."

"And?" Lady Woodbine leaned closer, as did her maid.

"We had one child survive," Nora admitted, her voice low. When she said it aloud and thought of the two dead mothers, the prospect seemed black as pitch. "I'm afraid it is very dependent on the circumstances."

Lady Woodbine glanced at her maid, whose white face and wide eyes instilled no confidence. Inhaling and running her finger across an ivory prayer bead she said, "Please ask Dr. Croft if he will join us. I believe we have no choice but to proceed."

"Fundus is thirty-five centimeters high. According to Lady Woodbine's information, she's about thirty-six weeks into her pregnancy. The sacrum is disconcertingly long and the subpubic arch narrow. I would say it's impossible to tell how much the bones will loosen in labor, but Horace says she labored two days before miscarrying, without the child advancing into the birth canal at all. He had to perform a craniotomy. Left on her own, I can't believe this time the results will be any different." Nora rubbed her forehead, wishing the evidence wasn't so discouraging.

"They'll be different," Horace growled. "This time it'll kill her. I told her not to risk—"

"We can't put broken eggs back together," Daniel interrupted. He drummed his fingers on the table. Horace sat opposite him, his right hand wringing his left, as if coaxing the nerves back to life—it had become his habit—and staring fixedly at the remnants of their supper. He and Daniel had demolished the plum cake Mrs. Phipps had returned to the menu, to that lady's great satisfaction. Every minute or so, she bestowed a smile on the empty plate, between sips of after-dinner coffee, just one of the Italian rituals she declared she had no intention of giving up. She'd brought back an entire set of brightly decorated Turkish demitasse cups.

Two would have been enough, Nora reflected. So far, everyone else remained suspicious of espresso.

Harry stood propped against the mantelpiece. Other than Julia, who'd ducked her head and made herself small in the corner of the table, he'd been the quietest so far in this discussion. Only Nora was unable to remain still, punctuating her opinions with a strident forefinger and pacing the length of the dining room table.

"She wants a cesarean." Nora swallowed in spite of herself, remembering the last time. "I know it's risky."

"It damn well is. To you, not just her." Horace pinched his lips together, giving up his next words reluctantly. "If she dies in labor, no one will question it. They'll think it tragic, but unpreventable. If she dies under your knife, you may never practice again."

"*When* she dies in labor, I'll have to live knowing I didn't use my knowledge to save her." Nora ran a hand across the back of her tense neck, blowing a frustrated breath to the ceiling. "And to your point, Horace, we have no idea if I'll ever practice anyway. I still haven't approached the surgeons' college. What is the point of all the sacrifice and expense if I don't use what I've learned?"

"If Lady Woodbine agreed to the craniotomy now—" Harry began.

"She won't consider it." Nora met his unsettled eyes and he nodded in grim understanding.

"She should have done it months ago to have a reasonable chance of success. At this point, I think it's almost as risky as the cesarean," Daniel said.

"Those are bold words," Mrs. Phipps snapped, dropping her fork. "You all speak like you know what's best for her. If it were your wee one, you'd sing a different tune."

"Thank you," Julia murmured almost silently. Nora hadn't seen how tense she held her shoulders until they lowered.

Harry looked to his wife with a concerned frown.

"Whatever your sentiments, her doctors have convinced her labor is less dangerous than the surgery," Horace countered. "Idiots. If she were poor, we'd not even be debating. You could do the surgery. But Lady Woodbine? Her husband is in the foreign service. Her father is ambassador to Rome. The story could spread from here to Europe. The risks are too great, Nora. You haven't even finagled your license yet, and the minute you do, all eyes will be on you. If you operate in defiance of two reputable physicians and fail, you're done for."

The room seemed to darken with his words, evening shadows climbing the wall ominously. Nora heard the words Horace held back. *They'd all be done for.* If Horace, Daniel, and Harry helped, and the surgery failed, the lawsuits would tumble in on all of them. At the far end of the table, Julia was drawing tight circles on the tablecloth with a fingernail. She was newly wed and trying to settle; she didn't need her husband at the center of a controversy.

"There is one alternative." Daniel laced his fingers and rested his chin on them before continuing. "Clearly explain the risks. If Lord and Lady Woodbine want to proceed, ask them to keep the procedure quiet. If they want you to do the cesarean, you must have them sign a contract of secrecy if it does not work."

Nora sifted through his words, probing for vulnerabilities.

"That's sound," Horace muttered.

"They may lose confidence in me if I suggest such a thing," Nora pointed out.

"It would be their choice." Daniel kept his stare steady,

giving her the same grave consideration he would give any seasoned doctor. Nora straightened, hiding the way his serious gaze made her breath hitch.

"I hate that we have to beg secrecy, but I think it's the only way. I could send a letter explaining my conditions—"

"A letter could be used as evidence." Julia's quiet voice barely reached across the table. She did not lift her eyes. "Don't write it in a letter."

"Clever," Horace praised, giving Julia a rare look of approval. "You must have them sign an agreement which you alone retain."

That meant confronting Lord Woodbine in person. Nora's chest filled with heavy reluctance. She'd stood up to countless snarling, disapproving men over the last two years, but this brief respite with Horace and Daniel and Harry made the prospect seem more distasteful than ever. She looked over her roomful of allies. In her mind's eye, she added Magdalena to the empty chair Harry had forfeited and placed Pozzi at the fireplace, leaning his skinny body against the mantel, just feet from Harry. Somehow that small addition fortified her wavering courage. "I'll go see him."

"No. *We* will." Horace didn't look the same with his left eye soft. Nora hated this disruption to his sternest frown, the one that usually sent wound dressers running.

"But you aren't ready—"

"Girl, I sent you to school to order others around with your knowledge. Not me." Horace sniffed, his cheek only lifting on one side.

Nora swore she heard Pozzi laugh.

"There are three of us to help prepare and assist," Harry interjected at last. "I give it fair odds. And if Nora pulls it off, we'll be at a formidable advantage."

"How so?" Nora asked.

"The first doctor in England to accomplish such a feat? You'd raise all our stock. Nora, you could lecture. Forget being a woman; you could be a troll under a bridge and they'd still come listen to you. If you succeeded."

"He's right," Daniel agreed quietly. "But we can't let that possibility make us overlook the risks. To you, to us, to Lady Woodbine." His level gaze clearly told her *It's your choice.*

"Let's not get ahead of ourselves. They haven't agreed. I haven't succeeded," Nora said.

"Yet," Horace said, tearing off his napkin. "But we can fix that. I'll send my card and a note over right away."

Nora stopped pacing and lowered herself into her chair, her legs no longer fit to hold her. A crippled old man and a female doctor proposing an unheard-of procedure? If Harry thought their odds were fair, he was a worse gambler than she realized.

CHAPTER 37

THE ORDERLY HAD STOKED THE STOVE IN THE CLINIC generously. Nora noticed special care from everyone—cook to maid—when it came to the diphtheria patients. There were two at present, but both appeared to have mild cases and their mothers were staying with them, doing a fair amount of the nursing. The large house was unusually quiet, and Nora, struggling to stay busy while Horace waited for Lord Woodbine's reply to their request for a meeting, was suffering from the unfamiliar circumstance of having too little to do. It had only been a day, but the hours stacked one atop another, growing heavier each time she checked a patient, a ledger, or a store cupboard and found all in perfect order. She could think of only one thing still unfinished. Pressing her portfolio under her arm, she searched the empty rooms and found Daniel at last, in his shirtsleeves, bent over the microscope.

"An interesting cyst taken from a patient yesterday," he said, stepping aside to offer her a look.

Nora peered into the eyepiece and adjusted the focus. This cyst was a fine representation of the fibroid type. "What are you using for stain? The features show up so clearly."

He pointed to a bottle on the table, then cocked his head in the direction of her portfolio. "Is that your application for the surgeons' college?"

"Umm-hmm." She'd rather talk about slides and stains, but her application was more important. Abandoning the bottle of unfamiliar liquid and the microscope, she untied the ribbon fastenings and spread her papers out on the table. Though she still felt elation every time she glanced at her degree, it diminished next to her apprehension for the task ahead. Degree or not, it was unlikely that the Royal College of Surgeons would simply admit her.

"What are you thinking?" Daniel lifted his eyes from the parchment, met hers and added, "Dr. Beady."

"I like the sound of that." She moved closer.

A throat cleared behind them, loud as a mail coach on a bad road. Nora turned. Harry was leaning against the doorframe and grinning like a five-year-old. "Does Horace know you're using his microscope as an excuse for canoodling?"

Daniel made a face. "What does that even mean?"

"You're a smart man. Figure it out. I picked up the term from your American student, Jeffers." He winked. "Good one, isn't it?"

Nora rolled her eyes. "I'm consulting Daniel about strategy. Any canoodling is my own business, not Horace's."

"Or yours," Daniel added.

"What isn't my business?" Horace, whose hearing was clearly unaffected by his apoplexy, stumped down the hallway and pushed past Harry, favoring them all with a fierce glare. Though he accepted the necessity of accepting Harry into the household, he was still making a show of annoyance to protect his pride. He was also carrying, not using, the walking stick Nora had pressed on him, repeating his question and punctuating the words with stabs at the air. So much for a quiet, private discussion.

"I suppose this might as well be a committee meeting." Nora sighed. "Come in, both of you." Daniel caught her eye and wheedled Horace into a chair.

"This isn't about the practice or Lady Woodbine," Nora told them. "Not directly, at least. I need to plan how to apply for English credentials. I can submit my application to the college registrar, but I'm concerned he may remember the name Beady and the circumstances that drove me from London."

"Why don't you apply to one of the counties first?" Horace suggested. "Hertfordshire, perhaps? They are a small body."

London surgeons were stern in their rejection of country practitioners, though they often took it upon themselves to practice outside the confines of their jurisdiction, like when Horace traveled to attend to wealthy patients.

"If you are already licensed in one of the counties, registering in London will be easier," Harry added.

"I can't work in the counties," Nora said. "You need me here."

"Then it has to be London." Harry shrugged. "We don't know what will happen until you try. Daniel or Horace or I can recommend you for membership. If the surgeons' college turns you down, try the apothecaries."

Nora tapped her finger on her parchment. "If one of you recommends me, it's more likely the registrar will remember who I am."

Horace frowned. "I suppose there's Dr. Thompson. He seemed to like you well enough, but—"

"But none of that matters, really." Harry spoke up. "If the queen recommends a doctor named Eleanor, it's not going to pass, is it?"

Nora could tell he didn't like the fact, but no one else was willing to voice it. "That's exactly what I've concluded. I have a reference from Professor Perra." In the bright specimen room with a brass microscope and polished soapstone counters, Perra felt more fable than reality. "I never thought of it until now, but…" Nora fingered her skirt and raised her eyes to Daniel's. "He never wrote my full name. Not even on my official degree." She was simply E. Beady.

Daniel moved closer, frowning as he examined the paper again. "That's odd. Why—"

Horace grunted from his chair. "Clever."

"Do you see?" Nora asked them. "No guild here will expect a woman to have a medical license and apply. Perhaps—"

"An ambush." Harry grinned wickedly. "Brilliant."

"Would that work?" Daniel asked Horace. "They could withdraw her license after they find out."

"That might take a good long while," Harry said. "The guilds and colleges are far too busy quarrelling amongst themselves. If I read one more angry letter decrying the quacks and calling for stricter governance or a new act of Parliament—"

"They're never too busy to fine or punish the unqualified," Daniel pointed out.

"She's qualified." Harry shrugged.

"But she still needs a sponsor," Horace said. "And Trimble,

that should be you." His eyes gleamed. "No one will expect you to help the woman you maliciously threw over in an act of selfish cowardice."

Harry rolled his eyes at the jab, and Nora placated him with a covert smile.

"There are other guilds. Apothecary guilds that would be less stringent. Apply to several, along with the surgeons' college," Daniel suggested.

Nora considered. There were other guilds for different medical specialties—as Harry said, they tended to be constantly quarrelling—and not all of them scrutinized candidates as much as the surgical guild. It was far easier to register as a physician or apothecary, which would at least get her practicing.

"If you get it, I can't promise they'll let you keep your surgical registration, but they'd look like fools and end up fodder in the papers for those feminine groups if they fuss and try to take it away," Horace said.

"So it's decided?" Daniel asked. "We attempt a Trojan horse? They accept E. Beady and get Eleanor instead?"

Nora gave a nod, her chest tight and giddy.

"I'll write up the sponsor letter now," Harry said, pointing toward the drawing room. Nora gathered her precious papers while Daniel supervised Horace's clumsy walking.

"Daniel will write out your application," Harry continued, adding with a smirk, "It should be in a masculine hand, but Daniel's will do."

Nora laughed. Except for her, Daniel had the finest penmanship among all of them.

"At least mine will be legible, Harry. Maybe Julia should copy out yours," Daniel said.

"An excellent notion," Harry agreed and pretended to dictate aloud. "Dr. Beady is a strange-looking man, but studious."

Nora would have told him to stop if she hadn't been laughing so hard. "Just get them to accept me, and I don't care what you write."

"That was a piece of luck, that reference from Perra. Or a good deal of foresight on his part," Daniel said once Harry and Julia had set out to deliver the application to the registrar's office and Horace had been persuaded—forcibly—to rest upstairs. Daniel picked up her hand—interrupting her anxious finger-drumming—and brushed his ink-stained fingers across her knuckles.

"I was surprised he gave it to me," she admitted. Her voice dipped. She'd wondered if she'd tell him, but now, on the point of it, it didn't seem difficult. "He didn't want me to come home."

Daniel's eyes tilted in confusion. "Why not?"

Nora hesitated. "Of course, for me there was no question…" She shook her head, dispelling the feel of Perra's warm hands, the pain of ignoring insults, assumptions, and sideways looks. She forced a smile. "He is not you."

His gaze withdrew. "He propositioned you? Despite being married?" Anger was an emotion he rarely entertained, but Nora sensed it in the quiet, deceptively gentle words.

The truth was causing him pain, but she could only soften it so much before he'd know she was lying. "He did," she said plainly. "But he accepted my refusal and still gave me my degree. He knew I loved you, Daniel."

His mouth hitched at the corners, but his eyes tightened. "You're certain?" His thumb rubbed the edge of the table. "I don't want you to regret anyth—"

"Daniel…" She swallowed and tried again, wondering if this quick, clutching fear was the same that seized you when drowning—the compulsion to instantly strike out with all your strength for safety, for shore. "We haven't had a chance to talk. With Horace, and the house—"

He opened his mouth to speak, but she forestalled him with a raised hand, certain that if she stopped now, she'd never finish. "When I left, you and I hoped to eventually marry, but it has been a long time with so many changes and I would never hold you to a prom—"

"Nora Beady." He gaped at her. "Surely you know—"

She studied his brown eyes. "Tell me."

At some point his hands had tightened into fists. They spread open, palms toward her. "Since you left—no, even long before that—it has never been a question of me wanting to marry you. My only doubt was that you would have me."

Her eyes pricked, her breath too unsteady for speech.

He flashed a shy smile, his words coming in a rush. "I was going to wait. Let you catch your breath, but since we are talking now and for once no one is interrupting—" He broke off, still an arm's length away, devouring her with his focus. "Will you?"

She wouldn't choke. She wouldn't cry. Nodding rapidly, she managed: "Yes."

CHAPTER 38

N ORA CLUTCHED THE TERSE NOTE AND TRIED NOT TO
gape as the footman escorted her through an intimidating
grand hall with a soaring domed cupola that dwarfed the velvet sofas, making them look like child's furnishings. Beside her,
Horace clumped unceremoniously. He was probably imagining
how many surgical rooms he could fit in such a well-lit space
instead of wasting it on statuary and dress balls. The servant led
them to an airy library, dominated by a graceful mahogany desk
positioned in front of the high windows.

A young man, clean-shaven, his stiff collar digging into
his soft jawline, looked up as the footman introduced them.
"Miss…" The footman paused, eyeing Nora skeptically, though
her name and qualification was clearly printed on her card.
"Miss Eleanor Beady and Dr. Horace Croft, at your invitation,
my lord."

Lord Woodbine stood, signaling them toward two empty
chairs opposite him. His youth hampered his stern impression.
Just as well. The house and the footman were intimidating
enough. "You are the lady surgeon trained by Dr. Marenco?"
He studied her severe gray taffeta skirt. "And you've brought
Dr. Croft."

"It seems you did not remember my advice," Horace said.

A muscle jumped in Lord Woodbine's cheek.

"That's neither here nor there," Nora interjected. "We've come to address the current crisis. Lady Woodbine is in danger and will not consent to a craniotomy. We must discuss an alternative."

"Why now? I wrote to ask your help two months ago. If this delay is to satisfy your own showmanship—"

"Not at all, sir." The lines in Horace's face deepened. "I suffered an illness that made it impossible to attend, and my convalescence took longer than expected."

Lord Woodbine swept his eyes over Horace's cane and the looseness of his skin from his lost weight. "I see," he said, not unkindly.

Horace continued. "I admit I was angry when I discovered Lady Woodbine was carrying a child again. I like her. I felt—I feel—considerable fear on her behalf. I did not recommend she avoid future pregnancies lightly."

"How is Lady Woodbine?" Nora interjected. "I hoped we might see her."

The man's eyes shifted back to her for the first time since he'd addressed Horace.

"She exhibits no symptoms of trouble whatsoever, but she has informed me of her private consultation with you." Her cheeks warmed under his scornful glare. "When Dr. Seagrave recommended killing the babe, we consulted Dr. Traffet and Dr. Vickery. Traffet sided with Seagrave, but Vickery was more encouraging about a successful labor. He is more experienced than Seagrave or Traffet. He claims any scheme for a cesarean operation is madness. A woman is made to bear, and while

Athena failed the first time, he assures me her body will succeed at last."

Horace grunted. "Dr. Vickery is well beloved for his devotion to outmoded tradition. He will still bill you when your wife and child die."

"That's a serious accusation, Dr. Croft." Lord Woodbine narrowed his eyes. "My wife is afraid, a victim of grief. Memories of before are upsetting her unduly. Dr. Vickery says if she will cease worrying—"

The rest of his words were lost beneath the pounding in Nora's ears. "The diameter of her pelvis will not change whether she worries or not," Nora interjected. "Have they even measured her?"

Lord Woodbine's face twisted at her words. He retreated a foot by pushing himself into his chair. "She has submitted several times to the distressing procedure, and while I admit the number is not encouraging—"

"Not encouraging?" Nora demanded.

"Impossible, more like," Horace snapped at the same time. "I like Seagrave. He's a skilled and sensible man. If he and Traffet are advising you that a normal delivery is too risky, I beg you to listen to them. Your wife—"

"Would be better off if you hadn't filled her with false hope of a painless surgery that would give her healthy son."

"I never said painless!" Nora's voice rose with the heat in her cheeks. "Nor a son, for that matter—"

Lord Woodbine continued as if she'd not spoken. "I expect you to tell her you were wrong and to allow Dr. Vickery to proceed."

"But you know yourself what happened the first time," Horace's voice expanded, reverberating off the high ceiling. "I invite you to my home to see a female skeleton so I can instruct you in the details of the pelvic bones and birth passage, but the simple truth is that I know from experience that your wife's bones do not loosen and spread at birth. To try to expel a child is certain death to both of them. History has shown your only chance—and it is *only* a chance—for a living child and a living wife is the cesarean."

"Dr. Marenco is able to save one out of three women who have the surgery performed," Nora said. She fought for control, steadied herself against the burning in her throat. She wished her record were as good.

"Poor odds," Lord Woodbine argued. "My wife admitted you haven't saved any."

"Dr. Marenco and I saved a child," Nora said. "And the other mother who died was not killed by the surgery. It was an emergency, and we had to administer ether without proper equipment. None of these circumstances would apply to Lady Woodbine." Her voice turned pleading. "We could operate soon, before the child grows larger and before labor begins. She would not come to us exhausted with her life already hanging by a thread. We will be prepared with the best equipment, working in your own home, where she is protected from the infections that afflict hospitals. It is not a simple procedure, but her chances are so much better."

"It doesn't matter," Lord Woodbine said. "I will not allow it. I'm more interested in my wife's well-being than you making your name with a risky surgery. My wife's chances are better with Vickery." He spoke with finality. "I've made arrangements and want no more interference. You are not to contact Lady Woodbine again."

Nora rose. "Your faith did not allow you and your wife to abort when you had a chance to do it safely, but this will be your only choice in the end. I pray for your wife's sake it will be done in time."

Lord Woodbine's nostrils flared, his lips vanishing beneath the force of his anger. "Dr. Traffet and Dr. Vickery assure me—"

"Yes, but they're wrong," Nora snapped, interrupting.

"You forget yourself!" He thumped a hand on the desk and rose to his feet, his face white. "I order you to tell her you've reconsidered and that the surgery is not required. Once her mind is at ease—"

"I will not." Nora glared at him as if the weight of her gaze could push him back. "You just ordered me never to speak to her and then ordered me to tell her your plan is best. I am a trained surgeon, not a teller of fairy tales, as such a lie would surely be. My oath as a doctor, to do no harm, would not allow me in any case."

"Your faith in yourself is unwarranted," Woodbine spat. "You haven't succeeded once, and I will die before I let you experiment on my wife. You may have turned traitor to your sex, but my wife knows she was made by the Almighty to bear children and has faith in the blessings of the church."

Traitor to her sex? Nora blanched as if struck. The confidentiality agreement crumpled in her clenched hand.

"Then you have no need for any physician," Horace said quietly and rose. "You may persuade your wife yourself and with the assistance of your holy ghosts and saints bring them both through safely. Dr. Beady has given her opinion and will not retract. Nor should she. She is correct in every detail. God save your wife, sir. We wish you good day."

Nora took his arm, holding back his retreat. "But Lady Woodbine wants—"

"It's not up to Lady Woodbine," Horace muttered through a miserable, stiff mouth. "And he is so blinded by his ability to command others that he thinks he can command nature and the human body as well. It is a failing I've seen far too many times." He propelled her from the room, not looking back, but Nora took a last glance at Lord Woodbine. He was tugging his coat into place, pointedly ignoring them.

The footman, waiting in the hall, wordlessly conducted them back the way they'd come. This time the house and all its trappings might have been invisible.

"I pity him," Horace whispered. "But perhaps he realizes there are plenty of wealthy women with more advantageous hips to replace her when she is gone."

Nora flinched. "Don't say that. How can you pity him? Pity her!"

Horace squeezed her arm. "Believe me. I do. Would that it helped."

⁓

"Arrived just now by messenger," the hallboy announced, brandishing the envelope at Nora, who'd been in clinic three hours and the waiting room still held a good crowd. Whenever they finished with one patient, it seemed two more appeared.

Nora glanced down. Probably just an order for… Her eyes scanned the address. *The Royal College of Surgeons of England.* She froze.

Daniel halted on his way to the waiting room. "What is it?"

"You," she said, extending it toward Daniel and then retracting. "No. Me." She looked up at him. "I can't."

He took the envelope and inhaled. "You can." His lips were straight, calm, but she knew he was as tense as she was. Pulling her into the empty exam room, he handed her the medical scissors to snip the string.

"If it says no—"

"Then we wait until one of the guilds says yes," he promised.

Nora cut and drew out the papers, closing her eyes to prolong her hope. Her letter of recommendation and degree from the University of Bologna were both included. It was the third sheet she hesitated to read, her fingers trembling.

"No," she breathed.

"What?" Daniel asked, pushing closer.

Her voice came out strange and unfamiliar to her own ears. "Dr. E. Beady is a member of the Royal College of Surgeons of England."

Daniel snatched the paper away, but Nora didn't trust her first perusal. She could have misread. As he let out a cheer, she took it back, checking again.

Nora's lungs expanded, the room swelling around her.

Daniel's mouth pressed to hers, and she tasted victory on his lips.

"It won't last," she warned him when he pulled away, beaming.

"They can't take away that piece of paper." He pointed to it in her hand. "Careful how you clutch it; we're having it framed like the Botticellis in the National Gallery," he insisted. "We must go tell Horace."

"The clinic—"

"Is closed for the next hour. I'll have tea sent to those still waiting." Daniel led her past the waiting patients and gave the orderly instructions to bring refreshments. "A moment's rest and a bit of food is better medicine for half our patients than anything else," he reminded her when she cast a backward glance.

She couldn't argue with that, nor could she concentrate on a case with her head buzzing like a sawmill.

They found Horace in the library, poring over renderings of South American lizards.

"Have you convinced Lady Finnely to have the lump removed from her breast?" Daniel asked.

"She's considering it. Why are you grinning at me like that? It's not a lump of gold." Horace snorted.

"Not at all." Daniel stuck his head in the hallway as he spoke. "Harry! Mrs. Phipps! Julia!" he called before turning back to Horace. "I'm grinning because I happen to know the perfect surgeon for the job." Daniel nudged Nora forward.

She heard footsteps approaching, building like the crescendo of nerves in her stomach. Harry appeared first, his eyebrows raised in question, followed closely by Mrs. Phipps and Julia.

"They registered me." Nora waved the paper before their curious eyes like a regimental banner. "Of course they don't know it's *me*, but it's my degree, my letter of reference, my name."

Horace dropped his book. "Blazing devils," he whispered in disbelief. "It worked."

Mrs. Phipps dabbed her eyes, which was a great show of emotion for her, and Julia clapped her hands. Nora was buffeted by Harry's arms as he took her in a gruff hug. "The tatties are o'er the side now," he said, laughing.

Nora looked to Daniel for translation, but he shrugged.

"That means we're all in for trouble." Horace grinned and rubbed his hands together as they all looked to him. The old flush was on his cheeks and a rare flash in his eye. "Just the way we like it."

CHAPTER 39

Nora was bent over her book when Daniel appeared in the library wearing his dressing gown, his hair wet from washing. For him, this was unexpectedly bold. Nora froze, unable to look away from him and his flamboyantly patterned silk, her hand arrested midway through turning the page.

"I've not seen that before," she said with a grin.

"Harry gave it to me as a honeymoon gift to embarrass me. I'm parading it around just to gall him."

"It doesn't gall me." Nora lifted her eyebrow and patted the sofa next to her.

"It's absurd, but it did get you to smile. You've been unusually quiet, for being England's first licensed female surgeon."

"I'm licensed." She sighed. "But the more I think about it, the more I realize it won't make a particle of difference to Lady Woodbine."

"There will be others to help," Daniel reminded her.

She nodded and rubbed the back of her neck. "My turn for a bath, I suppose." If Daniel was dressed for bed already, it must be late.

"I've cursed Horace's spending on this house time and again, but never right after taking advantage of the hot-water plumbing." He grinned at her, while pushing the damp hair off his forehead.

"I don't think Harry was trying to embarrass you when he gave you this dressing gown. I like it." Nora waved her hand at the robe.

"I suppose it's early for you to see it. We haven't chosen a date." But banns had been called in church last Sunday, asking if anyone objected. Since his parents lived in Richmond, no one had protested. They could marry in another two weeks if they wanted. Nora did, very much, but she and Daniel had concluded it was better not to change her name immediately after receiving her registration. If she asked the board to change the name on her certificate now, it would only draw more attention to her brazen tactic. In a month or two, they would have a better idea of the college's reaction to her—and proceed regardless.

"It's very…vivid," Nora said, fixating again on the muscles of his neck, visible above the dull-gold border of his robe.

"Should I change?"

It would certainly be helpful if they were going to talk, but… Nora thought of Magdalena and decided not to be a prude. "No need." She adjusted herself on the cushions, angling closer. "You look handsome."

"I'm sorry the meeting with Lord Woodbine went poorly," he said.

"I keep thinking of what is certain to happen and how helpless I am to prevent it. She is due to have the baby any time," Nora said, staring at her slippered toes. "She has such a wonderful smile, Daniel. I can't believe she found Magdalena's book on her own."

"You feel a kinship to her. It's perfectly understandable."

"If I were in her place—and I could be, someday, especially if you wander around in that dressing gown—"

He grinned and rubbed her thumb soothingly.

"I would want to choose my own doctor and the treatment to take."

"You would," Daniel said. "How can you doubt it?"

Nora tightened her grip on his hand. "And I know with you I would have that freedom, but how can I be satisfied knowing how many women do not?"

He slipped his arm around her shoulders and pulled her in to his chest. "No manner how many precedents you obliterate, you won't solve every injustice. But the world is changing, and in the meantime we can work at persuading one case at a time. After all, you persuaded me." His eyes crinkled at the corners, reminding her what a feat it had been to coax anything but scorn from him when he'd first discovered her.

Nora's lips twitched in a feeble attempt at a smile. "But she'll die, Daniel. This isn't the same as you supporting my wish to study."

"I think it is. Yes, the consequences to you might not have been fatal, but in its own way, it was life and death to you."

She inhaled, holding the air in her lungs as memories of the past two years flooded her.

His face lengthened and he sighed. "For now, you've done all you can, and if not tomorrow or next week or next month, there will be other women who need you. Lady Woodbine will not be the only one. You can't afford to lose your license or earn the displeasure of men like Woodbine. For the sake of other women, you must be ready and able to fight for them, too."

Nora rubbed her forehead, but it didn't make her any less tired. "You make it sound so strategic and sensible, and I just want to—" she broke off, shaking her head. "Well."

"I know. I feel the same way."

Daniel remained in the library long after Nora left him. As he said, she'd done all she could. So had Horace. Lord Woodbine had made his opinion clear. What more could be done?

Maybe one thing.

Next day, after his round of morning calls and a dispiriting hour answering bank correspondence and wrestling with the ledgers, Daniel washed and put on his best clothes. Harry was lecturing at the hospital, Nora was busy in the clinic, and Horace in the laboratory, swearing as he struggled to prepare his slides. No one noticed when Daniel left the house, hailed a hackney, and directed the driver to take him to Mayfair. He had no great hopes, so preferred to keep this errand secret.

At Lord Woodbine's palatial home, Daniel presented his card, scrawled with the message—*Our fathers were acquainted. Will you see me as a favor to them?*—to a butler with more self-consequence than the queen. The servant vanished, returning with disappointing speed. A refusal, then. Resigned, Daniel turned to go, then started when the butler murmured, "If you'll come this way, Dr. Gibson?"

The walk to the library seemed a mile. Daniel rehearsed his words until the butler left him standing on the brink of a beautiful Persian carpet, yards away from Lord Woodbine's desk. Lord Woodbine looked up from a piece of paper, his face heavy with care. "I remember your father. That is the only reason I've granted this interview. How is he?"

"In good health. Still residing in Richmond. He misses the hunts with your father. Please accept my condolences."

Lord Woodbine's eyes, partly obscured by a pair of gold spectacles, dropped back to his desk. "It is perhaps better my father is gone. He was very fond of my wife. Her near death during her first labor and the loss of our child was the beginning of his decline."

Daniel bowed his head. "I would like to help you avoid such tragedy again."

"I already told your *colleagues*"—Lord Woodbine lingered unpleasantly on the word—"that I've no interest in making a spectacle of my wife."

Daniel ignored the dismissive and unwelcoming notes in the lord's voice. He let silence settle before gently lifting it. "My lord, I am confused why you will not consider the cesarean. There is considerable risk, but no more than the craniotomy she has already survived. It is the only course of action that could end favorably for mother and child." Woodbine kept his eyes trained on the blotter. Daniel remembered that his father had been an inordinately tender man and hoped his son retained the trait, though he seemed adept at concealing it.

"Whoever heard of a man giving a woman permission to slice open his wife's stomach and pull out a child in an unnatural way? Nothing about it is allowable, Dr. Gibson." He glared at Daniel, his eyes narrowed with suspicion.

"It is not ideal, admittedly. I'm sure your wife wants desperately to bear a child in conventional ways, but this procedure has been honed in Italy, a place where your pope's word is the people's law. Surely if he approves—"

Woodbine drummed his fingers impatiently on his desk. "But to have a young woman wield the knife! Who could countenance such a thing?"

Daniel took a steadying breath, ignoring the insult to Nora. "I understand your reluctance. I've shared it in the past. I knew nothing of Dr. Beady's talents when I came to work with Dr. Horace Croft. I knew he was brilliant, eccentric, unorthodox, but I did not know he had taught a young woman to practice medicine. But he did, and he taught her well." Daniel shifted his eyes to the side as images of Nora's work rose in his mind. A small huff of wonder escaped him. "If ever you have marveled at a woman's needlework, you will know the care and precision of her handiwork."

"But what manner of woman would wish to inflict such horrors?" Woodbine grimaced and glanced at the window.

Daniel's fingers ran over his knees. He must not betray the least sign of temper. "A fine and brave one, sir, I assure you." He ventured a smile, though it was not returned. "For that matter, what kind of man pursues surgery? I can only answer for myself. I chose this discipline not because it is pleasant, but because of the potential to help. Having observed Dr. Beady and Dr. Croft, I venture their motivations are the same. We live in a strange and wonderful world. Buildings stretching to the sky, factories powered with the finest machines, and surgical miracles we could only imagine before, thanks to the discovery of ether and chloroform. Your wife is one of the first women to live in a time when we might save her from this terrible fate."

"She is due to have the child any day," Woodbine whispered. "Traffet says if it goes badly, we can tell her the child is dead. If she believes it, she can have no objection to another craniotomy. Traffet says if we drug her, she cannot resist…"

Daniel held back a shudder. "Please do not do this thing against her will. I fear it would be disastrous for you both. There is a doctor with the knowledge and skill to perform a once impossible surgery. She was trained by one of the greatest surgeons in the field and studied at one of the most renowned universities in the world. And she stands ready to help your wife in the way your wife wants. Will you let her?"

Lord Woodbine dropped his head into his hands. "I don't know." His muffled words wandered the room, forlorn and lost.

"There is no time left for indecision. Examine your objections. It's not enough to decide against the surgery because Dr. Beady is a woman and not a man. If, like your wife, you've read Dr. Marenco's book, you know survival for mother and child can be as high as sixty percent in favorable circumstances. None are more favorable than yours." Daniel stood and straightened his sleeves. "Listen to your wife. You are too wise to waste such an opportunity." Daniel held the man's eyes, softening his own in pity for the fear he observed. "At least I believe you are. Good day, my lord."

"Dr. Gibson—" The man's shoulders fell in defeat. He looked little more than a broken boy. "My wife wants the surgery."

Daniel's breath caught. "Are you willing?"

"I wouldn't be, but I overheard Traffet and Vickery conferring… Traffet is not as confident as he made out to me and clearly feels the need to defer to Vickery. I haven't confronted them. I—" His jaw clenched, but when he raised his eyes, they were helpless to the point of breaking. "Athena and I were matched when we were children. She is unbearably dear to me and has been my whole life."

"I cannot promise success. No one can. But if I were in your place, I would trust Dr. Beady. And remember she won't be alone. She'll be accompanied by one of the greatest surgeons alive today. And me," he added quietly. But this brought him to the most difficult point. "But I am afraid Dr. Croft insists on one condition." Daniel withdrew the paper from his pocket. "Our services are offered to you, but you must agree to tell no one of the cesarean if the results are unfavorable." His lip quivered at the appalled expression on Lord Woodbine's face.

"This is too much," the man declared to the ceiling, sending his complaint directly to God himself.

"You know Dr. Beady would be blamed and destroyed, even if she did everything perfectly. No one controls outcomes. You must agree not to assassinate her character."

"I think she's done that herself, with your help," Lord Woodbine added, his face mottled.

Daniel didn't respond. He stared steadily ahead, forcing Lord Woodbine to choose the next move.

"If she insists on secrecy, she must not be confident."

"She faces considerable prejudice within the profession. I'm sure you can understand," Daniel said evenly. "You face your own share of prejudice, do you not?" Daniel's eyes flicked toward a medieval crucifix on the wall.

Staring at his hands, Woodbine laced the fingers together

in a twisted snarl, touching them to his nose, then his lips, then his chin. He scowled as he reached for the contract. When he finished reading, he dropped it to the desk, his face a mask. "When could she do it?"

Daniel reached out to lay a hand on Lord Woodbine's clenched knuckles, recollected himself, and stepped back. "Forgive me, my lord. I'm greatly relieved. Dr. Beady recommended trying as early as possible. I believe she could be ready to perform the surgery tomorrow."

Woodbine's neck muscles hardened. He took up his quill, blotting the ink away before closing his eyes and signing his name. "Send instructions and I'll have the staff prepare what you need." He opened his mouth to say more but swallowed and clenched his teeth. Daniel ducked his head and collected the paper. "I will see you tomorrow, my lord."

CHAPTER 40

NORA LIFTED HER GRAY WOOL SKIRT WITH HURRIED carelessness and then discarded it for her black bombazine. Even with her heavy apron she must plan on bloodstains. She'd take a taffeta to wear while nursing after the surgery. Her fingers shook as she trailed them over the light fabric. *After the surgery.* She said a silent prayer in Italian that there *would* be two patients to nurse. Her trunk was only half inhabited with clothing. The rest of the space had been given over to Magdalena's books, useful journals, and a notebook to record the outcome of this endeavor.

She'd asked Daniel to hold on to the discretion contract as soon as he'd returned with the impossible news that he'd convinced Lord Woodbine to proceed on their conditions. She didn't trust herself not to lose it in her haste to prepare. With only hours left in the day, she had to make herself a whirlwind of activity and still somehow wipe her mind of frenzy and fear before the morning appointment.

"Nora?" The low voice made her startle. She turned and saw Julia's apologetic face.

"I didn't mean to interrupt. I wondered if I could help you pack." She hung back, as she always did when there were medical matters afoot. "I don't know the proper attire for a woman practicing medicine, but I thought it likely that Lord Woodbine would expect you at dinner at some point if the stay is long."

Nora blanched. "Surely I'll just take a tray."

"Perhaps." Julia approached, her eyes surveying the clothing laid on the bed. "But if he does want you and Daniel and Horace to eat with him, I think it best to be prepared. He will see you as heroes, not servants."

If... Nora let the doubt rest unfinished. "Would my taffeta skirt do?" she asked, pointing to the bundle rolled up inside her trunk.

Julia bit her bottom lip and shook her head. "You'll need a bit of color. And a dress. You should take a wrapper for tending to Lady Woodbine afterward. It will be loose and light for movement, but still look lovely. Just be certain to change for dinner." Julia's voice trailed off at Nora's expression. "I could loan you my dove-gray silk wrapper. It would look beautiful with your skin."

Nora wrinkled her nose. What doctor on earth worried about the color of their clothes? But then she remembered Magdalena's magnificent dresses in oriental fabrics. Frowning, she opened her wardrobe. "Pack whatever you like. I doubt you'll find anything satisfactory."

Julia surveyed the collection, reaching for Nora's one fine dress in dark-green silk. As she pulled it out for inspection, her loose sleeve fell back and Nora glimpsed the skin of her wrist, not smooth and creamy like her face, but twisted into red, angry, ropelike scars. With Nora's quick intake of breath, Julia's eyes fell to the floor, and she shook her sleeve back into place. There had been moments when Nora wondered if she should ask, but she hadn't, unsure how to broach Julia's brutal past.

"May I?" Nora asked gently, afraid, but they'd stumbled into this moment. Julia knew that she'd seen.

Julia's hands clenched together, the fingers twisting. "I don't usually—"

"I know. Your cuffs are always buttoned at the wrist," Nora said calmly.

"They remind me—" Julia muttered.

Nora shook her head, an automatic negative. "You survived a crisis. Not everyone does. Maybe you could be proud of your strength? Perhaps the scars could remind you of that instead?" Normally she'd phrase it as a statement, not a suggestion, but she didn't know Julia like Magdalena or Mrs. Phipps, though she knew, bone deep, what both would say to this young woman.

"Harry always says how proud he is of me." Julia shook her head. "Of course he says that—"

"He doesn't lie." Guessing that Julia would never give permission, Nora reached for her arm. She flinched at the touch but surrendered it reluctantly. Nora turned the wrist over, tracing the inflamed tissues crisscrossing the pale-blue veins. "It's lucky he had enough time," Nora murmured. Harry must have worked desperately as life flowed from this poor torn arm, but Nora couldn't help thinking that if Julia had been her patient, she would have left a kinder scar. Men didn't think of such things—

"I have a salve that will help. Let me show you how to rub it in. It takes time, but we could flatten these scars. Loosen them a little. They'll fade over time, too." Nora smiled. "But you don't need to hide them."

"I'd like the salve," Julia said. "And...I'll think about the rest," she finished quickly. "But we still haven't solved the problem of your clothes."

Making things prettier, it seemed, was one of Julia's comforts. Nora smiled at the flowers gracing her nightstand. "I trust you implicitly, but I can't spare it another thought." She grabbed another book, her movements clumsy. "Perhaps you could finish packing this trunk? You'll know what clothes I need better than I. I'll go double-check my medical supplies."

"I'd love to." Julia's eyes lit with genuine enthusiasm. Maybe the girl was more like Nora than she realized; she needed a job to do.

"*Grazie*," Nora said sincerely. "You'll probably spare me some embarrassment with the Woodbines."

"You're never an embarrassment, Nora. But these people..." She hesitated. "You have enough stacked against you. You don't need to give them any reason to criticize something as trivial as your dress."

A vision of Magdalena came again, her green walking dress glinting in the sun as she passed through the piazza to Santa Maria della Vita. Her clothing was exquisite nearly to the point of being ostentatious.

"You're right," Nora said softly, understanding. "Let's not give them any more arrows for their quiver. As for embarrassment..." Nora hesitated. "I'll wear what I must, if you won't be ashamed of the scars," she said awkwardly. "At least not with me." She patted the injured wrist, waiting anxiously, but Julia answered with a quick, tremulous smile, which firmed as she clasped Nora's hand.

There was no more time to spare for thoughts of clothes or

any person other than Lady Woodbine. Nora left Julia to her task and paced her way to the surgery, her stomach electric with nerves. Her supply of scalpels, silk thread, and bandages lay in a neat row where she'd arranged them last night. Nora smoothed her skirt and let out a heavy breath. If she failed, she'd be home, disgraced, before dinner tomorrow, and there would be no need to worry about wardrobes. Perhaps she should wait and have her trunk sent in the evening, if necessary, just in case.

CHAPTER 41

Normally Nora would have noticed the impressive view of Regent's Park from her carriage window, but this morning she registered neither the drumbeat of rain on the roof, nor the dull, black winter trees. In the tight confines of the chilly carriage, her eyes were turned inward, viewing only the impending surgery. Though Daniel's arm bumped hers when the carriage rocked on the pitted roads and Horace drummed his fingers on the door handle, both men were specters to her, ghosts intruding on the vivid scene inside her brain.

When the carriage stopped, footmen materialized from the wet drizzle and helped her alight, their umbrellas guarding her from the petulant weather. While Daniel gave instructions for unloading the delicate ether equipment, Horace struggled through the small door and down the carriage steps. His mobility and dexterity were improving, even if his endurance was poor. Just yesterday, he'd managed his bootlaces and celebrated by breaking into a Verdi chorus. Frequent practice had restored his competence with the vapor apparatus, so long as someone was on hand in case he tired.

Nora did not wait for them to organize themselves, but made for the shelter of the front door, a footman on each side of her. Though clean air and quiet in the country would be better for Lady Woodbine's recovery, Nora hadn't wanted her to risk the four-hour journey, and this home was grand enough to provide every comfort a patient and her surgeon could require.

"Thank you for coming." Lord Woodbine entered at the far end of the dimly lit hall, apprehension in his stiff arms and frozen expression.

"We're grateful you allowed us," Nora said.

"We'll see to these cases," Daniel said, taking the wooden box holding the vaporizer from a footman. "The ether equipment is fragile." He smiled gently at Lord Woodbine. "You surely didn't sleep well last night. I hope you know your wife is in good hands."

Lord Woodbine didn't seem capable of reply. Even his nod was jerky and reluctant. His eyes slewed sideways as Horace entered, shaking one foot that looked to have sunk in an ankle-deep puddle. "Dr. Croft," Lord Woodbine said, his face brightening fractionally.

Horace left off tending to his wet shoe and straightened. His sharp eyes took in the man's pale face and shadowed eyes. "I've brought you my best surgeons," Horace said without so much as a greeting. "If someone will help us with our equipment, Dr. Beady can prepare Lady Woodbine."

Lord Woodbine nodded again, his face painful in its longing to be reassured. "I'll show you myself." He waved back the butler and matched his steps to Horace's gait. Nora and Daniel followed.

"She's quiet today," Lord Woodbine said as they passed a portrait of an imposing general, answering a question no one had asked.

"Has she had any pains?" Nora asked.

"I don't believe so, but her maid would know more. She always tries to be brave when I'm with her," Lord Woodbine answered as he led them into a large bedchamber.

Nora took note—he must be naturally uncomfortable with such things or Lady Woodbine wouldn't try to spare him. She'd have to limit and modulate any medical descriptions for him. She thought of Venturoli's insistence that a patient be told as little as possible. In spite of her own opinions, today she would follow his advice.

Lady Woodbine was seated in the bed, dressed in an orchid-colored wrapper with her maid standing guard at her shoulder. Her face was paler than the last time Nora had seen her, a symptom of anxiety she recognized and hoped wasn't mirrored in her own face. Lady Woodbine managed a smile, but no one felt like exchanging happy greetings, least of all Nora. She swept forward and laid a firm hand on Lady Woodbine's arm. "I'll take every precaution," she promised, looking into eyes dull with worry, "and do my very best."

"Thank you." Lady Woodbine clutched her hand briefly. "Let's not fuss. I'm not worried." She raised her eyebrow a fraction in her husband's direction and Nora seized on the hint.

"Nor should you be," Nora lied, reminding herself again to heed Venturoli's advice. She had explained the risks earlier, and both Lord and Lady Woodbine knew them. In this moment, both needed her to exude confidence. Nora glanced around the room, judging the space to move, the height of the bed. She wished they hadn't put such fine covers on it. Soon there would be stains of every kind. She moved toward the maid. "Have you linens prepared?" she asked, hoping no one guessed her reasons for the question.

The maid pointed to a stack of white sheets on a chair in the corner.

"Very good," Nora said. "If I could have a moment alone to examine—"

Lord Woodbine slipped through the door with a worried backward look, but the maid didn't move, just knotted her hands in front of her and looked pleadingly. Nora nodded at the maid. "Your assistance with Lady Woodbine's clothes would help." She turned and looked a question at Lady Woodbine.

Together, she and the maid unwrapped Lady Woodbine down to her silk chemise. Nora applied her stethoscope. The baby's heart was beating steadily, and twice Nora felt a nudge of a surprisingly pointy little elbow. "The child is moving and the heartbeat is strong. As is yours." She smiled at Lady Woodbine, glad to give any good news, however benign.

Nora took her time measuring the uterus and feeling the position of the baby. The head was well down in a beautiful position, the little buttocks pressed hard above the navel. If she was wrong, if Lady Woodbine's pelvis would loosen and release during birth, it should be an uneventful delivery. Wishing she could tell the future as well as she could assess a baby's position, Nora started an internal exam, using olive oil scented with lavender as Magdalena had taught her.

Her eyebrows lowered in concentration as she probed. "Your pains began already?" she asked in surprise.

"No," Lady Woodbine insisted. "Nothing yet."

Nora rotated her fingers. There was no doubt. "You're

halfway begun." The soft cervix gave as she carefully stretched her fingers apart. It was at least six centimeters.

"She's not had any major pains," the maid echoed. "Just backache this morning."

Nora frowned. She'd expect this kind of loosening in a woman who'd had several children before. But although the cervix was widening, the waters were intact. Masking her confusion, Nora focused on where she was certain. The pelvis felt wrong. Far too long front to back and too narrow. "We're doing the right thing," she said through tight lips. "You are halfway through labor without even knowing it, which is convenient for pain, but I don't like it. I cannot bring a live child the natural way. I have no doubts."

Though solemn, neither Daniel nor Horace contradicted her.

Lady Woodbine closed her eyes as Nora smoothed the chemise back in place. She looked smaller and younger without her elegant trappings. Her face had the swollen quality of late pregnancy, enhanced by the worried pout of her lips. "When do we begin?" she asked with false courage.

"Now," Nora said, her voice bracing. She sent the maid to fetch Lord Woodbine, but he was at hand as soon as the door opened, pacing the corridor. As he stepped in, she noticed the rosary almost hidden in his fist except for a few polished beads that had escaped the confines of his fingers. "I can promise one miracle," she said to them both. "The surgery will cause no pain. I've used the ether myself. As have many hundreds of people. You will fall asleep and be unaware of all that passes. You will wake to find a baby beside you. Lord Woodbine may stay until we are ready." She smiled at the gentleman in question. "Is there anyone who will wait with you? I don't want you alone with your imagination."

"Our priest is coming," Lady Woodbine answered. "Father Allis will stay with him."

Nora swallowed, trying not to feel the tremor of anxiety working its way through her veins. She fervently hoped the priest's presence would be merely a comfort, not a necessity.

"In the meantime," Lord Woodbine said, "I will wait outside with Nurse Green."

Like a hive, the room began humming with softly orchestrated activity. As Nora helped the maid change the linens, she couldn't help noticing the quiet smiles exchanged by Lady Woodbine and her husband, each trying to reassure the other. While Horace bent over Lady Woodbine and told her what she'd experience breathing the ether, Daniel set up the vaporizer and waited until the mix of boiling and chilled water came to exactly the correct temperature.

Lord Woodbine and the maid arranged Lady Woodbine comfortably in the newly made bed.

"I'm ready," Lady Woodbine said.

Her husband's sigh cut out a piece of Nora's chest. "Then I suppose I must—" Breaking off, he bent and kissed her forehead. Then he was gone.

The maid, however, lingered by the door. Nora stepped close to urge her outside and saw tears collecting against her lashes. "I can see you love her very much," Nora told her, "but you should wait outside."

The woman swallowed, nodded, and disappeared.

Somehow this time, the walk was longer between door and bed. "Are you still ready?"

Lady Woodbine nodded.

"Good." Horace gave Lady Woodbine's cheek a fatherly pat and measured out the dose. "Dr. Beady?"

Nora met his eyes. "Yes. Let's begin."

CHAPTER 42

HORACE NODDED AND TOOK HIS PLACE, CANE IN HAND, ON Lady Woodbine's right side, across from Nora.

Lady Woodbine accepted the inhaler calmly but pulled away almost the instant Daniel had it positioned.

"I know the smell is—" he started.

"No. Not that. I want the child named Charles, please." Her eyes had a frantic shine to them, as if trying to collect every sight and sound.

Nora's heart gave a painful thud. She nodded, unable to promise more.

"And tell my husband I love him very much and I don't regret anything."

Horace huffed quietly but held his tongue.

"I'll tell him. And when you wake, he will tell you if it really is a boy." Nora spared the smallest teasing smile. "Are you sure you want to inflict that name on a daughter?"

"Charlotte for a girl," she said, and then Daniel had the mask back on her face. Her nose wrinkled beneath the glass inset that fogged with her rapid breaths, but it took only a half minute before her eyelids grew heavy. A muffled moan was swallowed by the mask and the hiss of the vapor as her eyes struggled for one last glance before drawing slowly, inexorably shut. Daniel set down the mask.

"Pulse is eighty-five," he said, bent over Lady Woodbine's chest with his stethoscope.

Nora held out her hand for it. "I'll locate the placenta. Daniel? You'll confirm?" She'd explained the technique months ago, by letter, and though all had practiced it, they'd never needed to be sure before now.

"Horace's ear is better," Daniel said, adding nothing more, but all three of them knew the risks of a misplaced cut. Without a pause, Nora bent and trained her ears on the wooden stethoscope. Her own pulse was fluttering, roused by Horace's grim face and Daniel's firm jaw. Nora closed her eyes and strained her ears, letting her own heart settle so she could focus on finding the muffled soufflage caused by the placenta.

If only Magdalena were here. All Nora's striving under Magdalena's careful tutelage couldn't stifle her qualms today. She'd never been as quick, as confident as her teacher, and every innocuous noise—a creak of the floorboards beneath Horace's shoe, the brush of her skirts against the sheets—was unnaturally loud.

She let out a breath and left her lungs empty to keep her ears clear, passing the stethoscope over Lady Woodbine's belly, round as a globe, the straining skin marked by a circle of violently red lines. There... No... Maybe... She circled the stethoscope nearer to her target and listened again. She'd found it, but held back from committing herself yet, sliding upward and left, where the fetal pulse was strong and she'd not detected the placenta.

Nora lingered, then straightened, passing the stethoscope to Horace. "When you find it, tell Daniel. If your conclusions agree with mine—"

He nodded, comprehending. "Good plan."

If Horace drew his conclusions independently, it minimized the risk of either of them imagining noises to fit one another's results.

As Horace listened—in this, nothing would hurry him—the seconds crawled over Nora's skin. She didn't dare twitch. He moved from where she'd last listened, frowned, moved again, smiling when he found what she believed was the right place.

He stood and passed the stethoscope to Daniel. "We all need to know how to do this."

"This isn't a teaching case," Nora retorted. Her heart was racing again. She pressed her damp palms to her skirts and circled her shoulders to ease the tension settling like a yoke on her neck.

"Every opinion strengthens our prediction. We have time."

Horace might never have done a cesarean, but he'd done thousands of surgeries. Nora gave a quick nod. He was right, and she heard his favorite maxim without him having to say it. *You must treat everything quietly.* How many times had he told her that?

"I hear it here," Daniel said, indicating the lower curve of Lady's Woodbine's belly, off to the right.

"So do I," Horace said. "Nora?"

"That's where I found it." She smiled, feeling easier than she had since concluding that the surgery must proceed. "We'll cut one and a quarter inches left of the umbilicus." The extra quarter inch would give them more space if the placenta angled medially toward the cervix.

Horace laid a hand on her arm. "I didn't like to say anything in front of Lord Woodbine. But you are sure?"

Nora grimaced. "She's six centimeters dilated. And you can see how well the child is positioned. But her pelvis has not spread at all. There's simply not enough room. I'm sure."

Horace nodded.

Daniel steadied her with his eyes as he deliberately placed a handful of sponges and a pair of retractors in front of him. He passed her a knife—her favorite one, the blade fresh and sharp. "When you are ready."

Bless him. Nora took the knife, reassured by the familiar weight in her hand.

Horace, back at the top of the table, set his watch down where he could see it. "It's eleven minutes past nine. Let's change British history."

Nora grinned but kept her eyes on the skin to be cut and the point of her knife. "On my count. One, two, three…"

Her hands were sure, as confident with the scalpel as they were with brush or pencil. "A little more light," she said, but Daniel had already anticipated her, adjusting a mirror one-handed while cleaning her field of view with a sponge. "Thank you."

"How long?" he asked.

"Six inches," Nora said through closed teeth. It was a shorter incision than Magdalena's but hopefully long enough to safely extract the child. Extending the incision later, if necessary, would be easy enough. A "quiet" surgeon would cut as little as possible.

Skin and muscle parted. The sharp point of her blade had etched along the exterior wall of the uterus. Nora traced the line, angling her blade deeper, but—hopefully—not deep enough to nick the child. The cut widened, spilling fluid, then widened more as Daniel applied his retractors. Nora wriggled her hands inside, gripped the baby's thighs and tugged. "I can't... He's not coming."

Like her, Daniel had caught a glimpse of the baby's scrotum just beyond a purple, rather pointy pair of baby buttocks. Horace, denied the close-up view, grunted. "Charles it is."

The light comment didn't ease Nora's frown or the pucker on Daniel's forehead. "I'll try again," Nora said and pulled with cautiously increasing pressure, easing the infant's bottom past the incision and sending another wash of blood-tinged fluid running down his mother's sides. "He won't budge."

"Look at his color." Daniel's warning was steady in pace and inflection, but she caught his anxiety all the same. "Perhaps the cord... Can you find his neck?"

Ignoring a sudden chill, Nora plunged a hand deeper, over spongy tissue and the infant's slippery, firmer contours. She stretched out a forefinger. "It's the cord. It's wrapped around his neck." Her voice was high and sharp as a whistle.

"Shh," Horace cautioned. "There's always someone listening at the door. The color is changing—"

Moments before, she'd felt the baby elbowing against the pressure of her hand on his mother's skin. Now he was blue and still, even when she squeezed him.

Daniel's breath left him in a long hiss. "Can you lift the cord over his head?"

She wriggled her finger into the crevice between cord and neck and tugged. "Not enough slack."

He pushed the child down, and blood surged from the

incision, but Nora was working by feel. Even if they had extra hands for sponging, there was no way to see where she needed. Nora hooked the cord over the chin, past lips that remained still, a nose and forehead. She pushed it free, found the thighs again, pulled, and though the child moved, he didn't move far.

"Check again," Daniel said.

She delved once more, molding her fingers over the tiny, tightly packed body, trying to make sense of these travels. There were those still lips again. Nora swallowed. "The cord must have slid back." Even to herself, she sounded unsure.

"Might have been wrapped around the neck twice. I've seen one wrapped four times before," Horace suggested. "Found it postmortem."

Her fingers were moving before he even finished. Again, she squeezed a finger beneath the cord, dragged it over the child's face. "It's coming easier this time. Pull, Daniel!"

He abandoned the retractors and reached for the scalpel, opening the cut another inch. Keeping her tenuous hold on the cord, she held her breath as he lifted. The child came free, upside down, the cord trailing behind him. Nora clamped and cut it in a blink.

"Here." Horace held out his arms. "Nurse!" he shouted.

The door burst open and a red-haired woman rushed in.

Horace transferred the slippery bundle awkwardly into the nurse's frightened hands. "Turn him over. He's not breathing yet."

Nora dragged her eyes away, reminding herself how many times she'd seen Horace slap a baby's back or suction lung fluid with a rubber bulb to start its breathing. She still had to help Lady Woodbine, and the work was far from finished. Daniel was toiling, swabbing, tying off a leaking vessel where he'd widened the incision. Nora found the cord's attachment, followed it to the root, probed, scraped, pulled again, and lifted away the placenta. She checked—"See any pieces missing?"—and passed it to Daniel. He held it up to the lamp, examining it minutely.

"It's whole."

Relieved, Nora glanced at the baby, but Horace was bent close to it, blocking her view. Murmuring a quick prayer, Nora closed the sides of the uterus and reached for a needle threaded with silk. "Continuous sutures for the first layer, and then we'll use a second layer of double-locking sutures. Magdalena thinks closing the uterus in two layers results in a stronger scar."

"Yes!"

She paused at Horace's exultant cry and spared a look at the baby. His lungs swelled, his face puckered, his limbs flew out in startled surprise at this rough handling after being yanked from his dark nest. A fierce cry tore through the air, more glorious than the hallelujah of a heavenly choir. Nora shared a glance with Daniel, a sigh of relief, and began suturing.

Working from one end and Daniel the other, they stitched intently, accompanied by the baby's howling. He settled when the nurse finished wiping him down and swaddling him, seconds before she and Daniel met half an inch below the umbilicus. Nora wiped away a trickle of blood, straightened, and knuckled the small of her back. "Pulse?"

"Sixty," Horace answered. "It's been twenty-one minutes. She's going to stir soon."

"She's alive," Daniel whispered under his breath. "They're both alive."

"Whatever happens, you have that," Horace said as Nora ran a soapy sponge over Lady Woodbine's swollen but empty belly. The bloodstains came away with the warm water, and Nora's eyes grazed over the row of stitches, the dark catgut dimpling the red skin. Lady Woodbine gave a low moan but didn't open her eyes.

"We won't know for days. In Bologna they washed the wound with wine or olive oil." Nora's eyes searched the room.

"I've rum in my bag," Horace suggested.

Nora rolled her eyes. "I've brought my own red wine," she said as she unstopped a small glass bottle. She tipped the liquid out, the pink drops spilling over the closed wound and running down Lady Woodbine's bare sides like an anointing.

"Some olive oil to soothe skin and then only God can proceed," Nora said as the slippery green oil pooled against the sutures.

"Her eyes are open, but she can't see us yet," Horace informed them. Nora laid a loose linen bandage over the wound to catch the water and blood slowly oozing from the incision and replaced the shift, which had not escaped unmarred. Vibrant bloodstains defaced the snowy silk. "Pulse is speeding," Daniel said. "Color is weak."

A shiver took hold of the fragile body, and Lady Woodbine woke with chattering teeth and wet eyes. "How?" she asked, her eyes still blank and her pupils contracting.

Nora beckoned the nurse from her place in the far corner of the room and steered the woman close to the bed. Understanding her intent, the woman unfolded the blanket to reveal the baby's face and leaned over to give Lady Woodbine a close view.

"Charles is here," Nora said in her ear, trying to swallow back the knot in her throat, but when her glance strayed to Daniel, she saw his eyes were pink as well. Perhaps it was not a feminine failing after all.

Lady Woodbine was too confused to answer, but her gaze fell on the baby and her bright blue eyes fought to focus.

The pain would be intense once the ether left her veins, and she shouldn't be in any hurry to meet it when it did. Nora put a gentle hand on her shoulder as her eyelids sank shut and her face went lax again. "Everything is well in hand. The best thing you can do now is rest."

"Athena?"

Nora turned. Lord Woodbine was standing in the open door, his face ghastly pale.

"You have a fine son, my lord," Horace said, smiling proudly. "Just look at the size of him."

"Bring him here," the man said, as if he did not trust his feet to carry him another step.

The nurse detached herself, ignoring the baby's flailing fist, and held him out to his father.

"He has all his fingers and toes," Horace said dryly, "but it won't hurt to check again while Lady Woodbine rests and gathers her wits."

CHAPTER 43

Nora, Daniel, and Horace waited so anxiously for the faintest flicker of an eyelash or contraction of a muscle from Lady Woodbine. As the moments wound together like a tightening noose, Nora's breaths grew shallower. "It's been too long," she said with a plaintive look at Horace, whose frown was too troubled for comfort.

"We've done all that we can. All is stitched and returned to its rightful place. Now we must wait and see if her body succumbs to the shock."

Daniel did not join the conversation. He was too busy listening through his wooden stethoscope to Lady Woodbine's swollen abdomen.

A fractional parting of the lips jolted them from their anxious reveries as Lady Woodbine gave a feeble, broken cry.

Nora lowered her head almost until it touched the woman's face, wishing she could block out the pain about to overtake her ravaged body. "Your son is safe. As are you. The surgery worked."

The blue eyes opened, dimmed by a film of confusion. Her first sounds did not resemble words, though she raised her arms as if searching for something.

"We can't keep her awake long," Horace murmured. "The

damage is too extensive. Let her blood oxygenate, and then we must keep her sleeping as long as possible." As he reached for the ether, Nora stopped him with a hand on his wrist.

"Wait. She needs to see her son. She needs to understand." Her first brief awakening had been too blurry to make sense of anything.

"Son?" The word was anguished, and Nora turned back to Lady Woodbine to see her eyes brightening with tears.

"Yes." She was about to ask Daniel to get the nurse and bring the child, but he had already reached the door.

Lady Woodbine made the mistake of trying to sit and let out a stifled scream.

"No movements of any kind," Horace growled. Then softening his voice, he placed a strong hand on her shoulder. "This is the part where your strength matters. You must marshal it all and use it on the inside. Do you understand?"

She blinked an affirmative, pushing out a bewildered tear.

Lord Woodbine, still clutching the baby, pushed past Nora in his rush to the head of the bed. "Athena?" he gasped.

The pain had begun, evident in the trembling taking Lady Woodbine's fingers. It would soon advance through her limbs and torch her body with a blinding, burning agony. Nora had seen it before. Gripping Lord Woodbine's sleeve, she whispered hurriedly. "You must keep her calm and let her see the child, and then we must get her back to sleep."

"They're both alive." He spoke like a man walking in his sleep, his eyes glazed.

"They are." Nora accepted his dazed congratulations. "The surgery was successful. But the next days are crucial. And they will be painful."

He caught the urgent notes in her voice and lowered the downy head to Lady Woodbine's disbelieving face. She inhaled, her focus sharpening until she realized that the sleeping baby held proudly before her was, in fact, her ousted tenant. She shuddered, sighed, and stretched out a shy finger, as if the child was as unsubstantial as a soap bubble floating in the air. Tears ran down her cheeks, silent and ceaseless as a trickle from a faulty tap. Nora's sharp eye picked up a tremor under the blankets. Athena was shivering.

"He's a miracle," the new mother whispered.

Nora didn't allow her to gaze for long. "You must rest," she said when Lady Woodbine opened her mouth in protest. "Dr. Croft and Dr. Gibson and I will do all we can to speed your recovery, but Dr. Croft is right. Everything depends on you now. You must regain your strength and be patient. Your family needs you."

Lady Woodbine nodded then, letting her head fall back from where she'd strained it upward to see the baby leave in the nurse's arms. Lord Woodbine pressed his lips to her head, and she closed her eyes. Nora had never seen relief portrayed so profoundly in the simple shutting of an eyelid. While Nora measured the temperature of the water for the inhaler, Horace and Daniel supervised the careful changing of Lady Woodbine's linen.

"Nothing but broth for twenty-four hours," Nora said, but Lord Woodbine was anxiously following the progress of the servants attending his wife. "My lord?"

He dragged his eyes away, focusing on Nora with effort. "Forgive me. It is all so—"

"We will watch her in turns," she assured him, deciding to spare him the details of his wife's diet. "So far, every sign is good."

He heard that well enough.

"You may sit with her, so long as you remain quiet," Nora told him. "I believe your presence may soothe her, and it's important she be kept comfortable."

He nodded once, sharply, then sank into the creaking bedside chair with the grace of a tiptoeing elephant. Hiding a smile, Nora turned her attention to the ether.

Later, when she was wrapped in more comfortable clothes and there were no traces of blood on her hands, not even under her fingernails, Nora made her way back to Lady Woodbine's room. Daniel looked up from his fireside chair, nibbling a ham sandwich.

"They brought a tray when I told them we could not leave her to attend dinner tonight. They said Lord Woodbine is too restive to sit and eat anyway. He keeps coming in and staring at her."

Nora veered toward the bed, checking Lady Woodbine's color. Too flushed, but that was probably better than pale.

"We gave her a bit of broth, but I don't think she's at all hungry." He held out a sandwich, and Nora pushed herself into the spare inches of the chair beside him.

"I've never seen anything like that, Nora. I never even imagined."

Nora laid her head against his warm neck. "But we still don't know the outcome."

"We do. There is a healthy child. It's half miracle, half madness." His throat vibrated against her cheek when he spoke, and she didn't want him to stop talking. "At any rate, your case will be published in every paper. Harry is right. You will be able to lecture."

She sighed, wishing she didn't have to say her next words. "Let's wait and see. At least one of us should go home. It's not fair leaving everything to Harry."

"I know. I'm leaving soon. But I hate not being here the first three days. You know the rule."

Nora did. Somehow, miraculously, bodies often fended off even the worst infection for two days, but by the third a doctor often knew the truth about the trajectory of a patient.

"After that, if all is well"—Daniel rapped his knuckles on the carved arm—"we can take it in turns to visit. In the meantime, I'll keep things afloat at home." He shifted her weight off him so he could stand. The soft down of the cushions felt much less comforting than Daniel.

"I'll send word if we need you," Nora said.

He bent and kissed her hair, inhaling once again. "You are her best chance now. Whatever the outcome, it was a marvelous surgery."

She looked up into his eyes, ready to confess her fears. "I still can't relive it. I'm more anxious remembering than I was doing it, as if I will remember making a mistake and that will be what really happened."

He put his fingers against her cheek. "I was there. What really happened was a wonder. Relive it a hundred times, Dr. Beady. You will amaze yourself every time." He smiled and her shoulders went slack, her mouth widening.

He squeezed her hand and turned toward the door. "Send word if there is news."

"I promise."

One week after the surgery, Daniel received word that Nora was returning home. Though Lady Woodbine remained weak, she no longer required Nora's constant attendance. The servants of the house had learned how to check her bandages and massage her legs to keep her blood circulating. Lord Woodbine knew to send for Nora at the least sign of change, and she would return to examine Lady Woodbine every morning and evening.

The news, while not unexpected, filled Daniel with relief.

Nora might even be home already, because her message had arrived before his round of afternoon house calls. Daniel gave up trying to enforce dignity on the speed of his steps and slipped into a jog when the house neared, like his sister Joan's horse, who showed twice as much life once the stables were in sight. Eager to see Nora and exchange news—he wished his own were better—he didn't see the knot of men until he was climbing the steps. Snagged by some overheard words—"after I take possession"—he stopped as if tugged by a string and wheeled around.

The tallest of the four was facing away, wearing a cloak and hat, but Daniel knew the wide back of Silas Vickery.

"Gentlemen?" Daniel asked, his eyes narrowed.

Silas turned, pulling up a smile as he registered Daniel. "Dr. Gibson." He gave no explanation, though two of the men beside him wore working clothes and were busy with notes and yardsticks. The third, in suit and hat, was poleaxed, as lifeless as Horace's stuffed zebra.

"Can I help you, Dr. Vickery? Measuring another man's windows is unusual." Daniel let his tone carry all the other adjectives: presumptuous, rude, tasteless, inappropriate.

"Mr. Holwell from the bank," Vickery said, indicating the stuffed man at his side. "I believe you may have met. He assures me the sale looks likely. But I didn't come for your thanks."

"Thanks?" The cluster of men parted as Daniel drew closer.

"Holwell assures me there will be a good deal left over for Horace from my generous offer. He can retire comfortably." Vickery's gracious smile did nothing but enflame Daniel.

"Who said anything about retiring? He's hardly reached his prime. You are wasting these men's time and mine." Daniel advanced, his heart racing despite the bland annoyance he put on. Silas's hand reached out and blocked his path, pressing into his hot chest.

"He's crippled and old, Gibson. If you support him in this madness, you will only help him die a pauper. Be sensible and take the offer. Consider it charity for your charity clinic."

His tone twisted the benign words into a threat.

"Would to God your intentions were charitable, Dr. Vickery. It's plain—as it has always been—that you're jealous." Daniel squinted against the slanting afternoon sun, its rays scattered by the smoky London air, blurring the distant buildings. "Build your own hospital. This one is not for sale."

"Are you certain? My offer, as you know, only stands until tonight. Tomorrow, my offer will be a hundred pounds less. And it will be a hundred pounds less the day after that. You will regret your stubbornness. When you first arrived at Bart's, you were much more reasonable." His assessing eyes passed over Daniel, cruel in their disappointment.

Daniel swallowed the bitter reply welling in him. Vickery's pressure couldn't have come at a worse time. It was too early to claim success with Lady Woodbine, and his sister had no more money to lend to tide them over. He could refuse Vickery's offer now, but in another four days the next payment was due. "You will all of you leave before I call a constable. You've no permission to inspect this private home."

Vickery sighed theatrically, turning to his friends. "Well, that's inconvenient, but I suppose I can afford to wait."

Daniel flinched but didn't move his feet, stubbornly waiting until the four men trailed around the corner out of sight. Then he went inside, slamming the front door with none of the dignity of a gentleman and all of the passion of a student of Horace Croft.

The sound brought Nora running from the drawing room, Harry and Julia at her heels. "What's wrong?"

"How is Lady Woodbine?" Daniel sidestepped, too helplessly angry to speak of it yet. Nora had just come home, and in days they'd have to leave it.

"I think of almost nothing else, hoping, too afraid to be sure. The wound is redder than I'd like. Professor Venturoli would say there is a discouraging lack of pus."

Her hands floated up to his shoulders as she searched his face. "It's not—?"

"Vickery," Daniel growled.

From the corner of his eye, he saw Harry twitch, but the first to speak was Julia, interjecting firmly, "Come sit down."

Daniel's eyes slid to the window, half expecting to the see the man with the yardstick back at work, muttering numbers. "Is Horace in bed?"

Nora nodded as he sat down. Best not tell him this part and risk any fit of temper. Nora could help him think of a gentler way to give Horace the news later. As for Harry and Julia— well, for months now Daniel had assured Harry he had the situation in hand, and he always had, barely. But there was no point in hiding the truth now that they were on the brink of having to leave Great Queen Street. The full extent of Horace's private financial woes could no longer be concealed or avoided.

"Do tell us," Julia said, smoothing her skirts over her knees. In the place beside her, Harry was frowning at his knuckles, looking troubled.

Daniel paused, wondering how to dole out the worst of the news.

"Is it the house?" Nora asked.

Daniel met her sober eyes. "Vickery was just outside, measuring our windows. I sent him and his workmen away," he added, forestalling her rise from the chair. "But the next mortgage payment is in four days, and we don't have the money. If we take Vickery's offer now, Horace will walk away with something in his pockets. If we refuse..." Daniel rubbed his forehead. "The offer will decrease by a hundred pounds a day."

Now he'd begun, the rest kept coming. "My sister has no more money to lend, and I've already exhausted her funds and mine, hoping some miracle in the next months would keep us afloat." He forced a smile at Nora. "Well, we've had miracles enough—your safe return, Horace's continued recovery, Lady

Woodbine's surgery—so this one was probably too much to hope for. My inheritance is tied to my father's estate and won't be available until he dies, and no matter how intractable he can be, I'm relieved to say I don't wish for that."

"Of course not," Nora mumbled, her eyes roving over the graceful moldings and framed prints of exotic fern branches embellishing the room. "It's only a house."

Daniel didn't believe her for a moment, and her bravery stabbed deeper than any complaint would have. "I went to see Joan, on the off chance she could spare another few hundred pounds, but my father—"

Harry's head jerked up. "Is that what's needed?"

Daniel frowned. "Is what—"

"How many pounds, exactly?" Harry pressed while Julia looked at him in confusion.

Daniel's eyes flicked to Nora. If she heard him say the sum aloud, she'd know how hopeless it was and he wasn't ready to see the light in her face extinguished. But Harry was waiting, his eyes focused and glinting. Daniel sighed. "Another four hundred."

"And that would—" Harry asked, his hands held open in question, the sum not even giving him pause.

"That would cover not only the fees for late payments, but put us ahead on the mortgage and pay off the remaining loans for the workers and finishings." Daniel avoided looking at Nora and threw up his arms. "But it doesn't matter. It's a huge sum, and even if Joan *did* lend it to us, if Horace doesn't recover, our salaries cannot keep a house this size with the expenses of clinic and nurses and orderlies." Daniel sighed and sat down in a chair, too dejected to gather Nora close. "If I lost my sister's money in the gamble, I'd be…" He didn't have to finish. Silence enclosed them in individual cells of misery.

"What if you lost mine?" Harry asked after a moment.

"Your what?"

"My money. Three hundred pounds." He grasped Julia's hand and gave her a querying look.

"What three hundred pounds?" Daniel asked irritably, not in the mood for humor.

"The money Vickery blackmailed me with…" His voice softened and he stroked Julia's hand with his thumb. "After all, that's what started this mess." Harry raised his eyebrows and circled a hand waiting for some sign from them. "You told me you were managing things. If you'd told me the truth, I would have offered earlier."

"Do you mean you never spent—" Nora finally asked.

"Never," Harry answered. "It's blood money. I nearly threw it in the Thames, but I wasn't drunk enough. I thought of giving it to nuns, but since one paddled the tar out of me in school in Glasgow, I couldn't bring myself to that, either. I threw it into a real bank instead of the river bank and settled that I'd figure out something later." He was standing now, pacing across the newly stained carpet. "Could you make up the rest?"

"But you're married now. You could rent a home—a nice one, not rented rooms in Lambeth—for two years with that much money." Daniel pointed out with irritation.

"But we don't want it," Julia whispered, her voice soft but steely. "I won't live in a house given to me by that man."

"But Julia—" Avoiding her eyes, Daniel tried to reason with

her. "With that sum, Harry could buy into a practice that will provide for your family for the rest of your life. It's precisely what he should do."

"I think I can figure that for myself." Harry's voice was gruff and unbending.

"Mrs. Phipps and I have thirty pounds saved from allowances we didn't spend," Nora interjected slowly, color fastening to her cheeks.

Daniel frowned, looked to Harry, then shook his head. "But there is no guarantee we could pay you back." *Another loan, another debt—*

"I'd not take it," Harry said. "We've set up here these past two months, and it's closer to St. Bart's and a sight better than our rented rooms. Julia likes that she sees more of me, and so long as we're not treading on anyone's toes—"

"Not likely, in this enormous house," Nora interjected.

"We'll take the free room and board and call it even," Harry finished.

Daniel shook his head, not in refusal, but to clear the mess of words crowding at once into his brain. "It's too much," he said, his voice thick. Harry had never had the luxury of wealth. Daniel could not confiscate his entire fortune.

"Daniel's right," Nora joined in, her words despondent. "That's enough for you to set up practice. We can't."

"Why should I set up practice elsewhere?" Harry's ruddiness deepened and his voice turned rough. "Couldn't I buy in here?"

"Join the surgery?" Nora's head lifted, her eyes widening.

"It's the only place I ever wanted to practice. There isn't a surgeon anywhere with Horace's knowledge or skill."

Daniel looked to the window to see if the sun had burst out of its winter hiding place, but all he saw was a wet, gray square. The brightness was dawning inside him, not out.

He glanced at Julia and saw she was nearly as anxious as Harry.

"That is more possible," Daniel said. "I can't take your charity, but I can collect your fee for becoming an under surgeon with us." He met Harry's eyes, seeing clearer the new lines that had appeared since their days as youths in medical school. "But it's a tenuous business you buy into. I don't know how long we'll hold—"

"Danny boy, I'm the gambler, not you. It's a good hand. If you think you can convince the old man."

"Consider it done," Nora said. "Horace—if he has any sense at all—will be honored at such an arrangement. If need be, I'll remind him until it sticks. But under surgeon? Perhaps..." She met Daniel's eyes, conferring silently. "Director of the clinic?"

"No," Daniel cut her off, more sharply than he meant. He softened his tone. "No, Nora, that title is meant to be yours. Why do you think Horace built this place?"

"Partner, then." She smiled at Harry, who lifted his empty coffee cup from the side table.

"Ho!" he cried out with a satisfying stamp of his boot. "I wish I'd taken five hundred pounds from that miserable man now!"

Daniel froze, only his nose wrinkling, followed by his brow.

"What is it?" Nora asked, her face coated in worry by the change in Daniel's expression.

A grin waxed wider and wider on Daniel's face. "You realize

it's Vickery's own money that is keeping him from getting the place."

"Zeus," Harry whispered. "I must be there when he finds out."

"I'd buy a ticket," Daniel agreed. He reached his hand out to Nora, tightening his grip around her warm fingers.

"Let's call on him now," she said, nodding decisively. "We'll all feel better once this is settled, and"—her eyes crinkled—"it is only courteous to inform him promptly of such a disappointment."

"Julia, get your cloak," Harry said, rubbing his hands.

"Is Horace—?" Daniel glanced at the ceiling.

Nora grinned. "He'll murder us if we make him miss this."

A sizable and unseemly giddy delegation, they crowded into a hackney and, after much jostling, arrived at Silas's tasteful and unostentatious home on Harley Street.

"Is the doctor in?" Daniel asked as the door opened, and Vickery's manservant recoiled away from the crowd on the doorstep.

Harry didn't wait for an answer, just pushed his way inside. "Silas? Where are you?" Daniel followed, with Nora fastened tight to his arm.

"His library's that way," said Horace, motioning with his thumb to one side of the hall.

"If you would please—" The flustered servant gave up trying to stop them and sprinted instead for the library door. "Dr. Vickery! Dr. Vickery!"

"You'd think we were the horde marching to Versailles," Horace muttered, rolling his eyes. Julia, who'd chosen to take Horace's arm, stifled a giggle.

The library door opened. Vickery, looking as vexed as the stuffed ostrich Daniel had sold two weeks ago, halted on the threshold, his eyes widening.

"Hello, my friend," Horace said cordially.

"Croft," Vickery returned stiffly.

Glancing past Vickery into the lighted room beyond, Daniel said, "I see you have Mr. Holwell with you. How fortunate. We'll be spared a second call."

"What is this?" Vickery hissed.

Daniel stepped forward. "Mr. Holwell, I have your money. Given Dr. Vickery's impatience to dispossess Horace from his property, we felt it advisable to find you both without delay. Here you are." He held out the purse—Harry's bank draft, Nora's thirty pounds, five each from Mrs. Crawford and the orderly, John, and sixty from the modest nest egg of Mrs. Phipps. "You'll find it all there. If you'd be good enough to count it and write me a receipt, I'll forward it on to Horace's solicitors. I'm afraid Mr. Jamison, hearing of your close negotiations with Dr. Vickery, here, doubts that you've been dealing with us in perfect good faith."

Vickery, more thunderous with every word, stepped up to Daniel, fists clenched, but was forestalled by the sputtering banker behind him. Holwell had gone quite pink.

"This is a mere social call, Dr. Gibson. I wouldn't—" Holwell sputtered.

"And your visit to Great Queen Street together? I'd swear you were loitering outside with particular purpose."

"Out for a walk," Holwell answered wildly.

"Have anything to add, Silas?" Horace turned to the surgical chief with raised brows.

"I've done nothing wrong," Vickery muttered sulkily. "I've made an offer—a very generous one—for your property. Naturally I am interested in seeing it up close."

"You could have asked for an invitation," Julia said. "I believe that's how it's generally done among friends and colleagues. But—" She broke off, glancing wide-eyed between Silas and Horace. "Oh, did I misspeak?"

Horace patted her hand. "Not at all. But I'm afraid, Silas, I must decline your offer. Your generosity would send me to the poorhouse."

"I don't believe it." Vickery scowled. "How did you come up with the funds?"

Harry hooked his thumbs into his waistcoat pockets and rocked on his heels. "This will surely surprise you, but poor man that I am, I happened to have three hundred pounds in the bank."

Vickery leaned forward, violence in his black eyes. "My three hundred pounds?"

"It was once, yes," Harry answered. Nora's smile flickered and Silas raked her with glittering eyes.

"You? Back in London and playing at medicine again? I hope you haven't killed anyone."

"Not at all," Nora said. "But I was recently called in for one of your patients, who I'm happy to say is recovering. Lady Woodbine has a beautiful son."

Vickery looked like a kettle about to blow.

"Dr. Beady's account of her successful cesarean section has been accepted for publication in the next edition of the *Provincial*, Silas." Horace dropped this as if it were a detail he'd carelessly forgotten. "I'm sure you'll find it instructive."

They'd played with their food long enough. "That receipt, Holwell?" Daniel asked.

He checked, then pocketed Holwell's hastily scrawled paper. "I believe that concludes our business." Daniel nodded and touched the brim of his hat.

CHAPTER 44

THIRTEEN DAYS LATER, NORA WAS CONFIDENT LADY Woodbine was making a good recovery, though she still called daily on her patient. Today she found Lady Woodbine sitting in bed, using cold compresses as prescribed, leafing through a book on exotic birds lent by Horace.

"I should love to see a bird of paradise," Lady Woodbine said, sighing and closing the book.

"You shall," Nora said. "Hasn't Dr. Croft promised you a view of his collection? If you keep on at this rate, you'll be paying calls again in a matter of months. Let that thought inspire you when you feel tired of this room." It wouldn't do for Lady Woodbine to chafe at her convalescence. Though Nora was pleased with her recovery so far, it was wise to be cautious.

Lady Woodbine glanced at the cradle beside her bed. Her husband sat next to it, his hand resting next to the sleeping baby inside.

"No fear of that, Doctor," Lord Woodbine said. "I don't believe either of us need more encouragement than this."

"How is the baby?" Nora asked, breaking the spell between them.

"Charles is remarkably well," Lady Woodbine said. "But we haven't christened him yet. When we thought—well, happily, there is no need to hurry, and one of his names is still missing." Her eyes, animated and clear, in spite of her thin face, exchanged a shy glance with her husband before they settled firmly on Nora's. "Lord Woodbine and I agree. We want him to have one of yours."

Nora masked her astonishment by bending over the child. He was pink, plump, and breathing easily, nestled in folds of— for now—spotless linen. "He's very handsome. I wish you would reconsider," Nora said without looking up. "I can't think of a single masculine equivalent of Eleanor, and I haven't a middle name."

"You have a family name," Lady Woodbine persisted.

Nora smiled, convinced she'd now persuade her. "Beady. But—"

"Our son will be proud to share it." Lord Woodbine spoke with too much certainty for Nora to contradict him.

"Charles Benedict Beady Rawlston," Lady Woodbine said, nodding. "It has a nice sound. If you permit."

"I don't know what to say," Nora said. "It's too great an honor."

"Not at all," Lord Woodbine said. He bent and inhaled the baby's scent, his breath ruffling the halo of soft hair. "I—" he paused, gathering himself and transferring his gaze to Nora with effort. "I have never been so happily, completely wrong as I was about you. Please accept my apologies." He swallowed. "And my thanks for the lives of my wife and my son."

Instinct would have made her declaim modestly, but Nora remembered she had Horace and Daniel behind her. They both—and Magdalena, for that matter—would advise her to accept her due. Gathering her courage, Nora faced Lord Woodbine eye to eye, smiling at him until his quivering lips settled. "I'm happy to have helped."

Lord Woodbine nodded. "Beady is a name he can be proud of."

CHAPTER 45

WHEN THE FRONT BELL RANG, NORA LOOKED UP FROM her notes and checked her illustration on the slate board behind her. She tried to recall Horace's expression when students arrived for a lecture. Was it bored? Dismissive? Certainly not terrified, as she felt. She looked to the bench beside her where Mrs. Bratt and Mrs. Dobbins were seated, looking as anxious as Nora felt. They needed as much shoring up as she did.

"Ladies, I asked you specifically because of your reputation and skill. Dr. Croft has long endorsed your abilities. I know it is intimidating to educate surgeons—"

"I don't mind a bit telling them what they don't know." Mrs. Dobbins wrinkled her bulbous nose in an attempt to be blasé. Nora resisted a smile. She'd worked with the stern woman plenty of times and remembered her rants about childbirth being women's work. When births grew dire, Mrs. Dobbins never screamed for a doctor; she was fearless.

"Good," Nora declared, looking to the much more timid Mrs. Bratt. She had eleven children of her own and an uncanny intuition when predicting which women would have trouble during birth. Though she was shorter than most children and walked with a limp, the women of her district swore by her quiet methods. "Mrs. Bratt, whenever you have something to add, just dab your nose with your handkerchief. I will pause to ask for your insights."

Mrs. Bratt gave her a doubtful glance.

"Remember, if you don't tell them, no one will. And one day they may attend the birth of someone you love. Would you want them bumbling through something you could have taught them?"

Her time for preparation was past. The sound of footsteps and chatter grew closer, and Horace appeared in the doorway, sweeping his arms around the nearly empty room. "My lecture theater, gentlemen."

The dark-coated men filtered in, their faces alight with admiration and jealousy as their heads turned up toward the skylights and then to the extravagant gaslights glowing above the dissection table.

"I heard it was fine, Croft, but this puts the hospitals' facility to shame." The doctor who spoke studied the drain in the floor and the waterspout projecting from the wall. His lips moved soundlessly, and Nora knew he was tallying pounds.

Dr. Adams grinned at her and took the seat closest to her as two younger doctors followed and joined him. "Miss Beady, it's been quite some time. May I introduce Dr. Lake and Dr. Holbrook?"

Daniel spoke up from behind her. "You must call her Dr. Beady now, Adams. At least for two more weeks." He winked at her and her apprehension softened.

"Forgetful of me. Apologies." Dr. Adams nodded and then frowned. "And congratulations. I hear there is a wedding planned."

Nora was grateful she was too busy to count the number of doctors milling in the room, swelling each time she checked. Their voices blended into a soft hum as they shuffled into their places.

Dr. Holbrook had settled his questioning eyes on the midwives, and the others soon noticed and followed.

Nora cleared her throat. "Gentlemen, I am Dr. Eleanor Beady, and these are women you have perhaps heard of or even worked with. Mrs. Bratt and Mrs. Dobbins are two local midwives endorsed by the pioneer surgeon himself."

The men made grim, polite nods in the midwives' direction, but Horace gave a hearty *ho* that made Mrs. Bratt startle.

Time to dive in. Nora straightened, clutching Horace's favorite pointer in her hand like a talisman. "I've no desire to waste your time or insult your intelligence," she began. "Midwives attend the majority of births in your districts and should be seen as critical partners in your endeavors. I've asked Mrs. Bratt and Mrs. Dobbins to join us for the entirety of the course. They will be able to add greatly to your case studies. There is nothing they haven't seen in their decades of practice." Nora saw no signs of objection in the doctors. Pressing back against a smile, she continued. "And they certainly would be benefited by your formal education and expertise. I believe we should begin with the methods of the cesarean and then go into detail about when to consider such a drastic surgical intervention."

The doctors leaned closer and several opened notebooks, their pens poised, waiting for her next words.

Horace caught her eye and flashed her a secret grin that bristled his unruly beard. Approval and amusement flicked across his face. For a moment Nora saw the scene from a bird's-eye view: the shining lecture room, the burning lamps pushing back the London night, the attentive row of surgeons and Horace watching her point to her chalk drawing of a child bulging against a full uterus. Horace's smug expression, as if he had orchestrated all of it. Her voice hitched for a half second as she drew in an extra portion of air.

Horace seemed to catch the change in her face, the suspicion in her eyes, and gave a yawn before interrupting. "I believe you rendered the pubic symphysis too narrow for this stage of pregnancy."

Nora wrinkled her nose as she turned and studied her chalk outline. She'd been so proud of it. *Blast him. He was right.* But she'd never give him the satisfaction of hearing it. "As you well know, Dr. Croft, the pubic symphysis is prone to dysfunction and misshaping at this stage of pregnancy. Something we will address later in the course. Now if you'd all kindly refer to this model—"

⁓

"How the devil did you find me out here?" Horace raised his head from the knee joint he was studying. The arborvitae that protected the garden from view made a small thicket at the back corner of the lawn that hid his small bench.

"Well, I knew you had a new knee to play with, and you weren't in your room or the dissection theater. Seeing as it's a cool day, I guessed you were here instead of hiding in the carriage house."

"It's warmer in there, but I wanted to be alone," he growled.

The knee clicked as he rotated it. "I can't believe this man walked naturally his whole life. This growth should have been debilitating." He gazed in wonder at the clean bones.

Nora grinned and took the empty corner of the wooden seat. "The human body will never cease to make fools of us." She pointed with her chin to the knee joint in his hands. "But I see you are moving it well. Your fingers hardly lag at all anymore."

He grunted and ran his fingers over the misshapen femur.

Nora adjusted the lace at the cuff of her sleeve. "Do you think you will be able to operate soon? Your dissection work is satisfactory."

"Satisfactory?" he barked. "When have I ever settled for satisfactory? It must be meticulous. Impeccable."

Nora let her eyes roll to the side in exasperation. A stiff breeze pushed a handful of sycamore leaves into the wall of arborvitae, the glossy new leaves skewered against the spiny green branches. Her free curls wrapped their soft strands around her neck.

"You can do with your one hand what most surgeons fail to do with two. Daniel and I both agree it's time you return to the table."

Horace pursed his lips, and the bones he'd been manipulating stilled. He gazed at the troubling bone growth. "With ether I could have removed this."

"Without a doubt," Nora agreed.

Horace huffed out a breath and tapped the tibia against his shoe. "I've grown fond of research."

"You love the scalpel as much as it loves you. And the world is growing impatient for the pioneer surgeon to return. I dare say the medical world is becoming quite dull without you. The lectures at Bart's drone on without anyone hurling jars or dancing in glee."

"I never danced!"

"On the contrary. Your celebratory steps are famous. You pranced like a ballerina when you got going."

Horace snarled but Nora only laughed.

"It's time you stop playing the furious old man with me. I know all your secrets."

He snorted. "Then I taught you too much." Horace ran his fingers over his own knee, studying the shape and movement of it.

"You have discoveries yet to make." She drew a long breath. "The guild can't revoke my license, not while I have Lord Woodbine's backing. But they've changed their regulations. From now on, women—even with medical degrees—are barred from joining."

Horace grunted. "Their fault, not yours."

She lifted her eyes, wondering if he saw how much it cost her. "Does it matter whose fault it is? What about others like me? I cannot be the only one."

"Teach those fusty owls their mistake," Horace said, turning his attention back to the knee. "And keep teaching your midwives. If there are other women like you, trust they can find their own way."

Nora bit her lip. "It would be easier for them if they had a great surgeon to lead them. You can teach them like you taught me. I would never be what I am now if—"

Horace met her gaze, causing her momentary grief when

she noticed the new wrinkles gathered around his bright and burning eyes.

"A great surgeon will lead them," he told her. "Even if I never make another cut." Nora tilted her head in confusion.

He rubbed his wild beard. "My dear, don't you realize by now? *You* are that surgeon." He patted her lap with his thickened fingers, and for a moment she feared his eyes were as misty as her own.

But Horace turned his head toward the muffled sound of the street traffic and cleared his throat. "Now let me get back to my bones. I've work to do."

Nora obliged, taking note of how his left hand, thinner than it had been, cupped the patellar surface of the femur as if it comforted him. Liver spots dotted the backs of both his hands, and the sun shone on the unrelieved silver of his hair.

She rested a hand on his shoulder—of course he was wearing his favorite shiny and threadbare coat—and kissed the top of his head.

The flexing joint stopped. "What was that for?" he demanded.

"Nothing," Nora said. "Go on. I've work to do, too. If you need me, I'll be in the surgery."

HISTORICAL NOTE

If we were to stroll down the streets of Bologna today, navigating the shade and stalls of the porticos and slogging through the warm, humid air of the red city, I would pluck at your sleeve and direct your attention to a building just over your shoulder. Through the maze of arched alleyways, it is difficult to tell where one burnished brick building ends and another begins, but this particular edifice must be entered. Watch your step on the crumbling curb. No one ever counted how many toes have caught on the broken bricks, but suffice it to say that men and women in lace-trimmed breeches and hoop skirts have cursed them under their breath as fervently as the tourists today.

Inside, we enter the cool and dim Palazzo Poggi Museum. Everything captures your attention, but I must press you on to the pièce de résistance. We are here to see *her*. Her own three-dimensional self-portrait, executed in wax like all of her anatomical sculptures. Her full face with a rather fine chin is unapologetic as she shifts her gaze slightly to her left, her lips supple and undisturbed by whatever has interrupted her work at hand. At her fingertips is the seat of human intellect—a brain nested in an open skull, much as kings used to serve turtle soup in the poor creature's own exquisite shell. Her salmon-colored gown adorned with draping lace and ruched satin does not seem to impair her work at all. Nor do her layers of pearls or large diamond rings. Her dark, soft curls rest provocatively at her neck, and she will go back to her business of discovery after giving you a quick glance.

She did, after all, entertain many guests in her day, from Pope Benedict to Empress Catherine the Great, all who came to see Anna Morandi Manzolini. They insisted on meeting the woman who married Giovanni Manzolini, sculptor and anatomy professor, and went on to become not only a great sculptor in her own right, but also a skilled anatomist who had no fear of dissecting the human body. This woman helped put the floundering city of Bologna back on the cultural map in the mid-1700s.

Perhaps it shouldn't surprise us that such a woman is found in Italy. From Anguissola to Fontana to Sirani (forgive our name-dropping, but the Italian names are too beautiful and impressive to resist), female artists found refuge in this birthplace of the Renaissance. Properzia de' Rossi was a Renaissance sculptor who earned the title of the first female sculptor of Europe. Whether that is true or not is difficult to say. Women's names have a way of fading from history as if written with delible ink. But the Italians had long frequented churches with masterpieces painted by women and sculptures carved by women, so perhaps it was not such a leap to think a woman capable of sculpting the *inside* of a human body as well as the outside. Anna Morandi Manzolini practiced side by side with her husband, writing texts and teaching hundreds of students, and continued their work after his death. It is for this reason we sent Professor Perra to fetch Nora across the sea to this land of possibility.

The University of Bologna boasts an impressive history

where women are concerned. It was there in 1732 that Laura
Bassi became the world's first female university professor after
being granted a degree in philosophy and was appointed to the
chair of physics. Considering women wouldn't vote for almost
another two hundred years, it is a marvelous feat.

But before we paint the picture too rosy, let us put on the
spectacles of truth that bring things into sometimes unpleasantly sharp focus. While Nora attended the University of
Bologna, she would have been one of exceptionally few women.
Women pursuing higher education took a steep dive after the
interference of a small, sharp-nosed man named Napoleon.
And even at the height of Anna Morandi Manzolini's fame, she
was awarded a far smaller stipend than men, struggled finan-
cially, and was berated by certain physicians of her day. Her way
was not paved with roses, but it was *her way*. That in itself is
extraordinary.

As for the cesarean section—we all believed the fable telling us that this was the way Julius Caesar came into the world,
but it is doubtful considering his mother lived to see some of
his conquests. The name likely derives from the Latin words for
cut and *child* (*caedare* and *caesones*), though Greek law did decree
that all mothers who died in childbirth should be cut open in
an attempt to save the baby.

It is said that a laborer in Switzerland cut open his wife in
1500 after a multiday labor and both mother and child lived to
ripe old ages. Beware, dear reader—a great many things are *said*.
The procedure was named in medical texts of the 1500s and
1600s, so it must have existed in theory at the very least. Few
attempted it, and even fewer survived. Not until the discovery

of ether and chloroform did it truly become an option. And not until the much later discovery of sulfonamides and eventually penicillin would there be a way to combat the almost inevitable infections. But people and their bodies do the most remarkable things, and some women and babies did indeed survive and recover despite all odds.

Daniel's battle with diphtheria introduces another heartbreaking tale of history. This highly contagious disease was known as the child strangler. It is caused by a bacteria so toxic it secretes a thick, gray waste product that forms a membrane over the tissues of the throat and mouth. This pseudomembrane can slowly choke a child to death, they being particularly susceptible due to their small airways. Daniel and Vickery were both correct to some degree. Bringing diphtheria patients into a ward did put other patients at risk. Ignoring them and sending them home was also a death sentence. Keeping the airway open until the body could overcome the bacteria gave the children a fighting chance. Tracheotomies were performed in Nora and Daniel's time, but more often to save people who were choking. Most often, in diphtheria cases, tracheotomies were attempted too late or under conditions that introduced new infections to children barely clinging to life. They were not the routine, safe, lifesaving procedure they are today.

Today children are given a single, almost painless shot that saves them not only from pertussis and diphtheria, but also from tetanus, the unforgiving disease that took Pozzi's life. Tetanus is a cruel bacteria that makes you see the scythe of death swinging ever closer until it cuts you down, slowly and painfully. The muscle spasms are so intense they can break bones. Let it be known that Jaima and I took no joy in Pozzi's death and shed tears. It is simply the tragic truth of his day and time, when doctors and medical students routinely died from diseases they sought to treat in their patients.

Today more than eighteen million lives are saved every year through cesarean sections. Cases of diphtheria in the United States have plummeted from 150,000 annually to a mere two over a thirteen-year period, miraculous numbers that would have made Nora, Magdalena, Daniel, and Horace weep with joy.

It is inspiring to know how things were, how things became better, and to envision what might yet come.

—Regina Sirois

READING GROUP GUIDE

1. Discuss the ways that, despite her admission to a prestigious medical school, Nora still faces oppression.

2. Compare Nora and Magdalena. In what ways are they similar? In what ways are they different?

3. Vickery refuses to let children with diphtheria into St. Bart's, as the risk of contagion is very high. How did you feel about his decision? To what extent do you agree or disagree with it?

4. Characterize Nora's relationship with Pozzi. How did their friendship develop?

5. While women like Nora and Magdalena are unconventional, there are plenty of women in this narrative who have limited agency. Discuss these characters. How do you think they feel? In what ways are they restricted? Do they seem satisfied with their situations?

6. While today the cesarean section is a common procedure, at its inception it was considered controversial. Why is that?

7. As the only female student of medicine, Nora faces many obstacles. What are they? Do women in STEM still face any of them today?

8. Daniel and Croft network with the elite to raise funds for their research. How did you feel about that? Did you view it as dishonest or a necessary evil?

9. While the largely male medical establishment was determined to keep women out, many female professionals still contributed to the field. What kinds of work did they do?

10. Though her gender is often a barrier to opportunities, in some ways, Nora's identity as a woman gives her advantages while treating patients. What are they?

A CONVERSATION
WITH THE AUTHORS

Historically, women's health has not been the primary focus of male medical professionals. So, what made you choose to write about cesarean sections and women's autonomy?

J: After reading the contemporary case histories, it was impossible not to write about it. I was haunted by the stories of these women and what they endured—a world away from the choices and medical care many of us enjoy. I used to take so much for granted. Women's health and reproductive rights continue to be hot-button issues today. I have been intrigued by how much technology has changed, while many of the surrounding issues—and stances about them—have stayed the same. Culturally, we tend to repeat ourselves more often than we think.

R: For much of medical history, women were treated as smaller versions of men with a few different parts. The intricacies of our exquisite, unique bodies were not known or actively investigated. The men who studied the miracle of childbirth took very little time to ask women about the process. At times, their arrogance as bystanders was astonishing. I love the study of the cesarean section for two reasons: First, that surgery saved the lives of two of my sisters-in-law and six of my nieces and nephews, along with many friends. It is a lifesaving, family-saving, world-changing procedure. Second, in the early 1800s, childbirth was one of the few entry points into medicine for women. Midwives were a necessity of life, and midwifery allowed skilled women to practice medicine in a profound way at a time when all other avenues were closed.

It's not easy to write a romantic subplot when your love interests are thousands of miles apart. How did you navigate that?

J: It wasn't easy! Especially without falling into the trap of excessive pining and daydreaming—I hope we got the balance right. Real romance isn't the lightning resolution of two hundred pages of stubborn misunderstandings topped with a sunset kiss. (I love reading romance, but in this book, we were trying to move away from genre conventions. Believe me, it's harder than it sounds). Strong relationships take commitment and shared goals and supporting each other. Nora and Daniel "discovered" each other in *The Girl in His Shadow*, and this story was a chance for them to navigate some hard tests. Even though it took us a lot of revising, I enjoyed portraying a "real-life" love story where the partners are more than the sum of their individual selves. Ultimately, I think that's the kind of relationship we all want and work toward.

R: It was easy when you love Nora and Daniel as much I do. They were each too rare and special to forfeit to a temporary separation. It was also satisfying to show the readers who they were individually and how they grew on their own when put in challenging positions. In their growth as people, I believe there was more to love when they came back together than when they parted. It was also good to make it clear that this is not a romance novel. Their bond is core, but it is a part of a bigger story.

You clearly did extensive research to ensure the descriptions of medical procedures are accurate, but did you find it difficult to describe some of the more graphic scenes without being too gruesome? What does that balance look like?

J: I'm not sure what this says about me, but I don't find it difficult to write about the procedures. It's easy to be there in my mind. Not so in real life. I found the anatomy labs and the surgical procedures I observed as an occupational therapy student intensely challenging. I will never forget the smell of bone dust or the greasiness of dead flesh. Useful experiences for writing, but I am so glad my day-to-day work as a clinician is tidy!

R: For me, I concentrated on telling the truth. What would it be like to stand right there in that moment? And if that is gory or graphic, it's also the truth of the human body, which is a marvelous creation. Accurate descriptions of life and death have never felt gruesome to me. Are they overwhelming for the senses and emotions to process? Absolutely. But never gruesome. I learned this when I fell in love with *All Quiet on the Western Front*. If you are being honest and not being gratuitous, there will be beauty even when relating the most disturbing circumstances. To borrow a famous phrase from John Keats, beauty is truth, truth beauty. It is in some of the most gut-wrenching accounts of our novels that I feel the closest to the people of the past—their courage, their loss, and their fortitude.

What's next on your to-be-read list?

J: That's a hard and an easy question. I read a lot, and I read quickly. Unless I'm very busy with work, I read one or two books a week. Before the days of e-readers, I would sometimes go through eight books in a week of vacation, which was really problematic—I would bring books, buy more while I was away, and then have to decide which ones to bring home because I couldn't put them all in my luggage. Right at this moment, I'm rereading *The Winter Sea* by Susanna Kearsley, which I love, and listening to Ben Philippe's *Sure, I'll Be Your Black Friend*. I just finished the *The Thursday Murder Club* by Richard Osman and can't wait for the sequel, which releases next month. And at the end of this month, Helen Hoang's next book, *The Heart Principle*, comes out, and I've been looking forward to that one, too. I'm also midway through *Why They Marched* by Susan Ware, and next I'm diving into *Rebel Girls: How Votes for Women Changed Edwardian Lives* by Jill Liddington.

R: David McCullough's book *The Pioneers* is calling to me, as well as *The Girl Explorers* by Jayne Zanglein. I love books about intrepid adventurers! Alexander Von Humboldt is a little obsession of mine.

In many ways, this is a book about mothers. As parents yourselves, was the interest in this theme informed by your own experiences?

J: I never thought about that aspect of the book until I saw this question! In some ways, I think it an incredible tribute to women that caring, nurturing, and mentoring is called mothering. But that's also an oversimplification that can be hurtful. Magdalena, as friend, teacher, and role model, fills a much different need for Nora than Mrs. Phipps, and neither woman is related to her. We all need mothering from many different people, and not all of it will (or should!) come from women.

That said, I loved writing the women who play such important roles for Nora, and it was important to me to populate this book with impact-making women.

R: I had never thought of it as a book about mothers, but I love that observation. Motherhood is woven throughout the book—the loss of Nora's mother, Mrs. Phipps's mothering, Magdalena's unconventional motherhood and career, the patients fighting for their lives and the lives of their children, and even the Mother Mary of the Christian faith. And I believe that is exactly what motherhood does—it winds powerfully and essentially through all things. As a work-at-home, homeschool mom, the time I spend empowering, teaching, and nurturing my daughters is the work of my life. Nothing comes close to it in importance, magnitude, or power. I believe it is a calling. A difficult, sometimes miserable one, but a miraculous one as well. My extraordinary daughters are my boldest ambition, my greatest creative work, my living magnum opus.

What do you hope your readers take away from this story?

J: I read to discover and to experience the emotions of other people, so I hope we've succeeded in providing both without the discovery part being off-putting or dry and with emotions that are real and relatable.

R: Knowledge! Knowledge is not proprietary; it is free for all. I hope at some obscure moment a reader will intrigue someone in a conversation by saying "the use of ether in the late 1840s was met with controversy" or "it's important to get your tetanus boosters because it can cause muscular convulsions strong enough to break bones" or "actually, the oldest university in Europe is in Bologna, Italy." I want the knowledge I curated over years through books, research papers, and antique documents to now belong completely to my readers, for their use, benefit, and enjoyment.

ACKNOWLEDGMENTS

This book owes much to the first readers, our agent, Jennifer Weltz, and our editors, Jenna Jankowski and Anna Michels. Their enthusiasm and love for our characters was always encouraging, and we couldn't ask for sounder advice or better advocates. Thank you for the gift of your talents.

Thank you to Barbara-Lynne Furler, MScPT, for generously sharing your clinical experience and helping us understand how a stroke would impact Horace.

We are also indebted to the friends and advocates of "Audrey Blake," including Ariana Philips, Diane Dannenfeldt, Heather Hall, Cristina Arreola, and Molly Waxman. Thank you for shining your lights on this book and our first endeavor, *The Girl in His Shadow*.

Thank you to the readers, booksellers, bloggers, librarians, and book clubs who've recommended our stories, and everyone who's journeyed with us to the University of Bologna and Great Queen Street. Writing doesn't work without readers. Until a new imagination lifts words off the page, they are just shapes in ink or lights on a screen. Reading lets us make more together.

As in our first book, the medical cases discussed in this novel are based on firsthand accounts of illnesses and treatments in the mid-1840s in Europe, and so we are deeply in debt to the men and women of the past who were cases or who wrote cases in such vivid detail. And we owe so much to the female scholars of the University of Bologna. If you wish to learn more about these "impossible women," an excellent starting place is the article "Women and the Practice and Teaching of Medicine in Bologna in the Eighteenth and Early Nineteenth Centuries," by Gabriella Berti Logan, in the *Bulletin of the History of Medicine*, Fall 2003. As ever, we tip our metaphorical hats to these brave women who knew they were healers long before the world acknowledged their talents.

For more about the people who inspired our characters, as well as a list of books extremely helpful to our research, please see the historical note in our first novel, *The Girl in His Shadow*.

Lastly, to our families, whose support and encouragement encompass much more than writing, words are truly inadequate to express our thanks. Pie and undying devotion might just suffice, though a pastry offering worthy of Jeff, Justin, Ivy, Audree, Blake, Juliette, and Edward is a real test of the imagination.

ABOUT THE AUTHORS

© Justin Sirois

© Alexander Aulenbach

Audrey Blake has a split personality—because she is the creative alter ego of writing duo Jaima Fixsen and Regina Sirois, two authors who met as finalists of a writing contest and have been writing together happily ever since. They share a love of history, nature, literature, and stories of redoubtable women. Both are inseparable friends and prairie girls despite living thousands of miles apart. Jaima hails from Alberta, Canada, and Regina calls the wheatfields of Kansas home. Visit them online at audreyblakebooks.com and on Instagram @audreyblakebooks.